Brown Ridge: Shootin' Noise

BRADLEY DAVENPORT

ISBN: 978-0-9997967-3-3

for Jason Davenport

Brown Ridge: Shootin' Noise

Also by Bradley Davenport

Monster Fantastic

Disclaimer

This is a work of fiction.
Resemblances to any peoples is purely coincidental

BRADLEY DAVENPORT

GROOVY TIME

ONE

1991

On a clear day in January, Johnny Womack, ran down Valner Street, ducking behind empty parked cars along the narrow street, as a single gun fired into the morning. I first saw Johnny as he walked out of Lucky Mackey's Donuts on Palmer. As soon as he saw me he dropped his bag of fried bread and ran. I called his name a few times, but he didn't turn around. The city was nice and bright. A single plane glided through the sky above. Stores and shops lined both sides of the street. The city bus roared a few blocks over. The sun bounced off my sunglasses as I ran after Johnny. Two small beads of sweat inched down my back. My legs were burning and tired. If I had thought about it, I would've just got in my car and run him down. He hooked a right on a sidewalk beside a restaurant called Janko's—it was there where I tackled him to the ground.

"Don't move," I shoved my knee in his back.

"Okay, shit," he groaned. "I'm not going anywhere. Damn, man, just calm down. We know each other."

"I have you now."

"Fuck you."

"Now, is that a nice way to talk?"

"Why'd I get outta bed today? You're such a fuckin' asshole! How can you live with yourself?"

"That's what they all say."

"You don't know who you're messin' with, Sean."

"Looks like a damn fool to me. Someone who's run out of luck."

"You'll be sorry," his voice hung in the air. "I've got a lot of connections. If something happens to me, they'll track you down."

"What, you steal from them, too?"

"No," he said.

I punched him.

"Wait, wait, wait!" he screeched. "I can explain. You have to let me talk to Joe. He's a businessman. He'll understand."

"I'm not the one who messed up."

"You don't know anything."

"Listen, I'm not the one who stole. Yeah, man, if you go to Joe I'm sure he'll put a bullet in you himself."

He sighed.

I picked him up by the collar and slammed him against the side of the restaurant. I punched him in the gut two times. He dropped, coughing and grabbing at his stomach.

He looked up at me. "Go to Hell."

"Think I'm there already."

"Serves you right."

A stream of blood rolled down his dirty face. I felt sorry for him for a minute, but then, I kicked him in the face. His head jerked to the side and fell on the pavement. A tooth covered in blood rolled out of his mouth.

I knelt in front of him and slapped him in the face to see if he was still alive.

"You okay?" I asked. "You gotta stay with me on this. Come on, that'll be over shortly. I can promise you that."

"I'm good," he wiped the beads of sweat off his face. "Probably had it coming.'"

"You know how to make enemies," I said.

"What do you mean?"

"You have me out here running after you for about two miles."

"Sorry about that."

"Yeah," I said. "You wasted a whole bag of donuts.

How much did you pay for those? Hope they weren't chocolate, that'd be a shame."

"Three bucks," he said.

"That's too much."

"I know."

"That's gonna be the last bit of money you spend."

He raised his brow. "Really?"

"It's double because you made me run."

He looked at me. "They say runnin' is good for you. It helps you stretch your insides. Keeps you fit."

"That's what I hear," I said. "I get all of it I need. Glad you take an interest in my health."

"What are friends for?"

"Friend? I wouldn't go that far."

"Really? Why's it gotta be like that?"

"You're no friend of mine."

"You're breaking my heart."

"Shut up."

"Okay."

"Good."

"But..."

"I said shut the hell up," I looked him over. "Sorry about the tooth."

He shook his head. "You ought to. I'm gonna have to get this fixed."

"I wouldn't worry about it."

"Why's that?"

I gave him a shove.

"A nice day," he tilted to the sky. "I like this time of year. Everything's fresh. Just seems like everything's clean, you know, buddy?"

"I'm not your buddy."

"And they say you're nice. Just sayin' how nice of a day it is."

"Good," I looked around me, then back at him. "Well,

better take it in now because I've gotta put you down," I tore out the gun from my jacket pocket.

"Really? Out in the open like this?"

"I'd wait, but you've pissed me off. You could've made it quick on yourself, but you had to run. I don't even have the right shoes on."

"Sorry if I wasn't thinking of your Goddamn footwear when I started running. You scared the shit outta me."

"You and I are gonna take a little walk behind there," I pointed to a small abandoned building across the street from Jankco's. "Nothing personal, it's just business."

"Understood. You don't have to do this. You can tell 'em I don't know... tell 'em I took off."

"I can't do that," I pointed the gun at him. "If I don't kill you, then I'm dead. I won't like that much. I may just have to come back and haunt you. Now, you better start walking."

"Come on, why can't you give me another chance? Just tell Joe it'll never happen again. I promise."

"Those are just words. You don't mean anything you say."

"You can trust me."

"Don't say anything."

We walked behind an old brick abandoned building; the only building on the street that wasn't open for business. I was familiar with the area. The place beside the abandoned building was an upscale burger joint. There was always a lot of noise going on in the kitchen, and no one would hear anything. He kept pleading for his life as we walked into the building. No matter what he said I had to get the job done. The building, because it was hollowed out, had a fine echo.

I kept the gun trained on him. "Johnny, you did a bad thing. We both know I can't let you walk away. You know the rules of the game. This sort of debt isn't easy to clear. And if not now, it'll get to the streets that you're nothing but a cheat."

He started to cry. "Tell them you couldn't find me. I promise to leave town. You have my word."

"Can't do that."

"Yes, you can."

"You hit a top guy and you expect people to turn their heads the other way? Sorry, shit doesn't work that way. Don't make me out to be an asshole."

"I have the drugs. Come on, he was askin' for it. You know it was only a matter of time before someone popped him. It… It… It…was an argument that got out of hand."

"The guy you shot up: wife, kids, nice house, someone has to pay for that. He was an upstanding guy."

"It's upstanding to kill people, is it?"

"There's all different kinds out there."

"Can't we talk about this?"

"No."

"Know who I'm friends with?"

"Think I give a fuck?"

He gulped air. "You should."

I grinned. "I'll take my chances."

"You'll be sorry."

"I doubt it."

"Come on, man, just forget about this."

"And how's that go?"

He shrugged.

"You knew better."

"Go back to them, I'll do anything they want. I'll make sure nothing like this happens again," his eyes lowered. "I'd take it as a personal favor. Anything you need, I can make that happen. I don't want this to be the end," his face turned red as he started to wrinkle and cry. "I beg you!"

He had fear and dread in his eyes.

I sighed. "I'm sorry."

"We can work something out."

"And how are we supposed to do that?" I kept the gun on him.

"I don't know. We can figure something out. I'm sure Joe can forgive. I have money."

"What am I supposed to do with that?"

"I could give it to you."

"Why?"

"For letting me live."

"I can't do that."

I had known Johnny for awhile. He stole from his friends. With someone like that, they couldn't be trusted again. He would go down as being a thief. His greed became greater than his life. He liked to run around town, bragging about things he'd never done, spreading lies like a girl's legs on prom night. His luck ran out when he took cocaine from my boss' organization. Joe heard that he took the drugs to sell to some of his friends for some quick cash.

I pulled the trigger, launching a bullet that hit him between the eyes. He fell to the cement floor. I walked over to his body and lifted his wallet for cash. I figured he couldn't spend the money dead. After I put two thousand of his money in my wallet, I turned and walked out of the building.

I walked to where my car was parked, got in, and sped down the street. I stopped at a filling station to use the payphone. The guy on the other end picked up. I told him I took out Johnny. He told me I did a good job then hung up. I walked into the filling station to get some cigarettes and something to drink. I got back in my car, dug around in the backseat, and found a half bottle of whiskey. I took off the lid and drew the bottle to my mouth, taking a long drink. I rested the bottle in my lap while I lit a cigarette. I took a few more drinks before putting the top back on and throwing it on the floorboard. I went to Johnny's place and got the cocaine.

 The guy Johnny shot was a good friend of mine, Steven Tippit. He had stolen a briefcase of cocaine from Steven and then shot him. Steven worked for Joe Butler, my boss. Everyone in the city, most people anyway, knew who Joe was.

Johnny knew he'd made a major mistake, a mistake he just couldn't walk away from. Plus, he killed a really good friend of mine. It was fucking terrible, he was an only child, and at the funeral his parents were all crying to me, looking for some sort of answer. Because of an oath I'd taken, I couldn't say a word.

 I went to Johnny's place for the cocaine and anything else I could find. I was there for about forty-five minutes before I left. I had to go back to my place and get ready for the gig that night.

two

    I was standing outside a bar called The Shack waiting for my band-mates to arrive. I was in a pool of light by the side of the building. The building was completely brown on the outside. A set of stairs were on either side to get to the double-doors that led into the dive. Neon beer signs hung in the front windows. The parking lot was a gravel pit mixed with dirt.

    I walked out of the pool of light, and sat on the front steps of the place while I waited. I looked at the different cars and trucks that were pulling into the place. I liked the idea that my band and I were going to play music for those people.

    Some guy staggered up to me and asked for a cigarette. After I gave him one, he started to tell me about this party he came from, and how all the girls there were whores. I told him he should've brought some with him.

He shook his head. "Nah, I couldn't do that."

"Why, man? Sounds like it'd be a good time."

"I have my girl with me."

"Oh, that'll change things."

He laughed. "If it were up to me, sure, I'd bring a truck load of 'em bitches. Whenever I get a chance... They are really nice."

"I can imagine."

He cleared his throat. "What are you doing out here?"

"Waitin' on some people. I play guitar in the band tonight."

"Really?"

"I never lie."

"What do you guys call yourselves?"

"Stoned Monkey."

"That's a cool name."

"Thanks."

"You guys have good music?"

"I think so."

"Guess I'll find out for myself, right?"

I shook my head. "Should be a good show."

"Let's hope so."

"Yeah."

"How many hours you guys gonna be around?"

"A few hours."

"That's good."

"Fun for all."

About that time a women walked up to the both of us. She looked at me. "Who are you?"

"Sean," I said. "I'm just talkin' to your man. Tellin' him I'm in the band playin' tonight."

"That so?" the woman said.

I nodded.

She said, "I'm sure it's gonna be a good time."

"I hope so," I said.

"If you've never been here, this is a nice place. Always good music, good time. We live over there a mile down Skunkhead Road," she pointed down the road, into the darkness. "We come down here whenever we get a chance."

"Seems like a nice place," I smiled.

She turned to the other guy. "How much beer money you have?"

"I have enough," the man said.

"You better for your sake. I want at least six beers tonight. Damn, Lee, told you to bring the rest of that case of beer with you. We paid for it. It's not like they were gonna offer us to take the rest of it. Damn, you don't think sometimes."

"Suzie, baby, don't start one of your fits. I was bein'

nice to those guys, that's why I left the beer. I mean, shit, they let us party with 'em, eat their food, smoke their dope."

Suzie hit him on the arm. "You're a good man, but you can be a dumb motherfucker at times. You always give to others."

"Thanks, babe," the man said.

I said, "You guys need some money?"

"No," Lee said. "We're fine as wine. Don't pay any mind to her. She gets herself in these fits. She's crazy as a kitty-cat. She's harmless, a push-over. Her bite isn't that strong."

She pointed a finger at me. "That's not true. Don't believe all of that mess. I'm not that bad, I can tell ya that."

"I didn't think anything," I told her.

"That's wise," she muttered. "You don't wanna hear it from me."

"I'll take your advice."

"Nice," she turned to her man. "I'm gonna go in. I need a drink."

"Okay," he said. "I'll be in shortly."

Suzie mumbled something as she walked passed us. She went up the stairs, opened the one side of the double-doors and disappeared inside.

Lee pointed at the door. "That girl's nothin' but crazy. Mark my words on that one."

I laughed. "I'll keep that in mind."

"You do that."

"The fuck I'm supposed to do with that?"

He dug in his pocket and pulled out a pack of cigarettes, lit one. "Better get in there. Don't want her comin' out here bitchin' at me."

"Don't blame ya."

"I'll see ya inside," he walked up the stairs and through the front door.

I wondered if Lee and Suzie would've stopped to talk to me if they knew I killed a guy earlier.

A slight breeze crept in the air. The winters in Arkansas were pretty tame, not too cold or hot. You never knew what the days were gonna bring. Ten more minutes passed before my brother, Jason, showed. He climbed out of his truck and walked toward me. He, like me, was tall and lanky. He was thirty-six. I was thirty-four. He was taller than me by a few inches. We both had brown hair. A lot of people would always ask if we were twins.

"Sean," he called over. "How's it going?"

"Can't complain," I told him. "Guess I could but who would listen, right?"

"Sounds about right."

"You know how it is."

"Indeed."

"It always is."

We shook hands.

"Get stuck in traffic?" I asked.

"Not bad," he said. "The 150 was a little busy."

"Ah, I went the other way."

"How was it over there?"

"Someone got arrested on my way up here."

"Anyone we know?"

"Just some guy who broke the rules of the road," I said. "Not really sure. Guess he had a warrant out or some-thing. Saw the cop cuff him on the side of the road. Cop had two other guys with him. Guy probably had drugs."

"That'll do it."

"Yeah," I pointed my finger at him. "Those cops, we need to keep a low profile. I'm sort of surprised I haven't gotten pinched yet."

"For what?"

"For anything."

He lit a cigarette. "Don't start that talk."

"That's something I don't need."

"You and me both."

"They'll lock both of us up."

"Yeah," he said. "If we can go through this life without going to prison, that'll truly be amazing."

"If our parents could see us now, right?"

He turned and blew a chunk of smoke toward the light. "It'll be one hell of a story."

"I think they would've prefer if we'd became lawyers or bankers."

"You're right about that."

"Hell, you have a lawyer, that's about the same as being a gangster. Most of them are corrupt at some point. Shit, you can never tell these days."

"Money always talks."

We laughed.

"What did you do today?" I asked.

"Not much, really. Met up with Viggo about noon. Went over to Brown's and watched the game. Think I had too much beer, though. When I got back to the house I had to take a nap."

"It happens to the best of us."

"Guess so," he said. "You know he got a new girl?"

"That's what he was sayin' the other day. I didn't meet her. I figure he'll have a new one by the end of the month."

"Probably."

"He runs through 'em pretty fast."

"You have to have verity."

"Can't argue with that. Just too many good lookin' women out there."

"That's about right," he threw the stub of his cigarette on the ground. "Won't ever see me tied down to just one girl, you know? Hell, they probably say the same thing.

But like all of 'em, that one day comes along where they want security and all that bullshit. They end up gettin' married to some poor fool."

I laughed. "And there's the sad commentary for ya."

He lit another cigarette. "I dunno, I look at this other shit we're in, wouldn't wanna bring a wife into it."

"Good point."

"I wouldn't want the girl to be a widow down the road or anything, to get that call early in the morning sayin' they found me face-down in a ditch somewhere."

"That wouldn't be good."

"It would fuck 'em up for life."

"And they'd spend the rest of their days poppin' pills, drinking like a fish, and bangin' anything with two legs."

"Shit, there are a ton of 'em that do that now."

"They are all wild."

He glanced out at the road, then back at me. "You see that one guy today?"

"Johnny?"

"Yeah."

"I did."

"How'd that go?"

"It's a done deal."

"Good thing."

"Guy had to go. You can't just go and do whatever-the-fuck you want. He knew he was playin' with fire."

"It was bound to happen sooner or later. Good work, man. That'll make some people happy."

"Don't know what'll make Joe happier, the fact Johnny's gone, or, that I got his snow back."

"Both."

"It's a lot of cocaine."

"Where's it now?"

"My apartment."

He laughed. "Keep it safe. Don't snort any of it."

"I value my life, don't worry."

"That's good."

"Don't wanna be in a hole any time soon."

"Don't think any of us want that."

"Wouldn't make for a very good day."

"You can say that again."

"Well, Sal and Joe got what they want. There won't be anyone in holes or ditches."

My brother laughed.

I looked off into the dark, then turned to my brother. "Hope this show goes good. I need good vibes, know what I mean?"

"Ah, it will," he said. "It's all about staying positive. The more shows we do, the more exposure we get, the closer we come to some sort of a record deal."

"When you're right, you're right."

"Always am."

"Ever since we were little you'd been there to tell me things were gonna be okay."

"Well, thanks, bro."

I sniffed some air. "Things need to start hooking up fast. I dunno, either the band or the crew. Looks like for now I have both."

"If you had to pick just one what would it be?"

"It's too late to pick."

"But, if you could?"

"I'd go with music."

"What about this?" he made his fingers in the shape of a gun. "You thinking about getting out?"

I shook my head. "Looks like we're in it till the end."

"I just wonder how this'll play out."

"One never knows."

"That's what makes me nervous.

"I wouldn't really dwell much on it."

"I forgot, you know what the future holds."

"It's the optimistic style in me."

"I should try more of that."

"You should."

"Someone has to be realistic about things."

I pointed a finger toward my chest. "I just envision the better outcome."

"That outcome may come with a price."

"It may."

My brother stared out onto the highway. "The thing we have to do is prevent that from being the way it folds."

"Those things can be tricky."

"You're telling me."

I looked at him. "It's fucked."

He shook his head. "Just this itch that won't go away..."

"At least we're in it together."

"For how long?"

"That's the all important question, isn't it?"

"Yeah."

"One day passes, another begins; that's all you can do."

"It's a great time to be alive, right?"

My other two band-mates, Clarence Dunn and William Glover, showed a few minutes later. Clarence was skinny, sporting long hair. He was thin like my brother and I. He had a wiry face that was clean shaven. Girls always told him he should be a male model. He was always a favorite when it came to the ladies. William was a bit shorter and a little heavier with a full beard. William was always a sort of quiet guy.

"Hey, man," Clarence came over. "What a night for a party, eh?"

"Guess so," I gave a nod. "Couldn't think of anything better."

Clarence gave a big smile. "If I didn't dig it, I wouldn't

be here."

 "Know what ya mean."

 "Just wanna have a blast tonight."

 William said, "Live it up! Rock n' Roll is gonna save us all, yeah!" he threw his arms into the air, and gave a howl into the night.

 I nodded at the building, then at the parking lot. "Looks like it's a packed house. I like the big crowds. It's all about exposure, you know?"

 Jason shrugged. "You're not just telling a tale out of a children's book."

 "You're crazy," I said.

 "I've heard that before."

 "Yeah."

 William lit a cigarette. "Guess we should check how this is gonna go."

 "Eager to start," Jason looked at William. "Can't fault ya for that. I had this nice honey I wanted to fall all over tonight."

 "I'm sure she'll still be there when you get back," Clarence laughed as he took a cigarette from his pack and lit it.

 "Oh, she'll wait," Jason said.

 "Sure that girl's real?"

 "Your mom's real," Jason replied.

 "Don't make me fuck your sister."

 "Nice," Jason said. "Better be glad you're my friend."

 "And just what were you planning on doing?"

 "Throw you in a ditch somewhere."

 "How harsh."

 "I have my moments."

 "Get the fuck outta here with that shit."

 We laughed

 "Think I'll try to get one of those girls tonight," William said. "Girls always love guys in bands."

"Tell them you just recorded an album. Learned long ago sometimes you have to tell little lies to get what you want," Clarence said.

"I'll do that."

"It works."

"I never said I doubted you."

"No offense, but you need to do something. Hadn't seen you with a broad for a few week."

"I know what I'm doing," William said.

"If you say so."

"You think I'm full of it?"

"Never said that," Clarence said.

"But you were thinking it."

"All I can tell you is what I see."

"And what's that?"

"A homo."

"I see what you're tryin' to pull."

"What would that be?"

"You're tryin' to deflect the fact you're gay by sayin' I am."

"But, William, buddy, I get girls all the time. Tell me, true or false, in the past few months have you not seen me with eleven different women?"

"Sure."

"And those are only the ones you know about."

"How many others were there?"

"Double the number."

William said, "Sure you're not makin' that up?"

"Oh, pretty sure."

"How do I know?"

"Guess you'll just have to believe me. I mean, if you want I could always teach you a thing or two. It's up to you."

"I'm good."

"That's why you have a girl?"

William sniffed. "I'm in between girls at the moment."

"Just like I'm gonna be in between your mama's tits tonight."

"The fuck?" William snapped. "My mom's busy with your dad."

"My dad's been with your sister."

"Doesn't surprise me, she's a whore."

We all laughed.

Jason said, "I was thinking about it, there's this new riff I came up with. Think I'll do it at the end of 'Arkansas Blues' after William hits the last two symbols."

"How long would it take?" I asked.

"About two minutes."

"Sounds pretty hardcore."

"Thanks, bro."

"When did you come up with that?"

"A few nights ago. I was just playing a little, and then I just started doing this little cord progression. I thought it was pretty good. When I played it, I was thinking, 'Man, I can't wait till the guys hear this. They'll dig it'"

Clarence said, "Can't wait to hear it."

"Me, too," William added.

My brother shrugged. "I was bored."

"That's when the best ideas come to us, right?" I said

"It makes sense, "Clarence said. "They say that's how some of the greatest artists made their art, under the in-fluence."

William looked around at all of us. "You think we should spark up?"

I said, "Think we should wait until after the show. We need to stay focused."

"I get your point."

"Then we can party like there's no tomorrow," I said.

"Won't get any complaints outta me."

"Good."

The four of us walked across the parking lot, through the doors into the establishment. The interior was all wood: floor, walls, tables, chairs, bar, everything was wood. The house musician was on his last song. He was a tall man with a white suit and a shiny black guitar. He had a deep scratch to his voice. He told the crowd his name was Dolan Buck, and that he grew-up in the area. He told the fine people that the only thing he'd never play would be Country and Southern rock. After he was done with his set he walked over and introduced himself. He was telling us how he was a fan of our music and we were on our way to greatness. Before he walked away he told us we should do a song together sometime. We thanked him and waved him on. I told the other guys that I had no intention on doing a song with that old bastard.

There were drunks everywhere. Cigarette smoke floated around all four corners of the room like fire stabbing its way through the night. There were laughs and chuckles from all directions. As people noticed who we were they started introducing themselves, and then they started telling us about how much they liked our music. After we thanked them and talked for a bit, we moved ourselves to the bar and ordered a few beers.

We told the barkeep who we were, that we were the band. She said she'd have to get the manager. She picked up the phone at the bar, pressed a button, waited a minute then started to talk to someone on the other end. She hung the phone up, came from behind the bar and walked to the back of the place. A few minutes later she returned with a heavy-set bald guy.

He walked over to us. "Hey, boys, the name's Roy Green, and this is my place."

"Not bad," Clarence said, looking around. "It's packed

tonight, Roy."

"That's what I like to see."

"I hear that's good for business."

"I know," Roy snorted. "All of these people equal money. Hell, that's the only reason I got this place. You have to keep 'em comin' in to spend money," he let out a big grin as he looked out onto the crowd from beside the bar. "It's about having good booze and music, that's what makes this place run smoothly."

"Hopefully, we can help with our music," Clarence said.

"I hope so. The last few acts to come here ran people off. They were a lousy bunch. It sounded like they just started the band that day," he laughed. "Well, you gotta know how to play the damn instrument, you know? Not really something you can learn in a day."

"Oh, that's not good," Clarence said.

"Not really."

"We'll try and be better than those guys."

"I'd appreciate that. If they like you I'll ask you guys come back again, then, if you want, we could work something out to make you regulars."

"What about that Dolan guy?" William asked.

Roy said, "You know, that guy's okay, I guess. I need some fresh faces in here. I can't have the same tired music," he shook his head. "I've heard a few rumors about him. Don't know if they're true or not."

"What did you hear?" Jason asked.

"That he's a pervert. Heard he raped a girl."

"Shit's crazy. You better get to the bottom of that."

"Something like that wouldn't be good for this place. I'd already sank too much money into this place. It'll work itself out. Change is always good, right?"

"That's a shame," Clarence said.

"Yeah," Roy said. "I'd hate to lose this place. Let's face

it, though, people can drink anywhere. Figuring out new things to get people in here is key."

"That's what any good business needs," I said

My brother added, "We're just glad to help. I know I'm excited. Can't really speak for the other guys."

"I just wanna play," William took a drink of beer.

"That's what I like to hear," the owner said. "More people I get like you guys in here, the more money I can put back into this place. In the next month or so I'd like to do some remodeling. It was pointed out to me I need to make this place bigger."

"Don't see where that would hurt anything," I told him.

My brother said, "Have to look at the big picture."

"Anyone can be bought," William added.

"Hell, boys, enough of my problems," Roy went on. "I might as well just piss in the wind. You guys just need to worry about having a good show. Can't wait to hear you play," he looked away from us at a women who pointed at him from the back office, then he looked back at us. "If you guys will excuse me, there are some things I need to tend to."

"We can see that," Jason said

Roy nodded at us, turned and walked away.

As I stood by the bar a little blonde bumped against me. She asked if I would buy her a drink. It turned out she was Roy's daughter. After a little back-and-forth I bought her a drink. She had a perfect smile.

"Thanks," she said.

"Glad to do it."

She looked at me. "You guys any good?"

"Huh, what do you mean?"

"Your music."

"Should be a good time."

"Hope so, for your sake," she smiled. "If you're not good my dad will shit-can you, never have you back.

You guys might even get a bad word spread all around. My dad knows a lot of people."

"I'm sure he does."

"And people like him."

"Hope they do."

"And they will tell all their friends."

"But we're good."

"Really?"

I laughed. "What, honey, you don't believe me?"

She looked me in the eyes, cocked her head to the side."First off, my name isn't Honey; second, I'll have to see for myself. You might be saying that to try and get into my pants."

"Trust me, I have better moves than that."

"I bet you do."

"Wanna find out?"

"You'd like that too much."

"What is your name?" I asked.

She ran her fingers through her hair and smiled. "Nikki."

"Nikki what?"

"Green," she laughed. "I told you my dad was Roy."

"Oh," I said. "See, I guess I should've put that one together."

A smiled. "You're funny."

"I've heard that a few times."

She smiled again. "Guess one more won't hurt."

"You gonna stick around for the show?"

"I can't."

"Why?"

"I'm going with a friend to another bar."

"Oh, that so?"

"Yes, sir."

"I see."

"Guess I'll have to catch you guys again. Guys shoulda

been here last night. The band that played, they weren't that good. Think people were a little mad. Then again, it was only a two dollar cover."

"That wasn't bad."

"I didn't think so."

"Can't go wrong with that price."

We talked about Stoned Monkey for a bit.

After the drink she left. I told her I would call her the next day. I never called the next day. I lost the piece of paper. The other guys kept telling me I lost it on purpose.

We were sitting at the bar when Roy came over and told us we should get ready to do our set. We went out to our vehicles, unloaded the equipment and brought it inside. They had a small wooden stage tucked away in the corner. It looked as if it would collapse at any minute.

At first, I thought it wouldn't be big enough to fit all of us. It was gonna be tight. After we got everything setup, I looked around at the crowd, everyone looked eager for a night of good music. They seemed to have all the momentum and energy for a great show. It was our job to show them a good time, to give them something to remember.

I played a note on my guitar; it screamed through the bar like a mad drunk. I followed it by sliding my fingers up the neck. I started to play this little riff I made on the spot.

Jason walked over with his bass. "Can you believe all these girls here?"

"The talent looks good," I said.

"It does."

"I might get laid tonight."

"Anything's possible."

"Got that right."

He nodded. "William might even find himself a girl."

"Even him?" I muttered.

"Anything's possible."

We laughed.

We looked back at William, but he wasn't paying attention to us.

Clarence walked across the stage and grabbed the microphone from its stand.

"Hey, guys. How are you tonight?" he said to the crowd. "I think we're gonna have a great Saturday night. There's nothing we like more than playing in our home state of Arkansas. I'm glad you guys are having a good night, drinkin' beer and going crazy. Hope you like the show. For those of you who have no idea who we are, we're Stoned Monkey. And we're here to rock your fuckin' night."

Yells and screams came from the crowd.

"Don't think we'd be here if it wasn't for you," our singer continued. "The best way to pay you back is to play a great show. Y'all sure look great!"

As soon as Clarence finished talking, Jason started to pluck the strings of his bass. Low tones thundered across the stage. William started a slow beat on the drums, and then he hit his symbols a few times. Clarence opened his mouth into the microphone and I joined on guitar.

A rhythm started to move through the crowd. People started to sway to and bop to the beat. Girls and guys started spinning around in circles, putting hands on hips. An excited chant manifested through all corners. The smell of beer ran through like a fierce snake, slithering and crawling in all directions.

There were smiles everywhere.

A few people in front started stomping on the floor as they danced. They threw up their hands in a fit of excitement. People in back came up front and started to mimic the others.

For the next few hours we played our hearts out.

After we were done with our set, we hauled all of our equipment back to our vehicles. We talked to the owner for awhile, then spent the rest of the night drinking at the bar, listening to another band.

"Music sounded good, guys," Roy told us.

"Thanks," I said. "Glad to hear you say that. We always try our best."

"Yeah," Jason added. "It's a groovy ride when we get on stage and play. One-by-one, we're getting as many followers as possible."

"That's the aim of any good artist, right?" Roy said "There was a time when I was in a band doin' the local scene."

"Really?" William asked. "What happened?"

"We had a few disagreements along the way. We only lasted about a year or so. It was a lot of fun. The guys I was playin' with got big egos and stuff; that's the thing that tore the band apart."

"That's a shame," Clarence said. "Ever think about picking it up again?"

"Not really."

"Why?"

"I wasn't really good at it. I basically just got in it to get girls. Once I got my girl, I lost interest."

"That's a shame."

"Maybe," Roy said. "Enough about me, I think you guys have what it takes to go all the way."

"Think so?" I asked.

"Of course," he said. "I think you guys could really go far if you keep at it."

We sat at the bar telling stories with patrons. It was around two in the morning when the place closed. We walked out into the parking lot. The breeze before had picked up, and turned into a cooler wind.

Shootin' Noise

We ended up going to this diner on the other side of town. We spent the next few hours eating, guzzling coffee, and talking energetically about the future of the band. We talked about the life of crime we'd come to know over the past few years.

When we started the band, we would play to a small crowd in the back of William's house. He had about half an acre with woods. As word spread the crowds grew every weekend. At their peak, there were about three hundred people at the shows. People would bring lots of dope and beer. At some point during the night someone would always start a bonfire, and then everyone would start yelling and howling. The party normally wouldn't die out until about three in the morning.

Soon after, we started to branch out and get gigs all around.

three

I got a call, from a guy I know, James Burton, who asked me to meet him at Highlife; a club in North Brown Ridge. I got in my car and sped away. I turned up the radio and rolled down the windows. The sun stretched its arms over the open road as I flew down the streets. I pulled up in front of the club and walked in.

I was sitting at a table in the corner waiting for the guy on the phone to arrive. I lit a cigarette and stared at the dancers on stage; they were all in G-strings and lace. They looked nice; no fake breasts or anything. The place was dark. A set of neon lights wrapped around the stage where the girls danced. After a minute I glanced down at a glass of whiskey, picked it up, and took a drink. There were about thirty people in the place, all drinking, smoking, laughing, enjoying the dancers

A waitress came by and asked if I wanted another drink. She was a beautiful girl named Madison. She had dirty blonde hair and a sweet smile. Ever since she started working at Highlife, I have been attracted to her. She wore a tight red T-shirt and a black leather miniskirt. She had bright green eyes. I loved looking at her.

"You know I do," I said. "I'm still waiting for someone to show."

"They running late?"

I shook my head. "About ten minutes."

"Maybe they aren't showing?"

"Nah. He'll be here. Probably got tied up in traffic or something. I can never really tell with that guy."

"Oh," She smiled. "You want anything else while you wait? Something to eat? It's all free to you guys, you know?"

"Yeah."

"So, anything?"

"Just the drink."

"Okay, then."

"I'll be fine."

She said, "Can I interest you in something later?"

"What time are you getting out of here?"

"Midnight."

"I'll be here."

"Sounds good."

"We can go to my place if you want. I'm sure we'll figure something out. I have a few things to do, but yeah, I'll be back here."

She leaned closer to me. "You know, I have a break coming up, if you want we could sneak into the back room."

"That's tempting, but I can't. I need to meet with this guy."

"Guess we'll have to wait till later."

"I guess so."

She licked her lips. "I'll make it worth the wait."

"I bet you will."

"It's a date, then."

"If you wanna call it that."

"What would you call it?"

"You know, two people enjoying each other's company."

"I'd like that."

"I knew you would."

"I always do."

I patted the top of the table. "Take a load off."

"Maybe for a minute."

"Hey, if anyone has a problem with it just let me know."

"I'm not worried about it."

She sat.

"Why should you?" I asked.

"I know you guys take care of things."

"No problem," I said. "That's just what we do."

"I know the other girls appreciate it, too."

"Glad to do it."

"I've heard them talk about it."

"It's a guy's job to do anything that protects women."

"That's sweet."

"It's just the right thing."

Madison smiled again. "If you need anything at all just ask. I'll be here or back in the kitchen," she moved closer to me and placed her hand on my leg. "I know where the cocaine's at in the place, you want some?"

I laughed. "You're too kind, but I can't. Wish I could. I have some stuff to sort out with this guy. We can do some later."

"Promise?"

"I always do."

"You better."

"How was your day?" I asked.

"Pretty good. It's been steady. I made twenty bucks so far."

"Well, there ya go!"

"And I didn't do much."

"You didn't tell them to come in. Hey, they didn't have to part with their money."

"True."

I shook my head. "Better for you."

"Yeah."

"You should go over to Tunica."

"Gamble? I'd probably lose."

"You never know."

"I never win at the casino."

"There's a first for everything."

She chuckled. "Yeah."

"I could go with ya."

"Sure."

"It's never a gamble with me, babe."

"Oh, I know."

"When you wanna go?"

"Wish I could," she said. "I have to stay and work."

"Maybe next time?"

"That'd be nice."

She asked how my day was.

"Not much. Jason and I just ran around town, getting shit done. It's all in a day's work"

"How exciting."

"It was."

"Break anyone's legs?"

I nodded. "The day's not over yet."

"You better not," she chuckled.

I lit a smoke. "After we got done running around we went to his place, worked on some music."

"How'd that go?"

"Not too bad."

"Can't wait to hear."

"Soon enough."

We talked a little longer before she was called away. She said she'd be back shortly with my drink. As she walked away she blew a kiss.

About ten minutes later, a tall thin man wearing a suit approached the table. He put his finger on the chair opposite me.

"This seat is taken?" he asked.

"It's all yours," I told him.

"Thanks," the man said. "Sorry for the wait, Sean. I was over at my sister's place. It turned into this whole thing. I tried to get out there as fast as I could. She needed a family. Her guy slapped her around some. Tuned her up pretty well. She was afraid he'd finish the job. I got to her house, she had a busted lip and a swollen face. It wasn't a good thing."

"Shit's not right," I exhaled a stream of smoke. "You gonna take care of it?"

"Told him I wasn't, but I'm gonna surprise him tomorrow. Short and quick. Element of catching a person off guard is key to this business."

I shook my head. "Something like that, you need to catch him when he least expects it. The guy probably walks tall thinking he's something big beatin' on people smaller than him. You gotta let that maggot know, knock him down a few pegs."

"You can believe when I'm done with him he's gonna pray for a bullet."

"That's the best way," I put my cigarette stub out in the ashtray. "You gonna need any help with the guy?"

"Thanks, but I'll be fine. He's not that tough. I've dated women stronger than him. No, you won't have to worry about me. After I give him that beatin', I'm gonna let him know if it happens again my sister won't know what happened to him. There's a lot of places to get disappeared to."

"Very true."

"He won't know what hit him."

"If you need help tomorrow just give me a call. I don't think I have anything on the agenda."

"Don't think I'll have any problems, though."

"Backup?"

"It'll be fine."

"Okay."

"And that's personal, a family matter. Best if nobody else gets involved."

"I understand."

"That's the thing, cops won't do shit. Most they'll do is throw the guy in the slam for a night or two, then he'll get out and do it again."

"Yeah."

"And the cycle goes on."

"It's fucked."

"People say we're the bad guys. Hell, I've seen more cops that are corrupt over the years. They're people, too. Maybe they got a few more screws loose than we do, who the fuck knows?"

I nodded. "I've come across people who've told me about that kind."

"Yeah, they're out there."

"You need to put some of them on the payroll."

James gave me a hard look. "You okay, kid? You look tired."

"The guys and I were out till early this morning. We did a show at Lakeview. It was a pretty good time."

"The bar over there?"

"Yeah. Wiggles, they had drafted for a dollar."

"Sorry, I missed it. You can't beat that price for beer. Guess I'll have to catch the next time you guys play."

"Don't worry about it."

He coughed. "Everyone needs something to do other than this stuff. For me, I like to read. This can be a pretty dangerous life."

"I like to read."

"It's good for the soul."

"I'd have to agree."

"But when talking about music, women swoon to stuff like that. It shows them you have a creative side to ya."

I nodded. "That's one of the reasons we got into it."

"Don't blame you."

"It's a way of life."

"I'll drink to that."

"It comes with the territory."

He turned his head to look at the dancers, then back at me. "I used to like going to the Jazz bars when I was younger. I always met some good women in those places."

"Can't go wrong with jazz."

"There used to be this place downtown, DeLona's, it was good but closed about ten years ago. You ever go there?"

I nodded. "Must've been before my time."

"It was a nice place. That was the last in a handful that closed around here. Someone told me they were gonna open another Jazz place. I'm not sure if that'll happen."

"That'd be nice if it did."

"We need more places like that around here. It was a nice little getaway. Just sit in the dark with a whiskey or whatever and taste those fine notes."

"I could get into that scene, no problem."

He pointed a finger. "You should open a place of your own."

"Really?" I laughed. "Why did you say that?"

"You have a good ear for music. You know what young people like these days. You could run a business if you put your mind to it. Hell, I ran a few things in the past. If I can do it, anyone can. Get them in the door... All the booze and women they want for a price," he laughed. "I can see it now in big neon letters."

"Maybe."

"Something like that could provide a good cover. It's a legit way to mask the business. Like what Sal did with this place."

"I can see that."

"Something to think about."

"Thanks."

"I didn't get where I am based on good looks."

Shootin' Noise

I laughed.

James was an older gentleman, about sixty or so. His face was old and wrinkled. He had deep blue eyes that held a lifetime of pain. He had always been part of his life since he was fifteen. He was a tough guy who knew his place in the world. He never lied to anyone about who he was. The first time I met him, was a few days after Joe and Sal first sat me down for a discussion. To me, James came off as a nice old man.

He looked over at the girls on stage and chuckled. "Those are some beauties, aren't they?"

"They are."

"You should take one of 'em to your place. Have some fun with her."

"I might do that."

"You better," he said. "When you get my age you'll wish you had. I have more days behind me than I do in front."

Madison came back with my other drink.

She apologized for taking too long. I told her it was no problem. She asked James if he wanted anything. He gave her a nod and waved her off.

As she walked away, I gave a little smile.

"You got a thing for her?" he asked.

"Not sure yet."

"Not sure?"

"I'm gonna take her back to my place tonight and see what happens."

He laughed. "Sounds like you have a thing for her."

"You think?"

"Sure."

"I guess so."

"Oh, don't give me that bullshit. Either you have a thing for her or not. There isn't a big riddle behind it."

"I'll just have to see how things play out."

"I know this, if you don't take her someone else will."

"I don't doubt it."

"You'll be shit outta luck then, buddy."

"Guess I'd better make my move."

"I'd advise you do."

"I'll take that."

He leaned back in his chair as I lit a cigarette. I glanced over my shoulder and caught Madison's eye. She gave me a wink.

"What did you call me here for?" I asked James.

"First things first, did you get the briefcase back?"

"It's at my apartment."

"At least we got that in our corner. That's a lot of snow."

"It looked like it."

"We have to sell it and get that cash."

"Shouldn't be a problem."

"It's sad when you think about it."

"All these fuckin' junkies, you'd think someone's giving the shit for free. Who gives a mother's fuck anymore? Look at it like this, if they're out there doing drugs, running the streets, stealing, killing, the next step is where we're sitting. New solders."

James said, "I just ask they don't leave me in a ditch somewhere."

"I know what you mean," I took a drink. "I always told myself I wanna get shot in the back of the head. I don't wanna see the guy that's gonna take me out."

"To be honest, I don't care. I just want everyone to know what I did when I was alive."

"I'd let 'em know."

"Thanks," he said. "It doesn't look like I'm gonna have anyone carry on my name when I kick."

"What are you talkin'? You're not going anywhere."

"Maybe. You can never tell."

I said, "Think someone's after you?"

"Nothing like that."

"Wouldn't wanna be the man who stands up to you."

"That's the thing, a man knows better. A little kid, they'd probably have to be taught a lesson."

"I hear ya."

"These new guys, they have to show respect, you know? I didn't get where I am without paying dues. I put in my time."

I nodded. "Just like a big business."

He laughed. "With a retirement plan not worth a shit."

"So, back to this other job you have for me?"

James turned his head to make sure no one was listening, then leaned into the table. "I have a little work for you. A nice little payday. I'd do it myself, but the big guy wanted me to give this one to you. One step closer to being a legitimate gangster."

"Who's the guy?"

"How do you know it's a guy?"

"I'm lucky, what can I say?"

"Can't pull the wool over your eyes."

"Not really."

James reached into his inside pocket, pulled out a folded piece of paper, and handed it to me. "Guy's name and address. He's gonna be home tonight. He's a real pushover. It should be really easy; no kids, no wife, he lives alone."

I read the paper, then looked at James. "Looks like Mr. Bryan is in for a surprise. Hope the last meal he eats is a good one."

"With him, it's the drink."

"I know him."

"You do?"

"For a few years now. When I first met him he would always try to get me involved in some of his shady deals.

He was always one for wanting to make a fast buck."

"That's what got him in trouble."

"Knew it'd happen sooner or later."

"It always does. They never think it will."

"How bad is it?"

"I wouldn't wanna be him, that's for sure."

"I know that's right."

"I saw our friend leaving the liquor store last night. I would've popped him myself, but there were too many people around."

"Oh? Might have to take some booze after I get rid of him."

James laughed. "There ya go."

"I don't have a problem with it."

"I bought him a case of booze last Christmas. He didn't get me anything."

"Think I would've shot him then."

"I was a little hurt."

I leaned into the table. "What about after, is there anything else?"

"We're gonna have a gathering at the warehouse tonight. Think the boss wants to talk over a few things. You know, touch base with everyone."

I shook my head. "Seems right. What time are we meeting?"

"Around eight."

"Should I bring a cake or pie?"

He laughed. "Nah, nothing like that. Tell those guys you run around with about the meeting."

"I can do that."

James slapped his palm on the table. "Why can't some of the other guys follow orders like you can?"

I shrugged. "Couldn't tell ya. I just do what I'm told. I've learned not to ask too many questions."

"That's the smartest way to go about it. I've seen too

many guys, friends of mine, end up dead because they didn't know how to do that."

Madison came back by with another drink for me and one for James, telling us they were on the house.

We thank her.

She gave me another smile. "You gonna be here at midnight?"

"Of course, baby," I smiled back.

"I'll be waiting."

"Okay."

"It'll be a time to remember."

"With you, every night should be remembered."

"Oh, you're such a charmer."

"I get that a lot."

"It's a good way to be."

"Oh?"

"Yeah."

"I'll have to keep that in mind."

She looked at James. "Make sure nothin' happens to this guy."

"I'll do my best," James said.

"I wanna keep him around for awhile."

The older man said, "Yeah, he's a good kid."

"He is that," she said. "Has he been over here saying good things about me?"

"You know he has."

She turned to me. "I like it."

"That's the kind of guy I am," I shrugged.

The three of us talked some more before she walked away.

James eyed me. "A woman like that, that's the kind you need to settle down with."

"I'm not ready for that just yet."

"Better worry, pretty soon she'll be with another guy."

"I know."

"The hell you waiting for?"

"Good question."

"Take my advice, kid."

Highlife was one of our hangouts. The place was owned by a man named Sal, a guy in the origination. He was a close friend of Joe's, the boss. Sal Alford was next in line for the boss. I'd heard some talk from people who said Sal would make a better boss.

"What did Bryan do?" I asked. "There's no telling when it comes to that guy."

James grinned. "He borrowed some money from the big guy, about sixty large, and didn't pay it back. If he has the money, that's good. If he doesn't have the money, give him a ticket on the bullet train, and paint the walls red with him. You can't pull that shit on the boss. He's a nice guy, but not that nice. Everyone who borrows something has to return it. He needs to be made an example of. He might be a friend to some people, but… and if I were you, I'd be pretty snappy about it."

"I can do that," I said. "You don't have to worry about a thing."

"When you get done just come back by the warehouse. We'll be there."

"Anything I should know about the place?"

"Can't think of anything. The doors creak, so you won't be able to sneak around the place."

"Other than that?"

"There's nothing."

I put the piece of paper in my pocket. "Consider him gone."

"You got your heater, right?"

"I carry it with me wherever I go. Don't wanna get in another jam again."

James smile. "You would've been fucked if I hadn't

been there. Would've been in the fuckin' ground."

"I owe you one."

"It happens to us all," James lit a cigarette.

I looked down at my glass for a minute, then back at James. "Think I'll go over there about six. That way I can just go to the meeting from there."

"Just make sure it gets done."

"That won't be a problem."

"If it doesn't get done, you and me…shallow grave."

"Understood."

"You're an ace in my book. If they have a problem, just tell those little bastards I'll be after them."

"Thanks."

"It's not a big thing."

"Well, at any rate..."

He eyed me. "You and your brother, you guys are good fucks. I'd do the same for him."

"He always liked you."

"Why wouldn't anyone like me? I'm the tough-as-nails, old, sweet gangster. I'm just having the greatest time I can."

"That's the way it should be."

"I have more years behind than I have in front."

An hour passed while we sat talking. James stood from his chair and said he had to leave. He wished me luck and headed for the door. After I finished my drink I stepped outside to the brightness.

I went back to my apartment and took a little nap.

Around six, I drove to where Bryan lived. He had a small house on Squirrel Road, on the outskirts of North Brown Ridge. He lived in a little white two-bedroom house. The house had black shutters and two bushes along the walkway leading up to the front door. I pulled in the drive and killed the engine. I thought he would peek his head out the window to see whose car was outside, but he never did. I took my gun out of my jacket to make sure how many bullets I had: ten, plenty for the job. After I was done checking the bullets, I put the gun back in my jacket and stepped out of the car.

I rang the doorbell. After a few seconds, footsteps came from the other side. The door opened and Bryan stood in the doorway. He was a short guy, not very strong at all. He was wearing a T-shirt and jeans. Booze and cigarettes were on his breath.

"Hey, Sean, how the hell are ya?" he extended his hand to me.

We shook.

"Not much," I said. "I was just in the neighborhood, thought I'd stop by."

"What were ya doin' over here?"

"Visiting a friend."

"Who?"

"You don't know him."

"Fair enough," he said. "Come on in. There's no fuckin' strangers here, buddy!"

I walked in.

The living room was small. The shag green carpet was tasteless. The four white walls had cracks in them. A black and white TV sat on a stand in the corner of the room. He had been watching cartoons. A plate with food on it was lying on the brown couch.

"Caught me at kind of a bad time," he picked up the plate and took it to the kitchen counter.

"Sorry about that, Bryan. Didn't mean to interrupt your cartoons."

"Oh, that's fine," he said. "I just got in about an hour ago. Went to the casino up in Morrison. Lost it big today."

Shootin' Noise

"How much?"

"Just over fifty large."

"Really? Damn. Sounds like you need better luck."

"I know," he said. "Thought I was doing good. Got too greedy, I guess. I was up and then down again. Need to play smarter next time."

"Sounds like it."

"Or cheat."

"That always works."

He hit me on the shoulder. "We all have a bad day, am I right?"

"Sure," I smiled.

"Hope next time I go back I win it big. I'll get back what is rightly mine," he laughed. "People call it a sickness, but the way I see it, everything's a sickness these days. Am I gonna die from gambling? Don't think I'm gonna go out like that."

"Maybe you're right."

We walked into the small kitchen.

We sat at his kitchen table.

"On that topic," Bryan said, "how would you wanna die?"

I sat back. "You wanna kill me?"

"Nothin' like that. Just talkin', you know?"

"Yeah."

"Come on with it!"

"I always wanted to go out in my sleep, nice and silent."

"Where's the glory in that? I always dreamed that I'd go in some sort of shoot-out with a bunch of crazy fuckers. I've played it out in my mind at least two hundred times. The shit's fuckin' beautiful, man."

"Really?"

"Why not? I'd be remembered for doing something noble. Fuck. They might make a day in my honor."

"I hate to rain on your parade, but I think those are re-served for guys who aren't criminals."

"Never hurt a politician."

"Good point."

"I'll be the peacemaker, the one who'll off the bad guys and blanket peace over the masses."

"Interesting. It could happen."

He asked if I wanted anything to drink

"What do ya get?" I asked.

"Brandy or beer."

"I'll take a brandy."

"You got it, partner."

"Thanks."

He smiled. "I want you to know my place is always open. Make yourself at home anytime."

"I appreciate that."

"It's the least I can do."

He got up from the table, walked over to a cabinet, and took a bottle from the top shelve. He dug into the cabinet beside it and brought out two glasses. He put both glasses on the counter and filled them.

He turned and walked back to the table with both glasses.

He handed me mine.

"Man, I gotta tell ya, I think I fucked up big," he said.

"Really?" I took a drink. "What makes you say that?"

He looked down at the table for a few seconds, then back at me. "That money I lost, it was supposed to go to Joe. I'd borrowed the money to pay back another debt. Either way, I'm dead."

"Who's the other debt?"

He took a drink. "Ted."

I lit a cigarette. "Ted?"

"I didn't want anyone knowing."

"You just told me."

"I trust you."

"Why do you trust me?"

He shrugged. "You just seem trustworthy."

I took a long drag on my cigarette and exhaled. "How much do you owe Ted?"

"Over seventy."

"Thousand?"

"Yeah."

I rubbed my hand along my chin. "That's a lot. You gonna be able to pay it back?"

"Not really."

"Damn."

"I'm pretty nervous."

I flicked my ash in the blue ashtray on the table. "What are ya gonna do? Somethin' like that, there's not many options."

He stared at me again. "Can you help me out?"

"I'm tapped. Even if I did, you'd end up owing me money."

"You're right, I guess."

"I have my shit to take care of."

He nodded. "Oh, that's okay. I'll find another way. Sorry, I brought it up."

"Never hurts to try, right?"

He nodded.

I drank the rest of my glass.

"Mind if I get another drink?" I asked.

He took my glass and walked to the counter.

I took my gun out of my jacket, pointed it at the back of Bryan's head, and fired. Blood splattered on the cabinets and he fell to the floor. I put the gun away got the brandy bottle and took a few swigs. As I walked back into the living room, carrying the bottle, I noticed a few spots of blood on my right hand. I went to the restroom to wash my hands.

I walked out of the restroom back into the kitchen and fished around the lifeless body for a wallet. I took the money, two grand, and then threw the wallet in the puddle of blood. For the next hour, I ransacked the place, looking for money, drugs, jewelry, whatever I could get my hands on. I found a few hundred dollars and some marijuana. After I was done I walked back into the living room, shot the TV, and left.

four

The warehouse was on Magtana Road, headed out of town by Pine Lake. As I made my trek along the road, I looked out the window at the lake; it was such a lonely place. The moon hung in the night, illuminating the open space.

I pulled into the parking lot of the warehouse. There were about ten cars in the lot. The street light above was dim. As I stood in the lot, I saw a car approaching. It turned into the gravel parking lot. The driver's door swung open and a figure crawled out. It was Sal Alford. He staggered up to me and asked how I was. He asked for a cigarette before he went inside. Sal was an aging guy with jet-black hair and a sharp jaw. He was always dressed well in a leather suit and tie. Sal was second in command next to the boss, Joe Butler.

"How the hell are ya, Sean?" he asked, extending his hand.

We shook.

"Oh, just tryin' to get through the day," I said with a grin on my face.

He chuckled. "Boy, don't I know how that goes. If I can get through the day without dying, that's the best day."

"Let's hope your days last. You're one of a kind."

"Thanks," Sal's eyes lit up. "You're a good man. We need more like you in the world, Sean. People can always rely on you."

I nodded. "I just do what needs to be done."

"That's good," the man said. "Now, let's go in here and see what these guys are getting into."

"Probably drunk?"

"I wouldn't put it passed 'em."

After Sal went inside the warehouse, I turned to see someone get out of another car, a guy by the name of Robert Spikes. As he slammed the car door shut, he looked over to me and let out a big smile. Robert was an idiot. The first time he ever got arrested, he broke into a church to steal a few bottles of wine. He got caught, as he always did when he tried to commit these dumb crimes. Robert almost got shot one time when he robbed a bank; for that, he got a five-year sentence. He was re-leased two months prior. I didn't like the guy that much. As he passed I gave him a nod.

Robert was a heavy-set bald guy with a dark thick mus-tache. He stood six foot three, three hundred pounds, something like that. He was always dressed in a dark suit and tie. I made the mistake of going to dinner with Robert once. After he sent back his meal a few times, he broke into a rage, yelling at the waiter, and cussing the other guests. The owner asked us to leave. We went to another restaurant and he ordered enough food to feed an army; half of which ended up on his shirt. He was a messy bear of a man. And the guy always seemed to sweat. With all the sweat it amazed me he was as heavy as he was. He talked in a low voice.

"Nice night," the fat man called out.

"That it is," I said.

He walked over to me and opened his arms big. "What do ya know?"

"Not sure," I said. "Don't know."

"Oh, come on, man, you gotta know what's going on. What the hell have you been doing?" he put down his arms. "Any rumors? Tales? Anything? You don't have anything for me?"

"Afraid to disappoint."

"Something's always happening in this city. I'd be amazed when something didn't happen. Like that thing last night."

I raised a brow. "What thing?"

Robert said, "Somebody busted this kid bad with a bat."

"What kid?" I asked curiously.

"Oh, that Thompson kid, Kyle Thompson. Worked over there at the liquor store off Pike."

"Don't think I know him," I said. "Who beat him?"

"A couple of hillbilly boys from what I heard."

"Damn."

"Sent him to the hospital."

"Hope he makes it."

"If that was my kid they beat, I'd hunt them down and take them out. There's too many crazy maniacs out there."

"You got that right."

"The world's a dangerous place," he muttered.

We stood in silence for a moment.

"Hillbillies, huh?" I said.

"That's right."

"Think they're from over by Midway?"

He shrugged. "Can't say. That would be a long way to come from just to beat someone."

"Was Kyle connected to anyone?"

"I'm sure he was."

I sighed. "Not good."

"Yeah," he said. "It was probably drug-related or something. I just happened to see his name on the news. They ran the story. Didn't say who did the beating."

"You know how things spread around here."

"I know."

"It's a sad thing."

He patted me on the shoulder. "It's a crazy place, my friend."

"You can say that again."

He gave me a hard look. "We need to do more jobs together."

"Sure," I said. "Name the time and place."

"I'll have to keep that in mind."

"You do that," I said. "I don't want any of your bullshit crimes."

He laughed. "I wouldn't do anything like that to you."

"I've heard that before."

"You don't have to worry about me. I'm done with the stupid shit."

"That's what they all say."

He waved me off.

I looked at the warehouse, then Robert. "They tell you how long this is gonna be?"

"Not sure," he said. "Hope it's not too long. I wanted to go out for some tacos."

"Where were you thinkin' of going?"

"El Romo."

"Never been there."

"They're pretty good."

"I'll have to check them out."

"Tell 'em I sent ya, they'll give you a discount."

"Thanks."

"Don't mention it."

I knocked on the door three times.

The door opened, and I saw James.

I shook James' hand, then walked through the doorway. Robert followed.

James and I exchanged a few words, then he asked how it went with the guy before. I looked at James, smiled, and told him everything was good, that it went easy. I left out the part about me ransacking the guy's house. I asked James how long the meeting was going to be, but he said he didn't know.

As soon as Robert walked in, he darted to the other side

of the building to talk to someone. My bandmates were sitting around drinking. I walked over and sat with them. Clarence was telling the others about this girl he met at this party three days earlier, and how lovely she was. As soon as he was done with the story, they moved to other topics.

The warehouse inside A hollow shell of something that seemed to be important at one time. A few chairs and couches were spread out in the open area. A fridge with beer inside sat against the far wall to the right. A long table sat in the center. In a little room off to the side was a restroom, nothing fancy. The guys were all sitting around the table talking, drinking, smoking, and passing time until the big guy, the boss, showed up. Joe hired a guy to put air and heat in the place

One of the guys looked at me and pointed to the fridge. "Want a bottle?"

"I'll get it," I told him. "A cold one sounds right about now."

"Cold ones are always good"

"True."

"It's just what the doctor ordered."

"I can see that. I know what you mean."

His name was Tony Wright. He was a bull of a man, strong, very respected on the streets. He took shit from nobody. He could be very intimidating when he wanted to be. When I first started coming around to the hangouts, he scared the hell out of me. There was just something about the way he'd look at you sometimes. He looked like a younger version of Sal. Tony was beside Sal in rank.

There were a bunch of us in the crew: Macho Machine, Robert Spikes, Tony Wright, Tomato Head, James Burton, Sal Alfred, Icy, Jack the Garbage Can, Mike the Hammer, Miles, Jumper, Tyson, Clown Face, Dizzy,

Christmas, Rooster, Clyde the Blade, Eyeball Frank, Jerky, Wise Guy, Blind Mouse, Sicko, Fishy, Toe-Foe, Jew as Ronnie, Hog, Minute Man, Popper, Dave the Man, Lester the Girl, Frog, Conley, Skully, Peppers, and two dozen others. Most of them had nicknames, and those names were what everyone called them. In a lot of cases, I knew what their real names were. For the most part, they were all nice guys, nice until you crossed them. They all had big personalities. At first, a lot of them were skittish about my friends and myself. You had to make sure they could trust you; if not, you would disappear and get spun off the world.

 I walked over to Eyeball Frank. He was sitting in a chair by himself, smoking a cigarette and drinking a beer. Frank ran card games and two whore houses: one on Riverside, and the other on the opposite end of North Brown Ridge, Country Hill. It was a good location for a business, off the beaten path. The place was surrounded by a sea of land. He had a plan to open more whore houses.

 "How the hell's it going, Frank?" I asked as I walked over to him.

 He put down his beer and looked at me. "Hey, hey, there he is! Sean, Sean, what do ya know?"

 "Not much," I said.

 "I hear ya, just waitin' for the damn meeting to start. Do you know what this is all about?"

 I shrugged. "No idea."

 "I was over at Riverside all day. You know, just makin' sure things go smoothly. I didn't want the shit that happened last week coming back and spooking the girls. They shouldn't have to put up with that thing. Sorry, it happened to begin with. Anyway, I was about to leave, that's when Sal came over and told me about this here."

 "James told me," I said. "He didn't give that much information, you know? Just said to come here."

"Probably just wants to touch base," he stood from the chair. "Looks like we got a full house tonight, boy. I should've had some of my girls come and entertain."

"That would've been good."

"Maybe next time," he said. "You hear about that new girl?"

I looked at him. "Which one? You have like four of them."

He started counting to himself on his fingers. "Mindy…Tara…Lulu… No, it's Tara," he put his fingers down. "Nah, you need to come see this new girl we have, Tara. She came over a week ago. She's a nice brunette with a tight body. Amazing tits."

I smiled. "I bet she does."

"You know it's always on the house. Just come by whenever. I can even give you her phone number."

"I'll just come by."

Frank nodded.

He got his nickname from when he took a man's eye out with a knife. The guy was an ex-boyfriend of a girl that worked for him. I guess the ex tried to get the girl back and wouldn't leave her alone. Frank beat the man with a pipe. People said Frank kept the boyfriend's eyeball in a jar at his house.

"Those guys come back today?" I asked him.

"Not today. That's why I hung around all day. I didn't know if those crazy fucks were gonna come back or not."

"Well, that's good."

"Yeah."

"There are enough problems on the streets without people stealing territory. It's a shame shit like that happens. There's a lot of money out there."

"True."

"I've come a long way to get to this point. It's a legit thing, you know? I don't need cops crawling around."

"Cops are nothing but a headache. They start snooping around, if they don't go away someone's going down."

"And that's not going to be me, you know? I fought hard for everything I got."

"At least you get free pussy out of the deal."

"One thing I can't complain about."

"Who would?"

"One of those assholes."

"Assholes better not come around me."

"Yeah."

We talked a little more, then he ran into someone else.

I walked around the room, greeting people and talking about nothing important. I talked to Dizzy and Tomato Head, they hijacked a truck the morning before. Things didn't go as planned. The driver, they weren't supposed to kill but it happened. Tomato blamed Dizzy. They got away with the truck. The body was left on the side of the road. They knew cops would be all over it. And they were both worried they'd get killed because of it. They told me Joe wasn't happy when he heard about it. I told them they shouldn't have anything to worry about if no one saw them shoot the guy. They seemed to be at ease when I told them. I talked to them a bit longer then they sputtered off somewhere to talk to someone else.

At the other end of the room, I saw Rooster drinking a beer. As soon as he saw me he started to come over. They called him Rooster because he had red hair that he put gel in. He was a handsome fella, tall, skinny, sharp jawline. He wore a black sports jacket and a big smile. He had wiry glasses.

We shook hands.

Rooster, whose name was Ned McGehee, was a pretty nice guy despite the fact he was a psychopath, a cold murderer. Rooster was a local drug deal. In all, he had twenty dealers spread all over Central Arkansas. Ned was in a very dangerous business. He assured Joe he was on top of things, that he'd never get caught. When he had dealers or anyone he was connected to become unstable, he had them taken out.

"I gotta tell ya, can't help to think I'm bein' called to the principal's office every time I come out here. The place sort of freaks me out."

"You don't have anything to worry about."

"You sure? Out in the middle of nowhere? I tell you what," he pointed his finger at me, "I wouldn't put it passed Joe to lead us here to kill us."

I waved the idea away. "I don't think anything like that would happen."

"No offense, what you don't know about Joe can fill a building. I've known him longer than you, and I don't trust that slimy fuck a bit."

"Maybe," I said.

"I just like to keep a good distance."

"Not for nothing, but you can see Joe's frustration, right?"

"I guess."

There was a lot of chatter among the crew about what was going on in the streets. A lot of killings and robberies have been happening. Dealers and pimps were always claiming new territory. The streets had gotten worse in the last five years than they had been. The city was nothing but a huge ghetto.

I walked over to the fridge again, got a bottle of beer, and sat on one of the couches. "Any good news today, fellas?"

Tony looked at me and nodded. "Same shit. Another day in paradise."

"Likewise," I said.

"It's good," he replied. "All manageable."

I nodded.

"Everyone thinks they're a wise guy," he continued. "Shove a gun in that motherfucker's face, show him what's what."

"What do you mean?"

"A gun pointed at them and they're cool as a cat, you have a stand-up guy, if he starts to cry and piss his pants you may as well shoot 'em. Living here, a guy's not gonna get far being weak."

"Interesting point."

"You can't respect a guy like that. They're no good to anyone. They'd be better off dead."

"I've heard that before."

"They aren't right in the head… I dunno... Shit's not right."

"I couldn't agree more."

Business was good. I had no complaints. I did my job and I did it well. Whenever someone messed with us, we messed back and won. It was a good thing. In our line of work, you were always faced with danger. But you always had to ignore fear in front of the other guys. I did my part so Joe wouldn't turn on me.

The door to the warehouse opened. A man dressed all in white walked in. All of us stood as he came in as a sign of respect. He was tall and lanky with a beard; that was Joe Butler. He was losing his hair. A man rushed over to Joe with a glass of liquor and handed it to him.

"Thanks, Eddie," Joe said.

"My pleasure," Eddie said in his screechy voice. "Anything else I can do?"

"I'm good," Joe gave Eddie a little smile.

"I'm here if you do."

"Thanks."

Eddie nodded.

Joe put his hand on the man's shoulder and looked out among us. "Anyone mess with this guy, you'll have to answer to me."

Eddie smiled.

Joe walked around the room, greeting everyone, shaking hands, and joking. After he finished, he told us to grab a drink and take a seat. He told us he needed to talk business. He pulled a bag of cocaine out of his inside pocket and tossed it on the table.

"Help yourselves," he said. "Took it of some stupid kid today. He's not gonna be needing it."

Someone grabbed the bag and started to pour it out, and then he started cutting lines.

"Listen," Joe said. "I'm gonna have to make this short. I forgot about some things I have to do tonight. We need to find ways to make more money. Cut and dry. I mean, fuck, that's why we all got into this, isn't it? I've never met anyone in this life who can't find ways to get what they want," Joe took a seat at the table. "You guys need to be smart about things. You don't wanna get put in prison or worse. You are good guys. I'd hate to see anything bad happen to anyone. Truth is, I depend on you guys. If you respect me, you'll get the same from me. No bullshit. If you look at past leaders, the good ones anyway, they took care of their men. Just want you to know if you need anything, you can come to me. Hey, in the end, we're all on the same side. This is the thing that keeps us alive. As for another order of business, I got information from my guy inside that the cops are still lookin' for whoever killed those three guys at that one place last week. You know what I'm talking about," he nodded at Sal and me.

Sal shrugged. "Must've been kids or something. There's always something going on at night. Kids these days, they're a bunch of wild animals. You can't control anything. All of them, are always on dope. They should lock 'em all the-fuck-up."

Joe smiled. "Things happen."

"That they do," Sal said. "Damn shame, young kid comin' up in the life, didn't even have a chance to enjoy the fruits of it. Fuckin' drug addicts anyway..."

"Agreed," I said.

Joe leaned back in his chair. "At any rate, it's the price of doing business. Some people aren't cut out for this. You have to find out what sort of man you are. It's a tragic thing. It's all about street smarts. Some have it, others... they don't get that many chances. It's a tough way to go. Back to what I was saying, if the cops ask no one knows anything. Let the cops do their job. If you do talk," he shook his head, "I hear people jump from bridges all the time."

Robert howled. "And that's not good at all. Heard about a kid, Eric, going like that. Bad deal for everyone. I was over at Pony's and over-heard a few people talking about it. They were mid-twenties, I guess."

"Heard about that guy," James said. "There was something about his girlfriend, right?"

"I guess," Robert said. "The girl he was seeing was fucking another guy."

"Really?" James said.

"That's what I heard."

"Some crazy shit, that's all I'm saying. I'd never kill myself over some stupid girl."

"Know what you mean," I said. "Women are everywhere. If one becomes a problem just go out and get another."

"They're always trouble," Joe said.

I took a drink of beer. "Took out a girl the other night. We were having a good time..."

"But?" Sal asked.

"She said she didn't wanna come back to my place."

"Why not?"

"Said she didn't wanna sleep with me the first night. She said she didn't want me to think she was a whore."

"Did you think that?" Sal asked.

"Sure, but that's beside the point."

All of us laughed.

Robert lit a cigarette. "It's always best to use 'em then leave 'em. That's what I always do. They always bring feelings to the table. I don't need that noise. They say there are good women out there. I have yet to see it. Probably never will," he stood up, went to the fridge, and grabbed a beer. "I just take a stripper or hooker when I wanna get off," he sat back down. "They can only go so far, know what I mean?"

I took a drink of beer. "What happened to you the other night?"

"Me?" Robert asked. "What do ya mean?"

"The gig we had at The Shack, you said you were gonna be there."

Robert shrugged. "Yeah, sorry, I ended up getting drunk and passing out. Sorry."

"No problem," I said. "You missed a good show."

"I'm sure I'll catch another one."

"We'll have more," I told him.

We talked more while the booze flowed like fine rivers in our veins. There were a few shootings and some drug deals gone bad they were talking about.

After everyone was quiet again, Joe went on to tell us a few other things. It was all pretty much in code because you never knew if anyone was bugged or if anyone would rat on you. In this life, it was hard to trust anyone.

After about an hour of talking Joe dismissed us.

As Joe was walking out the door, he motioned for me to follow.

Once we were outside, he said, "So, Bryan, I hear you paid him a visit?"

I nodded. "I did."

He patted me on the shoulder. "He was making a lot of complications for me. That degenerate fuck. He wasn't any good anyway. A guy like that is bad for business, bad the whole way 'round."

"I think the right measures were taken," I said.

"Glad to hear you say that. He was building a reputation of being a failure."

"I agree."

"How did you do it."

"Short and sweet."

"You don't want things to fester long. In, out, on with your day, that's the best thing you can do about that."

"Some good advice."

"Yeah."

"I popped him in the back of the head a couple of times. House looked all shitty. He said he lost a bunch of money at the casino."

"Yeah, my money."

If Joe wanted Bryan gone, why didn't he do it himself? Why did he ask me? What was Joe's plan? I wasn't a fan of Bryan by any stretch, but I didn't want the fool to die. Before I killed him, I entertained the idea of skipping out. If I had run the crew would've hunted me down and killed me. And if it was gonna be Bryan or me, it was gonna have to be him. I wasn't gonna have anyone get the better of me.

Joe dug out an envelope from his inside pocket.

"You've earned it," he laughed. "Don't spend it all in the same place," he handed the envelope to me.

"I have bills like crazy," I said.

"This'll help with that."

"I'm sure it will."

"Without a doubt."

"Thanks."

"I don't want ya to be homeless or anything."

"Yeah."

He gave a light chuckle. "But if that ever does happen you can stay at my place. I have an extra room. You can even fuck the neighbor lady."

"Really? She looks good?"

"Yeah, I've slept with her about a half dozen times."

"She has your approval, huh?"

"Yes."

"Think I'll have to pass on that one."

"Your loss."

I nodded.

"Part of that is the other job," Joe nodded to the envelope.

I shook my head. "The briefcase is at my place. I would've brought it, but I didn't know."

"That's good," he said.

As he walked away and got in his car, I looked at the envelope. I smiled at the ten grand I saw.

I stuffed the money into my jacket as I walked back into the building. When I got back inside a bunch of the crew were sitting around the table playing cards. They asked if I wanted in. But I shook my head, got a beer, and sat on the couch. I sat in the same spot for almost two hours bullshitting with some of the guys. Even though they were crooks and murderers, they were good people. It was around one in the morning when I told myself I needed to go home. I said goodbye to everyone and staggered out the door.

five

I spent my whole life in this city. All my friends were from here. We grew up and went to school together in North Brown Ridge, Arkansas. I was sunken in. You can tell a lot about a person by where they come from. My friends and I had been through a lot together. We were a tight family. If you messed with one of us, you could bet your ass the others would hunt you down and make you regret being born. There was a certain code we lived by. We looked out for each other and the community.

My brother and I were well-known in the area. Everyone liked and respected us. Everyone wanted to be near us. You can never have too many friends.

I was working in a bar called Exit on Lavender Street, across from my apartment, when I first met Joe Butler and Sal Alford. It was around six o'clock on a Friday night when they walked into the bar with three other guys. They sat at the bar and ordered beers. I'd always heard stories here and there about them; some of it I believed, some I didn't. A few people I knew had run-ins with him. I'd seen him from time to time around the city. I did my best to avoid them. I just got the drinks like they asked. They each gave me a hundred-dollar tip. I was bartending the next few nights they came in. One night I was leaving the bar and got jumped by two guys in my car.

After I fought the guys off, a black car pulled up, and Joe and Sal got out. At first, I thought they were going to shoot me, instead, they took out their guns and dropped the two guys.

I was shocked.

Didn't know what to think.

"That's how you handle that," Joe lowered his gun.

Both men helped me to my feet, then, they asked if I would join them for a drink.

We went to a place, Highlife. We sat at a booth in the back. We ordered and started talking. Joe Butler headed a gang called North Side Boys. Joe coined the name due to the fact he ran all of North Brown Ridge. There was nothing that happened on his side that he didn't know about, or, if he didn't when he did find out, he would either shut it down or demand a percentage of what was made.

Joe told me he liked the way I handled myself with the fight I had just been in, along with a few other ones. He was quick to point out the fact that not everyone wins them all. He asked if I wanted to join their outfit. I told him I'd think about it, and tell him at the end of the conversation. Joe went on to tell me about him and Sal. They grew up in North Brown Ridge together. As teenagers, they broke into cars and mugged people. The two of them, along with a group of friends, started their street gang in the mid 60's. After awhile what was little grew into a city-wide organization. By the end of the night, I told them I wouldn't be a part of their gang.

I said, "Thanks for what you did for me back there, but I can't be a part of what you guys have going on."

The two guys looked at each other and laughed, then looked back at me.

Joe smiled. "See, that's where you're wrong. You will join us or we might have some information about the guy who killed those two outside the bar."

I slowly shook my head. "No."

"This is how it has to be," Joe said. "We can't run a risk of you getting loose lips. If we go down, you go down."

"Sorry, kid," Sal said.

"You can turn the other way," Joe said. "You can turn

away, but be prepared to get shot through the head," Joe shrugged his shoulders. "I like you, Sean. I'd hate to see anything happen to you. People talk, things always have a way of getting back to me. If I were you, I wouldn't get wise. Feel lucky we didn't just shoot you when we did them. Oh, man, you have to decide here and now. I mean, I don't wanna rush you, you know?"

Joe went on to tell me more about Sal and himself.

I felt it was in my best interest to join them.

As the weeks unfolded, I found myself taking steps in the crime world. Days started to run together. I told the guys in Stoned Monkey about the other people I was hanging around. They didn't seem to mind. Finally, the day came when they started asking me about Joe, about getting into the origination. I arranged a meeting with Joe. Before too long we were all working for Joe. I started by going with some of the guys on burglaries and things. The hours my friends and I were around Joe Butler's guys grew. Stoned Monkey had a meeting to see if we still wanted to play music, or, run the streets full-time. We decided to do both. We could figure it out as we went along. I knew I wanted my friends on my side. I trusted them. I only told my brother that I was black-mailed into joining.

six

This one morning, I was outside Jason's place waiting for him in my car. He'd asked me to come with him to collect from a guy who owed money. Usually, he could handle his own, but, I thought that this case was something different, something he hadn't dealt with before. Jason lived in a white two-story about three blocks from my apartment. The house was only a couple of years old. He inherited it after our parents passed away. I decided to take money as my inheritance. I sat in my car listening to the radio for about ten minutes before he came out. It rained earlier that morning, and the pavements and sidewalks were water-stained and peppered with little puddles. There were some faint rumbles in the pale sky. Stable droplets of rain hung on the corners of the windshield. Jason came out of the front door. He shambled down the drive, opened the passenger door, and fell into the seat. He looked as if he had been up all night. A small fragrance of alcohol hovered on him.

He looked at me as he slammed the car door shut.

"What have you heard? Things good with you?"

"Start drinkin' a little early?" I handed him a grin.

"Figured it might help take the edge off," he leaned his head back on the seat. "Started last night and didn't stop till a little bit ago."

"Well, shit, you should've brought the bottle."

"It's in the house."

I considered it. "Nah, that's okay. I'm good."

"You sure?"

"I'm okay."

"Okay, then. I offered."

"And a very generous one."

"Anything to help."

"Next time," I told him.

"You got it, buddy!"

I turned the key in the ignition. "You guys go out last night?"

We pulled out of the drive and took a left.

"Went to River House," he said. "Viggo and I. They had a pretty good band. Met a couple of good girls."

"That's good," I said. "How long were you there?"

"Till about two."

"Really?"

"You should've come out."

"I'd rather of done that than what I did."

"What was that?"

"Oh, I talked with Joe. I guess it was more like a meeting."

"What about?"

"You know how he is, he just wanted to talk about the business, about my commitment."

"Commitment?"

"You know how he feels about our music. He was going on about how I need to make a choice, that old shit. As he talked I just nodded my head. We all know we've heard that ramble before."

"Wish he'd knock that stuff off."

"I know," I said. "Think he's just worried about us talking to people about criminal stuff, about what happened outside the bar that one night. We know a lot…would be embarrassing if it got out. People would go to prison for a long time, it wouldn't be good."

"What did you say?"

"I told him we would never talk. I was a little offended by it. I mean, we'd had the conversation a few times. If I wanted to say something to the cops I would've already."

"I know what you mean."

I glanced at him. "He's always been a little paranoid. You know, he'd been at the business for a long time," I looked back at the road ahead of me. "I just ignore it. One of these days he'll stop talking about it."

"Until then?"

I patted the steering wheel and sighed. "We'll see."

"We're stuck."

"You could call it that, I guess."

"Come on, the guy's got us by the balls. There's nothing we can do. No matter what we do we're dead."

"Afraid that's the case, brother."

"We both have blood on our hands."

"I know."

"If we went to the cops, it'd be over for us."

"We'll have to think of another way."

"Better do it soon. We could be next."

"Don't say that."

"Why? You know it's true."

"I know, it's just so depressing."

"Sure, no one wants to die."

I sighed. "I have too much to do to worry about that."

"I know what you mean."

A silence fell over us.

Jason shook his head as he dug out a cigarette. "Met this fine girl, Cassey."

"You don't say?"

"Tried to convince her to come back home with me, but she gave some lame excuse."

"Don't you hate when that happens?"

"Gave me her number. Told me to call anytime."

"At least something good came out of it."

Jason said, "I got a kiss outta her. Hope I can get more soon."

"When are you gonna see her again?"

"Maybe tonight, maybe tomorrow."

I nodded. "If it works out, that's all you can hope for."

"When you tell a broad you're in a band, they get hot for you."

"That's the main reason we started the band, right?" I laughed. "We should rename the band Pussy Monsters."

"Love that name. Just so I'm clear when you say Pussy Monsters, you mean we're the monsters who like pussy, or you mean that we're huge pussies who go around scaring people?"

I laughed. "You crazy bastard... The first one."

"Oh, well, that makes sense."

"Back to this girl," I said. "She like you?"

"Pretty sure of it. She let me buy her some drinks, guess that's a sign. She bought drinks for me. If she doesn't like me, I'll make sure she will in time."

"That's the spirit," I said. "You have to take your chances when you can."

"I guess."

I pulled up to a traffic sign and waited for a couple of people to cross the street.

"What about Viggo, he gets a girl?" I asked.

"He left with some redhead about an hour before I did. Sure I'll get all the details soon."

I laughed. "I'm sure you will. Guy has to tell ya about every piece of tail he gets."

"That he does."

"Some of the girls he gets with are just downright disgusting, you know?"

"We've all been with regrets like that."

"That's funny."

"It happens."

"Some may say," I said. "I just chalk it up to experience. Gotta take the good with the bad."

We sat in silence for a few minutes as I drove down a long street, passing big houses with small yards. A few people were jogging down the road; some were greeting the morning by sitting outside on their porch.

"Thanks for helping, Sean," Jason said. "It means a lot."

"No problem," I said. "That's what family's for. I'm just glad I can help. I figure after we get this little job done we can go back to your place, call up the guys, and have a jam session if you're up for it. Might as well do something today that doesn't involve crazy maniacs. Something that doesn't deal with this shit. I need to get to that pure place today. It's been an interesting week."

"Sounds good," he said. "I don't like dealing with this guy. Last time I was over there, the guy made me pretty nervous."

"How so?"

"Just had this crazy look about him, like he'd kill you if you looked at him funny. That guy, he's one crazy fool."

"Does he look funny?"

"Sure," he said. "I think someone beat the shit out of him too much. He seems to have some sort of complex. Not sure what that's all about."

"Hate when that shit happens."

"And no telling how many guys he has with him."

"How many did he have last time?"

"Three."

"Three?"

"He looked like a mean bastard."

"Three guys, huh?"

"No telling how many thugs are with him," Jason said. "We need to be on our guard, prepared for anything."

"No argument from me. I don't feel like dying today. It's a fuckin' jungle out here. You never know what's going to go down. Think we should call for backup or something?"

"We shouldn't," I said. "We're just collecting money. Shouldn't come to that."

"If it does?"

"What are we, fuckin' cops? Call for backup? How are we supposed to do that when we're in the shit? You are my backup, I'm yours, that's how it is. I'm not worried. Should be pretty easy."

"It's better," he looked out the window.

"Why are you so worried, anyway?"

"You never know," my brother said into the window.

"That's why we have each other."

He looked back to the road. "We have that, at least."

I pressed down harder on the gas as we zoomed down the street.

Jason said, "I'm starving. Hadn't eaten anything today. Think I may have drank too much."

"You think?"

He laughed. "I'm not as young as I used to be. Doing that hardcore drinking is good sometimes. I can't do that type of drinkin' all the time."

"You only live once."

"I get what you're saying, brother."

"We'll have to go out sometime."

"No doubt. Booze and girls, it doesn't get much better than that. That's some of the best company you could find."

We turned down Orange Street. About halfway down Jason pointed to a red brick house with two black cars in the drive. "That's the one."

I parked on the side of the road and killed the car. "Well, here we are."

"You got your gun?" he said.

"The one in my jacket and the one in my sock."

"I need to start carrying one in my sock."

"It's nice to have a backup."

"People don't expect you to have a heater stuffed in your sock, right? Good idea."

I looked outside the window. "Nice lookin' place."

"It is," he said. "I need to get a place like it."

"Think your place looks better."

"Always thought it would be nice to have more than one house."

We got out of the car.

I looked at the cars in the drive, then turned to Jason. "Looks like a full house, this should be fun."

"We're just a couple of party fools," my brother gave a small laugh.

"We wouldn't want to make things boring, would we?"

We walked to the door and knocked. A tall African American man with a blue suit answered. "Can I help you?"

I would've expected a deep voice from the guy, but a small one came out. He was too big for his voice.

"I need to see Nick," Jason said.

The man looked my brother up and down. "What's your business with him?"

"That's between him and I," Jason snapped.

"You're not gonna see him unless you tell me what you want. He's a busy man and doesn't have time for every fuck who wants to pay a visit. Shit, what do ya think he is, some lazy-ass white boy? I tell you what, mother-fucker, that's one hard-workin' man in there. It's my job to scan everyone that comes here. You have a problem with that, guess your business with him wasn't that im-portant," he shook his head at my brother. "Shit, man, get the fuck outta here. We have a lot to do today, talkin' to assholes isn't one of them."

"Cool your jets, buddy, it's just a little matter of a debt," Jason said.

"It won't take long," I added.

"In that case, you better talk to him. Debt isn't an easy thing to shake. I'd sure hate to see anyone get hurt over some green paper," he looked at me. "Who the fuck are you?"

"Your prom date," I smiled. "I didn't get you any flowers or chocolates, didn't know what you liked. We can take in a movie later if you want?"

"Funny," He said. "You're a comedian, aren't ya?"

"I've been told that a time or two, sure."

"I'm not laughing."

"People don't appreciate good comedy these days - shame if you ask me. You have all these people out here tryin' to make people like you laugh... they get nothing."

The man said, "That so? How 'bout I shoot you dead right here on the porch? Think that'll be real funny, wouldn't you?"

"Not really," I said. "It would make my day a little gloomy, I won't lie. Friends will have to go to a funeral, they don't want that. You'll have people cryin' and feelin' bad. Tell me, what's your name?"

"Fuck you," the man said. "I don't have to tell you shit."

I said, "You have to be like that? We didn't do anything to you. Don't have to act like a hard-ass or anything. I know you have to do this whole tough routine, but you can stop. I've seen it all before. Now, what's your name, man?"

The man just looked at me.

I said, "We can go 'round and 'round if you want."

The man nodded and shifted his suit jacket revealing a gun on his waist. "We gonna have a problem?"

"Not with me," I said.

The man looked at my brother.

Jason said he didn't have a problem.

"What's your name?" I asked.

"Derek," the man said. "You wanna know my name before I kick your ass?"

I shook my head. "That's not gonna happen, and we both know it."

"Look guy," Jason said. "I don't think you want a problem with us. We don't have anything with you. I suggest you let us in."

He said, "Why the hell should I? The way I see it, you need to get the fuck out here. You don't need to talk to him, goofy motherfucker. Guess his debt will have to go a little longer."

Jason frowned. "Now where's the nice hospitality, guy? We don't have any issues with you. My brother's just fuckin' around. We can always get into some shit if you want," Jason flashed his piece. "Somehow I don't think you'd want that. You wanna get all shot-to-fuck today? With one phone call, I can get twenty guys over here. Your call," I gave him a hard look.

"I'll be keepin' my eyes on you two," Derek said.

"You do that," I said.

Derek shook his head and moved from the doorway.

"That's what I thought," Jason walked through.

"Nick's in the office, last room," Derek said.

We walked down a small hallway. there were three doors on either side of the hallway. The door to the office was open so we walked in. Cigarette smoke and coffee lingered in the room. Two guys were in chairs in front of a desk, and one guy was sitting behind the desk. A bag of cocaine was on the desk along with a few notebooks. I glanced at the wall on my left: stacks of albums and books were leaning against a stereo. The guy sitting in the chairs; was African American, and the other was white.

I felt a small lump form in my throat.

Nick greeted us from behind the desk. He had slick black hair and a black jacket. He was unshaven. He didn't look opposing at all. He was smoking a cigarette, flicking his ashes in a dark green ashtray on the desk. He spoke with a pronounced Southern accent.

"What can I do for you guys?" Nick asked.

"You know why I'm here, Nick," Jason said.

Nick shrugged. "Guys wanna buy dope?"

"No," Jason said.

"How much?" I asked. "We always have the money to get high."

Nick pointed at me and laughed. "A man who knows what he wants, that's what I like to see."

Jason hit me in the shoulder. "No, no dope for us," he looked at Nick. "You forget that money you owe me? Slip your mind?"

Nick smiled. "Just a little memory lapse. You want your money, right?"

"That's right," Jason said.

"What would you do if I told you I'm not gonna pay?"

"What?"

"I know."

"You ass."

"It's a shame."

"What?" my brother said.

"I think you heard me."

"Think I've suddenly come down with a hearing disor-der. You just tell me you weren't paying?"

"See, your hearing is fine."

"Why?"

"I have my reasons," Nick said.

"What would those be?" my brother asked.

Nick said, "Oh, you don't need to know that. I had a lot

on my plate."

"Okay," Jason said. "let's have it."

"You need to get outta here while you can still walk," Nick said.

"Why?"

"I don't think I need to explain myself to you."

"Please, just this once?"

"Think you better leave. This is a business for big guys, you aren't that. Do yourselves a favor and get out. Go back to the school, boys."

As Jason and I moved toward Nick, the two guys stood and blocked us.

"I'm sure you're looking for some kind of explanation?" Nick continued. "No matter what I tell you, believe me, you won't like it. I know what it's like, you expect something then it doesn't come to pass," he put his cigarette stub out. "It's a bitch, a headache, something that tunnels its way into your mind and festers. Yes, that stays with you for a long time. Oh, I've been down that road many times."

"We had a deal," Jason tilted his head at Nick. "You borrowed money, and I'm gonna collect," my brother pulled his gun and aimed at Nick.

The other two guys took their guns out and pointed them at Jason and me.

"Wait, wait, wait," I held my hands up. "There's no need for this. We're all adults, right? Surely we can work something out. It's just about money. We don't have any problem beyond that. We aren't bad guys."

Nick looked at me. "Don't think I even caught your name."

"Because I never threw it," I said. "I wasn't ever good at baseball."

"What's your name, smart guy?"

"Sean," I said.

Nick said, "Good to meet you," he stood from his chair. "You'll have to forgive my two friends, they don't exactly get along well with others. They get a little trigger-happy when other people start pullin' guns. I'm sure you guys can understand. Wish we could've met under different circumstances, Sean."

The two guys nodded at Jason and I.

The African American guy smiled. "Y'all planning on mixing it up with us? Be prepared to be in a world of pain. My boy and I will fuck you up!"

The white guy laughed. "That's right, Leon never lies."

Jason lowered his gun. "We don't want any trouble. We just want the money you owe me, Nick. Come one, we have a busy day, just give us the money."

I chuckled. "We're hungry. Haven't eaten anything today. My blood sugar gets outta whack when I don't get something."

The African fella said, "I can relate."

"I bet you can," I looked at him.

"There's some cupcakes in the kitchen if you want," he told me.

I waved off the offer. "Nah, that's okay."

"Can't say I didn't offer."

"I'm good," I said to the guy as he gave me a funny look.

A thunder crashed down the hall, and Derek came into the office. "Hey, boss, guys need me? I heard a noise and whatnot. With all these guns, you lookin' to kill someone?"

"No," Nick said. "Everything's fine, Derek. Nothing to get excited about. We were just having a friendly chat."

"Okay, then."

"You can go back to the front. If we need you, we'll let you know."

"Yes, sir, boss," Derek glared over at my brother and

me. "These guys makin' any trouble, boss?" he opened his suit jacket just enough to display his gun. "It can be dealt with."

 I showed Derek my gun. "What the fuck's your problem? Ever since we got here you've been a huge asshole."

 "I'm doing my job."

 "Your job being a dick?" I asked.

 Derek gave me a little push. "You've just walked into Hell."

 Nick told Derek to leave the room.

 Derek turned and started to walk out the door.

 "Before you leave, Derek, can you come over here?" Nick said. "I want you to stay and visit. Think you guys might've gotten off on the wrong foot earlier."

 "Sure, " he walked over to Nick's desk and faced us. "Think you two need to go home. You don't wanna mess with the big boys."

 I looked at Derek. "Big boys? Some sort of music group you guys started? I've never heard any of your music. Guys have a record or anything?"

 "We might have something, you never know."

 "If you do, let me know."

 "I'll do that," Derek told me. "You always have to think of the end game, you know?"

 "Yeah."

 "If we kill you, though, you won't get to listen to any of our music."

 I laughed. "That won't ever happen. You won't kill us today or any other day

 "You think?"

 "Don't worry, Derek," Nick stood beside him. "You aren't gonna have to hurt 'em," he reached into his desk, pulled out a knife, and held it beside Derek's neck. "Sorry about this," he moved the knife to Derek's throat and cut to the other end.

I couldn't believe what I saw.

Ruby-red blood poured out as Nick struggled with him for a minute. After the last drops of blood squirted out, he threw the lifeless body on the wood floor in front of us. Nick kicked the body.

"See, boys, there are advantages of not having carpet," he held the knife for us to see the fresh blood on it.

The other two guys, like Jason and I, stood in shock. I looked at their expressions; eyes wide open, faces grew pale.

"The fuck's wrong with you?" I said.

Nick laughed. "I think you guys know I don't mess around. This could be you two on the floor if you don't act right."

"You sure are a sick motherless fuck," my brother looked down at the body, then back at Nick. "How can you kill this guy for no reason?"

Nick shrugged. "Had to get your attention. Can't have you guys thinking I'm a pushover. Plus, to be honest, never really liked him that much."

"So, you kill him?" I said.

"It happens"

I said, "Remind me not to join your ranks."

Nick laughed. "This guy lying down on the floor, my sister told me he tried to have his way with her," he pointed his finger at me. "You better not try to sleep with my sister."

"Hey, no problem from me," I said.

"If it wasn't me, someone else would've done it," Nick said. "He was getting sloppy with business. He'd done a few bad deals I had to clean up, the shithead. You can't get good help these days. I had big hopes for him. About a week back someone stole a brick of cocaine from him."

"That's not a good thing," Jason said.

Nick grabbed a napkin off the desk and wiped his knife. "Blood, it gets so messy; it's a hassle to clean."

Jason and I looked at each other.

Nick told the two guys to clean the mess up. Nick told them we'd leave them to do their job, and we would talk business in the kitchen.

Nick told Jason and I to follow him. We walked into the kitchen. He told us to take a seat at the table.

"So, start talking," I lit a cigarette. "What about the money? We didn't come over here just to see you kill somebody."

Nick asked if we wanted anything to drink.

We told him we didn't.

"Sure you don't want a beer? I brew my stuff. It's pretty good," he said.

"No," Jason said. "Just get on with whatever you wanna say. I have a full schedule today. Don't have all the time in the world."

He smiled at us. "You guys act like a bunch of tough guys, waltzing in here and demanding shit. I tell ya both, if you were anyone else you'd be dead. I like you guys. Don't wanna see you get hurt."

"Appreciate that," I told him.

Nick opened the bottle of beer and sat with us. "The debt I owe, I'm not paying. No matter what you say."

Jason moved in the chair. "You better start making sense."

"My brother is getting out of prison next week," Nick took a drink.

"What the fuck's that gotta do with us?" I asked. "We don't involve ourselves in matters of families. Did you need the money to throw a party for him? Want us to bring some girls over? Hey, buddy, I know a couple of girls that'll fuck you dry. Just say the word."

Nick continued. "No, thanks. His getting out of prison, has everything to do with you guys. My brother was arrested in 1980. At the time he was running pretty much everything in North Brown Ridge. Your boss, Joe, dropped a dime on him. It seemed Joe Butler had gotten busted for runnin' heroin. Your boss was facing twenty-five years. They offered him a deal to walk and he took it. Instead of facing his time like a man, Joe spilled the beans about my brother. For the past decade, I had to go to Cummings to see my brother. Word of Joe moving up in the business got back to my brother. He worked hard to get to where he was. Hell, he made a joke inside. Everyone thought it was fuckin' funny. My brother lost the respect he had."

"What's his name?" Jason asked.

"Max," Nick said. "Max Roark."

I said, "I've heard a few things about him. They said he didn't fuck around back then. I've heard he once killed a guy just for looking at his girlfriend. He went to the guy's house, killed him, and then skinned him on the front lawn. That stuff true?"

"Oh, it's all true," Nick took another drink. "He was feared by a lot of people. He was ruthless but fair. He was, and is, a very smart guy. He knew how to get respect. Everywhere we went... He was like a God. Whenever someone wanted to challenge him, sorry, they lost. Next thing I know Max got sent up-state. The whole thing was a sad story. The last time I saw him, he told me to start telling people he was gonna get out and to start collecting his money.

"That's a nice story and all," Jason glared at him, "but you still haven't told me what I want to hear."

"Don't you get it?" Nick shook his head. "Joe owes Max money. I told myself that I'd start taking from his guys. Asked you for the loan knowing I wasn't ever gonna pay you back. It's just all about good business."

"Thanks for letting us know," my brother said.

"And Max, he's gonna want what's his"

"Is that right?"

"He's gonna get everything he wants," he slammed his hand on the table. "Nobody is gonna stop him. As for Joe, he's got something special in mind for him. Max said to tell Joe if he wants a war he has one."

My brother said, "That was my money. I was nice enough to loan you that money. You told me you'd pay me back. Come on, we had a deal. If you would've pulled this shit with anyone else you'd be dead. Joe had nothing to do with me giving you that loan."

"This is true. I figured it was gonna filter through his fingers sooner or later. We're gonna start a big blood bath over this."

I shifted in my seat, revealing my gun. "Are you threatening us? We don't take kindly to ugly fuckers like you making threats."

"Oh, I don't threaten," Nick folded his hands on the table. "The dead guy in the other room would tell you I don't mess around. The other two guys in there, they'll shoot you dead without hesitation. My brother figures the time he was inside meant lost income. I tend to agree with him. We don't play that well with others."

"We'll have to see what the boss says about this," I said. "Why doesn't he just work on the boys on the south side?"

Nick laughed. "You guys are funny, really you are. Well, see, we have no problem with Ted Lavery. Max just has a problem with Joe. I have a problem with your boss. If your guys know what's good for him, what's good for all of you. He'll have a sit-down and figure all this stuff out."

"We'll take this to him, but he's not gonna like it," Jason said. "Come to think of it, we should shoot you and then go in the room back and shoot those two ugly fuckers."

"I strongly advise against doing that," Nick took a swallow of beer. "You'll be very sorry. I have good connections."

I sighed. "That's it, then? Nothing else we can do?"

"That's about it," Nick said. "Well, I'm sure they may need help cleaning all the blood in the office."

"No, thanks."

Jason and I stood from the table.

"We've gotten all the bullshit today we need," I said

Jason looked at Nick. "I'll be in touch, buddy. When did you say Max was getting out?"

"Next week."

"We'll make sure the boss gets the message."

"That's good," Nick sat back in his chair. "I hate to bring this on you guys."

I said, "Joe always told me he started running things."

"That's not entirely true," Nick said. "Yeah, Joe took everything over when my brother went on the inside. Your boss has a lot of explaining to do, the prick. It seems that he'd been lying to you about a few things. True, they came up together but they parted ways a few years later. I guess Joe got jealous of my brother and the steps he was taking. I expect he'll deny any wrongdoing."

Jason said, "If what you say is true, then why didn't you step in?"

"When my brother went away I wasn't in the position to do anything. I was only twenty when Max went away. The first time I visited him in that place, he said he didn't want me to get in the middle of it. Over the years I sat back and watched, finally, it got to be too much. I couldn't sit back and do nothing. I had to let him know Joe was taking more and more. As I told my brother these things I was busy making my crew. Started from the ground up. Now, look at me."

I nodded. "Looks like a fine life you made here."

"You are a funny guy," Nick said.

"I've heard that before."

"Just run, tell your boss what I said."

My brother said, "This is bullshit. We came all the way here for no money. It's not fair."

"Live is seldom that," Nick stated.

"Tell us about it," I said.

We walked to the front door.

Nick called from behind us. "Wait a second."

We turned and faced him.

"Do you guys know anything about what happened to Johnny Womack?"

Jason shrugged. "Have no idea who that even is."

"Really?"

"That's right," Jason looked at him. "Should I know him?"

"He ran with the same crowd you do."

"That so?" Jason put his right hand in his jacket pocket. "What happened to him?"

"I didn't say anything happened to him."

"Well, you said *ran,* past tense."

"Someone shot him the other day. Left him in the street. Cops found him. They came around asking questions," he said. "You know anything about this?"

"No clue," I said.

"Of course you don't," he said. "I'll be lookin' for whoever shot Johnny. If I were you guys I'd put word on the street. When I find out who did it, that guy's gonna pay. I'll put out his eye before I kill him."

"Pretty harsh," I said. "Why do you care so much?"

"Why do I care?" he looked and me, then at Jason. "He was a good friend of mine. We grew up together. We were five or six when we first met on the playground. He had a problem with a kid, and I picked up a rock and threw it at him, cracked his skull good. Since then we have been good friends. He was family. Tomorrow, I'm gonna have to stand with his parents at the funeral. It's a shame when they go out with a bullet. I'm gonna figure out one way or another who did it. I feel sorry for whoever pulled the trigger when I got to them. I guess they didn't realize just how many people would suffer."

"It's the life we choose, right?" I said.

"Yeah," Nick muttered.

I turned to my brother. "We should get out of here, eh?"

Jason shook his head.

I told Nick he had a nice place.

Nick said, "You guys don't be strangers, now. You guys need to run along and go tell your boss about our little conversation. I'm sure he'll see it'd be in his best interest to give my brother what he wants."

Jason said, "We'll let you know."

"Yeah," I agreed.

"And don't get any wise ideas," Nick warned.

We walked out the front door.

In the car, Jason said, "He'll be pissed when he finds out you killed Johnny."

"I'm not too worried about it. When he finds out I'll take care of it. That guy seems like a pushover to me. He just wants us to be afraid, that's why he killed his guy."

"You make a good point."

"We'll get this sorted out."

We sped away.

seven

We stopped at the first payphone we saw. After about twenty minutes of trying to track him down, calling all of the hangouts and his house, we finally tracked him down at Sugar, one of the crew's hangouts. It took us ten minutes to get to Sugar from where we were. The place was dark and neon inside. There weren't that many people around, just a few guys drinking away the afternoon. One of the dancers, a sexy tattooed Blond, Smooth, told us Joe and Sal were in the back office. She asked if we wanted anything to drink. We thanked her but said we didn't want anything.

Smooth said, "If you guys want anything just say the word."

"We will," Jason gave her a wink. "You'll be the first one I call, believe that, babe."

She let out a smile and cupped both her hands behind his neck. "Oh, I can't wait till that night. Oh, baby! A secret is behind every corner."

"Well, they have to be somewhere, I guess," my brother put his hands on her waist.

"Oh, a funny man," she took her hands from his neck and started to slowly run a finger down his chest. "Why don't you got a girl? Someone out there is missing you…wishes they were with you."

"There's just something about me," he padded her side with his left hand. "We need to see the big man. This'll have to wait."

She moved out of the way.

We passed.

We were about to the office when my brother turned

back at her. "I'll call you later. We'll get drunk or some-thing."

I hit him in the arm. "You seriously wanna get with her?"

"Fuck no, bitch probably has more diseases than the CDC has cures for."

"Think I'd have to agree with that."

We knocked on the office door and heard someone say to come in. I opened the door and saw Joe and Sal at the desk. Sal, with a handful of money, glared at Jason and I. He was quick to put the cash in a big envelope. I couldn't ever seem to understand Sal. You couldn't read him like you could with some of the other guys; the same could be said for the boss. They put me on edge from time to time.

"There they are!" Sal howled. "Come on in. What, school let out early today, boys?"

The two of us walked through the doorway and closed it behind us.

"Funny," I said, "Funny guy," I smiled.

"How are Arkansas' finest hoodlums today?" Joe said.

"Can't complain," I said.

"Just makin' it all happen," Jason added.

Sal snorted. "We need more of that these days. Too many people pissin' in their shoes out there."

"What can I do for you guys?" Joe sat back in his chair. "Guys caught me in between phone calls. You know, business never stops. They're running me crazy today. Shit, someone has to do it. Do you want coffee or any-thing? I can have them brew a pot out there. The girl brought in homemade cookies," he pointed to a table on the other side of the room with the cookies on it. "The girl, Bridget something, brought her in to work the bar on weekends."

"She any good?" Jason asked.

The boss grunted. "Oh, she's okay, I guess. How hard is it to mix some drinks and fetch beer?"

"You'd be surprised," I added.

Joe said, "I can get Smooth to make you some drinks or whatever. You could probably even talk that dirty girl into a good fuck. Heard she doesn't care who you are. Damn girl, last night skipped out here with a couple of redneck boys. They probably had their way with her and sent her down the street."

I said, "We don't need anything. She already asked when we came in."

"She already tried to get with me," Jason said. "Let me ask, why do you keep a girl like that around? She's a nasty slut. I mean, I dunno, if you want that hangin' around the customers."

"Oh, she gets to ya, did she?" Joe said. "You need to watch out for that one. Some of the people who come in here like the trashy ones. I agree, that girl, she has a way about her. Maybe she didn't have a father figure in her life. Most girls like that come from a broken home, you know?"

Jason said, "Had to be a dirty daddy."

"Maybe so."

"There are some sickos out there."

"You got that right, buddy."

I lit a cigarette

"Oh," Joe said. "Well, what about a burger? You guys need meat on your bones. Have to have energy to run around the world."

"That's okay," Jason said. "We just had a couple of burgers."

"Fair enough."

"We have news you're not gonna like," I said, eyeing Joe's coffee cup on his desk. "It's not that great. And just so you know, the burgers here need to improve. I don't know what kinda meat they're using in that kitchen."

"Sick cow, maybe?" Sal offered.

"That's what I've heard," Joe said. "I'm still here. I've had a few since we got that new kid back there. That guy burnt the shit out of his hand the other night. The burgers at Highlife are a lot better. Maybe I need to start ordering that kinda meat for here."

Sal shook his head. "I'll give the guy a call."

Jason interrupted. "Think you're gonna want a stiff drink for this one, Joe."

"What is it?" Joe said. "Someone gets shot or something? I always hate asking. One thing after another around here. Like a spinning wheel, round and round we go."

"No," I said. "Well, someone got his throat cut. It was probably the guy's suit. It wasn't something I'd never wear unless I was in the circus. I don't know who dressed that guy, but they had no fashion sense."

"Sounds interesting. Just tell me what it is. Take a seat if you want," Joe pointed at the two chairs in front of the desk. "Relax. Stay around for awhile. Ease your troubled minds. Let the weight of the day drift away. We were just talking over some future investments before you guys showed."

"And what's that about?" I asked.

"We'll let ya know when the time's right. There's this heist we're planning. If it all goes, a big payday."

"I can get behind something like that."

"Good," Joe said.

Jason said. "I've always been a fan of money."

"Aren't we all?" Joe laughed.

We sat.

"We went to see Nick to pick my money up," Jason cleared his throat.

"Always workin' these guys," Joe nodded to Sal, then back at us. "Did he make good with the dough?"

"He didn't," Jason said.

"That's why you went over there, no?"

"It was. Didn't get too far, though. Nick told us he wouldn't give us the money. He told us a crazy story. His brother, Max, is getting out of jail in a few days. Nick said you guys have a history. I dunno, he sort of sounded like a real bad guy."

"He thought he was," Sal said. "He always wanted something he could never have, and he would never stop. Greed got the better of him. A sad story. He won't get any sympathy from me."

Joe shrugged. "Really? Old Max. What do ya know about that? That sorry bastard finally getting out? We should throw that fucker a party, then beat him to death and grind up the body. I'm sure a lot of people wouldn't mind if we gave him that gift."

Sal said, "That's all we need around here, just when things were going good. We need to steer clear of him when he gets out. If the past has taught me anything, it's taught me that Max should've died back in the seventies."

"Nick told us Max wants everything that's coming to him when he gets out," my brother said.

"That so?" Joe lit a cigar. "He wants everything, huh? That should make things interesting. I knew this was coming sooner or later. Yeah, we'll give him everything that he has coming. We'll give him a bullet to the back of the head, or, a butcher's knife to the back."

"And this Max character is pissed at you. Nick told us they'll go to war if it comes to it. He also told us you dimmed Max to the cops."

Joe puffed on his cigar, and smoke surrounded him. "When I woke up today Max was the furthest thing in my mind. I wondered when I would hear that name again. I used to play this in my mind, how things would be when he got out. Guess we're about to find out."

"How did it go in your mind?" I said.

Joe snorted. "It was fuzzy…unclear. I'd be a fool if I were to say he'd just keep to himself when he got out."

Sal leaned on the desk and pointed his finger at me. "That's bullshit. That's not how things went down. Max is a liar. He'll say anything to make himself look good. Don't ever trust a thing he says."

"That's just what they said," Jason added. "We know you, Joe, you'd never do anything like that."

Joe laughed, patting Sal on the side. "It's okay. Cool it down. The guys didn't mean anything by it. Don't worry, I'm not going anywhere."

"Is it true?" I asked.

Joe sat up in the chair. "What happened to Max was his fault. He did own all this at one time, but when he got locked up he lost everything. The whole north side was up for grabs. Truth is, that rat fuck was turnin' on his guys. He got caught, so to reduce his time he started talkin' to the FEDS. They had him for murder, gambling, all types of shit. If he wouldn't take the deal that fool would've gone down for life. I tell ya, a lot of people wanted to see him dead. He made a lot of problems for us all. A lot of good guys were taken off the street."

"So, it's a lie?" I said.

"That would appear to be the case," Sal looked at the ceiling, then back at us. "That guy Max, he's no good. I'm surprised no one got to him in prison. He had lots of enemies that were with him, the prick. I wished I was in the same prison he was, I could've killed him myself. You may have disagreements, misunderstandings, hell you may not even like people in or outside your crew, but, you don't rat them out. You keep your fuckin' mouth shut. And if you get busted, you do your time like a man. It's sort of like this unwritten code. You have to respect this thing. You can't just go off and do whatever. People remember they remember every time a person wronged them."

"Should we be worried?" I looked at Joe. "He told us we're number one on Max's shit list. The both of them want you dead, no doubt about it."

"I wouldn't be worried," Joe answered. "If he does wanna cause a scene, which I doubt, then I'll take care of it."

"How?" Jason asked.

"We'll have to go to war if they give us no choice. But I figure Nick's just sayin' that to try and start some sort of paranoia or something. Some people you can read like a deck of cards, but others... then again... you can never tell. Everyone's different. You never know. If he doesn't kill you, he'll die trying. An all-out blood bath isn't what I want, but if it comes to it... Something tells me Max wouldn't want that either. Originally, we all got into this thing for money. Things, always get out of control. Before you know what happened, just have a list of regrets for days."

Sal said, "I'm always telling myself I should've gone to college when I was younger. Don't have to put up with shit like this teaching an English class," he gave a nod. "It's a damn headache no matter what you do."

I sighed. "Why would Max tell Nick you told on him? Just trying to get under our skin, do ya think?"

"I wouldn't put it past anyone. First of all, Max is a crazy guy. Probably said that so he could justify a war of some kind. You can never tell with guys like him. So, the brother says he's gonna be out in a few days? Well, if he wants to see me, I'm not going anywhere. I'm always around for a good fight. If you ask me he should try to get Ted's territory."

"You know, he and Ted were always pretty tight," Sal said. "It's gonna be interesting to see how things play out. A lot of the guys who were in Max's crew went to work for Ted when he went away."

"Ted?" I said. "We don't have a problem with him. There's been things here and there, but-"

"I said *were*. The tune might've changed now."

"It has been awhile since Max was on the streets."

"My point," Sal said.

I said, "Should we go to Ted about this, do you think?"

Joe puffed on his cigar a few more times, reaching for a bottle of whiskey behind his desk. "Guys want a drink?"

We told him we did. When we first came in I wasn't in the mood for a drink, but at that point I was. He turned to a cabinet behind his chair and took out enough glasses for us. He filled those glasses to the very brim.

We thanked him.

"This is the best stuff right here, guys," Joe told us.

We all clanked our glasses together.

I took a drink and put the glass back on the desk. "Yes, indeed. Can't find stuff like that everywhere.

"Anyway," Joe said, "I wouldn't go telling Ted. He'll know soon enough."

Jason said, "We're here to do whatever you want. We're on your team. Just let us know what you want us to do."

"Thanks, guys," Joe offered a smile. "I know you guys mean right. We'll see how things go. Thanks for being so loyal. All of this may disappear in a few weeks. It's been over ten years since I'd seen Max. From the sounds of it, he hasn't changed much, still an ego-driven freak. Thanks for telling me."

"Anytime," I said

"You got it, boss," Jason added.

"This put a cramp on your day?" I asked.

"Not really," Joe said. "Ran out of coffee at the house before I could get a cup, I knew it was all downhill after that."

" I always buy in bulk," I said. "I don't like to run out of shit like that, it gets my nerves in a twist."

Jason said, "I had no idea Nick had the connections he did."

"He was a young kid when his brother went away," Sal said. "He wasn't a threat to anyone. I guess he just wanted to follow in Big Brother's footsteps."

I said, "If he doesn't watch it, those footsteps may lead to a hole in the ground."

"I'm sure we can arrange that if it comes to it."

"Guess he planned on getting revenged," my brother said.

Sal said, "That could get bloody. We have enough problems now without this guy getting things started. We need to figure out a way to get him before he gets out before anything happens."

"We won't be able to get a message to any of our guys in time," Joe said. "The window's not that big."

We went on to explain to Joe and Sal what Nick told us about his brother, and how Nick had been in the shadows, quietly recruiting the whole time. I asked Joe if he knew what Nick had been doing in the past ten years. Our boss said that he had heard things now and then about what he had done.

After we talked some more we left the club.

eight

A few days later, I drove over to my brother's house. We were going to spend a few hours rehearsing. Before I went to Jason's, I stopped at a dealer's place to get some cocaine. When I pulled into my brother's driveway, William and Clarence were already there.

I got out of my car and walked to the front door. The door was unlocked, so I let myself in. A cool breeze mixed with stale cigarette smoke crept over me as I walked across the brown shag carpet. A white couch sat against the wall. A stereo and big screen TV were side-by-side on the wall across from the couch. I entered the kitchen and heard muffled music from the basement door. Three cases of beer sat on the counter. I thought about ripping a bottle open, and drinking the whole thing before I joined the other guys. I opened the door to the basement, and a chunk of cool air rushed over me. A dusty light bulb hung by a string from the ceiling. A few cobwebs were scattered in the corners. The slightest hint of motor oil and sweat lingered in the air. I walked down the brown creaking stairs. When I got to the bottom I saw they were huddled around a TV. I wondered what was playing on the box that could captivate my friends so much. I thought some sort of pornographic movie was on or something.

Jason turned and looked at me. "Hey, man, what's new?"

"Not much," I said.

"Same here."

"Seems to be common."

"Yeah."

I smiled. "That beer upstairs looked inviting."

"Take all you want."

"I'll have to do that."

Clarence gave me a nod. "Good, you could make it."

"Anytime," I told him. "I wouldn't miss it. What are you guys watching?"

"The news," William muttered. "They're talkin' about that Hussenin bastard. Shit's crazy. They should kill that fucker."

I said, "It makes you wonder why people do the things they do. People like that don't deserve to live. The guy thinks he can just force his way into anywhere he wants. He has no regard for human life."

William said, "I'd walk up to him and blow his fuckin' brain all over the place. Everyone would thank me. There'd be no love lost."

"Lord knows someone needs to do it," Clarence said. "You have to think this country is controlled by some of the biggest gangsters in the world; they should've figured it out by now, don't ya think? Shit, man, they need to send us over there. We'll fuck him up. Teach him a thing or two."

"They'll get him sooner or later," I told him. "They should bomb the whole fuckin' planet. Let us rule everything. Middle East, hell, they'll be fightin' after the world ends. Shit isn't gonna resolve itself overnight."

Jason chuckled. "Sounds about right, Sean. I'm all for that. Get a huge compound with a lot of girls all the time. Mountains of drugs and money at our disposal. No one will dare mess with us. We'll have guards and cameras all around."

Clarence and William agreed.

I said, "As soon as they take that guy out another is gonna pop up. It's just gonna keep going and going. It's never gonna end," I pointed to the television. "All those reporters, all they care about is their careers."

William said, "It's not good at any rate."

Jason walked over to a small wooden table picked up his pack of cigarettes, took one out, and lit it. "That reminds me, that guy over at Edge said he can only pay us a quarter of what we were asking."

"Really?" William said, putting his hands on his hips. "That doesn't sound right. He could just charge people at the door. All he needs to do is ask around, see if we're any good if that's an issue."

Jason shook his head. "He was also saying he would only be able to have us play for twenty minutes."

"He says why?"

"If I had to guess I'd say he doesn't want us to play for some reason."

"Think we should go and bust him up?"

"Nah," Jason said. "Nothing like that. His loss. If he doesn't like the music he can go fuck himself."

"That place is a shit-hole," I said, "cheap liquor, cheap everything. Last time I was in there I saw three fights. And the band they had, they split about halfway through. The people in charge were pretty pissed about that. Said they were gonna track them down."

"Why were you there if you didn't like the place?" Clarence asked.

"I'd never been there before. This girl I was dating dragged me in," I said. "We met with some of her friends. One of those girls, Audra, I ended up sleeping with."

"Really?" William said. "When was this?"

"When I was seeing Amanda."

"Had no idea."

"She wanted to get together again, but then she moved."

"Where'd she move?"

"New York, I think. She was gonna be a model for this company. Some sort of fashion thing."

"Why hadn't I heard this before?"

I shrugged. "Guess I forgot to tell you. You tell us everyone you sleep with?"

"No."

"Well, there ya go!"

"Okay, okay, if you say so."

"I'll be glad to hear any sex stories you have."

"Really?"

"No."

"Oh, man, that's some cold shit."

I laughed. "You know how that goes."

"I wouldn't say anything like that about you."

"You need to keep it that way."

"Fuck you!"

"Your mom."

We continued to talk and joke for about an hour before we started rehearsing. We tried to rehearse whenever we could. It became difficult at times, due to the criminal life we dedicated ourselves to. Whispers and rumors always crept into places we played. Some bar and club owners, even though they couldn't prove anything, had hesitations about booking us. We were careful not to let people know of our criminal activities. When we started with Joe Butler's gang, we thought that our playing music would serve as a cover; for the most part, it had. Rumors started because a few people we had dealings with had loose lips. Some people believed, others didn't.

All of our equipment was kept in my brother's basement. We kept all of the stuff there due to the fact there wasn't any space at anybody else's place. He had a fully stocked bar he built himself; it was tucked away in the corner. He had three couches that sat around the bar. A refrigerator stood against a wall. He always told us he wanted to build his recording studio in his house. I thought it sounded like a good idea. I brought up the idea of raising the money for studio time and doing it ourselves. But we found out that was a big investment. We all wanted desperately to get into the music business. We were just gonna see how things played out. Maybe things would work out, maybe not.

"I can't wait till you guys listen to the riff I thought of last night," Jason picked up his bass.

"Sounds about right," the drummer added. "I wanna hear it, man. You know what we should do, man? We should do a bunch of snow and make a whole album. We need to do everything fast and now. Fuck it!"

My brother looked at him. "It takes you on a ride through the rainbow waves, above sunshine moon skies. They're all good trips."

"I'll agree with ya on that one. You have some?" William asked.

"I do."

"We'll have to break into it."

"Sure."

"You want me to get it?"

"No, that's cool. I'll get it. Have to keep some things secret around here, you know?"

"Oh, sure, sure, sure. I wouldn't wanna be labeled a rat or anything."

"Well, Willy, we wouldn't want that."

"No kidding."

"Let me run and get it."

My brother went off and got some cocaine.

We all sat around doing some.

After awhile of joking around, we agreed we needed to start to play.

I was tuning my guitar as Clarence took out his notebook of songs. He showed us a few new lyrics he wrote. We talked for a little bit about what the music would sound like. Once we got an idea of what we wanted, we turned on our amplifiers to begin.

There was something about loud music that made me smile. The louder, the better. The equipment we had wasn't the best. We had to make the most of it. We bought new stuff when we could

William started with a slow drum beat, then back and forth, hitting the symbols. Jason and I joined in. Clarence started to sing into the microphone. We rehearsed for about three hours, stopping a couple of times for a cigarette and a beer.

"We should knock 'em dead tomorrow," I said, putting my guitar in its case. "It'll be a good show. The energy from the crowd is all you need. You can always pull someone out of the crowd to play for you, right?"

My brother clapped his hands together. "We have a real nice show for you tonight, kids. You'll have to see and hear it. They'll dazzle you with skill and technique. Yes, ladies and gents, you'll get your money's worth."

"That was pretty good," William started to dismantle his drum set. "We might get people to like us if you do that."

They both laughed.

"Or Four crazy gangsters," I said. "I'm sure that's every mother's dream to have her daughter ride off in the sunset with a hoodlum."

"Hoodlum?" Clarence said. "I'll be like that guy in *Scarface*. You know, I'll have a big mansion with tons of money, women every night. It'll be great. They'll respect me."

William said, "He got killed at the end of that movie, you know that?"

"They won't take me without a fight. I'll take a few of them out before I go."

"Just ambush all of 'em. That'll put an end to that business pretty quickly. Make sure you have enough guards.

I think that's the thing that was missing from that movie. Think about it, he had all the money to do all that fuckin' blow, he could've afforded more bodyguards. If he did that, he might not have died as he did."

"They can't have a ten-hour movie," the singer said. "It has to end sometime."

"I know. All I'm saying, he had his priorities all screwed up. He cared more about the powder than he did his own life."

"The whole thing was about excess, about not letting it cloud your judgment."

"That's crazy."

Clarence continued. "I've been called worse. It's all that powder, it made him twisted inside. In the end, he didn't know what to trust. It all got twisted. It's about thinking things out, planning, having a strategy in place, not deviating from it. If I had been in that guy's shoes that's how I would've done it. Doing it smart, that's what it's about. Here's another thing, what happened to his house? After he died someone had to take it."

"The cops, probably."

"You think?"

"Look, the house more than likely was bought with drug money. The instant he was taken out the cops seized the property. Either they tore down the house or sold it."

"I want a house like that," Clarence said. "Kingpin or not, that'll be my reality one of these days."

"Something like that comes with drawbacks."

"I can take it."

"Take anything, right?"

"You know it."

We went around the room giving ideas and thoughts.

Shootin' Noise

When I was a teen, I remember walking passed a corner record store, I fell in love with the sounds I heard. I walked in to look around. I was in there for a bit when I stumbled on the Rock section. There were a few Led Zeppelin albums I bought. I went home and listened to the albums two times each. The rhythm and sound was something I wanted to emulate. I went back to the store a week later and got some AC/DC and others. I always liked Joe Walsh, and I picked up some of his stuff, too. I liked the way Joe played and sang.

We all had big hopes and dreams about the future. We would watch music videos and wish it was us. We would record our favorite songs on the radio and figure them out by ear. I could never learn how to read music. I thought I could write music my way and sell it. What I would do, I would draw out the guitar strings on paper, and then I'd mark where the frets would be, after I was done with that, I'd play a few notes and then mark the finger placement on the paper. After awhile, though, I concluded that no one would buy my stuff.

Throughout all my years of guitar playing, I never did learn to read music.

The reporters on the television were still talking about the Gulf War. I lit up a cigarette as I watched. "This is too crazy," I said.

"We live in times of war, indeed," my brother said.

"But it's not our fight."

"Sooner or later it trickles down to everyone."

I turned from the television. "I can't watch this anymore."

"It's the world we live in."

I left Jason's a little after two in the morning. I didn't want to go directly home, so I took a long drive. I drove down the highway to a little park in Conway, the next town over. The park was quiet. There wasn't a single soul in sight. I could see a few houses in the distance had their lights on. But I didn't think they'd care if someone was in the park. I sat behind the wheel and rolled one of the fattest joints I'd ever rolled. I smoked the whole thing as I stared at the abandoned park. I rolled down the window. A silent blanket covered the early morning sky. A sigh from a car echoed down the main road leading to the park; its headlights bent through the trees along the road. At some point in the morning, I fell asleep.

I woke around noon to the sun pouring into the windows. I sat up and wiped the sleep from my eyes. I was hungry.

When I got back to my apartment I grabbed a shower and something to eat. I messed around the rest of the day until I had to get ready for the show. The show ended up being pretty nice. The next day I worked a few hours at Highlife, tending bar and cooking. At about eight o'clock I drove to a bar a few blocks away called Swango. I spent the evening drinking and talking to strangers. Two girls sat beside me at the bar and we started a conversation.

Their names were Amy and Heidi. Soon after they got there, Amy met a guy, and they went off into the night. Heidi and I had a nice time, drinking and telling stories, and getting to know one another. She told me she worked at a record store called Scratches in the Mullock Plaza. We talked for a few hours before I asked her out. We agreed to meet at a café the next day when she got off work.

nine

I pulled into the Mullock Plaza and parked in front of a
bookstore. The Mullock Plaza was on the south side of
Brown Ridge. I killed the engine, opened the door, and
stepped out of my car. There were two restaurants at either end of the plaza. There was a bank and a retail store
that, along with Scratches and Donna's, made up the rest
of the dark brick plaza. I thought I'd go to see Heidi before our date. I couldn't believe I had known about the
store and had never gone in.

I walked through the glass doors of Scratches. When I
got inside I was greeted with the familiar smells of music. There were speakers attached to the walls. Jazz music was coming from the walls. It was my sort of place,
full of good sounds and vinyl. Some of the other customers didn't seem to like the selection coming out of
the speakers. I never understood people who didn't like
jazz.

I saw Heidi was dealing with a customer, so I continued
thumbing through racks of albums. I thought of how
great it would be to see Stoned Monkey's debut album in
one of those racks. The next thing I knew a voice behind
me said my name. I turned around to see Heidi. She
asked what I was doing there. I explained I wanted to see
where she worked. I'd never been in the place before
and I wanted to check it out.

"What do you think?" she asked.

"Not bad," I told her. "I dig the music."

"Good. Well, if those great musicians hadn't recorded
all that material we wouldn't have any of it. So, you really should thank them."

I leaned against one of the racks of vinyl. "Fair enough.
One day we'll have our album in here."

"You in a band?"

"Yeah."

"Really? That's good. What's the name?"

"Stoned Monkey."

"That's the name?"

"Sure."

"You guys any good?"

"I think so."

"You have a demo?"

"We do."

"I bet it sounds good."

I gave a smile. "It'll be the best-selling thing in this place."

"What are ya waiting for? You just can't talk about it all the time."

"Very true."

She jetted out her hip and put her hand on it. "Of course. I love creative people."

"Good thing for me, right?"

"We'll see," she smiles.

I liked the way she smiled.

A small line started to form at the cash register.

She told me that she needed to do her job and take care of the situation.

We walked over to the front counter. She kissed me on the cheek and said she'd see me at the café when she got off work.

I walked around until it was time to meet at Donna's. I walked into the café and looked at the clock on the wall. It was a little after six. I secured a booth in the back corner. It wasn't that big of a place. There was a jukebox next to the entrance. There were only four tables occupied; one elderly couple, and three couples around my age. The conversations around the tables echoed wall-to-wall. I leaned back and lit a cigarette. It was nice to sit and relax. A small television was playing on the counter.

It was fifteen after when the bell on the door jingled as the door ripped open. I motioned to Heidi where I was sitting. She walked to the booth. She was wearing a white button-down with solid black pants that complimented her pale thin frame. She looked like she'd just walked out of a movie or a commercial. She was beautiful.

"This booth okay?" I asked.

"It's fine," she fell into the booth, setting her purse beside her.

She leafed through her purse for her cigarettes. She put a cigarette in her mouth, and I used my lighter and lit it for her.

"Thanks," she said.

"You're welcome."

I lit one of my own. "How was your day?"

"It was good. Busy and frustrating. I was ready to get the hell out of there, have a cigarette, and get off my feet."

"I know how that goes."

"Where do you work?" she asked.

"Highlife."

"I've been there a few times. Never have seen you. You like it?"

"It keeps money in my pocket."

"I guess that's the important part."

I shrugged. "It does. It can get a little crazy there sometimes."

"How's that?"

"On weekends, mostly. Fights and stuff like that. The things we do for money, right?"

"Have you ever been in the middle of any?"

"A few times."

"That's scary."

"A little."

"Next time someone can have a gun or something."

"I know."

"Do they call the cops when that happens?"

"No. They like to handle things themselves."

"Oh? That's interesting. Why don't they want cops involved? Are they doing illegal things?"

I laughed. "No, it's nothing like that. They just don't wanna be known as the place, the bar, the cops always have to go to."

"Has anyone ever died there?"

"I'm sure the cops would come then."

"I'd hope so."

"I mean, you know, they've had shots fired outside the building; they've come out then. Just drunks."

"I gotcha."

A waitress came over and we ordered coffee and pie. Heidi said, "Anytime is a good time for pie."

"And coffee," I added.

"A cigarette is good, too."

"When I'm at work and can't smoke it's like, 'look buddy, don't know if you know it but if I don't smoke this I'll hit you in the face. I need my nicotine.'"

A smile crossed her face. "I wanted to do that so bad today. Had a guy who wanted money back for a damaged album."

"Did he get the refund?"

"No."

"Why?"

"Because he did the damage. He broke it into two pieces. He claimed he broke it when he was mad."

"Really?"

"I had to stop myself from laughing. He started telling me about how his wife left him. So, he got drunk and

trashed all of his belongings. The theory he had was because this record he broke was bought at our store, it was
our responsibility to reimburse him. You know, because
we just go around to houses breaking albums people
bought."

"What did you say?"

"I told him after the merchandise leaves the store it's
not our responsibility. I told him if he wants to buy another copy, he's free to do so."

"What did he say?" I asked.

"He mumbled something and threw the two pieces on
the floor."

"That's pretty rude."

"That's what I thought."

"Sorry about that."

"Wasn't your fault."

It amazed me how beautiful she was. Something in the
back of my head told me I was very lucky to be there
with her. When she told me she would go on a date with
me I almost went into shock.

The waitress came back to the table with the pie and
coffee. She told us her name was Beth, and if there was
anything else we needed to let her know.

"Thanks, Beth," my female companion said.

"I'll be here till we close," Beth told us.

She walked back to the kitchen.

A little while later she came back with an extra pot of
coffee.

Beth went to the other tables to take care of the other
customers.

I looked at the coffee and pie. "Smells good."

"Sure does," Heidi grabbed the sugar jar.

As she was shaking sugar into her coffee, I laughed.

The white sweetness poured out of the jar in a thin
sheet.

"What?" she asked.

"You like sugar?"

"Yes, sir, I do."

"Same here."

"It's the only way to be. I dunno what I'd do if I didn't have my sugar with coffee."

"Know what you mean."

"It's so tasty."

I shook my head in agreement. "Indeed."

She took her fork and knifed off a piece of her cherry pie. "This was a good idea."

"It's good," I shoved a piece of pie in my mouth.

She wiped her napkin across her mouth. "How was your day?"

"It was okay."

"Really? What did you do?"

"Oh, not much. Rehearsal, that's about it. I didn't have work."

"Wish I could've had the day off."

"Jealous?" I offered.

"A little," she took another bite. "How is the music-making going?"

"It's good. Slowly getting there. Just have to play one gig after another."

"Well, that's good, though. You're getting yourself out there and making fans."

"Very true."

"And along the way, you could inspire someone."

"To do what, kill themselves?"

"No, no, no," she smiled. "Hopefully you'll inspire someone to go out and do some good. Make their art."

"Not sure they'd look to me."

"Why do you think that?"

"Just think there's someone more qualified for that job."

"I'd disagree."

"Thanks."

"You never know who you may touch in your life, who you may encourage to do great things. I think if you're given a gift, may as well try to share it with everyone you can."

"That makes sense."

"Now and then I make some good points."

I drank the rest of my cup, then poured a refill.

One of the other patrons in the café had put a song on the jukebox. The song was a slow piano number I'd never heard before. The bell on the door jingled a few more times as a few more people entered. The clatter of pans and dishes echoed from the kitchen.

I leaned back in the booth. "Must be nice to work in a record store."

"It's nice."

"I'd like to do that."

"You can have my job."

"No. That's fine."

"Thought so."

I took another drink of coffee. "But to be surrounded by music all day, that would be my dream job."

"We're constantly playing music in the store, and you get a feeling of the history behind it."

"How so?"

"A lot of what we play are the used records, and with some of them, you get all of those pops and scratches with the music. It's like every pop and scratch on that album tells its own story, its past, loves, addictions, successes, and sorrows. Every story tells a tale."

"Interesting."

"It gives the music so much meaning."

"I'd have to agree," I said. "I write a lot of the songs we play, and I put my own experience into them."

"Really?"

"I had all these great stories about things that happened to me and people I know. I told myself I needed some sort of vehicle to get it all out. I thought about maybe becoming a novelist. I still may write something like that."

"Sounds neat. Like your own diary."

"Yeah."

"I like it."

"I write poetry, too."

"I love poetry."

"That's how songs start."

"With poetry?"

"Of course."

" Used to write that stuff."

"You don't anymore?"

"Don't really. I do read a lot."

"That's good."

"At least it's something, right?"

"Sure."

"And that's the best thing."

"Right about that."

"In the future…who knows?"

"You're so positive."

"I try to be."

"I like it," I told her.

Heidi excused herself to go to the restroom.

I knew I was doing good because she hadn't left yet. I felt so good about myself that I thought about jumping up and dancing a jig right there in the café. In her absence, I looked around the place and gave a deep sigh. Everyone seemed to be on a caffeine high, chatting into the night. I'd always been somewhat pessimistic, thinking good things could never happen to me. And if good did happen, the other side would drop.

I refilled my cup and lit another cigarette.

Shootin' Noise

Some other guy in the café put on a more upbeat song on the music box.

Heidi came back to the table and sat down.

"Thought you weren't gonna make it back," I looked at her.

She brushed her hair from her eyes. "I see you're a comedian."

"That's me."

She poured herself some more coffee. "I'd love to come to one of your shows sometime. I love live music."

"We put on a hell of a show. I can't believe you've never been to one of the shows."

"To be honest, I hadn't ever heard of your band before. Don't take offense, I don't go to those places much."

"That's okay."

"When are you playing next?"

"We're playing at Dumons tomorrow night. Should be a good show. You should come and check it out."

"What time?"

"We take the stage at about nine."

"I'll have to check it out," she said. "A friend of mine, Sarah, wanted to go do something tomorrow."

I nodded. "You guys will love it."

"I'm sure we will, if not, we'll demand our money back."

I laughed. "Won't have to worry about getting the money back."

We spent the next couple of hours sitting in the café, trading stories, getting to know each other. She agreed to come back to my place afterward. We spent the night listening to music. At dawn we made love.

ten

Jason and I went over to talk with the owner of Bonzo. We had to talk to this guy because we had a show there that night. The guys and I always hated dealing with these owners: they were all hustlers and drunks for the most part. They'd say one thing and then do the opposite: a bunch of rotten bastards. The guy we talked to was named Danny Wright.

"People say you boys put on a hell of a show," Danny told us. "They say you know how to draw the crowds. That's what I want tonight, good old music. I don't want any wild business going on."

I nodded. "Anything you want, sir. We just wanna put on a good show."

"Good to hear," the guy told us. "The last group we had in here got too drunk to finish playing. Had to kick 'em out. Bastards tried to give me a bunch of headache over it, sayin' I had no right to end their show, threaten to kick my ass, burn down my house, all sorts of shit. Had to call the law on 'em. They were crazy guys. Don't want that sort of thing again."

He stared at Jason and I for a minute. He was probably thinking we were trying to put on a con.

"Oh? Well, we do all our drinkin' after the show," I said.

"That's good. Might have to join you boys for a couple later," he said.

"Sounds good."

"Do what you do best and help me put money in my pocket."

I shrugged. "Why not? I'm always one to support local

business."

"Glad to hear you say that."

"I'd want the same for myself. Hate to see anyone go bankrupt."

"At least it hasn't come to that yet."

Jason grinned. "There's a first for everything."

Danny looked at my brother and I. "There's only one thing."

"What's that?" I asked.

"I've heard rumors about you guys, that you guys have connections to a certain criminal element in the city. That Joe guy, I hear you're with his group. I run a clean place around here, and I don't need any trouble."

I looked at my brother, laughed, then back at Danny. "Rumors are just that, right? I can assure you, you have nothing to worry about."

"I have your word on that?"

"Of course."

Jason said, "My brother knows what he's talkin' about."

Danny pointed a finger at me. "If you're trying to pull something, I have a loaded gun in back."

My brother shrugged his shoulders. "You can never be too careful. There are a lot of crazy people out there. You can never tell, but, honestly, you don't have to worry about anything. We're professional."

Danny said he'd show us around the place. He showed us where they kept all of the beer and everything. He told us about how his father used to have a restaurant in the place before he died of cancer. We went back to his office.

Danny walked over to his desk and plopped down in his chair. "The thing about music is it's always changing. You have to stay with what's hip, have to know how the tide goes."

"We're finding that out all the time. So far, everyone

loves us. It's fuckin' great."

My brother told the guy we'd play there again if everything went okay.

"Sorry the other guys, Clarence and William couldn't make it to this meeting," I told him. "You'll meet 'em tonight. They had some things going on."

Danny said, "Hell, boys, Chuck White told me I'd like eating deer asshole, too."

"How'd that go for ya?" I said.

"I hated it."

"That sounds pretty nasty."

"It was."

"I don't think I wanted to hear that," Jason said.

Danny shrugged. "Hey, whatever works. The point is, I don't believe what anyone ever tells me again. I have to see it for myself."

"I guess."

"You'd be amazed at what I've seen," Danny went on to tell us.

"I guess," I said. "Back to what I was saying, you'll like the other guys."

Danny said. "I'm sure what they had to do was important."

"It probably wasn't," my brother said.

"Is it ever?" I chuckled.

"I know," Jason added.

Danny sat back in his chair. "You know, if this goes right I'll schedule ya boys for more shows."

"Thanks," I said. "I'm confident things are gonna be okay."

Danny continued. "We all need breaks once in awhile."

"Some people do," Jason said.

"This'll be a good move for you, Danny," I said.

The bar owner looked at us for a few minutes. "Just make it fun for everyone. I just want everyone to have a good time."

"We'll see what we can do," Jason said.

"Good, good, good! Repeat business is always a plus in this line of work," Danny said.

"I know all about it," I said. "I work at Highlife."

"Never been there."

"You should come by sometime."

"Any live music?"

"Sometimes."

The three of us talked a little longer.

Jason and I went to this small restaurant for lunch. After we finished eating we headed back to my brother's house until the show. We called the other guys over. I was telling them all about Heidi, how I thought she was the girl for me, about how they should meet her. Around eight o'clock we got to the bar. My brother and I assured the other two guys that Danny wasn't a bad guy.

Finally, the time came for us to perform. As soon as I hit the first chord on my guitar, I looked out to the audience and told myself it would be a good show. Our singer started his little opening speech to the crowd. He went on for about five minutes about how much he appreciated everyone coming out. No matter how many times I heard him give that speech, I never got tired of it.

We played fifteen songs out of our catalog. After our last song, everyone was cheering for more. We looked at each other for a minute. It was known to us we had a limited window to play in. But we started another song. Danny was over by the bar pointing at us and saying something. I couldn't understand what he said.

We were in mid-song, electricity spun across the room, everyone was roaring, and then the sound came to a screeching halt. Our instruments came back down to their bare sound. Clarence jumped off stage and raced to where Danny was standing. "Fuck you do that for?" my friend snapped.

"I told you guys what the deal was. I have a schedule to keep. I'm running a business here, buddy." Danny said.

"You're way outta line."

"And why's that?"

"Those people, we were playing for them. It's not our fault they wanted more. We were just giving them what they wanted. What the hell do you care?"

"You rotten fools," Danny snapped. "I should toss you people out on your heads. Thanks to that stunt I won't pay you guys. How do ya like hearing that? I don't give a hunk of shit."

"You better pay us. My friends and I will have to beat you if you don't pay. I'd hate to do that."

"I don't respond to threats."

"That wasn't a threat."

"Oh? Well, make your move, Bubba."

Clarence grabbed the guy by the shirt.

I stepped in to calm them down. "No one wants this noise. Let's all just go our ways. No harm done."

"We will after we beat you," Danny said.

"We?" the singer asked.

"Me and the bouncer, big guy."

Clarence waved his finger at the owner. "I'll fuck you up!"

Danny said, "You wanna go? We can handle this shit right here, little punk!"

"No need for all of that," I said. "You don't want us to get other people involved. Trust me, you don't wanna tangle with us."

"You bastards are all doomed," the owner said. "I'll tell every bar owner around how you guys do business. By the time we get done with you, you'll be lucky if you play at all. Maybe at a fuckin' rodeo, a candy store, what do ya think of that? Now get the fuck out before we start something you won't walk away from."

"That a threat?" my brother said.

"You better believe it!"

I said, "We want our money."

Danny nodded. "You crazy."

"That may be, but we're not here to talk about my philological state," I said. "Look, I'm sure we can work something out. What about half?"

Danny glared at me. "No deal."

"Why?" I asked. "We did our job."

"You did."

"Well, then, pay us."

"No," he said. "You're being disrespectful."

"What?"

My brother raised his fist. "I'll hit you in the face."

"If you hit me, I'll get the police out here."

William walked to Danny and spat at him.

Something told me we weren't getting out without a fight.

"You're gonna pay for that," Danny said.

Our drummer said, "Look, you don't want this, man. Can't we just leave?"

Danny shook his head. I could see the anger on his face.

A couple of big guys walked behind us to toss us out. They had crazy looks about them. Neither of them said a word. I knew if we were going to mix it up with them, someone would call the police and we would go to jail. After a few more heated words I lunged at Danny, hitting him in the face two times, then, kneeing him in the stomach. He fell to the ground. After he fell to the floor. one of the big guys was on me. He had both of my arms pinned behind my back.

From somewhere a voice called out. "Let him go."

"Who the hell are you?" I heard the big guy say.

I turned around, breaking the hold the guy put me in to hear the sound of someone cocking a gun. I Saw it was Nick holding a .45 in plain view. He had a tall guy beside him I'd never seen before. I thought about it for a minute and decided the other guy had to be Max; that, or another one of Nick's guys.

This was all we needed, to get in a mess with these two thugs.

Nick waved his gun toward me and the big guy. "Hey, let the guy go. I have business with these guys."

"And what if I say no?" the guy said.

Nick raised a brow. "You sure you wanna say *no* to a man with a gun? Think you better do what you're told."

The big guy tossed me aside. "Don't care what you do, just don't do it in here. If you need help kicking their asses let me know."

Nick chuckled. "No, that's okay," he turned to the patrons. "Sorry about the interruption. We were just about to take our business outside. Go back to your drinks, folks. We just need to talk to these guys about joining our record label. We'll take this outside."

Everyone in the bar seemed to be in a daze about what was happening. With all the fighting we forgot to get our gear from the stage. We asked Nick and Max if we could get our stuff before we left.

"Make it quick," Max nodded.

We made two trips to get everything off the stage.

I looked over at them as we passed Danny. "This isn't finished. We'll be back."

Danny smiled. "Sure you will."

Max turned to all the patrons. "There won't be any more music tonight. Just sing to yourselves or something."

We walked out the door with our gear into the welcoming night.

"How are you boys doing tonight? Sorry, we didn't see any of the show. Would've been here sooner, but we had to see a guy about some money. Maybe we'll come to a show sometime," Nick turned to Max. "If you're wondering this guy's Max. But something tells me you already knew that."

"What do you want?" I asked.

"Just to talk. Thought we'd pay you a little visit. You know, pick up where we left off. Something told me our last meeting wasn't long enough," he looked back at the bar, then back at us. "You guys gonna play these shitty bars forever? Guess Joe doesn't pay his employees that well, eh?"

"He pays fine," I said.

"Really? We could use you guys for work," Nick said.

"No thanks."

"You're makin' a big mistake."

"Then it's mine to make."

Nick looked over at my band-mates. "What about your friends, maybe? Guys wanna start makin' good cash?"

The other guys didn't say anything.

"Nick said, "Gave you guys a chance," he laughed. "Thought you guys were smarter than that. Man, does Joe have a bunch of dumbasses workin' for him, or what? Guys are fuckin' crazy the way I see it."

"Then that's our choice," my brother said.

"Fair enough. You guys have a change of mind, just come see me. Talk to my other guys, I'll treat ya right."

William said, "Thanks, but we have a good thing goin' now."

"I bet you do," Nick looked back at the bar, then at William. "Those guys in there, if we hadn't of stepped in, you would be in a world of hurt by now."

"How did you know where we were?"

Nick reached into his pants pocket and pulled out a piece of paper. "Saw your flyer," he unfolded the paper, threw it on the ground, and stepped on it.

"Hey, those cost money to make," I said.

"Tough shit."

Max stood in front of me: he looked around fifty, balding, thin, and in shape. He was wearing a blue jacket, black ball hat, and jeans. He was unshaven. Terror ran across my mind as he dug his cigarettes and lighter from his jacket. I thought he was going to pull a gun. He spoke with a rusty voice as he lit a smoke. "In prison you have nothing but time to think, to think about how you should've done things differently, to think about the people who fucked you over, to think about revenge, how you plan to fuck that person over. You sit in your cell and dissect every moment of your revenge plan to the point where you have it memorized in your sleep. I was in my cell one day when it occurred to me that I was too soft when I was on the outside. I mean, I dunno, trying to be a good guy, to be fair with all my people... shit didn't work out. Guess you shouldn't make friends with guys in your crew," he gave a sharp laugh. "As it turned out I'm the one that got screwed."

"Why are you telling us?" I asked.

"Your boss tell you guys about how he sold me out?" Max asked.

"He said you were the rat."

Nick said, "The nerve of some people..."

Max pointed to himself. "He said I was selling people out? I don't think that's how things happened. I was there and I know. Truth is, he was giving people up," Max exhaled a chunk of cigarette smoke. "But never mind all of that. He's just another fuck in a long line of greedy fucks. He waited till I was behind bars to take over everything. As far as I'm concerned I still run all of North Brown Ridge. I paid my dues. Hell, I remember Joe and I did hits together all the time. Those other guys, Sal and James, they were doing the same thing. We were like a killer gang or something."

Jason walked over to Max. "So, what do you want us to do? I mean, why are we here? Some sort of threat or something? You gonna kill us?"

"It's come to my attention that Joe and everyone who stays with him are gonna be problems. Now, as anyone who knows me will tell you I don't like problems. I'd like everyone to know what a nice guy I am."

Jason looked at Max and Nick. "I guess we're gonna be a problem for you? I don't betray friends."

"You sure about that?" Max asked.

"Pretty sure."

"We'll just have to see about that. It's interesting what you can make someone do when you have a loaded gun at their head."

"That so?"

"That's been my experience."

"Why, some guy has a gun to your head as you sucked his dick?"

I glanced over at Nick: he just shook his head.

Max threw out his fist, making contact with Jason's stomach. Jason fell to his knees, clutching at his belly. Max pulled his foot and kicked Jason on the side

"That wasn't very nice, son," Max said. "Sounds like someone needs to teach you some manners. If I wanted to I could kill you right now."

William and Clarence ran over to help Jason, as I tackled Nick to the ground. I got a few punches in before I heard a deafening ring. I turned to see Max firing a .45 into the air. He muttered something about guys staying in line as he put the gun back in his pocket.

"I'm gonna be nice and not kill you guys tonight," he said. "Get your friend off the ground. Next time he smarts off to me, well, he won't be as lucky. We understand each other?"

We nodded.

Clarence and I picked Jason up from the ground. He was beat up a little. He was a little stiff as he tried to walk.

Jason looked at Max and spat.

Max gave a sharp laugh. "You want another love tap, buddy? I suggest you quiet while both legs still work."

I took in a fresh gulp of air. "Look, we don't want any trouble. Why don't you guys just leave us alone?"

Max said, "We'll leave you alone for the time being. Nick and I have other matters to tend to tonight. We're done here. Runoff and put the word out that I'm back, and I'm not going anywhere."

"You girls need to get outta here before we change our minds," Nick pointed his gun at us. "I shot someone earlier today. Felt so good I may have to do it again. I might have to start with you, Sean. Just be thankful we don't do you guys in tonight. Watch your backs. We'll be out there somewhere in the night when you least expect it. See, I'm loyal like you guys. I just want the best for everyone."

Max said, "I'm one of the good guys, boys: in time, I think you'll come to see that. I'm just tryin' to get myself going again. It's just all about money with me. The thing with Joe and I, that's our thing we have to work out. The anger I have with your boss, it's something that I can't let go of. He cost me so much. If you guys are with him... Bad days for you. I'll stop at nothing to get what I want," he let out a little grin. "Now, you guys have a good night," he looked at Jason. "Hey, sorry about the beating."

Both men turned, walked to a car, and they drove away.

We spent a couple of hours drinking and talking about what we should do. I figured the guys and I would tell Joe about it later that day. I knew he wouldn't like the news. I didn't want to tell him, but I knew I had no choice. Truth was, I didn't know if I should believe Joe or Max. It was around two in the morning when I got back to my place.

We found Joe and Sal and told them about what happened.

eleven

I was spending every spare minute with Heidi. We couldn't get enough of each other. Every night we spent together we had hot sweaty sex. Most nights were at my place, some at hers. I just loved being with her, putting in the time, and getting to know every little detail about her. When I told her what I did for a living she didn't seem to mind. She thought it was neat she was dating some kind of outlaw, a guy who was connected. She just didn't want me to get hurt. She was asking why I didn't tell her from the beginning. I told her I didn't know what her reaction would've been.

 "I don't want you to do anything that's gonna get ya thrown in jail," she said.

 "Don't worry, babe," I lit a cigarette. "I'm careful about what I do. I'm not gonna get caught."

She stared at me for a moment, then opened her mouth. "Have you ever killed anyone before?"

"Only those who deserved it."

"Do people deserve to die?"

"If they intend to harm me or someone in my family, yes."

"I guess that's okay. Something has to be done with those sorts of people. You have to be some animal or something to want to hurt a family member. I'm just worried you might get caught."

 "I won't get caught."

 "You better not."

 "I'm not on any major radars. The band and job at the nightclub are good covers. Cops, they don't know my involvement. They won't ever find out. Trust me, I'm really careful. I'm not gonna get caught. They don't suspect me."

"Have you ever worked at Highlife?"

"I just work there on paper. Yeah, I tend to bar and stuff now and then. FEDS start snooping around it'll all seem legit. We try not to let any blood get into Highlife."

"How's that working out?"

"Pretty good," I said. "There were a few things here and there. Mostly, it was just minor stuff. We can handle it if things get too loud."

"I'm glad to hear that, dear."

"You don't have to worry."

"And the music?"

"The music was first. Who's gonna think a group of guys that appear in public all the time are mixed up in crime?"

"But when they do find out?"

"We'll deal with that when it happens."

"Has that ever prevented you guys from getting gigs?"

"A few. Guess those guys were too scared even if it was just hearsay. A few of the club owners heard and liked the mystery."

She smiled. "I'm fucking a gangster... Every girl's dream."

"Glad I could make that come true for you," I nodded.

"Thanks."

"Glad you like my work."

She walked over to the kitchen to make coffee.

I followed.

"How was the store?"

"It wasn't that busy," she said. "Just a few regulars. Nothing too exciting. I wasn't in the mood to be busy to-day."

"One of these days I'll make it so you won't have to work there anymore."

"How?"

"I'm makin' some moves."

"Like what?"

I glanced down at the floor, then back at her. "I promise I'll make enough money so you don't have to work, so you don't have to stand on your feet all day and take shit from people. I want the girl I'm with to have whatever she wants: I won't rest until that happens."

She opened a cabinet and took out the can of coffee and a bag of filters. "That's sweet. Anyway, I could join the club?"

"The crew?"

"Yeah."

I shook my head. "You don't want this."

"What makes you say that?" she fitted a coffee filter into the machine. "If anyone messes with me, I'll take a hammer to them."

"Remind me not to make you mad."

She laughed, as she put some coffee in the filter. "Better not piss me off."

"Thanks for the advice."

She made her finger in the shape of a gun and pointed at me. "You better watch it! I'm pretty ruthless."

I laughed. "I'll take my chances."

She laughed.

"Seriously," I said. "I don't want anything to happen to you."

"What about you?"

"I'm not going anywhere."

"Better not."

I ran my hand along the side of her face. "I love you."

"Likewise," she whispered.

We kissed.

After the coffee was brewed she poured two cups and handed me one.

"Thanks," I took a sip.

She put her cup on the kitchen table. "So, will you be able to get a better place?"

"What? You don't like my apartment?"

"It's a little small, don't ya think?"

"I dunno, I like it."

She picked up her cup and took a drink. "It's not in the best neighborhood, babe, I hate to break it to you."

"Like yours is any better? I had to fight off two homeless guys just to get down the street."

She laughed. "I love you, Sean."

"Love you too, kid."

"Thanks."

We put down our cups.

I moved to her, brushed her hair from her eyes, and kissed her. She led me to the bed where I ripped her clothes off. She snapped my pants open and unzipped me. I kicked off my pants as she fell on the bed. I fell on top of her and started to kiss her. I slid my hand across her naked breasts. She started to moan. I slid my hand down and tore off her panties. Her body was nice and warm. After we were done, hot and sweaty, I put on my pants lit a cigarette, and sat on the edge of the bed. I looked out the window as the outside sky started to fade to blue. She crawled over to where I was sitting and kissed me.

"What are you thinking about?" she asked.

I looked at her. "Nothing to concern yourself with. it'll get figured out in time."

"Are you in danger?"

"No, nothing like that."

I lied.

twelve

My brother suggested we go for a night in the town. We pulled into the parking lot of a place called Billingtons: one of many night spots in the area. The place was a big two-story building. As I got out of my car the calm air ran across my face. I was ready for a much-needed break from everything. I held the passenger door open for Heidi to crawl out. Everyone else in our company parked beside us. The street in front of the club was congested with roaring cars and loud headlights.

All types of people were gathered in front of the building. Laughter and smoke ripped across the parking lot. Everyone in my group was huddled around looking at the scene.

A tiny little blonde was running around yelling. "hey, I'm high. Anyone who wants me better come get me. I like to suck and fuck. I'll be the best you ever had. Any takers?"

She wore a purple shirt, black pants, dark eyeliner, a shiny necklace, and a few bracelets on either arm. She walked up to our group.

"Anyone here lookin' for a good time?" she said

A few yells and roars came from all directions.

I turned to William, patted his shoulder, and said he needed to try and get with her. He just looked at me and nodded. He needed to get himself a girl. The last one he had dumped him after she found out he shot someone.

"That's okay," he said. "From the sound of it, she's too wild for me."

"Is there such a thing?" I said.

"Guess not," he said. "I have to take a pass on her. Tell

ya what, Jason could say the right thing to her to make her his."

"I bet you're right about that one."

"He always gets the girls."

"Can't argue with that."

Jason turned to us. "Hey, I can dig that. Sounds good to me. She does look pretty sexy."

"Better you than me," William added.

Jason said to William. "I'll have to tell ya how it goes, buddy. You might wanna ball her after I'm done. I'll let you know if she's any good."

"Maybe."

Jason chuckled. "Willy, my boy, we need to get you laid."

William waved him off. "Yeah, yeah, yeah, if you say so. I can get my dates. Thank you for the concern."

"Your hand doesn't count."

"Funny."

We laughed.

"You guys are crazy," Heidi said.

"See what I put up with, Heidi," William said. "These jokers, think they're so amusing. I'm always telling them how they should be stand-up comedians."

Jason barked, "I'd rather be a sit-down comedian."

"That shit's funny," William howled.

"Standing in the same spot for too long gets tiring."

"I can see that, sure."

I slapped my brother on the back. "Hawke brothers, live in person. We'll be here all week long, folks! A grand routine we have for all of you! Everyone swoons to the spectacle that is us."

"Sounds about right," Jason added.

Clarence said, "Two acts in one. The 'song and dance' guys, conquering town after town."

I took a cigarette from my pack, stuffed it in my mouth,

and lit it with my lighter. "Going state-to-state, seeing the sights, beats the shit outta here."

We laughed and chatted it up more.

The blonde sauntered over to a group of guys around an orange car. I saw one of the guys take her to a van a few cars down. Some girl asked if I wanted to buy some cocaine. I told her she'd better go to her boyfriend's house before the police came and stomp her. She looked at me like a mad person and walked away.

We got to the door, passed through the turnstiles, and walked down a corridor. There were four rooms you could choose from. Each room had its bar and staircase that led to the second floor. We threaded ourselves over red cement to the back room. The room was full of cigarette smoke and tired souls. Patrons all around were talking, laughing, and drinking, on bar stools, and at tables. Some people were standing, huddled in groups. There were two billiard tables in the center of the room, across from our table. A pinball table and a few arcade games were tucked in the corner. Our table sat next to a full-length mirror.

We started commenting about the people in the bar. It was clear we were surrounded by two different groups of people: the first, a group of young college students, then, a group of people in their seventies or sixties; either way, you had two ends of the spectrum dwelling in the same space. The kaleidoscope of life swilling beer and seas of liquor.

The older people seemed to be disturbed by outbursts from the younger generation. In retrospect, I think they were there because they thought maybe they, somehow, some way, could recapture their youth, which, didn't work. Irritation was in every drink they took. A lot of them looked like drifters: lonely people looking for something they could never have.

Nights here were spent sitting at a table, looking, gazing, at the drunken fools who tried to get with women. A lot of nights they weren't successful. When they were tired of trying for the girls they liked to start fights.

Most of the girls that came to Billingtons, to me, seemed to be out of reach. They usually traveled in groups of four or five and weren't interested in the men. They wanted to be left alone. Now and then a girl would twist into the night with a man. For the most part, they kept to themselves.

Jason and I stood waiting at the bar while the barkeep finished making drinks for three young girls. They got their drinks and joined the drunken circus. After they left we told the guy what we needed.

"The booze is flowing tonight, eh?" the bartender snorted.

My brother and I nodded.

"It's a good night for it," the guy continued.

We brought the whiskey and beer to the table.

People were moving up and down the black wood stairs. Everything was loud, crazed freaks looking for some excitement and a good drink. The music from above was echoed down to where we were.

The sound of a guitar poured out from the top of the staircase and screamed its way across the room. We continued drinking, laughing, smoking, and conversing.

Behind the bar, liquor bottles were stacked underneath the blue neon light. Two drunk guys sitting at the bar got into an argument. The only thing I could discern was the fight had something to do with a girl.

In a way, I felt sorry for them. I was always told not to fight in public: it gives people a bad impression of you.

"Thanks for asking me out here guys," Heidi said.

"No problem," Jason shrugged. "I'm just glad Sean found a gal. I started to think there was something wrong with him."

She laughs. "He's just fine with me."

I looked at her. "Oh, thanks, I feel so special."

"Anytime, babe. That's what I do best."

We all leaned back in our seats and lit cigarettes.

"The show was good the other night," Heidi broke the silence.

"Thanks," my brother said. "We wondered if you liked it or not."

"It was good," she said.

"Always nice to hear compliments. Thanks."

"Yeah."

I looked at Heidi. "You know a good thing when you hear it," I turned to the guys. "Listen to that, boys, we have a fan with us."

"Don't meet them often," Jason laughed.

"Nonsense," I told him. "Do you see all the people at our shows? Man, in a few years, everyone will know who we are. We're on the right road. Just think of all those girls who'll fall at your feet. You'll love that, right?"

"Yeah," Jason muttered. "I just have a question, how are we gonna deal with our other business venture when we get big?"

"We'll just have to deal with that went it comes. You can't plan too far ahead."

Jason sighed. "Have to tell ya, though, when he hit me the other night I felt like killing him right there. I wouldn't have cared who was there."

"Just thank your lucky stars we were there," William said. "No telling how that would've gone down if we weren't. You could be dead right now, man. That's a heavy thing to deal with."

"William, you're a dumb-ass," Clarence said. "We would've been there no matter what. Does the show ring a bell?"

"I know, I know," William said. "I'm just saying, if we'd gone for some reason and he was there alone, that would've been a bad situation."

"As opposed to what did happen?" I said. "Need to start thinking before you speak, buddy."

"Fuck you."

"Fuck me? Fuck you."

William smiled. "Oh, hell, let's talk about it tomorrow. I don't have it in me tonight to get into that mess."

"I agree," Jason took a drink. "Things will get dealt with."

The singer in our group said, "Come on, it is what it is. Everything that goes in must come out. It's all trying. Things are tough all over."

Bursts of laughter came from the room above. People were yelling and screaming as the music played. People were still wildly moving up and down the stairs. Everyone seemed to be in comfortable hands.

William looked at the stairs and pointed. "I wanna go up there, ya dig? Seems like that's where all the action is. We can chit-chat up there."

"In a few," Clarence muttered. "We wanna drink here first."

"Fine with me. Just didn't want you guys spending all night down here. We need to find some nice women tonight, man. I have a powerful lust for it."

My brother nodded. "Oh, William, what are we gonna do with you?"

"What do you mean?"

"You're already twisted."

"This is true."

Jason said, "I'm not far behind him. Shit, I'm lookin' to get into someone."

"Jason," Clarence snapped, "we're in the presence of a

lady. She doesn't wanna hear you talk that mess. Show some respect," he looked over at Heidi. "Sorry about him. He doesn't have anyone to teach him manners."

Heidi laughed. "It's okay. Don't worry about it."

"Thought you might bring a friend with ya?" William said to her. "I was thinking that's what Sean told us."

"She was supposed to," Heidi told him. "My friend had to work. I promise I'll bring her along the next time."

"She looks good?"

"Yes."

"Good enough for me. I'm sold."

"I'll make a call and let ya know."

"Thanks."

"Don't mention it."

We spent the next hour or so drinking and telling stories. A little while later William and Jason looked in the direction of the stairs.

Clarence said, "Fine with me now that our drinks are gone. Let's go and see what sort of trouble we can find. Might be able to find a girl for William. You never know, anything is possible."

"Don't wanna get with a dirty one," William added.

Clarence smiled. "Not all girls who hang out in bars are skanks."

"Think I'll just keep my options open."

"What options?"

"I get around."

"I'll believe it when I see it."

My brother looked at me. "Guys wanna join?"

"That's okay," I told him. "We'll stay here."

"Hey, I'm not gonna stop ya."

"We might come up later. Someone has to make sure you guys don't get into too much trouble."

He laughed. "We can take care of ourselves. We're just enjoying the life."

"Can't argue with that."

They asked Heidi and me again if we wanted to join them. We both told them we were just gonna sit there and get drunk and talk.

After the three of them shuffled up the stairs, Heidi told me she had to go to the restroom. I told her I was gonna get some more drinks.

When I got back to the table Heidi was already sitting there. I sat a tray on the table that had a few glasses of whiskey and beer on it.

"Thirsty?" she asked.

I shrugged. "If it works..."

"Got that right."

I sat across from her. "So, what would you like?"

"Think I'd like one of those glasses of whiskey."

"You got it." I handed her a glass.

"Thanks."

"Anytime."

She let out a smile, and put the drink to her lips. "This has been fun. I liked meeting your friends."

"I'm sure they liked meeting you."

"Seemed like it. Guess I sort of promised to introduce William to my friend."

"He won't let that go until you do."

"Really?"

"He and Jason, both."

"Oh, I see."

"Yeah."

"Guess I'll need to do that."

"I think that would be best."

She laughed.

We talked and drank more.

"You know what would make the night complete?" she said.

"What's that?"

"If we ended up in bed together."

I raised a brow. "Really? That does sound good."

"I'd love it."

"We could go back to my place."

"No," she said. "I was thinking we should change it up."

"How do you mean?"

"I was thinking we should go to a motel."

"A motel?"

"Always wanted to go there and spend a night with a guy."

"You never have before?"

"No."

"Really? That's a shame."

"That's why I'm wanting to do that tonight."

"The Century is just done the street."

"I like the way you think."

We finished our drinks and took to the stairs. The top of the stairs spilled out to a large room with a white marble floor. A bar was on the right side with a stage on the left. The band, playing Blues and Jazz, were all long-haired guys. All sorts of people were dancing and drinking. Everyone was having fun. It took Heidi and I a bit to negotiate ourselves through the crowd. We spotted the guys in a booth in the corner of the room. They had a few girls sitting around them.

They introduced us to the girls. They were having a wild time. I told my brother that Heidi and I were going to the motel down the street. He looked at me and gave me a big smile. They all knew what we were up to. We were about to leave, but, Jason suggested we stay and have a drink with them.

A few drinks later we were on the dance floor. Heidi led my hands all over her body, swaying to the music. We started to kiss. After the dance, we went to the bar for a quick drink. We told the gang we'd see them later, and then, walked back downstairs and out of the building.

We got into my vehicle and drove down the street.

We walked through the lobby doors of the Century: it was bright inside. A small stone water fountain rested to the left. Thick tan carpet covered the floor. Fake plants and pictures in cheap frames lined the walls. A few chairs and couches were scattered to the left and right of the lobby. We looked at each other, then walked to the desk.

The place was like a tomb. We looked around and saw no one. At first, I thought the place might've been closed, and that they just had the door unlocked with the lights on. The faint sound of a radio came from one of the offices in the back.

I rang the gold platted bell. A few minutes passed when a woman came out from a door behind the desk. She was wearing a black suit with an orange mop on her head. She told us her name was Abby.

"Sorry about that," she said. "I was just getting some coffee. These night hours, they have a way of pulling at ya. It can sort of get boring this time when you're here by yourself."

"That's understandable," Heidi said.

"So tell me, how can I be of assistance to you two at this hour?" Abby asked.

"We'd like a room," I said.

She laughed. "We have plenty of those."

"Good news for us, whaddya know about that?"

"I'll see what I can do, sir."

"Thanks."

"Just doing my job."

She opened the log book and scanned a few pages. "I

have three rooms available," she looked up from the book. "All rooms carry a fee of forty dollars a night. If you don't check out by noon the next day you'll have to pay another day. Are you still interested?"

I displayed my wallet. "That's fine. We'll only be here for a few hours."

She grinned at the wallet. "I don't need to see an ID. I just need the name and fee. We get a lot of recreational visits here if you catch my drift."

"The name is Sanders."

Heidi smiled at the woman. "We've never been here before."

"Friends, lovers, affairs, see these things all the time. Your secrets are safe with me," she laughed. "Oh, boy, though, if these walls could talk. I could tell ya some stories."

"I imagine so," I said. "All those perverts who wanna get their action in."

Abby looked me over. "You're not one of them, are you?"

"No," I said. "Nothing like that. I'm an upstanding young man."

"He is," Heidi wrapped herself around my arm.

"If you guys say so," Abby said.

"We're telling the truth," I said. "You guys must get a lot of those types in here? Well, trust me, we'd never do stuff like that."

She passed the log book for me to sign.

"It's nothing like that," Heidi said. "We're out of town. We're married from Oklahoma on our way to Texas. The road gets weary after spending all day on it. We both got tired and needed a room for a few hours."

"I'd rather so," said the lady. "We do breakfast in the morning. You guys need anything just let me know."

"One thing," I pointed at the logbook. "Who's going to

see this?"

"What? Well, just me and the manager. Why?"

"Don't worry about it. Just forget I asked. The thing is, we don't want any kind of disturbance of any kind. I'm a very secretive person. I just don't want it published in the news or anything."

"Sir, you won't have to worry about that," Abby looked like there was something wrong with me. "That stuff is private. We just use it for our records. We don't publish things like that anywhere. Don't be crazy, sir."

"Good."

"We don't do any housekeeping till checkout. We like to keep quiet 'round here."

We thanked her. She pointed to the elevator and told us the room was on the third floor.

"The second room when you get off the elevator,' she handed me the key. "You two enjoy your stay."

We walked into the elevator.

We started to kiss each other.

A few minutes later we were standing in front of our room.

I unlocked the door and Heidi followed.

I flipped the light on and glanced around. "This is it. Our little piece of paradise."

"It's nice and cozy," she looked around. "Could be better, but it'll do. It's not like we're gonna be here long."

"It'll be fine."

"You can never be too sure."

"You got that right."

She walked across the brown floor to the bed. The bed let out a squeak when she sat on it. "I'm afraid to make it on here now," she smiled. "It might fall apart."

"Let's hope so."

"You're a funny man."

"That's what they tell me."

I walked over and sat beside her.

The heat from her body felt so soft.

I put my arm around her and kissed her.

She gave me one back.

We fell on the bed and made love.

After we were done we both lit a cigarette.

"Round two?" I asked.

"In a minute. I have to say, sir, you're a good lover."

"I do what I can."

"You're very good at it."

We talked a little more.

"Place is sort of a dump," I said.

"I agree. We should've thought about the location more."

I crawled out of the bed to the restroom. When I came back Heidi was sprawled across the bed. I walked up to the bed and fell on top of her. We made passionate love again. After we finished, we both lay in silence for a moment.

We were both staring up at the ceiling. As I was looking up I saw all of the brown stains and water damage.

"I have a question," Heidi broke the silence.

"What's that?" I asked.

"Have you ever cheated on a girl?"

"No."

"Not even once?"

"I've never cheated on a girl."

"That's good."

"Why's that?"

"I'll tell ya this, if a guy ever hurts me I'll shoot him."

I thought about that for a minute. "Would you shoot someone?"

"If they hurt me, yes."

"Remind me to never hurt you."

"I just did."

After we talked some more and smoked a cigarette, we spent another hour in the warm embrace of one another. After awhile, I got out of bed and put my clothes on. She walked over and kissed me on the cheek.

"Think I should go pretty soon," I said. "Have to get a few things done today. I have to go back to work tomorrow."

We gathered our belongings and headed out the door to the elevator. We got to the lobby and went over to the front desk. Abby was still working. She looked tired. She told us the next time we wanted a room for a short time she would only charge half price.

"Thanks," I offered Abby a smile. "We'll have to keep that in mind. Well, have a good day."

"Oh, don't worry," she said. "Next time you guys are in town just come one by."

I gave a nod. "That's not something I want to know."

We thanked Abby.

We walked out of the door to the morning daylight. As we stood on the curb of the motel, people were walking in and out of the building. A shaggy-haired man was walking along the sidewalk, talking to himself, carrying a cup, asking for money. A few people were tooling through the parking lot smoking weed.

thirteen

One of the guys from the crew, Viggo Gasper, a short bulky guy with a brown beard and a mustache, came to my apartment and told me about the sit-down Joe had with Max. I could see a hint of concern in his voice as he was telling me the meeting didn't go that well. I asked if he wanted a beer.

"Anytime is good for a cold one," he told me.

"Can't argue with that."

"After the day I had, I could drink a case."

"Know how that goes."

"It's a day in the life, right?"

"That's about right," I said. "What were you out doing?"

"Oh, I had to pick up some money. Joe, he, uh, wanted me to go talk to these other guys, the Finely brothers, about this credit card thing."

"Oh," I said. "That gonna work out?"

"I'm sure it'll be okay. I just hated talkin' to those two fools. I dunno, it's something in the water or something. They're strange."

"I've never met them."

"You're not missing much."

"That right?"

"A couple of shitheads who used to sell a little weed and blow, and now they wanna move up in the world."

"Or down?"

"Well, whatever."

"Little boys who want to sit at the adult table... Always nice."

"Shit," he said. "If I needed these fuckin' headaches I'd gotten a job in retail or something. I need a raise."

"Don't we all?"

"We should do something."

I nodded.

"They probably wouldn't even hire me, the store," Viggo said.

"Don't say that. You never know what the future holds."

"Sure."

"Of course."

"This is why I drink like I do, all this shit," he muttered. "I'm not sure about this anymore."

I thought about it for a minute. "The way I look at it, it's all about protecting people and things you care about."

"That's what I try to do," he said. "Dealing with fuckin' people constantly? I've done that long enough. Don't know if any of this matters."

"You can never give up."

"I wouldn't give it up for anything. It does get tiring, you know?"

"I see your point."

He laughed. "Like the one on top of your head?"

"Fuck off."

Another laugh. "You know me, just messin' around."

"Yeah, yeah, yeah, always the funny one."

"I try to be."

"Bet you see something funny every day you look in the mirror."

"Oh, hell, think Joe just hires all types of out-of-work comedians."

"Maybe," I said. "From what I've seen so far, that seems to be the case."

"You know what one I'm waiting for? The day I'm that big-time movie star."

"The old movin' picture, yeah?"

"Yes, sir."

"Good luck with that one."

"Thanks."

"Damn, makin' moves and music, you're gonna be pretty busy?"

"That's the point," I said. "I wanna get myself far from this shit."

"It won't matter. It'll follow you. These guys will track you down if you try anything."

"That's the thing that worries me."

"I hear ya," he said. "Let's try to get through this little patch first, okay?"

"If we live that long."

"Hey, I'm on your side."

"Thanks for that."

"What are friends for?"

In many ways, Viggo was like me. We were both the same age, about the same attitude and got into this business in sort of the same way. The difference is that he didn't almost get killed before Joe's guys broke up the fight he was in. They let Viggo kill the guy after they broke the two of them up. Before I got into the crew I'd seen him around the city a few times. At the time, I didn't think much about him. Little did I know he was part of a criminal circle. When I started running with the same crew we became pretty good friends. He, like me, had yet to get pinched for anything real serious. I'd seen Viggo in more than a few fights, and he tore the pieces out of all of them but three.

The whole time I'd known him I witnessed him kill ten people, and he pushed one off of a roof of a building. He was a nice guy, but you didn't ever want to get on his bad side.

I opened the refrigerator and took out two beers, handed him one. "Nice and cold."

"Thanks," he opened the bottle and set it in front of him on the kitchen table. "Just what I needed. Nice place ya got here."

I nodded, as I sat across from him. "It'll do for now. Haven't you ever been here?"

"Don't think."

"You weren't at the party I had last month?"

"No."

"Sorry about that. There were a bunch of people that night, and I'd had a lot to drink. I was pretty sure I told all of you."

"Guess you didn't."

"I'll make sure you're at the next one."

"Don't be sorry. You didn't do anything wrong. How do you like the place?"

"I don't have any complaints here. My neighbors are all pretty good. They keep to themselves for the most part. I needed to get away from the other place."

"It's good to change it up now and then. Can't get too comfortable in one place."

I took a swig of beer. "Keep telling myself I need to buy a house. One of these days..."

"Can't go wrong with one of those. When I finally got mine I was so glad. No one told me how much work it was, though. Having to fix everything that breaks down, all the yard work. But it's all worth it. You, pretty much, can do what you want."

"That'd be nice."

He laughed. "You know they gave me a bunch of shit when I paid with cash?"

"That just goes with business, right?"

"I guess."

"It's just me, I don't think I would've done that, even if I had the cash."

He shrugged. "Oh, well. They didn't lock me up. Every-one got what they wanted."

"That's a good thing," I took a bring of beer. "So, tell

me, how'd the sit-down go? Everyone shakes hands?"

"I can tell ya it got pretty heated," he said. "They brought Jack and I for muscle. Good thing shit didn't get out of control. I didn't feel like shooting anyone. Having to get rid of a body, and all..."

"I understand perfectly," I told him.

Viggo shrugged his shoulders. "But it comes with the job. Sometimes people have to go."

I took another drink. "Jack went with you guys?"

"Yeah."

"Was he sober?"

"No."

I laughed. "That guy, he'll drink an ocean of booze if you let him."

"Yeah. But he's an upstanding guy. I'm glad he's on my side."

I lit a cigarette. "Who did Max have with him at the meeting?"

"He had Nick and three other big guys."

"Three?"

"Yeah."

"Black guys? Yeah, I've seen them before. Well, I've seen two before. Jason and I went over to one of Nick's places to get some money - that was how we found out about this business with Max. Nick killed one of his guys in front of us. It was some sort of message or something."

"He seemed pretty calm at the meeting," my friend said.

"Anyway," I drank the last swallow from my bottle, got up, and went to get another bottle. "Want another?" I asked Viggo.

"Sure."

"You got it!"

"Thanks."

"That's something I have plenty of around here."

I walked back to the table, placed both bottles on the table, and sat down. He grabbed one and opened it.

"Nothing wrong with that. You can never have too much beer."

I grabbed the other.

"Oh, that's good. Hits the spot," my friend said.

I took a long drink, then set the beer down. "Tell me, what did they agree on?"

He lit a cigarette. "Not shit."

"Why not?"

"Ask me Joe should've taken Max out. I'm kind of surprised he hadn't done it. They talked about it, about a lot of things, about the old days. Guess there's still bad blood there. Max still says Joe turned on him and ratted him out. All that shit. Sounds to me like they want a war in the worst way."

"What about us?" I asked. "The fuck are they thinking? They just need to go over there and clean the house. I'm not up to bang it out on the streets with these guys."

"They could just be bored."

"Think they could do something else if they're bored, ya know?"

"Guess they weren't worried about what we thought."

"How long have you been around? You know how they do things."

"Looks like Max has already started taking our money. A few of the guys said they went to make their pick-ups but were told the money had already been collected."

"Really? They're starting to take things over."

"Yeah."

I took a swig of beer. "We need to convince everyone this thing isn't good."

"You got a plan, buddy?"

"Whatever it is, we don't want to have to deal with any cops on our end. I don't know."

"Do you even know how many guys work for them?"

"I didn't even know Nick was anybody. I just thought he was a low-life thug, a wannabe."

"Well, now you know."

"Wish I didn't."

"Everyone's okay for now."

"You know if they killed anyone when they collected money?"

"Hadn't heard. Know a few guys got beat up."

"Damn," I said. "Did Joe do anything about it?"

"No. I mean, he heard about it. He didn't know who they were with, probably. I'm sure if he'd known things would've gone another way."

"Who knows?"

"It's a crazy time. Something tells me this isn't gonna end well."

"I can see that."

We sat for a couple of minutes saying nothing. He was staring down at the kitchen table, then looked at me. "We could try getting some outside help."

"Like a hitman?"

He shrugged. "Something like that. That way, no blood on our hands."

I said, "That could work. I wouldn't even know where to look for someone like that, though. Guess I could run it by Joe and see what he says. I just don't wanna get killed over some bullshit I had nothing to do with."

"Know what you mean. I didn't ask for this. Messin' around with these fuckin' clowns 'cause of something that happened years ago. I have limits to what I'm willing to do."

I stood from the table, walked to the refrigerator, and took out some stuff to make myself a sandwich. "You hungry?"

"Nah, man, I'm good," he stood from where he was sitting. "I have to make a few more stops before I go home tonight," he stepped by the front door. "I just wanted to come by and let you know what happened with the meeting."

"Thanks. I'll run it by the big guy tomorrow when I go over there, and see what he says about it. We should stop this before it gets any bigger."

He opened the door and was about to walk out, then he turned back to me. "How do you think that'll go?"

"Guess we'll see."

"He's a pretty smart guy. He'll know what to do."

"Let's hope so, huh?"

"You never know."

"If he was smart he would've stopped this at the sit-down."

"We all have our reasons, I guess."

"Sure."

He nodded. "By the way, when's the next time you guys playin' a show?"

"Fox Lounge, day after tomorrow."

"I'll be there."

"Thanks."

"I like shitty music," he smiled.

"Fuck you."

A laughed. "Nah, man, you know I'm all about supporting you guys."

"I know."

I got a few more beers from the fridge. "Good livin'," I said.

Viggo just looked at me and laughed, taking one of the beers. "I second that. If only it was that easy."

"I know," I said. "Tell me, my brother said you hooked up with a piece of tail the last time you went out."

"When was that?"

"I can't remember now. All these days seem to run together lately."

"I don't know what girl he'd be talking about. There's been a few in the past month. Can you give me any more? I can't remember names."

"He didn't say anything."

He shrugged. "I have nothing."

"I hate when that happens."

"One girl got mad at me once because I couldn't remember her name."

"Can you blame her?"

"Not really," he said. "I told her I have a lot going on…stress and shit."

I cleared my throat. "Been there before. It's not fun when that little fine thing gets mad."

"Oh, I just talk away. Plenty of women out there."

"True."

After he left I ate the sandwich and watched TV. After awhile, I fell asleep. When I woke I stood from the couch, rubbed my hands in my eyes, and looked at the clock on the wall. At first, I thought it was later than it was. I had called Joe and asked him to meet me at Highlife.

Before I left my place I smoked a cigarette. Ten minutes later I pulled into Highlife.

When I walked in I saw Joe sitting at the bar. I nodded and slid into the stool beside him. He was drinking whiskey. Rick, the bartender came over. I told him I wanted what Joe had. Rick went to fix my drink. Rick was also a connected guy.

Joe and I went to the back office to talk. I told him about the idea of hiring a hitman to get rid of Max and Nick.

"A hitman?" Joe laughed. "What, you gonna pay for that outta your pocket? We don't need anything like that."

"We need to do something."

"What makes you think we need to do anything?"

"Do you wanna have our guys killed?"

"How dare you ask something like that. Of course, I don't want that. If it happens, though, would you blame me? It would all be my fault, right? Well, you better think again, son."

"I didn't say that. If we got a hitman that'd keep us clear from it. Let the guy do the dirty work for us."

He eyed me from across his desk. "When I was your age, I remember having crazy ideas like you."

"How?"

"What I'm saying crazy?"

"You just don't understand how it works."

"How it works? And, you do?"

"I don't wanna die on the streets if I can help it."

"Things aren't that bad. Yes, a few things have happened so far, not much."

"It's about avoiding conflict. We'll just wait it out. As much as Max and I don't like each other, I don't wanna have a bloodbath on my hands."

"I hope you're right."

He took a drink. "I'm right. For now, let's let monsters be."

"Hey, you know best! Why should anyone question you? Gotta tell ya, I don't like this."

"If you don't like it, you can go to Hell."

"Think we're going down that road."

"Whatever the case, however, this plays out, I'm the boss. I have the final say about how shit goes down. If you keep this up, I'll have to put you down. You understand? Would you want that? Two ways play out for ya, my way, or a shallow grave. Your choice."

I looked at him. "It's your game."

"Good. You can shut the door when you leave."

I walked out of the office to the bar, sat on a bar stool, and ordered a beer. Four beers later I decided it was time I went home. I crawled off my stool and said bye to the guys.

I got back to my place around midnight.

fourteen

We had a card game going in the back room of Highlife when Joe took me aside and told me he wanted me
to take out James. There were about twenty of us playing. A lot of times I'd lose. When I first started going to
the casinos in Tunica Mississippi when I was in my early
twenties I'd always lose at slot machines. After awhile,
it dawned on me I should start playing the tables.
 As the night grew and the game became long, the pot
got big, then small. I won some and lost some more. We
talked and laughed over drinks. The place was so
Smokey you would've sworn something in the middle of
the room was on fire.
 After the card game, after everyone was gone for the
night, I got in my car and headed to Joe's house. When I
got to the house, before I had a chance to get out of my
car, he opened the front door. It was around midnight
when I got there. The idea of a trap was in the back of
my mind. I wouldn't have put it passed him. I'd known
him to do things like that to other people. I was ready for
anything.
 I guess he had seen my headlights come up the drive.
 "Good to see you could make it," he said.
 "Had nothing else to do."
 He laughed. "Get the hell inside."
 "Don't mind if I do."
 We shook hands.
 I walked inside.
 I smelled coffee being brewed.
 "I disturb you?"
 "No," he said. "I was just about to watch some *Cheers*."

"*Cheers*?"

"You watch it?"

"Haven't missed it yet. One of my favorites."

"I have the VCR set to record it - that way I can watch it when I get in late."

"Good idea, that's what I've been doing, too. It took me awhile to figure out how to record. Almost threw the damn thing out the window."

"Yeah, that was a little tricky," he let out a grin. "Who would have thought, you a fan of *Cheers*?"

"That so hard to believe?"

"Thought you more of a Clint Eastwood sort of guy."

I shrugged. "He's okay, I guess."

Joe nodded.

"I'm more into *Murder, she wrote*. I was always into shit like *Miami Vice* when it was on. *L. A Law* is another one I like."

"Never really liked that."

"It's not for everyone."

"I can tell."

We walked into his living room. He had an armchair, a couch, and a television in the room. A fireplace was on the far wall: and an area rug laid in front of it. A rifle hung over the fireplace by little metal pegs.

"I've watched all of the episodes so far," he said. "Who would've thought, a show about guys in a bar?

I shook my head. "It's a pretty good show. That's the kind of shit I need to do, create a show like that."

He said, "Girls, they like those creative types. You want something bad enough, anything is possible."

"It's true," I said. "I bet the guys who write that show are rollin' in the girls"

Joe laughed. "I bet they are."

"You're right about that."

"A friend of mine once told me, he told me you

shouldn't settle for just one woman. The greater sex, they're a beautiful sight. A guy needs options. Sometimes your girlfriend or whatever can't always be there. You have to make an impromptu choice. Maybe it follows you for a bit, maybe not."

"I think I've mastered that art."

"I tell ya, it's a tough cookie to crack sometimes. If you're runnin' around with two at the same time and they find out about each other, that won't be good for you, buddy."

"Yeah," I said. "With me, I always cover my tracks. If they do find out, who gives a fuck? Both girls get what they want. I get what I want. Everyone wins."

He shook a finger at me. "That's not always true, through. You get a real crazy on your hands, she'll drive you fuckin' nuts. Next, think you know you'll wanna kill yourself over the broad."

"I've known a few people who got involved with that sort of thing. It didn't work out well for them. I never saw the attraction. One minute, talkin' about falling in love, getting married; the next minute, they hate each other. Don't understand why someone would put themselves through all that shit. Guess they like to suffer."

"Maybe," Joe said. "There are all sorts of sick people out there. You don't know what runs through people's minds."

I nodded. "It takes all kinds to make up this fucked world."

He chuckled. "You got that right."

He invited me into the kitchen for a cup of coffee.

"Coffee sounds like it's done."

"Okay," I said. "I could go for a cup. Think coffee is one of the best things ever invented. It ranks pretty high on the list."

"There was a time when I'd put a little cocaine in

mine."

"Bet that was good."

A laugh. "It was fuckin' fantastic."

"I'll have to try that sometime."

"You'll love it," my boss said. "You know, I know a guy, he would put a small sheet of acid in his to get him going."

"That makes a different ball game altogether."

"I'd guess so. I never tried it. He always kept telling me I should."

"I went to school with a guy who did some of that shit. He was never the same. They said something in his brain got fried, I dunno."

"What a shame," he lowered his head. "That's a tough way to be," he looked back at me.

I nodded.

The kitchen looked immaculate. A lot of cabinets and drawers were splattered around the area. A big round oak table sat in front of a big window.

Joe got two cups from the cabinet and put them on the counter. "How do you take it?" he asked.

"Lots of sugar."

A smirk. "That's how I took mine for a long time."

"Took?"

"Now, I'm fine with just straight black," he took the pot and filled both cups. "My father never drank coffee."

"Why?"

"Said he didn't like the taste. Guess he thought it was too bitter or something. My mother was the coffee drinker of the family. Back then, I was too young to drink it. My parents would never let me. These days, hell, I drink it every day."

"I'm the same way."

"I can't understand why people don't like the stuff."

"Something has got to be wrong with 'em."

Shootin' Noise

We sat at his kitchen table.

He asked if I wanted anything to eat. I wasn't hungry.

"You sure? It'll be no problem makin' something quick."

"No, thanks, I'm fine."

"Don't say I never offered."

"I had a burger awhile ago."

"Burgers are good."

"Yeah."

He nodded at me. "I could never trust someone who doesn't eat meat."

I laughed. "A little corny, no?"

"I dunno how people do it, these vegetarians."

I shrugged. "Beyond me. Your guess is as good as mine."

"They just hadn't ever had a really good steak," he chuckled.

"Bet that's it," I lit a smoke.

I took a drink from my cup.

"How'd you do tonight, win against those guys?" he asked.

"You win some, you lose some. Playing the cards you deal with can be hard at times. I was on a pretty good roll for awhile, but then… slowly lost it all."

"I've been there many times."

I took a drink. "I should've stopped when I was ahead."

"That makes two of us."

"Yeah."

"Love winning, hate losing."

"Think that goes without saying for all of us, right?"

"Guess you're right. It's this thing, that balances the world out. You can't win all the time."

"That's a rough thing to deal with sometimes."

Joe told me he lost at least ten grand that night. My eyes went wide when I heard the figure. I wish I had that kind of money to lose, I thought. I looked down at my coffee cup, took another drink, and then thanked him for the beverage. He just waved me off, saying something about depriving somebody of coffee is the equivalent of depriving someone of fresh air.

We sat quietly for a minute.

He took a drink. "I like it at night. Do my best thinking at night. Go out on my porch with some scotch and a cigar, stare into the darkness, and think."

"That's why I have my music," I said. "I don't know what I'd do without it."

Joe shook his head. "We all need outlets, that's for sure. It's good to keep your mind occupied with good things. You need a nice distraction from time to time. I've known too many guys off themselves over the regret this thing brings."

"Well, music's always been a part of me for as long as I can remember. I remember listening to music on the stereo and dreaming of the day when I'd be able to make great music."

Joe said, "I've never really been all that into music. Guess you could just chalk me up as an average listener."

"Really?"

"When I do listen to music, I like Classic Rock. 109.7 is a good station."

"I tune into that whenever I'm in the car."

Joe took another drink. "These neighbors next door would always blast that Rap shit at top volume."

"I like Rap. It's not for everyone, sure."

"It wasn't for me, still isn't. I'd rather listen to dogs barkin' all night."

I took a drag off my cigarette. "What did you do about them?"

"The neighbors?"

"Yeah."

"They'd lower the music when I went over there, swear they'd keep it down. By the time I'd get back in the house the volume would be blastin' again."

"What did you do?" Call the cops?"

He shook his head. "Cops can fuck-up a wet dream. You have to guide those fuckers to do anything. I'm surprised they can find their pricks to take a piss. The only thing they can do right is go to the donut shop."

I laughed. "There's something about fried bread..."

"About the neighbors, what happened was, a few of the thugs shot the house up one night. Everyone who lived there got arrested a few days later."

"Damn."

"Shame when things like that happen. Have to think what people are thinking when they do that stuff. It was all part of this drug operation. The guys who did the shooting got arrested, too. A few weeks after that, they started to find their bodies scattered all over Brown Ridge."

"That's pretty crazy stuff."

"It was their fault. They'd still be alive today if they hadn't done what they did. You know, sometimes I see shit outside or on the News, I think there are too many people in the world."

"Could be."

"Think that's gonna be the death of all of us. It's madness in every direction these days. Just hope we can make it out alive."

"You and me both."

"A friend of mine told me one time, he says, 'Only two ways to get out of this life: death or prison.' Which, you either get murdered or die from health on the inside. At the end of it all, we all die no matter what. What the fuck difference does it make, right? Soon we'll be gone and all of this along with it. Soon others will take our places. And then, over and over, the wheel keeps turning, you can't stop it. It just keeps repeating itself."

"I'm not going anywhere."

"Let's hope not. You have a lot of potential for more. You have to want this. You can't half-ass this shit. That thing with Johnny and Frank, you handled that like a professional. You have that evil streak in you that this needs."

"Really? I don't know about that."

"Sure you do," he said. "I've been keeping my eye on you since you've been with us. The way you handle yourself, Sal and I are impressed. I just wanted to let you know I appreciate it."

"Thanks."

I nodded. I knew Joe had something to do with the murder he talked about. He probably hired the guys who did the deed. I could never ask him, though. Things you weren't involved with were always very "hush-hush."; And even things you were involved in. You didn't want to take chances of someone getting arrested and becoming a turncoat.

"So," I said, "what's this thing about James?"

The boss said, "He's gotta be put down."

"Why?"

"I know you like him, but he's lost his touch."

"How's that?"

"He's old."

"Old?"

"Exactly."

"Why is that a problem?"

"He doesn't have many more years in front of him. People, when they get that age, don't have that much to live for anymore. He could turn on us all any day."

"But that could be anyone."

"He can't be trusted. There was a time, but those days have gone. I see him sizing me up sometimes. I know he has something up his sleeve. He thinks I'm a fuckin' idiot. I can tell when someone's hiding something from me. Another reason he has to be gone, he did something about eight years ago that hurt me - something I will never forgive him for. When this first happened I told him this day would come, that he would have to pay a great price."

"What did he do?"

"I can't get into it. It'll bring back a bunch of shit I don't wanna face. You think you know him, kid, you don't. He's just putting on an act for you. He wants you to think that he's on your side. He's a fuckin' snake, a hack, a piece of scum. Don't let him sell you a load of lies."

I raised a brow. "Really? What do you mean?"

"He's been in this life for a long time. He's done shit you'll never know about. I don't want to see you go down that road."

"Can you tell me any of this stuff?"

"Can't tell you that."

I thought for a minute. "You want me to kill one of my good friends, you won't tell me why?"

"That's about the sum of it."

"Look, all of us have our pasts in question. I need proof he did something to one of us before I pull the trigger, even then, not sure if I wanna do it."

"I'm sure I have the right guy. You do this, it'll get you one step closer to the top. Isn't that what your generation's all about, getting ahead?"

"What if I don't wanna be at the top?"

"What are ya talking about, why wouldn't you? It has everything you want, money, power, respect."

"This is a dying business, Joe, with all due respect."

"Right about that."

"I'm not sure I wanna move up. I'd rather be alive than get the promotion and get killed. The higher you are, the bigger the risk. I wouldn't wanna have to deal with that shit. You're in charge of thirty, forty guys, all doing whatever-the-fuck they want. Nobody listens to you. I don't wanna be boss."

"Being the boss, it's not an easy thing, I'll grant you that."

I laughed. "I'll still pass."

Joe sat back. "What's it gonna be, you gonna do me this favor?"

"I don't think he'd turn on you."

"The fuck do you know? I've known him for many years, and I can tell you I don't trust him anymore. It's too much of a risk to keep him around, he's got to go."

"Don't you think you're moving too fast? What, you want him gone but you won't tell me why?"

"Nothing you need to know."

"What does that mean?"

"Why?"

"There has to be another reason you want James out of the picture."

"There might."

"And again, what would that be?"

"I don't have to tell you."

I said, "What does that say for the rest of us?"

"What do you mean?"

"If you're willing to get rid of James just because of his age or whatever, just because you want him gone, where do we stand? How do we know you won't take us out for something stupid?"

"This is how the game's played, Sean. I'll say this, if you don't do this Job I'll have to get rid of you."

I could tell by the look in his eyes he meant it. He

would hunt me down and kill me if I tried to run or anything.

"That a treat?" I said.

"A promise."

"In that case, I'd better kill him, eh?"

"That would be the wise thing. I like you, kid. I'd hate it
if something happened to you. I have a feeling you'll last
long in this business."

"Honestly, I just wanna stay alive."

"We all do."

I took another drink of coffee. "When do you want this
done?"

"As soon as you can. Sooner is always better."

I looked at the time on my watch: it was two in the
morning. "Think I'll wait until nine or so. I need to go to
my place and get some sleep. I've been up for almost
two days straight."

"Just get it done," he said. "I knew you wouldn't fuck
things up."

"Thanks," I said. "What about the body, what should I
do with it?"

"Just leave it."

"Leave it?"

"Yeah," he said. "When they find him, cops will assume
Max and his guys were behind it. They know there's bad
blood."

"You sure that'll work?"

"Why wouldn't it?"

I shrugged. "It just seems too soon, don't you think?"

"Who, Max? Nah, not really. He's been out for a few
weeks."

"When the people in our crew find out... Not gonna be a
good thing. This, by itself, can cause a war."

"Oh, that's all you guys have been talkin' about, "war'
this, *"war"* that. Nothing is gonna come of it. Look at all

those people on the streets. They'll just think one of those poor assholes did it. Just have to not have anyone see you."

"You'd know best, right?"

"Of course," he said. "A lot of those people, you know, they don't have much to live for anyway. What's one less guy on the street?"

"I still think it could come back on us."

"Don't wanna think about things too much."

"How's that a bad thing?"

"Sometimes you gotta do things without thought, quick on your feet."

"Still sounds too risky."

"You saying you won't do it?"

"I didn't say that."

"What are you saying?"

"If I use a gun, it'll make noise."

"That's why you muffle the sound."

"How?"

"Use a pillow or something. Do I have to think of every motherfuckin' thing for you?"

"Why don't you do it?"

"I already told you, I want you to do it. Come on, sometimes I think you're the dumbest piece of shit who ever lived, you fuckin' cocksucker! Just do what you're told, what's so hard about that? I told you to do this, and if you don't I told you what would happen."

I looked at him for a minute. "Okay, you win. I'll do what you asked."

A smile crossed Joe's face. "That's what I like to hear. Good to know I can count on you, kid."

"Anytime."

We talked a little longer before I told him I had to go. Knowing I had to get rid of James, I knew I wouldn't be able to get to sleep. I spent the next couple of hours playing my guitar.

At nine o'clock I got in my car to visit James. When I got to James' place I told him he had to skip town, and that Joe wanted to kill him. I told James that Joe said it was over past issues. James said he didn't know what Joe was talking about. After a few hours, the old man was gone. He told me he had a kid up in Ohio somewhere. I told him we'd see each other again. I felt bad about the situation. I didn't wanna kill him.

fifteen

I needed to clear my head. Everything was starting to get a little foggy. I was getting twisted out. I needed something. I wanted my music. For the next two weeks every night, we had a show booked. Music has always been a huge source of relaxation for me.

We had a gig at The Shack: a place we'd played a few times before. It was a packed house. The show went great. After the show, we were sitting at a table in the back drinking and talking. A bartender came over and told us some guy wanted to talk.

The bartender called the guy over. The guy was of average height with shoulder-length brown hair. He wore wiry glasses. He looked like the type of guy who would steal from your mother in a heartbeat.

"Hey, guys, good show, loved it! I'm Morris, Morris Flynn," he went around the table shaking hands.

"Thanks for the kind words," I said. "What can we do for ya?"

Morris said, "If you guys don't mind, can I have a little of your time? I work for a record label, and I liked what I heard."

"Sure, take a seat," I said. "You telling us you liked our sound, that's the sort of thing we like to hear."

"Thanks for giving me some of your time," he said. "In my line of work, a lot of times I wanna sign someone, but, they don't. Their loss, I guess."

"I'd say so," William said.

"But that's what you get sometimes doing what I do. Everyone wants to be the next best thing, but, they don't have the balls to commit. The question is, do you guys have the balls?"

"Of course," my brother said. "We have huge balls, sir. We're ready for whatever you throw our way."

"That's good," Morris said.

"That's how we like to do things."

"I like it."

"We think it's the best way."

"If you want something done it is."

"And we have no problem with that," our singer added.

William said, "Pretty fearless here, man."

I was a little suspicious of this man at first. I didn't know if he could be trusted or not. We'd come across a few guys that had the same story in hand, about how they wanna put us on record, then, they'd disappear, never to be heard from again. We would try to make contact and fail every time, then, we'd hear that the guy had been running around, saying those things to other local bands.

The bartender came over and we ordered some drinks. Our new friend told us he'd pay the bill. He told us to drink as much as we wanted. He said he would put it in the books as a business expense.

"Thanks, man," William said. "Drinkin' for free is the best kind, you know?"

Morris said, "My bosses don't think anything of it. We're drinkin' on Ostellio's wallet tonight, boys."

"Ostellio?" I asked.

"That's the name of the record company I work for. I've worked there for almost ten years. I've seen a lot of acts in my time. You guys have a really good thing goin' on with this. I'm hooked."

"You liked the show?" my brother asked. "Have a good time?"

"I did. And I can tell you this, you guys have real talent. You can go far in this business if you want."

"Music Business?" William asked.

Morris said, "That would be the one."

"Like the sound of that."

Morris looked at him. "I never lie."

"Oh, yes, bring it on," Clarence said.

A waitress, a girl, brought a few pitchers of beer and some glasses.

We each filled a glass.

The next thing I knew, four girls ran over to our table, asking for our autographs. We signed their shirts. They told us that they wouldn't ever wash those shirts again. They told us how they loved the show and loved us. We asked if they wanted to join us for some drinking. They said they had to go back with their boyfriends.

Morris continued, telling us again about how he liked the music and how we had great talent. He told us that he's based in Texas, and he had been to Arkansas a lot, looking for people to join the music family, to join the record label.

He said, "I think Stoned Monkey would be a great addition to the Ostellio family. I've seen you guys play two other times."

"You like those shows?" I asked.

"Of course," he said. "I didn't know what to expect at first. I thought, it being a loud place, you'd be shit. I have to admit, the name, thought to myself, 'What the fuck is this gonna be?'"

I laughed.

"But you were good," Morris said. "You guys have a demo or anything?"

Jason said, "We have one. Need to make another one, put more songs on there."

"Mind if I listen to it?"

"Sure," I said.

"And if everything's good, I'll go back to the label and see about putting you guys on record."

"You fuckin' with us?" I asked him.

"No."

"That's good."

"I'm as honest as they come," Morris said.

"We've heard about offers before. All of those guys said what you're saying now."

"Hey, guys, you can believe me. I wouldn't bullshit you. I've been doing this for a long time."

"How long?"

"Ten years."

"That is awhile."

"You guys are being offered something few ever get," he pointed his finger down at the table. "If you wanna keep playing shit-holes like this forever, be my guest. But I can open you to the world. We can go beyond the stars!"

I looked at the other guys, then back at Morris. "What do you need from us?"

Morris took a swig of beer. "First thing, I need that demo. Take it back to the label so they can listen. After that, we'll book the studio time and go from there. A lot of business goes into this music thing. I wish it was all about the art of it all. This whole country's a business, and they decide if they want your brand or not."

We looked at each other, then asked Morris if we could talk in private. He agreed and went over to the bar. After about twenty minutes of talking between ourselves, we came to a decision. We waved him back to the table.

One of the things we had to worry about, we didn't want any of our criminal activities to interfere with our music.

"What did you guys agree on?" Morris asked.

My brother said, "We're coming on board. We just have

a few things."

"Of course, what would those be?" Morris said.

Jason said, "Just so we understand, you're willing to sign us, right?"

"Yes."

"Another thing, if we record the music and put it on a record label, do we still own it?"

"The music?"

"Yeah."

"You and Ostellio both own it. Like a joint ownership. All the details about everything will be in the contract. You guys wanna be rich, right? I can make it all happen for you. You just need to trust me."

"Okay."

"And the first thing, I need that demo. I'll give it a listen, then I'll give it to the label, and see what they say about it. If I had to guess, they should like it. They have a lot of smart people working there who have good ears."

"Should we be in that meeting?" my brother asked.

"Nah, not this one," Morris said. "If things go good, you'll come in and sign a contract. You guys know how many people playing in garages and bars wish they were you right now?"

"We do, actually," I said. "We've been at this for almost four years now."

"Four years is a long time."

"It is."

He laughed. "Good thing I came along."

William said, "I was havin' my doubts there for a bit. Didn't know when this was gonna come along. Was gonna hang it up."

"Glad you didn't," Morris told him.

"Me too. The reason we got into this in the first place was to get girls. We got all kinds of girls. I was getting laid every day."

"Think that's why everyone joins a band at first. Hell, I know I did. Just so happened one of the girls I slept with liked me sober. We were married for about ten years after that."

"She gets tired of your music?"

"You could say that. She's a whole other story I don't wanna launch into," he looked down at his watch. "You guys have two days to spare?"

"I've had a few of those myself," William said. "I didn't marry any of them. I was always told never to get too involved with a woman. My dad told me that when he left my mom for a younger model."

We laughed.

"I would've talked to you guys sooner, but I had to clear it. I manage a few other bands. All of them are from Tennessee and Mississippi. I have a few others in Texas. We're always looking for good bands. I have a feeling, something tells me we're gonna have a good partnership."

"How much money?" I asked.

"It depends. They'll cover all that with ya when we sign."

"But nothing in concrete yet?" our singer asked.

"That's right," Morris said. "I'm pretty sure things are gonna be fine. If what I heard tonight is the same that's on the demo, then we're all good."

"That's what I'd like."

"Do everything to make that happen. A lot of people these days, never get to obtain their dreams. You know, life happens, gets in the way of everything."

I shook my head. "Think any man would have to feel a little sad about something like that."

Jason looked at Morris. "What are some of your favorite songs?"

"I liked 'Madman Blues' and 'To The Academy.'"

"That's good," I said. "Those two are ones I dig, too. I like 'em all. But those two are great."

Morris shook his head. "Tell me, who writes the music and lyrics?"

"We all do," our singer said.

"Really?"

"We all take part in the creative process. For some reason, we don't write together. We can't write on a schedule. Something like that, it hits you at any time."

"Know what you mean," Morris said. "How many songs do you guys have on your demo?"

"Thirteen."

"That's a good number. How many songs you guys have in all."

"About a hundred."

Morris shook his head. "That's a lot."

"Thanks," the singer said. "We rotate them throughout all of the shows. We're always making new ones."

"Good, good. You guys have enough for about five albums?"

"Maybe."

"If it goes that far, right?"

"Something like that."

"That's the way to look at it, you can never be too sure of things," he eyed all of us around the table. "I know this is gonna be a good partnership. If the demo's a little good, you guys are in. Something tells me it's better than I'm thinking."

William said, "You aren't just having a big joke, are you? With all due respect, we've heard things like this from guys before. They tell us that they liked everything we did, promised us all sorts of things, then, they vanished like air. I don't know, I'm a truthful motherfucker, I'd hope other people would be as well. I'd hate that for my friends. Me, I do care. The four of us go back a long time. If you tell them a lie... That'll be the end of your career. We'd splatter your bad name all over."

Morris laughed. "It's a damn good thing I'm not a bad guy, isn't it? Nah, hell, I understand what you're saying, really I do. I'm the true article, the real deal, man. You're more than welcome to ask the people I represent: they'll tell ya I'm the real deal. I can tell you guys, I'll do everything in my power to help further your career."

"You mean that?" William asked.

"Of course," the man said. "Wanna talk to my other bands?"

"No, that's okay," William let out a little smile. "I trust you. I just had to get that out there."

"Fair enough."

"I didn't mean to offend."

"None taken."

"Good."

I stood from my chair and told them I had to go to the restroom. As I was walking to the restroom, I thought of the drunkards, trying to get with girls they can never get with.

I stepped into a sea of light when I got inside the bathroom. I heard someone mumbling something from the end stall, but, I didn't think anything about it. I walked to the urinal and took a leak. When I finished, I walked over to the sink and washed my hands. I heard the mumbling again from the stall. Then the person in the stall asked whoever was there to show themselves. I wasn't going to but I walked over to the end stall. The door was open. There were two skeletons of men shooting heroin.

I pointed at them. "Guys better stop that."

"Why?" one of them asked. "What business is it of yours?"

"Fuckin' kiddin' me here? Guys are doing drugs, pumping poison in your arms?"

The guy gave a blank stare. "Who the fuck are you to tell me what I shouldn't do?"

I shrugged. "I'm no one at all. I'm just some guy in the restroom talking to two dope-heads."

The other guy looked at me. "Hey, man, you were with the band tonight. You guys kicked ass," he took his needle. "You want some?"

"No, I'm good," I said. "Thanks for saying you liked the band."

"Good times. Sure you don't want any of this?"

"I should get back to my table. I have a few friends waiting on me."

"Have them come in here. We can all get high together."

I thought about that for a minute, then I said. "That would look a little strange."

"How's that?"

"A bunch of guys going to the bathroom."

"Let them talk."

"Maybe later."

"Maybe, maybe not. You never know how things are gonna end. For all you know, your friends out there might wanna get high."

"I doubt that."

"Somehow I think you'll come around. Shit, man, we all wanna high! A whole nation stoned... The way things should be. You always have to keep an eye open for new customers."

"That's okay, I got my sources," I said.

"Who?"

"Wouldn't you like to know?"

"Come on, man," one of the men said. "Tell me who he is, and I'll convince him one of his customers jumped ship on him," he laughed. "Hey, we all gotta eat, right?"

The other guy tied his arm off. "Sure you don't want in on this? That spike, that spike, oh that sweet spike! It's fantastic."

"I'm sure it is," I said. "Look, I didn't mean to intrude or anything. Seems like you guys are having a nice time. I'll just leave you to it."

The one guy, with long black hair, pointed the needle at himself. "The name's Jimmy," he pointed to the other guy. "That's Pete."

Pete had a shaved head, and no facial hair, he nodded at me. "Sure you don't wanna shoot?"

My eyes went to the needle, then back at him. "I don't think so."

"Why?" Pete said. "You think we're dirty, something like that?"

"Nothin' like that," I said.

Jimmy said, "It's not every day we share our drugs with whoever-the-fuck. It's a special day for my friend."

I glanced at my watch, then back at Pete. "Birthday? Graduate something?"

"Got married last night," Pete said.

"Oh, great," I said. "Glad to hear it. Where's the wife, shooting up in another stall?"

Pete laughed. "Maybe. I wouldn't know. Ran off with a guy awhile ago. Probably shacked up at his house."

"But you just got-"

"It's like one of those things where we're free to do what we want. It'll work for us."

"Whatever works, I guess."

"If you wanna meet her I can arrange it?"

"No, no, no, that's okay," I said. "Sounds too messy for me."

He threw up his hand. "Have it your way. You don't know what you're missing."

"Sure I'll regret it for the rest of my life."

"I bit you will."

The other guy, Jimmy, looked at me after he shot junk into his arm. "This is pure shit... Pure as the open sky. You're just... I dunno... vanish. Crawl out of your mind, and see what you find on the other side. Purple stains, they slither, cover you like a white blanket on a cold day."

"That's a nice thought," I said. "Listen, guys, I have to get back to my table."

"If you must," Pete said.

As I was walking out of the restroom door, they were still calling out to me, telling me to come back and bring my friends. When I got back to our table I told them about the guys in the restroom.

As the night grew on we drank a lot more and talked, sharing stories and joking. Morris told us about himself. He told us we didn't have anything to worry about.

We took the demo down where he was staying. He told us he was going back to Texas and would call.

sixteen

A few days later, he called and told us everything was good. He told us he'd book us for some studio time. I figured we were gonna be gone for a week. When I told Joe where we were going, he wasn't happy about it.

Morris gave us the address to the place where the studio was. We loaded up William's van and set off the next day. I wanted Heidi to come along but she had to stay for work. It took us about ten hours to make it to Morris' home base of Burk, Texas. When we first pulled into the parking lot I thought we'd come to the wrong place. There was a payphone on the side of the building, and I gave Morris a call. He told me it was the right place, to sit tight. Twenty minutes later Morris pulled into the lot. He got out of his car. We joined him. He went around and shook everyone's hand. We joked around for a bit.

The studio was a tan building.

Morris turned to the structure. "It's not that bad. It's only three years old. Think the owner got a lot of his money from scamming people. The bastard should be in jail. I forget what the actual figure was, but it was up there in the thousands somewhere."

I laughed. "That's not a very nice thing to do. Sounds like someone may need to teach him a lesson."

He shook his head. "If that piece of shit ever stole from me I'd beat 'em. I'd pour gasoline all over his house and light a match. Everything he owns would burn. Everything except him. No, I'd deliver my brand of hurt."

My brother stood with his hands in his pockets. "I'd walk up, point a gun right between his eyes. I'd just make him wonder if I was gonna pull the damn trigger or not, 'Now what's this motherfucker about to do? I can see it in his eyes, man, he's fuckin' crazy. Someone, please help me outta this shit. I see his finger on the trigger, he's gonna pull it back and I'm done, over, last fuckin' disco.' That's what I'd think he'd say. I'd still shoot him. Don't wanna have to worry about thugs trying to scam me out of my hard-earned money."

I agreed.

Morris tilted his head. "I got enough to worry about than havin' some bastard do that."

"What happened to him?" I asked.

"Prison."

"Scamming?"

"No. He murdered his girl."

"Really?"

"Put two holes in her belly."

"Wouldn't make for a good day."

"He got twenty years.."

"Wouldn't like to be that poor asshole."

"I'm sure he wouldn't either," William said

Jason muttered. "Or, even better, string him up by the toes. Dump a few buckets of water."

I looked at my brother. "They did that to him on the inside."

"Wouldn't doubt it," my brother said.

"After they beat him," William added.

Everyone laughed.

Morris pointed to the sign on the building, "I'd like to introduce you guys to Lordar Studios. I know, the name could stand to be changed. When you walk in, the big studio to the left, Studio B, that's where we'll be. The guy who'll be producing is a guy named Graffiti. He's been a friend of mine for years. Good guy."

"Graffiti?" Clarence said.

"Not his real name," Morris added.

"I'd hope not."

"Real name's Scott."

"Why don't they call him by name?"

"I dunno. He coined the name after trippin' on drugs."

"Really?"

"He's had a problem with substances and alcohol. All those drugs rotted his brain. Don't get me wrong, he's really intelligent and knows his stuff. He's been doing this for a long time. Just listen to what he says and you'll do fine. I've got every confidence he'll steer you guys in the right direction."

I studied the outside of the building for a minute. "He's not gonna go crazy on us, is he? I mean, he's all there, right? I don't wanna go in there, have the guy go all psycho on us."

"He shouldn't." Morris gave a nod. "You shouldn't have a problem. I think you guys will get along great."

My brother said, "Way to get wild, huh?"

"That sounds right," Morris said. "The sound of a thousand screaming voices at your hands. Just think, what you put on tracks in there will end up in the hands of a shitload of people."

Jason clapped his hands together and roared. "Hell, man, we'll rip this place up. Sure they've never heard anything like us."

"I can go with that," William said. "Think of it like this, we're standing where lots would love to be right now. Damn, we're some lucky assholes. What would the boys back home say about us now?"

Morris went on to tell us a few other things about what to expect. None of us had ever been in a real studio before. I just wanted to get the record done. We'd done a few demos before but nothing quite like this.

About the time we walked through the door and down

the white hall, the engineer came out of one of the rooms.

He was a thin-haired man. He wore jeans and a white shirt. He had tattoos all over his arms. We could tell he'd just finished smoking some grass.

"Guys," he said. "You must be those guys? Please to meet you. They call me Graffiti."

I shook his hand. "How's it going?"

"I'm doin' pretty good. Can't complain much. I was just in the studio messing around. Always workin' on one thing or another. When I'm not dealin' with other people's music, I work on mine."

"Good to know," I said. "You got a band?"

"Yeah," he said. "But we're on a break right now. I'm not sure if I'm gonna stay with those guys or not. I'm itchin' to get this done, and I don't think their hearts are in it anymore."

"That's a damn shame."

He chuckled. "Well, it depends on how you look at it. Good, bad, everything happens for a reason, right? Doors close, new ones open."

"Guess you have a point there," I told the guy.

"It's all about how you look at a situation. I mean, is going solo such a bad thing? Some would say it frees you up to do the things you couldn't under certain confines. Maybe it was a song, a note, a verse, those other three guys wouldn't let you sing. On the other hand, a group could make beautiful music that'll never die. I think music is important for the soul."

"I couldn't agree more."

Everyone introduced themselves.

"Why do they call you Graffiti?" Jason asked.

"Something about bringing out the best in people's music. This energy is very colorful, and it's my job to help facilitate those colors. Sprouts out like flowers and stuff... Forces behind a stronger force. You can imagine how it goes. They say I'm a master behind the buttons. And it has something to do with me trippin' my brains out a few times. I was explaining to a few guys I was hangin' out with about all the lights and colors I saw. It was magical."

"Interesting."

"You just smoked grass?" William said.

"Of course," he said. "You should've spotted that, right? I'm sure we'll get high together soon enough. My given name's Scott."

"That be great," our singer said. "Put it into the music, make that shit flow."

Scott walked over to Morris and shook his hand. "Hey, buddy, how's everything going?"

"Can't complain," Morris told him.

"Good to hear."

The two exchanged a few kind words to each other.

Scott turned to me and the other guys and nodded to Morris. "You trust him with your music career? You know he can fuck-up a glass of water? You guys are throwin' it all away!"

I turned and looked at the other guys for a moment, then I looked back at Scott. I saw he had a big smile on his face, as he patted Morris on the shoulder.

"We like to mess around like that," Scott said. "Him and I, we go back a long time."

"We heard," Jason told him. "How long is a long time?"

Scott looked off like he was thinking, then back at us. "About thirty years."

"Really?"

"Yeah, that's a long time for a couple of assholes to know each other, that's for sure. We've had great times, though. I'd never trade it for anything."

I nodded. "That's an important thing these days. Hell,

Jason's my best friend. I've known him forever. I could go on and on about what he means to me."

We all shuffled into the studio room we'd be using.

"Here it is," Scott threw up his arms. "I hope this is okay with you guys. The other studios in the place are bein' used. I don't think we should have a problem. The sound in here is really clear, you dig? You can get a good sound from all of these studios in the building. All are soundproof. Think you can get that from looking at the walls."

I asked Scott what type of music he plays as a solo act.

"I don't like to put music in categories," Scott said. "I like to think it has a Southern Rock thing. I don't want it to be known for that exclusively. I was playing some of what I'd done for some friends, and, they were telling me some of it could be called Alternative Rock: not sure about that. I just do what sounds good to me."

"Like that band Nirvana?" Morris asked.

"Not really," Scott said. "I've heard some of their stuff before, and I don't do that. Don't get me wrong, I liked the songs, but, I just don't think I could ever do that type of thing."

I nodded. "I get it. Yeah, I bought that album a few weeks ago. I liked it."

"Had to get the damn thing on cassette, though," he snorted. "Nothing will compare to listening to an album - it just sounds better. Think they should make those the only way music can be heard. Cassettes are okay. And now, stores are flooded with all these things, CDs; those aren't gonna last. They might be the latest craze now, but they won't last. Vinyl is where it's at. Mark my words, those compact disk things... Give 'em five years. After five years they'll be history."

"Read a thing about those," Morris said. "They say it's gonna be the wave of the future. Albums, 8-track tapes, cassettes, and now these CD's, compact disks... Fuckin' things look like mini albums with pictures on the one side. I don't care what they say, I'm not buying into the hype. You have to buy a whole other player just to play the thing. Just another way these companies can suck more money outta ya. I think it's all bullshit."

Scott nodded. "That's another thing, you have to buy that damn player. It's all just another way to get your money and try to fool you into something you already have. Next thing you know they'll beam the music right in your goddamn head. They'll make zombies of us all. After the music then it's the mind control... Those guys in black suits, just love to keep you on your toes, know what I mean? I wouldn't trust them

William said, "The future can be good."

I looked at William. "Get the fuck outtake here with that."

"You get the fucked out," he retorted.

Scott laughed. "Guess I just know what I like and won't change."

"Nothing wrong with that," my brother said.

I looked around. The room had red carpet on the walls and floor for better sound. The open space was huge. Scott took us into the engineer's booth and showed us the board.

Scott gestured to the board. "This here won't mean shit unless you have someone who knows what they're do-ing. The other part, of course, is you guys. You gotta make it work if you want it. I figure, though, you guys have come this far you don't want to piss it all away? Boys, you know, we can fuck this whole thing up, you know? I'm kidding, guys. I wouldn't do anything like that. It's not good for business."

"We'd hope not," Clarence added.

"Unless you guys piss me off," Scott added.

Morris gave a smile. "Don't worry. It's just Scott's way of putting you on edge. If I didn't already know he's the best I wouldn't have booked him. Nah, this guy standing here, he's a stand-up guy. I have all the faith in the world he'll do a good job."

I thought about it for half a minute. "If you say so, Morris. Hey, everything's a gamble, right?"

Scott shook his head at us. "It takes a lot to piss me off. I'm one of the most laid-back people you'll ever meet."

He continued to show us around the studio: all the different microphones and cables. He explained how everything in the place works. He asked what the name of our band was.

"Stoned Monkey," Jason said.

Scott said, "That's a pretty good name. Think you might need to change it sometime in the future."

I looked at Morris. "What does he mean?"

Morris said, "We can talk about that later."

"I don't wanna change the name."

Clarence said. "We aren't changing it."

"How did you guys come to the name?" Scott asked.

"I dunno, really," my brother said. "Guess we were all jamming one day and it just came to us. It might've helped we were stoned when we came up with it."

"I dig it," Scott said. "I was gonna say you had to be high to think of a name like that. It may not play well with people that may pay money for the music."

"Thanks," Jason said. "It's worked so far. That thing about not fixing something that's not broken, that comes to mind."

"You guys should've just called the band Potheads."

"That's a good idea," my brother looked at us. "Why didn't we think of that? We could've been Acid Eyes, Screaming Kaleidoscopes, Whispering Circles, something like that."

We agreed with my brother.

"Those are good names. I might have to use one of 'em sometime," Scott said.

"No, man, we might use those sometime. Sorry." William said.

"Fair enough."

Clarence walked over to Scott. "I'm the vocal power around here. All these other guys try but they never compare. I tell ya, my singin' will be the best you ever heard."

"You sure about that?"

"I am."

"I can't call it. Have to take your word. Hope it's a good one and not a bad word. All these folks in the world, you gotta watch yourself. You don't wanna get stuck in the back. I haven't heard you guys play yet live."

Scott went on, to tell us he liked the demo Morris gave him.

"Before we start this thing," the engineer said, "just let me tell ya what's gonna happen. I'm gonna do it all at once if you guys don't mind - it's just the way I like to do things. If you guys wanna do it one by one, that'll be fine with me. Feel free to do what you want. Hey, man, it's your dollar, baby!"

Clarence said, "We can just do it like a show. We get a good sound together. I think that'd be the best way to get this done. I dunno, to me, it just wouldn't feel right separating the sounds. Part of the vibe with us, we fuel each other's sound. I can't speak for the other guys, but that's how I feel about it."

He asked if we needed any drugs or anything to get started. We told him we didn't need anything.

Graffiti said, "Let's lay down some tracks and see what we get. Let me ask, ya have any idea about what kind of sound ya want?"

We looked at each other for a few seconds.

"Guess we hadn't thought about it," my brother said. "Whatever you say is good with us. If you're asking about sound, we have a rough sound in the bars and clubs. I know it's a whole different game than this."

"Yes, it is."

"What would you suggest?"

"I suggest you do what you want. Do you have any type of reference you could use to get any idea?"

"Like what?"

"A band you like, maybe?"

"We always dug the sounds of Dymot."

"Really?"

"Yeah."

"I recorded them."

"Right on!"

"Their first two albums," Scott continued.

"Those first two were great. The third one lacked something...I dunno," Jason looked at the

"It lacked me."

"Oh, was that it?"

"Probably."

"Ah."

"We can do something like that. I know sort of what you're talkin' about."

"I guess that's good," I said. "Think we might need a little inspiration from time to time. Hell, just snort a bang and go."

Scott put his hand up. "That's good with me. I learned long ago that fuels the art. People always talk about drugs being bad. I've never had a problem with 'em. They agree with me."

"Right on!" I said.

Scott looked at the guys. "I can go home and get more cocaine. We could get loaded. That might be pretty interesting. You guys can find stuff you never knew you had."

We told him not to bother.

Scott went and locked himself in the booth. A few minutes later he came back out.

"I almost forgot, can you guys give me a list of songs we're doing? Just so I know a little of what's going on."

I found a pen and a piece of paper and wrote down the list of songs.

I handed it to him and he nodded.

Thirteen days and thirteen songs later we had a full album worth of material. I was surprised we got finished so fast. On the last day of recording, we went out to celebrate.

Morris and Graffiti took us to a few of the local bars in Burk.

Graffiti invited us to a party at his house. He lived in a big two-story overlooking a lake in the town of Buckston, about an hour from the studio.

seventeen

Morris picked us up at the hotel we were staying at. The drive took about thirty minutes. As I sat in the seat of the car I watched the traffic glide down the street.

We pulled up to Graffiti's house. There were a lot of cars parked in the drive and on the lawn. We walked to the door and were greeted by a brunette in a white dress named Tonya. She was a small framed girl.

"Hey, guys," she looked at Morris. "It's been awhile."

"I've been around, honey," he said. "Hope you've been well."

"I have."

"Good for you."

They hugged.

"Good to see you."

"Same here," Morris said.

Tonya smiled. "Always nice when you're in town."

"I need to do it more often."

"You should."

"Work, you know how it goes, right?"

"Yeah, Scott's been on it lately. He keeps talkin' about wanting a bigger place."

"How much bigger does he want?"

"That's what I said."

Morris turned back to us. "You guys are looking at one of the most beautiful girls in the land. This woman and I go back years. Before she met Graffiti we were a force like no other."

"That's right," Tonya said. "Morris here, he's one of my biggest fans. I think bigger than my husband sometimes. I always get a kick outta him."

"She's got me there," Morris laughed. "You have to appreciate fine beauty - if everyone did that, hey, the world would probably be a better place."

"I'd second that," Clarence said. "There's a lot of sickos out there."

Morris looked at Tonya. "I miss those days. As I get older I start to miss them a lot more. Guess it just comes with age."

She smiled. "I know what you mean. Being around people we knew then keeps us young. Man, when I think about the first time Scott and I got together... It was special. That first week, I never wanted it to end."

"And where is the old man?" Morris asked.

She pointed to the back of the house. "In back. He's entertaining guests. You know, he has to be the king of the manner."

"Good," Morris said. "Yeah, he's always one to make a party."

"Those were some wild times," Tonya said.

"Every bit of it."

"Yes, sir," she said.

He gave her a little peck on the cheek. "I'd better make sure he's not already drunk."

"You can go through the house."

"Thanks."

Tonya looked at us. "So, you guys just made a record?"

"That's right," I said.

"I can't wait to hear it."

"Neither can we."

"Aw, it's an exciting time for you guys!"

"It is," I told her. "We'll just have to see."

"You'll be great. You have two of the finest guys on your side."

"That's what I hear."

She smiled and waved her finger at the front of the

house. "Welcome to our house. Make yourself at home. Anything you want, just ask"

"It's a nice home," Jason said.

"Sure is," added William.

Clarence also agreed.

"That means a lot, guys," she said.

She stepped aside to let us pass. There were all sorts of characters hanging around, playing music, smoking dope, and doing cocaine. In some far-off rooms, the smell of sex could be heard. We walked through the house and went through the double doors to the back lawn. People were drinking and doing drugs all over. Little white tables with people sitting at them were everywhere. At one of the tables, a guy was singing and playing guitar. He had a few girls on his side. I thought that was something I needed to get into. Tucked away in a corner of the lawn stood an outside bar.

Morris pointed at a small table where Graffiti was snorting lines. When Scott raised his head he told us to come over.

"Welcome friends," he said. "We have been waiting. Thought you got lost."

"Nothing like that," Morris told him. "Nah, I'd never forget where you guys lived. Think when I'm old and senile I'd still remember. I just had to take care of a few things fast. Gotta keep that good credit going."

"I see," Scott got up from his chair. "I know how that shit goes. Once you're in, they wanna keep you. No escape for the wild ones, right? We have to make that bread somehow. It's a fuckin' grind. We can't seem to get over the hump, but, hey, let's save that shit for another time, huh? Tonight we party like kings!"

"When you're right, you know it."

My brother walked over to Scott. "Nice place. Would you wanna sell it?"

"I'm afraid I couldn't do that," Scott said. "The damn money I sunk into this place, I'd be a fool to sell. You can have my wife if you want."

"Really?" I said.

"No."

"She's pretty foxy."

"That's why I married her."

Jason snorted. "Got any other girls around here?"

I laughed.

Scott took out a cigarette and lit it. "Just look out in the lawn and take your pick. You need to go find, someone. Hey, there's plenty of space in the house to roll around. I may have to cheat on my life tonight."

"Really?" I said.

"Tonya would cut my balls off and feed 'em to me. She won't have any of that mess."

Morris laughed. "Sort of wish I kept her."

"I bet you do, Bubba," Graffiti said. "Can't have her know. If you want we can't knock the shit outta each other over her again."

Morris howled. "Give it your best shot, sir."

"I wouldn't wanna put ya to shame."

"You mean put yourself to shame."

"Maybe."

Scott folded his arms. "Guys get a drink and enjoy the entertainment around. Just don't do anything to cause trouble. I don't want the cops here. Those rotten bastards already have it in for me."

"Thanks," I told him. "All this is nice. I can't thank you enough. Sorry, my girlfriend had to miss it."

"No you're not," he said.

"Why's that?"

"If she were here you wouldn't be able to see all the nice scenery, right?" he said, looking around at the girl's pass. "And there's a lot of 'em. They could give you material for new songs."

"Yeah."

"Happens every time."

"I'll have to take your word for it."

He laughed. "I dunno if you'd wanna do that. Hell, if I were smart I'd be in the house with Tonya."

"No one's stopping you."

"I should go and check on her. Said she was waiting to greet anybody that shows," he looked around. "Think we have enough here."

I shrugged. "Could do worse, I guess."

A grin. "There ya go! Oh, I'll check on her in a bit."

I talked to him a little longer as we smoked a cigarette and chugged a few bottles of beer. As I walked away he mumbled something to a girl about getting more booze. The more I walked the lawn, the more people handed me liquor. People were screaming and yelling, staggering across the yard, falling, and throwing bottles and glasses. Things were starting to get sloppy I stumbled on a few other people to talk the night away with.

When I was done being sociable, I stumbled to a piece of ground underneath a tree and fell asleep. I woke a few hours later but everyone was gone. I was still feeling drunk, so, I just smoked a cigarette and passed out again.

I opened my eyes slowly to a figure above me. I squinted, trying to block the glare of the sun. I blinked a few times as the figure came into focus, then, realized it was Tonya. She asked if I was okay as I climbed to my feet. She was wearing a yellow blouse and a dress. She gave a soft smile.

"I guess I'm okay," I said surveying the ground where I had laid.

"Too much to drink?" She asked.

"Among other things."

"I see."

"You?"

"I had fun."

"I'm sure you did."

"Just like to keep things lively."

"I hear ya," I said. "That was the night for it."

"I have no complaints."

I rubbed my left eye with my hand. "You throw one hell of a party. I didn't want it to end."

"Thanks. Glad you had a good time - that's what we like to see here."

"What's that?"

"People having a good time."

"I guess I'm still a little out of it. I really can't remember much."

"Join the club."

"I've been a member for years."

"Me, too. More so than you'll ever know. I guess Scott never told you."

"Told me what?"

"I used to always be the queen of the party. I was the nice girl everyone wanted to be with. As it turned out Scott finally won me over. We fell madly in love. The perfect match."

"That's nice."

She smiled.

"I take it I'm the only one who passed out outside?" I gulped fresh air.

"Don't worry. You weren't alone."

"That's good. Don't wanna give the impression I'm a crazed drunkard that always does this."

She laughed. "Aren't you a crazed drunk?"

"I guess."

"That wasn't a lie."

As I talked to her, I felt dirty and sweaty.

I asked if I could take a shower.

"Our showers broke," she said.

"Really? That's a drag."

"I'm kidding. Of course, you can use it."

"Thanks."

"Just make yourself at home."

I picked up the empty bottle lying on the ground beside me. "What a crazy night that was. At one point I ran into a prostitute."

"What was her name?"

"I think her name was Maggie or something. It was all sorts of foggy."

"That's funny."

"It is?"

"My sister, her name's Maggie."

"Was she here last night?"

"No."

"Oh, shit…who…who was that then? Damn, what did I do?"

"Don't worry. After a nice shower, you should be feeling a lot better. The woman you ran into was Lisa. She's an old friend of mine. Yeah, she's been doing that for about ten years."

"Prostitute?"

"Yeah."

"Never understood that."

"I've never really either. You know, she asked me to get into it right after she did. She'd brag to me about the money she was makin' and all of that."

"What did you say?"

"I considered it. After thinking about it over a few days, it wasn't gonna be something for me. Not to mention, I had Scott."

I shook my head. "That's always a good thing."

"And, if I wanna fuck someone I'll just do it for free."

I smile. "I'll have to keep that in mind. I'm not sure if your old man would like that so much."

"Oh, Scott," she laughed. "Yeah, I gotta tell you, though, if I knew you before I met him, I-"

"Really? I grinned. "Thanks. Well, I dunno if I'm at my best right now."

She looked me up and down. "Lookin' a little rough, I have to say."

"If that's the only thing then I'm doing good. I need some food to go with that shower."

"I can see what I can do about that."

"Thanks."

As we walked to the house we talked some more. I told her how much I liked the house, and how much I appreciated her husband recording us. She told me Morris gave him a case of beer and money to do it.

"He did?"

"Yeah."

"How much money did he give him?"

"A hundred bucks."

"That all?"

"It was good beer."

"I'm glad."

"You would've liked it."

"I'm sure."

We walked through the door into the kitchen. The guys were sitting around the kitchen table drinking coffee. I told them I was going to take a shower, and that I'd be back in a few minutes.

"Nobody's keeping' ya," Scott told me. "You smell like a twisted night."

"I blame the booze," I turned to walk away.

"Don't get lost," William yelled after me.

After my shower, I returned and joined them.

"See you made it back," Jason said

"Barely," I said. "I think I'm still drunk."

"I wouldn't doubt it. You had a lot."

Tonya cooked us some sausage and eggs. She was a good cook. I walked over and poured a cup of coffee. I looked through the window at the back lawn. I always wanted a place like that of my own.

About ten years before Scott lent his talent to the music business, he was co-owner of this little bar where they lived. Morris became a fixture at the dive. At one point Scott was trying to make a name for himself in the music scene, and he asked Morris if he would be his manager. Scott got a band together and played all over. They were pretty successful for awhile, but, like with everything else, it came to an end. Scott was so distraught over this that one night after closing down the bar he burnt the place to the ground. He used the insurance money to buy another bar.

Scott sat back in his chair. "Those were the days. I mean, I was part owner of the joint so I was always drinking on the job. It would've been kind of hard to fire myself. At that point in my life, it was all about having as much fun as possible. I met Tonya a few months after we'd opened. She was with this rotten asshole then. It was an interesting time, that's for sure."

Tonya's eyes darted towards him. "Hon, we don't have to get into that story now, do you? Sure they don't wanna hear all that."

"We don't," Scott said. "I was just gonna tell them about how I beat the guy outside the bar."

Morris lit a cigarette. "If I remember right, I helped you with that little piece of work," he looked at us. "The guy, that rotten pimp, had some goons with him. Had to take care of 'em. They never came around again."

Graffiti said, "In those days when someone messed with you, you tell the right people about it and the problem would vanish. In those days we had the world at our fingertips. Sometimes I wish we could go back to that place. It was special. I don't think we'll ever see anything like that again in our lives. You guys would've loved it."

I looked at Morris and Scott. "You talking about being a gangster?"

"Something like that," Morris said. "We just happened to have fallen in with a really tough crowd. Not full gangsters. We were just a bunch of kids who knew the street life. It was exciting a lot of the time. Other times, it wasn't really that inviting. In the end, I wouldn't change it for anything. That stuff made me the guy I am today."

Scott snorted. "It's crazy when I think about it, fifty-five years of life, I've seen a lot of things. People have come and gone, and stories told over the years. I've seen things I wished I could erase - some pretty bad shit."

"Sounds good," I said. "I wish I had been there. The boys and I, we would've had lots of wild times."

"It was great," Scott said.

Tonya asked all of us if we wanted a beer. She jumped over to get the beer. She came back with a bucket full of ice and bottles of beer. She was about to sit when Scott jumped to his feet.

"Hey, babe, we're gonna need more than this!" he bellowed. "We're gonna be at this all day."

She laughed. "I think this is good for now."

Something told me Scott would always play some sort of part in our lives. I already had it in my head that we would hire him to do our next album. He was a great guy. He and Morris were both crazy, but, we were all crazy.

We continued talking energetically about anything and everything.

At one point I asked Scott if he liked our music

"You guys have a nice sound," Scott said. "You need to keep at it. Recording you guys was one of the best jobs I've ever had."

"Really?" my brother said. "That means so much to us. We've been playing together for awhile, and it's nice to hear a compliment like that. With a lot of these guys who run these bars and such, you can never really tell if they're telling the truth when they say we sound good. Think they say stuff like that to help fill the bar."

"Those guys don't care," Scott said. "They're there to make money. Yeah, if enough people come and see the show they'll say you have a good band. They'll say you can get with their daughter... anything you wanna hear. Half of them are bullshit."

Morris cleared his throat and took a drink of beer. "In their defense, they're trying to run a business, get people in there, and sell booze. One way to do that is by offering good music."

"You saying our music sounds like shit?" I asked.

"No, no, no," he said. "I didn't mean it like that. You guys are great. I wouldn't have talked to you guys if I thought you weren't good. I was just saying that because that may be something they just say to get business. For all you know, they might not even like your music."

"I don't know how they couldn't like the music, those dirty bastards," William said, rubbing his brow.

Scott said, "When you guys hit the airwaves, you'll blow up big."

"Think so?" Clarence asked.

"I'd bet anything on it. You guys have what it takes. And I think you'll be around for a long time. Shit, man, I've done work for people, laid-down tracks, the album comes out and does pretty okay the first month or so, then, they can't even get shows anywhere. Pretty soon they fade away. A friend of mine, Mickey Leary, had a band called... um... hell... I forget the name... something about.... yeah... it was Welcome Friday. I don't know, guess he liked Fridays or something, I don't fuckin' know why he picked that name. Anyway, those guys, they paid me some money and I put them on tape. A few months later the music isn't doing as good as it does and Mickey hangs everything up and gets a job in construction. The other guys, go their ways. Days turn into months, moths turn into a year. The whole time I keep in contact with Mickey. He keeps tellin' me about how he's gonna bounce back, get another band together, blah, blah, blah, I'll climb back, all that shit people in his situation say."

"What happened?"

"He reached out to me about a month later. He wanted to hang out. I went over to his place and saw the drugs he was doing. Told me he had everything under control, not to worry about anything - when someone tells you that, that's the time you need to start to worry. I played it cool, 'Hey, man, no problem. If you say so. I'll mind my own business.'"

"And?"

"He was dead two months later. Some guy found him in an alley behind this one bar we always went to."

"Damn."

"So, I guess the point to that was don't ever give up. See, Mickey fell down a path of destruction. I'd hate to see you guys go down that path."

My brother looked at his bandmates, then Scott. "We wouldn't do anything to fuck this up. Think we'd all have to die before we gave this away."

"Good. I think that'll be great for both of us," he

pointed at Morris. "He needs this gig. Don't wanna see him become some homeless drifter."

"Thanks for that," Morris said.

We spent the rest of the afternoon getting drunk.

The next day we woke and went for a nice breakfast. We spent the rest of the day exploring the town. We talked to Scott and Morris to see if they wanted to join us. They didn't.

We talked about the future of the band. I was feeling fantastic. The overall conscience was that the recording process was a success. As usual, Jason started to flirt with our waitress.

After we finished lunch we called Morris and met up at Scott's house. Later that night we went to a few local bars. This next day we hit the road back to Arkansas.

It was around midnight when we crossed back into our home state. When we pulled up to my place. I called Heidi and she came over. I told her about the trip, and how much fun it was making the album. We opened a bottle of wine and celebrated.

eighteen

A week later we had a gig at Hill Top, about two miles out of North Brown Ridge, in a stretch of land known as Sharlo. The bar was at the end of a long quiet dirt road called Culley. Up from Hill Top sat a gas station. On the other side of the road was a huge field with an old dilapidated barn in the center. Beyond the field, a lonely tree line waited.

I'd been to Hill Top a few times before it was a nice bar that served good booze and cheeseburgers. The last time I was in the place I was thrown out for fighting. A few months had passed since that night, but it was still on my mind. At first, I was a little worried about entering for fear of them throwing me out again.

No matter where I went, I carried my gun on me. You never knew when someone was going to start something. On that night, however, I forgot the gun at my apartment. As it were, Jason and my other two friends didn't have their guns either. For the most part, we felt safe in the area. Of course, you never knew when evil lurked around the corner.

As we walked into the place I saw the crowd was loud and ready for music. Heidi smiled as she hung from my arm. Wild drunks were staggering around the place.

We headed to the bar for a drink.

I saw a few people carrying around the flyer we made: a few people wanted us to sign them. I thought it strange to sign a piece of paper for someone. But I told myself it was all for the greater good.

We talked to the bartender and some people who were sitting at the bar. One of the employees ran to get the manager.

The manager led us back to his office. He introduced himself as Stew. He was a brown-haired guy wearing nothing but black. He talked with a heavy Southern accent. As we entered his office we were engulfed in thick cigarette and marijuana smoke. A woman sat behind his desk with a bag of cocaine lying beside her.

"Where did you get off to?" the woman asked. "You ran off and left me here."

"Don't worry, you witch," Stew said. "I can do whatever the hell I want. Why do I have to answer to you every fuckin' time I take a step somewhere?"

"Don't have to get rude about it," the woman said.

Stew shrugged. "Oh, well, if someone would've taken you, they would've brought you back

"You shithead!"

"That's not nice to say, babe."

"What about fuck-face?"

"Oh, I like the way you talk dirty. You can talk to me like that all night long."

"Eat my pussy!"

He laughed.

"What?" she said. "Did I say something funny? Come on, I know you want me," she licked her finger and ran it over her right breast. "Are you man enough for me?"

Stew laughed. "Doll, we have company. Now, be a good little girl and be civil. I'm sure you can do that."

I learned her name was Sally.

She was a thin woman with black hair. She looked as though she was much older than she was. Sally spoke with a raspy voice. If I had to guess, I'd say she'd smoked for about thirty to forty years.

"Oh, baby, guess you drank the rest of the booze?" he said, looking at an empty bottle of whiskey on his desk. "I thought I told you about that, baby? Want these guys to see how freaky you get? Damn, baby, you have to slow it down," he turned to us. "If you give her enough booze and drugs she'll let you do whatever you want to her. Trust me, guys, you'll want some of that action."

"What's your point?" Sally licked her ruby lips.

"Guess I have to get more from the bar," Stew said. "You're gonna drink my whole inventory, baby. Have to make that money to buy you all those lavish gifts."

"You act like a damn Jew half the time, have to ask for everything."

Stew raised a brow. "I'll be right back, you drunk," he turned to walk out the door

She came from behind the desk. "And get a couple, you asshole. You know I gotta have it to put up with your business. And, who knows, maybe one of these fine men might get lucky tonight?"

I laughed and looked at the guys. "That was pretty funny."

"That's nice,' Stew said, as he turned back toward her. "You sound like a damn whore when you say things like that."

"Honey, you never had a problem being with me."

Stew threw up his arms. "At least you're good for something."

"Someone has to sleep with you tonight. I'll be dammed if I'll let you stick your dick in one of those waitresses out there."

"That's nice," he said. "Why should I get you more booze if you're gonna talk like that? Cocaine not enough?"

"Oh, baby, it's all about entertainment."

"I just don't understand you sometimes."

"You don't have to. Just have to do what I tell you."

"You're still pullin' that, huh?"

"Think you know the answer to that."

Stew looked at us. "It's not a good idea. She's on this self-destructive kick right now. I don't know, she thinks this whole 'crash 'and burn' thing is the way to go. Women, you can never understand them, am I right?"

My brother said, "That's about it. We love 'em all, but they can be crazy. I've had my share of crazy women."

Stew patted Jason on the shoulder. "Don't have to tell me," he laughed. "Sometimes I think to myself, 'Those women, those beautiful beasts, why do they play with us so?' They don't always play the game we want them to. They set and rewrite rules the way they see fit."

"That's right," Sally barked. "You guys shouldn't forget that little detail."

Stew gave her a nod. "You should watch these guys play in a bit."

"Just get the booze," she waved him away.

"You sure? Not gonna pass out like last night, are ya?"

"I might. Do whatever I want. You're not my boss."

"Better not."

"And what if I do?"

"Just might have to go see Miss Swayne down the street. Don't think I have to remind you she's had a thing for me for some time now."

"Just make sure you save some for me," she smiled, as she leaned back in the chair.

"Sure."

"That's all I ask."

"You're crazy."

She looked at us, and then back at him. "You find them at some back alley garbage pile somewhere?"

We laughed.

"No," he said. "They're a pretty good band."

"Nice. What's the name?"

I smiled at her "Stoned Monkey."

"That's good," she waved her hand at us.

"Think you'll like it," my brother told her. "We can draw the people."

"Oh, yeah. Well, hope you guys sound better than most people Stew gets to play. With what he pays, he can't get good bands. Anyone that's any good, they go to a nicer paying gig."

"What sort of music do you usually have here?" I asked.

Stew grinned. "All kinds. Don't pay attention to her. She doesn't know good talent if it walked up and introduced itself," he looked at her. "All she knows is how to drink and fuck," and then back at us. "Some of those perverts out there can't seem to keep their hands away. She's got the goods, that's for sure. I have to keep an eye on her. She's just gonna drink herself to death one of these days."

I laughed. "I'd watch myself if I were you."

"Why's that?"

"She might get pissed."

"Shit, I'm not afraid of her."

Sally moved to the doorway. "Don't worry, honey, I'll get the booze myself. Should just be married to myself. I need to get more cigarettes from my car, anyway."

"Don't get lost," Stew said.

"I'll try."

"And don't suck any dick out there."

She blew him a kiss. "I'll take the advice."

"I mean it."

"Whatever. I might just pick some random guy to go home with."

'Why do you talk like a whore all the time?"

"Because I am, isn't that what you always say?"

"It is."

She turned to us. "Guys better be careful around this fool. He'll screw you out of the money he owes you. I told him I know people who'll put him in the ground - he doesn't believe that" She let out a big smile. "You guys have a good show."

We thanked her.

"Don't listen to her," Stew told us. "She doesn't know what it's all about."

She kissed Stew before she left the room.

"Don't worry about her, guys," Stew sat behind his desk. "She a crazy drunk. I don't pay her any mind. She threatens to kill me all the time. There's this thing with us, I dunno what it is, it's was this strange pairing when we would get all whacked-out on drugs. It's a toxic combination. I'm afraid one of these days we're gonna end up killing each other."

"Ever think about getting some help?" William asked.

"Not really," Stew said. "I've never worried about it. That's just how she is. Hell, the first night we met she said she'd kill me."

"Really?" William said.

"And that was five years ago."

"You don't say?"

"New Year's Eve party, we were both drunk. She didn't mean it, I know that now. But at the time I didn't know what to think. Now I know it was just a big show."

"I see."

Stew offered us drugs. We passed on the offer, telling him we didn't want to get loaded before the show.

"More for me," he said.

About the time Stew snorted two lines Sally came back into the office with two bottles.

She threw the bottles on the desk.

Stew talked to us a little longer about the details of everything. We left the office and headed towards the stage area. As soon as we came on stage the lights came on.

The only color they used for stage lighting was white. I turned on the amplifier and started plucking my guitar. The sound bounced around the room.

Jason gave me a nod. "Look at all those fine women."

I gave a little smile. "Just picture yourself rollin' in a bed with them."

"Seems like we see them all over."

"It's nice, though."

"I wanna fuck all of 'em."

"That'd be nice."

Two redheads in front blew me kisses.

They yelled to me that they'd see me after we were done playing.

I moved my fingers up and down the strings. I started to play this little riff I came up with on the spot. William looked over at me from behind his drum set. It took him about a minute or so but he found a good beat. The screech of the guitar ripped through the crowd.

Jason let out a few low notes

Clarence spoke into the microphone. "Good evening, Hill Top. How are you guys doin' tonight? We're proud to spend the evening with you."

Hollers and screams came from the crowd.

Some people started to dance before we began playing a song.

I didn't quite understand why they were dancing. It was at that time I finally realized that we brought joy to people.

"No matter where we play, Arkansas will always be our home and favorite state to play," Clarence continued. "I know you people are here to listen to some great music, and we're happy to do that for you. We dig the fact you guys have been so supportive of Stoned Monkey."

We started playing.

I walked across the stage and did a little dance as I

played. The move seemed to get a lot of cheers.

They asked for more.

I danced two more times.

Then, Jason did a little boogie of his own.

Men grabbed women by the waist and grooved their bodies together. People were jumping up and down, twisting their bodies in all directions.

My soul spilled out through my fingertips as I mashed every note. I looked out in the audience and saw Heidi cheering and screaming. Our eyes met and we smiled at each other. I looked down, heard a muffled pop come from the audience, looked up, and saw Heidi's head fall on the table where she was sitting. Her body slowly dropped out of the chair onto the floor. Three men dressed all in black started shooting people in the crowd while others scattered and ran for the door. I jumped off stage, saw a chair, picked it up, and threw it at one of the men. He dropped his gun when he fell. I ran over and grabbed it, pointed at him, and squeezed the trigger. Out of the corner of my eye, I saw Clarence knock one of the shooters in the head with the microphone stand, and then start to strangle him with the microphone cord but the guy broke free, then, my friend shot the guy. One of the guys was coming after William. My friend took one of his drumsticks and poked the guy in the eye. The guy dropped to his knees and William ran over to him and kicked him in the face. William grabbed him by the head and slammed him against one of the tables. I looked behind me and saw Jason on the floor. He was holding his side. I walked over to him, knelt, and told him everything would be okay.

I looked down at the gun in my hand and stood. I turned around and the guy who got slammed against the table was back on his feet. I aimed the gun and shot him in the chest three times. He fell like a brick. A shotgun blast went off and a loud something hit the floor. I turned to see Stew holding the shotgun and saw the third shooter lying on the floor. A cloud of gun smoke hovered in the area as it slowly dissipated to nothing. A couple of patrons screamed and disappeared out the door.

 I looked at Stew. He looked like he had just seen a ghost or something, all pale and white. He put the shotgun on the bar beside him.

 "The fuck?" he said. "This is my fuckin' place, man! You guys got yourselves in some shit. I knew the rumors about you were true," he looked down at the bodies, then at us. "I shoulda never let you guys in. What did you do? The way I see it, I'm fucked here. Have to call this in. There's not much I can do," he looked over at my brother on the floor. "Your brother gonna be okay?"

 "I hope so," I told him.

 He looked at Heidi's body. "They got your girl?"

 "They did."

 "Shit's not right."

 "Nothing about this is right," I shook my head

 I looked at Heidi's lifeless body. Everything she and I shared flashed before my eyes. She had her whole life in front of her. She didn't deserve this.

 "That's it," I looked up. "Somebody's gonna pay. She shouldn't have gotten tangled up with me. Somehow I knew some shit like this would happen," a tear trickled down my face.

 I walked over to Jason. He was in the fetal position on the floor: hands covered in blood.

 I knelt beside him, and put my hand on his shoulder. "You still with us?"

 He looked up at me. "I'm still here."

 "At least we have that."

 "I don't wanna die here."

 "You won't."

"I hope so.'

He had a hole the size of a little rock in his belly.

I asked Stew if he had anything that would help my brother.

"I'm not a doctor," Stew said. "I have towels and shit 'round here. Don't have much here. I know there's some rubbin' alcohol back in the office. It's in there from when I burnt myself with a cigarette one night," he smiled. "I was drunk."

"Good. Get them. Anything would help.'

'You got it!"

He ran off to the back room to get some supplies.

All told, twenty bodies were on the floor.

A blood bath.

I'd never seen anything like it.

"I can't believe this," I muttered.

The good thing for us, since Hill Top was pretty much in the middle of nowhere it would take cops awhile to get on the scene—it bought us a little time.

William and Clarence were scrabbling around, getting the equipment to our vehicle outside. On their first trip back, Stew came back with a handful of towels and rubbing alcohol.

I ripped the towels from his hand. "This'll help."

Sally burst out of the office. I could only imagine what she must've thought as she looked at all the bodies on the floor. Her eyes looked tired.

"Stew, what the fuck's going on?"

Stew gave her a blank stare.

Her mouth opened like she was about to say something, but she just covered it and stood in silence. The glass she had in her hand dropped to the floor.

"Stew?" she said, sitting down at one of the bar stools. "What did you do? What happened? Heard something that sounded like gunshots. I passed out for a bit. I thought it was the radio. It took me a little to realize the radio wasn't even on."

Stew looked at her. "Aren't you the genius? Look around you. Yeah, it was a fuckin' shoot-out here," he pointed a finger at her. "Don't give me any of your psycho bullshit or I'll slap the piss outta you. We need to think about this."

"Why did they start shootin'?"

"I don't know, babe."

She looked at me. "Maybe they didn't like the music, ya think?"

"Maybe," I told her. "Hard to tell. We aren't for everyone."

"Guys shootin' noise to make the night complete?"

"Somethin' like that."

She sighed. "Oh boy, what a mess."

"I know."

She looked at my brother. "You need to get him help now. Don't want another dead guy on our floor. We Shouldn't have ever had you in here. Well, you're only getting half the pay. That's a fucking rule we have here. If you start a gunfight, only half the fucking pay. In this case, a fucking slaughter-fest, you don't get anything. We don't care what you say, who started, nothing. We know what you are."

"We didn't plan on all of this."

"But it happened."

Stew said, "We've never had that before."

"We do now," Sally said. "We opened this for beer and good music, remember? If you want anything else, we aren't the place, don't come here."

Stew looked over the bar room floor. "Think you better be quiet about this. We don't know what this is yet."

My eyes went to Clarence and William, they shrugged their shoulders. They, like me, didn't want them to know we knew who had been behind it. I thought it was best if we left out that piece of information.

"A fucked-up thing that happened. Boys, I'm going back in the office and get stoned. Need to forget about this. When I come out you guys better be gone," she looked at Stew. "What are we gonna do? I…I just…this is….I don't know. They…they're gonna lock us up!"

William said, "Don't worry, they won't take ya to jail for this."

I looked at William. "Sure about that?"

He shrugged at me. "Not really, no. I mean, I just assume. Never been in the middle of shit like this. For all I know they'll string us up, beat us to a puddle, then kill us. There are worse ways to go, I guess."

"Don't listen to him, babe," Stew told her. "We'll take care of it."

"How? You understand what? Do you think the cops might be on the way already? You don't know shit, Stew. Why do you always act like you know everything? We could lose everything, babe. We worked so hard…"

"It'll be okay."

She started to cry as she walked away. I felt bad for her. She and her old man didn't need any of this on their hands. They just wanted to run a small bar and make a little money along the way. We ruined it in a night.

William and Clarence were after Jason.

Stew said, "Guys better get outta here super-fuck-fast. The wife's right, someone probably called the cops. No telling where all those people went when they left. Not sure how long it would take for cops to get here. They've only ever been here twice in the past year. One of those times an off-duty cop was already here."

"Yeah," Clarence said. "We're sorry about this."

"Who was it?" Stew asked.

"I wish I knew."

"When I find out I'll kick their ass, slice a bullet through their heads, the fuckin' shitheads," he pointed his finger at us. "Your boss, whoever he is, tell him he needs to compensate me for damages. I'm gonna have to close down for awhile and clean up. I don't need this shit. I'm not a thug or anything. I'm just a businessman, a man of business, that's all. I've always been on the right side of the law."

I said, "Sometimes you have to ask what's the difference. Would you kill the man who hurt someone you loved?"

Stew shook his head. "I would."

"I'll tell ya, I don't care who it was, they'd be dead," I said.

Stew glanced around the room, then looked back at me. "Now what?"

Just then, the door to the office swung open and Sally walked out. As she got closer in front of me I saw the shotgun in her hand.

She cocked it and pointed at me.

I put my hands up. "Hey, hey, hey! Hold on! Sally, what's this? Put the gun down."

"No!" she snapped.

"Come on, drop the gun. We can talk about it."

"Someone has to pay."

Her hands were shaking as she held the gun.

Stew moved over to where she was, took the barrel of the gun, and pushed it away from me. "Baby, what the fuck you doin'? You don't wanna do this, trust me."

"Shut up, Stew," she said and then pointed the gun back at me. "Because of you, this happened. You know who did this, don't you?"

"I don't," I said.

"Bullshit! Guys like to keep everything hush-hush, but, I know you know."

I said, "Sally, I don't know who that was. None of us do."

"Guys were probably after ya. What, dope deal go bad, sound 'bout right?"

"Don't know anything about any dope. Look, I just saw my brother shot and my girlfriend killed. I don't have time for any of this shit. If we don't get Jason to a doctor he'll die. You can either move out of the way or wish you had."

Her finger ran slowly across the trigger. I hit her hard with my hand. She dropped the gun as she fell over. I was fast to pick up the weapon.

"You need to get her outta here."

Sally cried as she walked away to the office.

Stew said, "You gotta forgive her. She didn't mean anything by it. She's just rattled."

"Rattled?" I said. "She didn't have anyone she loved to die in front of her tonight."

Stew shook his head. "She'll get over it. Just give her a little time, and I'm sure she'll welcome you back in here like nothing happened. It's all that shit she puts in her. She's harmless."

I shook my head. "Yeah, seen that type of thing a bunch. Think she'd talk?"

"Nah, she'll sleep it off," Stew waved off the thought. "She'll feel better tomorrow. Nah, she wouldn't say anything 'bout this. If she does, a little slappin' I'll have to do," he laughed as he raised the back of his hand in a striking motion. "I'll put her in line."

I laughed.

William said, "We need to get Jason to a doctor. This isn't good," he was trying to stop the bleeding.

"Where we gonna take him?" Clarence asked.

"Joe knows people," I said. "We'll take him someplace safe. He can't die like this."

"Who?" Stew asked.

"A guy," William looked at Stew.

"A guy?"

"That's what I said."

"Won't tell me who?"

I looked at William and nodded toward the stew. "Certain people are here."

Clarence's eyes followed my nod. "Oh, yeah."

I looked over at Stew. "No offense, but we have to keep things on the quiet. Don't want to end up dead, do ya?"

"Not really."

"Good."

"Anything I can do to help?"

"Thanks," I said. "That'll help."

After a little discussion, Stew told us he didn't want Jason to bleed to death on his floor.

We carried Jason and put him in William's van.

After we got Jason situated, Clarence and I stood outside the van as Stew still wanted to go over a few things with us.

"What am I supposed to say to the cops?"

I looked at Stew. "Simply say you don't know anything. It's easy. It's the truth. Just tell them you were minding your own business when those guys started to shoot the place up. You've never seen them before. You didn't do anything wrong."

Stew shrugged. "If you say so. I don't wanna get involved in anything you guys have going on, all due respect. Have my troubles. I don't need anything else."

"This is a mess," I said, lighting a cigarette. "We truly are sorry, but with all due respect, you're involved now. We have to think about them coming after you. I mean, sure, we took care of the guys tonight but they had people above them. It's a good bet they might be back. Hell, we might even have to get a few guys to watch your place."

"They?"

"The bad guys," Clarence said. "We don't know who they are. If anyone tries to mess with you about any of this give us a call."

Clarence took a piece of paper from his pocket, asked Stew for a pen, and then wrote his number down.

"Give me a call day or night if anything happens."

"Think someone's gonna be after us?" Stew asked.

"They might," Clarence said. "You're a loose end. These aren't the type that like witnesses."

"That's not good."

"No, it's not, "Clarence said. "We can protect you, though," he looked at me."We better go. The boys in blue, they'll be here soon enough. We don't wanna be here for that shit. That'll be very bad."

Stew shrugged. "My livelihood was in this place. You know how long it took me to get this place off the ground? It's gonna take me a long time to get it all back. This is bad for my business, guys."

"Us, too," I told him. "If you want, we can see about compensating for the damages and whatever. If you want we can burn the place down, and make it look like an accident. You guys can collect."

Stew said, "That's okay. There won't be any need for that. Shit like this, you just never see it comin' till it's too late," he looked down at the ground, then back at us. "Now I have this. All a big nothing… Everything, this place is gonna have cops and shit all over."

Clarence said, "At least you and your lady are okay. Luck was on your side."

"They could've done me a favor and shot that bitch in there. From now till the day I die, all I'm gonna hear about is this night from her. She likes to bitch about everything. Sure you guys know what I mean, right?"

"I guess," I said. "We can help with that nightmare if you want?"

Stew looked at Clarence and I smiled and made his hand in the shape of a gun. "You mean this…bump her off?"

"Anything we can do to help," my friend said.

Stew said, "I appreciate the offer. Still need her around to put up with me. When she goes I may as well go, too. Not gonna ever find lovin' like that again."

"You need to make sure she doesn't talk," I said.

"Don't have to worry about that," Stew said. "Fear will keep her in line. I don't think she wants to get hurt."

"You need to talk to her, make things clear. We don't wanna see anything happen to you."

"I'll threaten her."

"Do anything you have to."

The back door to the van slammed open and William jumped out. He ran over and said we needed to leave that instant. He said Jason had lost a lot of blood and had passed out, and said he needed a doctor. We told him to give us another minute and we'd be ready to go.

He jumped back in the van.

"And you guys don't know who this was?" Stew asked.

"Believe me, we'll check around, and see if anyone on the street heard anything. Odds are, word got out some-where. People end up braggin' about stuff like this. They can never seem to keep their mouths shut."

Stew looked at my friend, then me. "Can I talk to your boss? Think I'll need money. I need some sort of money. I have so many things to pay - house payment, electric, insurance…all that shit."

"How much were you wanting?"

"How much could you give me?"

"We'll ask the boss, see what he says. Everything goes

through him."

"I understand. I don't wanna get in the way of any-thing."

I smiled. "No problem."

"I do have a question?" the bar owner said.

"Shoot."

"When you track down whoever was responsible, you give me a call?"

"I can't promise that."

He shook his head. "You gotta do what you need to, I guess. I'd like to kick their asses for what they did," he looked out towards the road. "My bet, someone used the payphone at the gas station up there. The cops will be here soon. Better leave now. I can handle things on my end."

We nodded.

Stew gave us his address, and we told him we'd visit him. As I turned to walk away, I looked back at Stew and told him to tell Sally we were sorry for what hap-pened.

As we drove away, I couldn't help but feel guilty.

nineteen

We stopped at a phone booth by a filling station and called Joe. We told him what happened. He was a little surprised. He arranged to have a doctor he had on the payroll to look at Jason. The doctor, Gene Sutter, had an office ten minutes away from where we called. We arrived at the office soon before Joe did. Gene worked at the end of an eight-business plaza building. He told us he'd have to take out the bullets and give him painkillers. He told us my brother would make it, that he'd just have to make it passed the next few days. When I asked the doctor if he had everything he needed, he directed me towards his cabinet full of instruments and drugs. Jason was awake and was screaming in pain the whole time. At one point the other guys stepped out of the room with Joe.

"Hope he'll be okay," William said.

"He's in good hands," Joe said. "Gene knows what he's doing. He's a good guy. We need guys like him around. I'd trust him with my life. What he's into us for a lot. We're gonna keep him forever."

"Sure about that?" I said.

"About what?" Joe asked.

"He knows what he's doing?"

"What the fuck did I say?"

"For all you know, he could let my brother die. Why should he give a damn?"

"What? He's never let me down yet."

"He's saved everyone he's ever worked on?"

"Well…there was a few…they…they were gonna die anyway. What the shit difference does it make any-

fuckin'-way? The point is, you need to trust me on this."
I shook my head. "Okay."
Joe glared at me. "You have a problem with that?"
"I'm fine."
"You sure?"
"I promise."
"Better be."

The lobby of Gene's office was plain - nothing too flashy or anything. A few brown armchairs were against one of the white walls. A brown couch rested against another wall. A few boring pictures hung from the walls. A little black table sat in the corner with a stack of magazines on it. A cheap blue carpet covered the floor.

"Guess it'll be fine," I said. "We don't have anything to worry about, right? Oh, I forgot, we could've been fucking killed."

"But you guys weren't," Joe looked me up and down. "Who you think it was?"

"No doubt in my mind Nick and Max were behind it," I told him. "They're going down. Those fucks killed my baby. When I'm done they'll pray for death. I'm talkin' about fuckin' torture. I'm gonna hunt them down and tare them limb-by-limb. They don't deserve to live."

"Heidi?" Joe lowered his eyes. "I'm sorry," he looked at me. "I know you loved her. She was a good girl, but, then again, she was trouble. Girls like her can complicate things. It's probably best she died. They tend to get in your ear a little too much - makes a guy go soft."

"The fuck?" I said. "How can you say that? You stand here and say some shit like that. I know you're the boss, but you need to watch how you navigate around this."

"I've seen girls like that before ruin business. She would've ended up getting someone killed. At first, it all looks good, but it's just a matter of time before she makes things difficult for you. So, tell me, what do you wanna do about it?"

"Find both of 'em and make them gone."

His eyes got wide. "That's your answer to everything, just kill everyone?"

"Sounds good to me."

Joe pointed his finger at me."I told you, that's not how I wanna handle the situation. Do you want things to get bloody out there? We'll have a big fat war on our hands. I've told you guys that this whole music thing would do nothing but cause problems. No matter how many fuckin' times I said something, you guys never believed me. Well, just look what happened, you stupid mother-fuckers! A fuckin' blood bath! You're the one that got your girl killed and your brother shot. What am I gonna do with you? You don't know what it's like to be me, what it's like to make the tough decisions."

"Better watch yourself, you bastard."

He squinted his eyes as he pointed his finger at me again. "Better watch who you're talking to. You guys call for this and expect me to be happy? I had a girl with me. She didn't want me to go. Left her at the house. She's probably lookin' at what she could steal. I'll put it to ya like this: You need to learn a little more respect."

"I respect people who deserve it."

"I don't deserve it?"

"Not in my book."

"That so?"

"And I'll tell you what, next time, I'm not gonna bring this to you. I'm gonna take 'em out myself."

"You better not."

"Try me."

"You'll be sorry."

"I'll take my chances."

"For your sake, that day better not come for you."

"We'll see."

As I looked at him, I started to feel a little nervous. I couldn't believe the words that came out of my mouth. At that point, I didn't care who he was.

Joe said, "You think you can just go over my head on this? I told you, I'd handle things my way. I was waiting for the best time to retaliate if it was needed."

"It was needed."

"Says you."

"Oh, okay, three guys shoot a place, and we're supposed to stand there and watch it happen? You just want some more people to die before you get off your fucking ass and take care of business? The fuck's wrong with you?"

"You better watch it. This is gonna be in the papers. See, it's things like this that open you up to the cops. Better pray ya don't go down for this. Those pigs are gonna come around asking me questions. I could just lie if they ask, who knows? Good thing for you I'm not that sort of prick. But you're going down for this no matter what."

"No, Joe, we're not going down for this. All they'll have is some people came in a shot up the joint. We just defended ourselves."

"And you don't think Nick's gonna go for another round, use some more guys to take care of you?"

"If that happens we'll deal with it. We don't have any other choice now, do we?"

Joe shook his finger at me again. "You boys… Well, I guess the war's started. Goddamn asshole! You see now, the music thing and our thing can't go together. You're out there like a big target. You're all marked men now. Any day they can come by and pop ya."

"I can handle myself."

"You think so, eh?"

"I know I can."

"Well, just walk out there and kill Max, Nick, and the whole fuckin' crew then. I should've let those kids stomp you to death that night at the bar. I tried to give you something you never had before. I wanted to build you into a man."

I tilted my head at him, then looked down. "I dunno what to say," I looked at him. "I used to respect you - all the advice, wisdom, you've given me over the years... Not anymore. I don't give a fuck. The way I see it, you're the reason Heidi was killed. I'll never take another order from you again. I fucking came to you and asked if you could put an end to this problem. I can never forgive you."

Joe looked at Clarence and William. "Believe this shit? What do you guys think about this? You think it's okay to go against me?"

Clarence held his hands in front of him. "All I know is he watched his girl get killed and his brother getting shot. You'll have to forgive him for being a little pissed."

"Is that it, Sean?" Joe asked.

"I do," I said. "What's the next step? Now things are fucked. The poor guy, getting his bar shot up. He didn't do anything. He was just trying to make an honest living."

"Guys tell him anything?" Joe asked.

"He asked. We told him we didn't know anything," Clarence told him. "We told him to tell the cops he didn't know who it was either. We might have a problem though."

"What's that?" Joe asked.

Clarence cleared his throat. "Nick or Max may send some guys after the bar owner after they hear about what went down. That could be very bad for Stew."

"Who's Stew?"

"The owner of the bar. If he's threatened he might go to the cops."

Joe shrugged at us. "I guess we have to stop that from happening."

"How?" I asked.

"Get rid of him," Joe said.

"He hasn't done anything."

"He can always turn on you guys. You can never be too sure about guys like that. It's just how things go."

"We told him everything would be okay, that we could protect him."

"He has to be dealt with. You don't wanna have any doubts."

"I wouldn't feel right about doing that," I said. "We told him we'd protect him."

"I dunno," William said. "I liked the guy. I'd hate to see him taken out."

The boss let out a sigh. "You sure he won't say anything?"

"He won't say anything," I said. "He's too scared they'll kill him."

"That's all they need," Joe said. "All it takes to get a civilian to run to the cops is a shooting. Even more so when the guy's livelihood is damaged. He's a risk. The little he does know is too much. We can't take any chances."

Clarence said, "Makes sense, I guess, but..."

"But what?" Joe snapped. "Do ya feel bad? Did you make friends with him? Did he let you fuck his sister or something? I say he's a fuckin' dead man. I want this done in the next few days. Was there anyone else there?"

"His wife."

"She has to go, too."

"Understood."

Joe raised his brow. "And hopefully, they'll be in a better place. Anything must be better than this shit."

I shook my head. "Got that right."

Joe said, "In all, how many people were killed up there?"

I thought about it for a minute. "About twenty-five or so."

"Was that everyone in the place?"

"Some got out."

"How many?"

"A few, I don't remember."

"It's a safe bet someone else spread the word."

The three of us agreed.

Joe told us he was going to check and see how Jason was. He walked through the door to where they were. While he was gone I looked at the other guys and told them we needed to talk after we were done with the doctor. Joe came back out the door. A few minutes later the doctor followed. He told us Jason would be okay, but he would have to take it easy for a couple of days, and that he would have to stay at the doctor's office.

After Joe was gone we shuffled into the examining room to see Jason.

twenty

A day later, news of what happened at Hill Top hit the papers. I guess a few people who were at the club called the local paper after they called the cops. Seeing that Heidi Lee was shot in print sent a shiver through me. Her lifeless body lying in a pool of blood was an image I would never be able to shake. The paper said the cops would start an investigation; from reading that, I knew they'd be grilling Stew, if they hadn't already.

The next day Clarence and I paid a visit to Stew. We drove over to Yellow Street where he lived. Stew lived in a blue one-story beside a railroad track. A rusty brown truck sat in the driveway. As we got out of my car I heard kids across the street playing. A guy to the left of Stew's house was mowing his lawn. Someone's radio was blaring out a window from a few houses down.

The sky was clear, and the sun was bright.

We walked the decaying wooden steps that led to the porch.

I knocked on the door two times and waited. A minute later someone started to move on the inside. The door swung open and Stew stood on the other side, beer and smoke in hand. At first, it looked like he was surprised to see us like he didn't recognize us or something.

"Oh, hey, what are you guys doin' here," he said.

"Just checkin' on ya," I said.

"Well, come on in, partners," he stepped from the door to let us inside. "You guys didn't have to come by. Sure you have better things on your agenda."

"Oh, it's not a problem," I said.

"We were in the neighborhood anyway," my friend said.
Stew shut the door behind us. "You guys doing okay?
Get ya something to drink or something?"
"Sure," I said.
"I can take something," Clarence said.
Stew said, "I was about to grab another beer, myself.
Guys have pretty good timing."
"We try."
The floors and walls of the place were all wood. An
ugly green couch lined one of the living room walls: the
television was on the opposite side. A few pictures were
hung beside a clock on the wall. We walked into the
small kitchen. As I quickly scanned the kitchen, I no-
ticed they didn't have a dishwasher.
"You guys don't even have a dishwasher?" I asked.
"Had one," Stew took a drag from his cigarette. "The
damn thing broke. We were gonna get it fixed, just
hadn't gotten around to it. Guess that's why I have the
little woman, right?"
"Guess so," I said.
"Have to make 'em good for something, eh?" Clarence
added. "They have to earn their stay/"
"Got that right! Sure isn't her cookin' skills, that for
sure. Bitch burns everything she makes. Hell, I end up
doin' a lot of the cookin' myself."
I said, "See, and they say a mother's supposed to teach
a daughter things like that."
"I think her mother taught her how to suck pole pretty
well. She can do some outstanding things, let me tell
ya."
I smiled. "That's sweet."
"We'll take your word for it," Clarence said.
Stew went to the fridge and got a few beers. "Man, I tell
ya, I'm glad to see you guys. You wouldn't believe the
shit rolling through my head," he handed us each a bot-

tle.

"That so?" my friend said.

"Yeah," Stew said. "I tried my best to keep calm. Guess I needed to smoke a joint or something. Those damn cops took me down to the station. Started asking all sorts of questions about it. Thought I was gonna go insane. I started to think they thought I was stupid or something, kept asking me the same thing over and over."

The three of us took a seat at the kitchen table.

Stew said, "Guys find the place okay?"

"Yeah," my friend said. "It wasn't any problem."

I said, "We grew up in the area. There's not a spot in this part of the city I don't know like the back of my hand."

"I didn't realize that."

"Yeah."

"Come to think of it, I don't know anything about you guys. I never got anything or heard anything about you guys."

"It never crossed my mind when we first contacted you."

"Oh, it's no big deal. Guys in the past just offered info when they first booked the show."

"Good to know for the future."

My friend took a drink of beer. "Thanks for the drink."

"My favorite kind of beer is the kind I don't have to buy," Stew laughed. "There's plenty of that where it came from. I have a deal worked out with my beer distributor."

"That's good."

Stew sat back and sighed. "I have to tell ya, talkin' to those cops, it didn't do much to calm my nerves. I thought I was gonna get sick from it all."

"What did you tell 'em?" I lit a cigarette.

"Man, what could I tell? I told 'em I didn't know anything. Just said a couple of guys came in and started shooting the place up... That's the only thing I could say. Told them the guys from the band split."

"They ask who killed the guys?"

"Yeah."

After a minute Clarence shrugged. "What did you say?"

"Told them I didn't know. I said that some of the customers fought back. Told them at the time I was in my office, and after I heard what was going on I ran out to see what I could do."

"And?"

"By the time I got out there, it was already over."

I let out a deep exhale of smoke. "They bought that?"

"Yeah, man," Stew smiled. "Cops are fuckin' dumb as shit. I can tell a good lie. They believed every word of it. I surprised myself. Made it sound very convincing."

"Don't underestimate anyone," Clarence said

Stew nodded. "This whole thing is fucked. Hill Top is gonna be a crime scene for the next couple of days. Until I see where this lands I dunno what to do. I put a lot of time and money into that place. Now, after this, no telling how my business is gonna be. Everything is gonna probably fall through the tubes. You spend time working towards something just to watch it go to shit. It's not right, not fair. All this for nothing. My daddy worked his whole life till the day he died. Worked his hands to the bone to give his family something he never had. I got my good work ethic from him. When he dropped dead he didn't have a dollar in his pocket. He was the type to never complain about anything. He was a good man. So, when I opened this place, I put my whole soul into it just to watch it turn to nothing. Shit's not fair... No matter how you look at it."

"The world's not fair," I told him. "The only thing you can do is hope for the best."

We sat in silence for a minute

Clarence sat back in his chair and looked around the room. "Nice place ya have here."

"Thanks," Stew said.

"It's cozy."

"I bought the place four years ago. Here, lately, Sally's been talkin' about how she wants to move. She keeps saying how she wants to be in a new place, new surroundings."

"Where would you go?" I asked.

"Conway, maybe Cabot. I have friends in both places."

"Cabot?" Clarence shrugged. "A lot of racist motherfuckers there. Dated a girl from there once. I never liked the town, though."

"Oh, I dunno, just something we've been talkin' about."

"How long have you been debating?" I asked.

Stew said, "Oh, it's been about six months, I guess."

"Well, the good thing is you still have time to decide."

"I guess," Stew said. "She gets all these plans and ideas in her head, hard for me to keep up. The best thing I can do is just to go with the flow. I can't seem to get anything across to her. Women, it's all a mystery, right? That's double when she's already off her damn rocker. When we first got together, nothing but sparks. We were on fire for each other day and night. It was pure lust at first sight. Now, not that much."

"Yeah, I caught that."

"She was a bit full."

"Understood."

"People find it hard to deal with sometimes. We stick to ourselves anymore."

"I know how that can go."

"let's go into the living room, okay?" Stew said. "It's nicer in there."

"Sure," I said.

We stood from the table and walked on the brown shag carpet to the living room. My friend and I sat on a big green couch, while Stew took a seat in a red armchair by the window.

"Where's your better half?" Clarence asked.

He chuckled. "Should be back any minute, went to the store to pick up some groceries."

Clarence looked at me, then back at Stew.

"What did she tell the cops?" I asked.

"About the same thing."

"About?"

"Yeah."

"What does that mean?"

"She had the same story I did," Stew blinked. "Of course, she was pretty upset when they kept asking questions. They had us together in the same room, then split us up. I guess they figured if we were lying, they'd find out easier that way. It shook her up pretty good," he sat back, glanced out the window, then looked back at us. "That's not what's on my mind, though."

"What's on your mind?" I asked.

"I'm startin' to freak out. How do I know we're safe? Don't wanna have to look over my shoulder every time I turn around. I need protection for my wife and me. When the bad guys find out it was my club, they're gonna come after me. I don't mess around with any of that stuff. You guys are gonna help us, right?"

"You have our word," Clarence said. "You won't have anything to worry about."

"That's a relief, thanks," Stew said. "That's a load off my mind. I don't wanna have to go into hiding because of some crazy guys. Would we have to?"

"You might. Just give us time to sort all of this out."

Stew made a fist and hit it on the arm of the chair. "Oh,

shit. Where would we go?"

"Not sure yet."

"You guys have any safe houses or anything?"

"We'll talk to the boss about it. Everything goes through him."

"Can I talk to him?"

"It's best you don't."

"By the way, I forgot to ask, how's your brother doing? Hope he's okay."

"He'll be okay," I said. "After we left the bar we took him to a doctor, patched him up. He should be as good as new before long. He's tough. Just been takin' it easy. Thanks for asking."

"And your girl, I can't tell ya how sad I am for you. That's something no one should have to deal with. The way she went out... It's a violent thing. Not sure what I'd do if someone did Sally that way. I'd probably do the same shit you did."

"Thanks," I said.

"It's the least I could do."

I said, "Bet the cops had a hell of a time cleaning that mess. No offense, but I don't think I could set foot in that place again."

"I get that."

Stew went to the kitchen for more beer. When he came back he was carrying a bucket of ice with a dozen bottles of beer in it. "In case you want more," he sat the bucket on the coffee table.

"Were you there when they took the bodies away?" Clarence asked.

Stew went over to his chair, sat down, and shook his head. "They took us to the station pretty quick. Said they had to lock down the place."

"How long they keep you guys?"

"About three hours or so."

"That's never fun."

"They had free coffee," Stew said. "Guess that's one thing to come out of this fucked-up situation."

"That's always the best kind," I said.

"I dunno, a cop made the coffee. Honestly, it could've been better."

Clarence said, "Don't they just drink that shit all day, eat donuts? That's why most of 'em are fat, it's like, 'Come on, guys, think about this for a minute. Need to be chasing more people... Lose some weight'"

"You should tell them that," Stew opened a bottle of beer. "Hell, when I was there most of those guys looked bored. And just think we pay all those guys to do a job. It made me a little pissed when I saw that."

The front door opened. Sally walked in with two paper bags full of groceries. She gave us a nod on her way to the kitchen. Stew jumped out of his chair, saying he needed to help her put stuff away. When Sally and Stew came back into the living room we talked with Sally - basically, we just asked her what we asked her husband. She told us how scared she was talking to the cops.

"I didn't get any sleep that night," she said. "They said they might be talking to us again about it."

"No need to worry," I said. "Cops like that, they like to scare honest people like you guys. It's just something in their nature."

Sally said, "They did a pretty good job at it."

"They're pigs," I said. "They like to shake people up, make you think they already know something they don't. Everything will be okay. Just stick to the story and you'll be fine."

"They shook me up good," Sally said. "I thought they were gonna lock me up for a minute."

"Cops are assholes," I said. "They rub everyone the

wrong way."

"If they would've rubbed me I was gonna have to hit 'em."

"Glad that didn't happen."

"Guess I was getting pissed."

"I can imagine."

"I don't wanna go through anything like that again. Bad enough we had to witness what we did."

I sighed. "We're still workin' on who that was."

Sally said, "You guys are gonna protect us, but, you don't know from who?"

I nodded. "That seems to be the case, yes. I wish I had all the answers you want. When we know something you'll know. We need a little more time to figure all of this out."

Stew said, "Is there anything we should do?"

"Keep a low profile," Clarence said. "Just be smart about things. Don't go out alone, stuff like that."

"We can do that," Stew cracked open another beer.

Sally said, "Sure about that, hon? You're stupid. You'll end up getting yourself fuckin' killed. You can't protect shit! You're just a dumb-fuck hillbilly."

Stew looked at his wife. "How can you say something like that? You're the one who was sleepin' with your cousin, Marv, last year. Yeah, tell that to these guys. I'm sure they'd love to know how big of a whore you are. Next thing I know, hell, you'll probably be lying with your brother. I can't have any two-headed babies runnin' around here, with six eyes and shit! When you talk that way to me, that makes me very mad. I care about you. I'm sorry I wasn't much help with this."

"You're a sorry motherfucker, you know that?"

Stew raised his voice. "Look, if you don't watch it, I'll slap you good. I don't care if they're here or not! I love you, but I don't want your shit. I got a shotgun in the back closet."

She started to choke up. "I…I…I'm sorry... It's all still shocking."

I said, "I talked to our boss about the money. He said he can get it for you."

"When?" Stew asked.

"Tomorrow."

"Thanks."

"No problem."

"What time tomorrow?"

"Around noon. We'll come and pick you guys up."

"Sounds good to me," Stew said. "We'll be able to thank him in person. He's a pretty nice guy, your boss?"

I shrugged. "He's okay."

"That's good."

Clarence said, "He may talk you into joining us."

"That'd be okay with me."

"Nah, man, you don't want any of this, trust me. It's more trouble than it's worth."

"Why do you guys do it?"

"Long story," my friend said.

I said, "Listen to the man, you don't wanna end up dead in a ditch somewhere, three bullet holes in your gut. For me, there was no other way. It was either joined or killed. I already knew too much."

"Why didn't you go to the cops?"

I shook my head. "Wasn't that easy? One of these days, maybe."

"I see," Stew said. "You'll get a hand on it one of these days," he rubbed his hand on his temple. "I was disappointed you guys couldn't finish your set. I liked the music. You guys need to stop fuckin' around with this street gang shit and fully commit yourselves."

I shook my head. "We'll take it under consideration."

Stew asked if he could catch any other shows. We explained to him due to the shooting we would have to take a break from putting on shows. He looked at us and said he understood. I could tell by the look on his face he didn't.

I looked at the clock on the wall and told Stew and Sally we had to go. Stew said he'd walk us out.

As we walked to the front door I noticed a picture on the wall I hadn't noticed before. The picture was of a young man, twenty or so, wearing a suit and tie.

I pointed at the picture. "Your son?"

Stew looked. "Nephew."

"How old?"

"He's twenty-two. He just got back from the Gulf War. He was telling us the other night about how he almost got shot."

"That so?"

"He's a brave guy, though."

"You'd have to be."

"Guess so."

"What's his name?"

"Chuck," Stew said. "Picture was taken last year."

"That's nice."

"We're proud of him."

"God bless America, right?"

"No truer words have ever been uttered. We are gonna have a big party for him this weekend. We're pretty proud of him."

"You should be."

We talked a little more.

He opened the front door and we told him to contact us if he needed anything, then, we walked to our car and got in. After he saw we were in the car Stew shut the door.

I put the key in the ignition.

"So, what do you think?" Clarence said, lighting a cigarette.

I looked ahead, beyond the windshield at the house for a minute, gave a sigh, and looked at him. "I know it needs to be done," then I turned my head and looked up the street. "Too much exposure," I looked back at Clarence. "A lot of people seem to be home."

"Then what would?"

"I have the heater with the silencer in the trunk."

"That'd work."

I slammed my head on the back of the driver's seat. "I hate this shit."

"I know."

The both of us got out and walked to the back of the car. I took my keys and unlocked the trunk, got the gun, slammed the lid down, and locked it. I stuffed the gun under my shirt. We walked back to the front door. I was about to knock on the door when it opened.

"You forget something?" Stew asked.

"You could say that," I walked inside

Clarence walked in behind me.

"What is it?" Stew asked.

When I got to the center of the room I pulled the gun and pointed it at Stew.

He raised his hands. "The fuck's this? Thought we were good, man, what's the deal?"

Before he had a chance to say anything else, I pulled the trigger, putting a bullet hole in his forehead. He fell back on the couch. I put two more bullets in his stomach. His wife came screaming from the kitchen. I turned around and put three in her head. She dropped to the floor with a loud *thud*.

I looked at Clarence. "And that's how things go, huh?"

"Pretty much."

I glanced around the room. "Before we go I think we

should take a look around. See if there's anything worth anything."

Clarence nodded. "Might as well."

We searched the house for any cash or anything. We thought it'd be better if we took it instead of the cops or any homeless that would squat. Before we left we wiped everything that we may have touched.

In the end, we walked out with a few thousand dollars and a few small bags of cocaine. Everyone can use a little extra now and again.

"We need to make another stop," I got into the car.

"What's that?" Clarence asked.

"Just remembered I needed to do a pick-up."

"Who?"

"Cigarettes."

"Oh, yeah, need those."

"You know it."

"I need to get some, too."

We pulled out of the drive and headed down the street.

On our way to the tobacco store, I couldn't help but feel a little guilty about killing Stew and Sally. I kept turning it around in my mind. I still felt bad about the situation. Joe told us it had to be done. They never deserved what happened to them.

The next day we got pulled down to the police station by a couple of portly cops. They asked a ton of questions. We kept to our story, telling them that we didn't have any idea who was responsible for the shooting.

twenty-one

After the police were able to identify everyone who got killed at Hill Top, they had the funeral. Instead of having separate services they only had one. A total of twenty people were murdered that night. I scraped together money to give Heidi a service all her own—it's the least I could've done. The clouds started to roll over the afternoon as the temperature dropped. The smell of rain was near. Most everyone was crying and weeping. I glanced over at the iron gate of the cemetery and wanted to run. A tear slowly glided down my face as I stood there.

After the service was over we stood around the cemetery talking. I was offended Joe didn't show. Even though we weren't fans of one another I would've thought he would pay his respects. Some of the other guys from the crew came to show their support. Jason came to the service. He was still sore from his injuries. Everyone wanted to honor Heidi's life.

Viggo walked over and patted me on the shoulder. "Sorry about this, Sean. She was a good person."

"She was," I said. "Thanks for coming."

"Anytime. It's all about the brotherhood. If you need anything never hesitate to say the word."

"Appreciate that."

"The least I could do."

"After we're done here we're gonna go to Jason's if you wanna come along. Have some issues we have to sort out."

"I'll be there," Viggo told me.

"Thanks."

Viggo nodded at Jason. "See you're still alive."

"I am," Jason smiled. "They're gonna have to try harder next time if they want me dead. Don't send armatures to do a professional job. This is nothing. I'll be fit in no time. It feels good to be moving around."

Viggo laughed. "Need a whole army next time, right? That's the way to be. But still, when I heard I wanted to kill those fuckers myself."

"They're dead now."

"That's what I saw in the paper. What the fuck happened over there?"

"We'll have to fill you in," William said. "It's a pretty good story if you haven't heard."

"Just know what the paper said. I gather that's not the whole story."

"It never is," Jason said. "Journalists are all full of shit."

"Got that right," Viggo said.

"It's the only way these days," Jason added.

The preacher who performed the funeral was shaking hands and hugging everyone. That old guy didn't understand a thing about how I was feeling, I thought. He didn't know how much I loved and adored Heidi. He would never know anything about me or my pain. I studied the ugly fool as he made his rounds, making small talk, trying to be a friend to us. I felt like walking over and shooting the preacher. His wrinkled face carried a look of somber as he got closer. I knew what he was going to say. When he got close to me, and opened his mouth to say something, I turned and walked away.

After we stopped at Mo's for a bite to eat, we headed to Jason's house. With everything that happened, we needed to decide what to do about it.

We filled Viggo in on what happened. He looked stocked. He told me again how sorry he was that Heidi died. He asked about the people who ran the bar. We told him that they had to be dealt with.

"My dad always warned me not to get involved in the life," Viggo said. "Now I know why. Shit like this…Nick and Max... Have a feeling a lot more people are gonna die before this is over. We could make a run till things cool down."

"That what you want?" William untied his tie.

"Not really, but I don't wanna die either."

"Don't think any of us do."

Jason walked over to the fridge. "You guys want a beer?"

He pulled a few beers and passed them around.

Jason fell onto the couch. "You know, I'm ready to shed some fuckin' blood over here. I can take whatever they have. Wherever, whenever. Fuck 'em. I could've died."

Clarence nodded at Jason. "I'm with him. Hell, we can't forget about playing music. As soon as word spreads about that, mark my words, no one will ever book us. May as well dive in this with everything we have."

I lit a cigarette. "I want revenge for Heidi. I owe her that much"

"We know," Jason said. "I got shot because of them," he pointed to the area of his belly where he got injured. "That should've never happened. I could've died. I didn't see a white light or anything, but shit... Look, I need this payback. We need to move carefully with this one. We need to get the other guys behind it."

William said, "Max, taking him out might cause another shit-storm we don't want."

"We need to plan it out," Viggo said. "These aren't your common street guys we're dealin' with. These are some tough guys."

Everyone agreed.

"No, not Max," I whispered.

"Then, who?" William said.

"Joe Butler."

As soon as I said his name everyone grew quiet and looked a me.

Viggo took a drink of beer. "Why him?"

"Because of him all this happened," I said. "If Joe would've dealt with this sooner Heidi would still be alive."

Viggo looked at me. "I don't know, I just think it's too risky."

"I'll take the risk."

"I don't want you to think I'm totally against you on this or anything. Don't you think it's a drastic measure?"

"Not the way I see it."

"Look, I'm your friend and all, but-"

"But what?"

"You really wanna start this over some girl? You could end up dead."

"I loved her, now she's gone. He didn't put the bullet in her, but he was the reason she died. He should've killed them when we told him to."

Viggo sighed. "You can count on me, no matter what. I'm your friend, and always will be."

"Thanks," I told him.

My brother looked at me and smiled. "I like the way you think, brother. We need to make that fucker burn! You know I'm with ya."

For the next few minutes, no one said anything, just the inhales and exhales of my friends as they smoked.

Viggo broke the silence. "And how do you plan to do this, just bust into his house and shoot him?"

"No," I put out the stub of my cigarette in an ashtray. "We can't have this traced back to us. We need a third party."

"Like who?" Viggo asked.

"Not sure yet. Thought we could sit around and discuss it. Any ideas? I'm not sure, we could throw some homeless guy cash to do it. We could kill him after, so he doesn't tell."

William said, "That could work. We could follow the homeless guy around, and after he kills Joe we could pop him. It'd be perfect. He'd never know anything. I can see it now. They wouldn't ever suspect us."

I shrugged at the idea. "I think we should get a professional."

"You know any of those?"

"No. You?"

"Not a clue."

Jason said, "We could reach out to someone up in Midway."

I shook my head at my brother's suggestion. "That's an idea. We'll keep that one on the list. Have to keep our options open."

"Agreed," my brother said.

William said, "How many people you know who'd do this? I mean, whoever does it, you'll have to make sure they won't ever say anything. There's a lot of trust that goes into something like this."

Clarence said, "The homeless guy doesn't sound bad to me. It could work."

"No," my brother said.

"Why?" our singer asked.

"He could still talk, and that talk could get back to certain people. We can't have that. It'd be very bad for a lot of people."

"Anything you say."

We spent the next hour or so discussing our plan to get rid of Joe.

Viggo snorted. "Okay, then, who would be boss?"

"Sal," I said. "As far as I know everyone likes him."

William said, "I can go along with that."

"I always thought he'd make a good boss," Jason said. "I was surprised he wasn't boss already. I never thought Joe had what it took."

William cracked open another beer. "You think so?"

"Don't you?" my brother said.

"I never really thought about it. It's all the same to me. Only thing I know, I don't wanna be fuckin' boss."

"Can't blame ya there."

"But, I guess, if it came down to it I would. Things would have to be fucked before I did it, though."

We laughed.

"I know some people," Viggo said. "A few guys that do this sort of thing. Contract killers, it's not cheap, though."

"Who are they?" I asked. "Call 'em up! We need to handle this."

Viggo sighed and patted my shoulder. "Sean, is this just about Heidi? I mean, this comes with risks. Sometimes it hits people connected to us."

"I know," I said. "Things are just going crazy in my mind. I can't help but think this wouldn't have even happened if Joe would've fucking listened to me. I told him we needed to deal with this before it got out of hand before anyone else died. He chose to ignore me and do nothing. He needs to pay."

Clarence said, "That's what we do then. Everyone here liked Heidi. She was a good girl. We all owe it to her to do this."

"Thanks," I shook my head.

Clarence looked at Viggo. "Make the call."

"Will do," Viggo said.

"Who's this guy?" I asked.

"There's a few of 'em. The guy I'm gonna call first, his name's Keith Wallace. When I was over in Memphis I met him at this thing one night. It was this party at a buddy's house. Think he'll be our best bet."

"Why's that?" I said.

"Because now that I think about it, I think the other guys are dead or in jail. Guess killing people for money didn't work out for them."

"That so?"

"Yeah."

"Then we need to make sure we get him before he's dead, too," my brother said. "Does Joe know this guy?"

"I don't think so," Viggo said.

"We might want to find that out. We don't need a double-cross. We need to be smart about this."

We all agreed.

William looked at me. "You ever been to Joe's house?"

"A few times," I told him. "Why?"

"No reason. I've never been. How is it?"

I shrugged. "What? I don't know. I guess it's about the same as anywhere else, you know? Nothing special about it."

"Oh."

"Yeah."

"Should we bring Sal or anyone else in on the plan?" William asked.

"No," I said. "Too risky. We can't let anyone outside this room know what's going on. I think we shouldn't even tell this Keith guy the whole story. Just let him know the target. Shit could blow up in our faces if we aren't careful."

The other guys shook their heads.

I continued. "We need to do this fast. The sooner, the better."

Jason said, "And because of that dumb fuck we're gonna have to give up the music. What a sorry motherfucker. I guess he got what he always wanted."

I shook my head. "He's never liked the idea of it."

"You don't think what happened will hurt us? It was in all the papers. How do you expect to beat press like that?"

I shrugged. "We can't."

"Then, what?"

"As far as people know it was just some random act. Those people won't ever find out the truth."

"Sure about that?"

"Not sure of anything anymore," I muttered. "If anything we can get the public behind us."

My brother looked at me and wrinkled his face. "How do we sell that?"

"Self-defense."

My brother raised his brow. "Interesting. That could work. If people start to ask, just tell them we had to beat 'em off. Wasn't our fault. We just didn't wanna die."

"Exactly," I said, as I looked around the room. "If any cops ask any of you about what happened, that's what you say."

Everyone understood.

Jason looked at Viggo. "You trust Keith?"

"Yeah. I've known him for awhile," Viggo said. "We'll be able to trust him. He won't say anything. He's a pretty nice guy."

"Okay, make the call," Jason told him.

"Will do," Viggo said. "He'll be glad to hear from me."

"Really?"

"Yeah," Viggo said. "He always liked me. The first time I shot someone I was with him."

"How'd that happen?"

Viggo's eyes lowered a little. "It was a drunken night. We'd been to a few bars that night before we hit this one. This guy, can't even remember what his name was, mouthed off to me too many times. We'd been shootin' pool. He got mad because I beat him at a few games. He and his friend who was with him waited for Keith and me in the parking lot. They jumped us and we fought them off. We leave, driving down the road, and their car shows up behind us. They ram our ass-end a few times till we can't get away. They pulled up beside us and showed us they had guns. When we saw that I told Keith to take the wheel. I pulled my gun out and got three shots in. Their car veers off the road and goes into a deep ditch. Keith stopped the car. We got out and walked over to the ditch. We had to walk down to where the front of the car was. I opened the door, saw they were both still alive, and fired two more shots at both of 'em. Once we saw both the guys were dead we left."

"Damn," my brother said. "Anyone see you?"

"Nah, that was the good thing. The whole time I was worried someone would come by. No one ever came down the street."

"You're lucky," Jason said.

"I know," Viggo agreed.

"If it was me," Jason continued, "someone else would've come along. I would've had to kill more before the night was over"

Clarence laughed. "I'm afraid that would be the case for me, too."

"You can put me in that club," William said.

twenty-two

Two days later, I was lying in my bed when the phone rang. I lay in my bed and let the phone ring four times before I staggered out of my bed into the kitchen. On my way to the phone, I stuffed a cigarette in my mouth. My head was killing me from the night before. Too much booze, I thought. I had the thought of killing whoever was on the other end of the line.

I picked the phone up. "This better be important."

"Well, hello to you," Viggo's voice came through.

"Nice way to answer a call, prick."

"I've heard that before."

"Sure about that?"

"Fuck off!"

"Funny," he said. "You sound tired."

"I am."

A laugh. "You know it's past noon?"

"Shit?"

"Yeah."

"Thought it was like eight or something."

"Long past that."

"That's what I guessed," I said. "Yeah, I had a night last night."

"Sounds like it."

"Yeah," I said. "You should've joined us."

"What, you guys go out with Jack?"

"At his place."

"Yeah."

"What were you doing?"

"Last night?"

"Yeah."

"I got me some of that sweet lovin' last night, you know what I mean?"

"Yes, I do."

"That's what I should've been doing."

"Don't you still have that free pass?"

"Yeah, but she had to work late. I went there. Said she had a headache and wanted to sleep."

"Better hope that's what it was."

"Fucker," I muttered.

He laughed. "Nah, I was just kidding."

Holding the phone with one hand, I rifle through a cabinet for some pills. My head was killing me. Too bad I was all out of cocaine, I thought. It was uncommon for me to not have a bag of powder.

"So, don't keep me in suspense, whaddya want?" I asked.

There was a small pause, and then. "We need to have a chat. I talked to the guy."

"And?"

"We need to talk."

"Where at?"

"My place," he said. "The other guys are here."

"Need me to bring anything?"

"Beer."

"How much?"

"How much money do you have?"

"I have enough."

"A case should be good."

"Be there in about an hour or so."

"We'll be waiting."

I hung the phone up and walked to the bathroom to shower. After getting ready I got in my car and sped away to Riverside Liquor, about ten minutes from Viggo's house. I got two cases of beer and some whiskey. Luckily, there was a tobacco store across the street, so, I walked in and got my smokes.

Viggo had a small brick affair at the end of a long narrow road. Every time I had gone to his house in the past, a girl who lived across the street would always flirt with me; this time, that wasn't the case. The girl's name was July. Her house was for sale and empty.

Viggo's door was unlocked so I walked in. After I chatted for a bit, I went back out to my car to get the alcohol.

I popped the trunk of my car, took out the beer, and slammed the lip shut hard. I was walking to the house with the cases I realized I didn't bring enough money to gamble with: I knew they were gonna be doing that later. That was always the case when we got together, always drinking and gambling. You'd win some, lose some. Money would go back and forth between us.

I put the cases of beer on the table. "What happened to July?"

Viggo grinned. "She moved a few weeks ago."

"Where to?"

"She got a new job on the other side of Brown Ridge. Some little store, don't remember the name."

I nodded. "Guess I'll have to make a trip over the bridge."

"Go for it! When you go over there, though, try not to get shot. Certain people over there don't like us that well."

"Yeah."

"That piece of pussy might get you dead."

"Good point."

"It happens from time to time."

"I think I'll be okay."

"You better," Viggo said. "We don't need any of that noise floating over."

"One of us might get shot."

"Yeah, they might."

"Maybe not, then."

"Hey, you can always take your chances."

"She was always a little firecracker, that one."

He looked at me and laughed. "Oh, man, she was. Always questioned why she didn't have a guy. Lord knows she could get any guy she wanted."

"You can never tell about women like that."

A few hours passed with us talking and playing cards. I asked Jason if I could borrow the cash to play with. I lost it all.

After the game we sat around talking more, joking with one another like school kids.

"I talked to the guy," Viggo said. "Called him from a payphone. Said he wouldn't have a problem doing it. The only thing is, he wants fifty grand."

"Fifty grand?" I said. "Isn't that a little high? You usually pay that amount for something like that, do ya?"

"Maybe," Viggo said.

"When do we need it by?"

"A few days. He was telling me he wouldn't do anything until he had the money, and he didn't wanna waste his time with amateurs. He's been doing this for some time. The guy is a pro."

William asked, "How are we gonna get the money?"

"We don't have that kind of cash," Jason said. "We'll have to figure something out. Any ideas? Steal something, maybe?"

I nodded to Viggo. "We might need more time to put something together. Sorry, I don't have any good ideas right now."

Viggo sat back in his chair, stared at the ceiling for a minute, then back at us. "I have an idea."

"You do?" I said.

"Yeah."

"What is it?"

"It might be a little risky, but it's something. How would you guys feel about knocking off a bank?"

No one said anything for a minute.

Jason finally said, "I can go along with that, sure. What bank were you thinking about? I'm sure you have one in mind or you wouldn't have suggested it. Those damn places, they can afford to spread around the wealth."

"First Sign Arkansas, the one over the river."

"I'm not sure about that," William said. "We'll end up in prison. Cops don't fuck around with that shit."

"Not if we're careful," our host said.

"Need to make sure we have a getaway car," my brother said.

"That'd probably be good," Viggo added.

At first, when he brought up the bank I couldn't believe my ears. As I was sitting there thinking about it, the danger factor was the first thing that flashed in my mind. I'd never been on a bank job in my life. I knew it was risky. I knew people who had been busted for bank robbery. We had five guys from our crew in prison for bank jobs.

"You Fuckin' crazy?" William said. "We don't rob banks. That's not what we do. Look at how many guys we know who've been pinched for that shit."

"I've thought about that," Viggo said. "If you guys have anything better, I'm all ears."

"I can't think of anything, really," William said.

"A bank," Clarence said, "that sounds fun. One thing, need to make sure no one gets hurt in this thing. Don't need bloodshed."

"I couldn't agree more."

As the day grew to night, we sat around Viggo's kitchen table hatching out a plan that could work. At one point, William suggested we hire guys to do the robbery.

Shootin' Noise

We decided against it.

The next day, we drove out to where the bank was to
check it out. We got there a little after noon. We parked
in a lot across the street from the bank. The parking lot
of the bank was spars. We took a vote and Jason was
elected to go in and check things out. At twelve-forty,
we saw a cop car circle the block, then leave. Jason returned to where we were about fifteen minutes later. A
different cop car came by around one-thirty. After he
was done circling the block, the officer stopped at a café
down the street.

"It's good, boys," Jason said. "Should be a sweet bit of
work."

We sat a little while longer watching the area.

After some more time, we sped away.

We got back to Viggo's place and piled into the living
room.

"How many people are in the bank?" Viggo asked.

"About fifteen, including me," Jason said.

"How many of those were employees?"

"Three tellers, bank manager, and a guy doin' loans and
shit."

"Loans? See, and they say what we do is illegal.
They're the biggest loan sharks out there. They charge
interest just like us. I've never fully understood what this
separation was all about. The way I see it, they all
should be thrown behind bars," he lit a cigarette. "Anyway, now what about security?"

Jason shook his head. "Not when I was in there, no. I
did see two cameras, though."

"Doesn't surprise me."

"Need to have enough guys to cover the doors on the
other side."

"I'm not sure that'll be a big problem."

"You think?"

Viggo shook his head. "Nah, the lobby isn't that big. I'm sure we can cover it."

"What about on the outside, any cops roll by?" Jason asked.

"They were half an hour apart."

"That close?"

"It'll be okay. Don't worry. It's easy. We're gonna be fast. Just have to make sure we get out before those pigs see us."

"The bank's gonna call it in."

"We're gonna be long gone by then. I already have all the gloves and masks."

"Sounds good."

Viggo unfolded himself from his chair and started to walk around the room. "Now that this is a real thing, I need to know you guys all wanna go through with this. If not, you don't have to go. No one will think any less of you. For me, I'm doing this because I'm loyal to Sean. His girl got killed. He feels like he was done wrong by Joe. His inaction was action as far as I'm concerned."

No one said anything.

"Good," Viggo said. "I'm sure Sean appreciates your support and loyalty."

"When are we gonna do it?" William asked.

"Tomorrow morning. We need a car or truck. We'll torch it after we're done. Ya know, now that I think of it a van might be better. Yeah, when you guys go boost something make sure it's a van. It'll work better."

"No problem."

Clarence said, "Sure this is the best idea we have?"

"We do," I said. "If you'd feel better about it, you can be the driver, Clarence."

"Sure, I'll get behind the wheel."

"We need a reliable driver."

"You can count on me," Clarence nodded. "I've never had a wreck."

"Never?" Viggo said. "What about the time that truck ran you off the road and you flipped on the side?"

"Doesn't count."

"Why doesn't it?"

"'Cause we were shootin' guns at each other. It wasn't my fault."

"Not your fault? You killed the guy's girl."

"Better her than me."

"I guess."

Clarence waved off that comment. "She had what was coming to her."

I took William in my car and drove about twenty minutes to Brewston where a parking lot was. This particular lot was used by people who wanted to leave their vehicles for days at a time. The whole time we were driving to Brewston I kept thinking what we would do if they didn't have a van. Luckily, for us, there were four: two red, a black one, and a tan one. We put our target on the black one.

I looked at William. "Still know how to hot-wire or do you need me to do it?"

"No," he said. "I still know how to do it. Some things you'll never forget."

"Okay, well, I'll wait here till you get the van started."

He looked at me. "The sooner, the better, right?"

He got out of the car and ran over to the black van. He popped the door open and crawled in. The whole time I was looking out the window to make sure no one was coming. About ten minutes later the engine turned on. William rolled down the window and gave a nod.

We pulled into Viggo's drive.

William drove the van into the garage.

That night we stayed up and played cards.

twenty-three

As soon as the sun rolled across the sky the next morning we got ready. We left the house at eight. I'd never committed a bank robbery before.

As with every morning, everyone in the city was making the morning commute - zooming cars and roaring trucks passed. We started across the bridge to the. As we made it to the other side I looked out the window at the water, and I saw a small boat moving slowly to somewhere, somewhere beyond what could be seen. For a moment I thought it would be nice to get in a boat like that and float away—maybe in another life, I thought. I lit a cigarette and leaned against the window. When we first planned this little heist we were gonna go in the afternoon. But after some debate, we thought it best to do it first thing in the morning. I mean, hell, we were gonna give those people a heart attack.

"Ready for this?" Clarence came from the front of the van.

"Let's just get this over with," I said. "Sooner-the-fucking-better."

"I agree," Jason said, as he took out a little bag of white powder. "I brought some candy. Thought we might need something to get right before the shit."

"Let me have some," I said.

Jason handed me the bag and a straw.

I took three long snorts.

Clarence said, "We're going to a fuckin' robbery. You guys are gonna get pinch for a little snow?"

"Calm down," I said. "We'll be able to get the job done.

No problem."

"You better."

"It's not like we're gonna get fucked outta our minds or anything."

"I want some," William waved his arms wildly in the air.

"Some quality stuff there," I handed William the bag. "Speed-o, Speed, speed, that's the name of the game. Shit will start now, start now. You can be anyone."

William vacuumed some. "Hey, that's good! I need to get some more of this, more of this white goddess," he rubbed his index finger on his left nostril and cleared his passage. "I can go like a fast motherfucker on more of that. More is best. Why don't we blow this gig and score some more pleasure powder?"

"After the job," my brother said. "We need to make sure everything goes okay."

"If everything goes alright?" William asked.

"Cops might very well be hot on our tail. I just hope this rust bucket will be able to outrun them."

"I can't go to jail," William ran his hand through his hair. "I'm too young. You know what they do to good-lookin' guys like me in those places?"

"At least you'll get laid," came our driver.

"Sure, sure. I hear you loud and clear, buddy. Is that all you guys have? You know, you guys always talk the same shit about me. What about coming up with some new fuckin' material? Keep ragin' the same shit over and over."

Viggo said, "Oh, Willy, we love you. If you were a woman I'd marry ya."

"That's okay. No need to go that far with it."

"Hey, that's my final offer," the voice from the driver's seat said.

William shrugged. "I just know I'm not gonna be anyone's bitch on the inside. They'll have to beat me. I'm not suckin' anyone's big hair dick."

"You never know, Willy," Jason grabbed the baggy

We laughed.

We continued to talk as we passed the cocaine around.

Viggo said, "You know what? I was sitting at home the other day going through my video tapes, just lookin' for something to watch when I discovered I didn't have my copy of *Return of the Jedi*."

"What happened to it?" Clarence asked as he zoomed us down a street.

"Not sure. Think I let someone borrow it. Wish I could remember who."

"Yeah, you might wanna track that one down."

"I need to. You know, the other two are there. Would've thought I had it with them."

"Unless it's at someone's house," William said. "I have all three at my place."

"Well, isn't that special," Viggo barked.

"Just sayin' you can borrow it."

"I'm good."

"I'm just-"

"I know, I know, you're just sayin' shit. Yeah, sure I can borrow it, it doesn't help my problem. I need mine back."

"Damn, son!"

"That's right. I'm sure you can sympathize."

"Seems to me, that a true fan would always know where all of his *Star Wars* movies are."

"Shit," Viggo turned to the back seat. "If I remember right, I turned you on to the trilogy. Don't tell me how that goes."

Jason chimed in. "Have to agree with Will on this."

"Well, he has no clue what the shit he's talkin' about," Viggo replied. "You know, now that I think of it, that

Lisa girl was over one night."

I said, "I'll never forget the first time I saw the first one. It was a Saturday night. I was three and it came on TV. It was great. We used to have all the action figures."

William said, "They say all those toys are worth money now."

"I know," I said. "I just wished we would've kept them."

"You and me both," my brother added. "We could be rich right now."

"Hell, you know there's always a market for that stuff. Some comic shop would pay a ton for those toys."

"Right about that," I agreed.

William said, "I lost count of how many I had."

"Think we all did along the way," I glanced at the time on my watch. "The thing about it, is you have to find someone who'll pay what the stuff's worth. I mean, hell, they can say what they want, 'Hey, yeah, I know they say so-and-so is worth this much, but I only have a certain amount - so, that'll have to do. Sorry. Take it or get fucked'"

"Never thought about that. Guess that'd suck if you didn't get the money you wanted."

"Nothing is guaranteed."

William laughed. "The grand mystery of it all, right?"

"Something like that."

Clarence took a right and headed down a street called Dotson. At the end of the street, he turned the wheel onto Eltwood. We pulled into the parking lot across from the bank. He killed the engine. We looked across the street at the bank. At that time in the morning, people were coming and going from the building.

I was a little nervous.

My stomach started to swirl.

I lit another cigarette. "I should've brought a bottle of

something. Think I'm gonna get sick."

"You'll be okay," my brother said. "Try not to think about it. This'll be over before you know it."

"Thanks," I said. "Hope everything goes as planned."

"We got your back," Jason took out his gun. "I have my buddy to get mine."

I let out a little laugh.

"You wanna go now or what?" Viggo asked.

"Sure," I said. "I need another snort before we go, though."

My brother gave me the baggy of cocaine and the straw. I took two long snorts. I raised my head from the baggy and instantly felt the loud rush.

"We have to go now," I said. "Just need to get this over with."

"Yeah," my brother said.

"Maybe we should've done a practice robbery."

Viggo said, "Okay, Clarence, if you leave without us we're gonna hunt you down and chop your fucking dick off. You'll be a fuckin' dead man."

The driver nodded. "Don't have to worry about me."

We flipped on our black masks and gloves, grabbed our shotguns, and broke out of the van. We ran across the street straight through the double doors of the bank. As soon as we got into the lobby we raised our guns, letting everyone know what the situation was.

I fired into the air. "Okay, listen, do what we say and nobody gets hurt!" I yelled. "We're here for the money! We don't wanna hurt anyone."

Jason and I walked to the counter, guns trained on the three tellers. William and Viggo were turned the opposite way behind us. They had their heaters pointed at the customers and the loan officer. You could see the fear in their eyes - sweat trickled down their faces. They stood frozen, looking at us.

"No one wants to be a hero here. If the manager doesn't show, we'll kill all of you," I said. "Come on, now, let's all play nice. Do everyone a favor. You make these people's day worse if you don't show yourself."

One teller, a dumpy hairy guy said, "O-o-o-okay, don't do anything rash. We'll do what you want. We don't want any trouble."

"That's what I like to hear. See, you play by the rules, everything will be okay."

The teller started to sweat. "Take what you want."

A couple seconds later a door beside the counter opened and a guy wearing a white shirt and tie stepped out with his hands up. "I'm the manager."

"Why didn't you come out sooner?"

"I dunno."

"Sure you do."

"Fine. I...I...I was scared. Please don't hurt us. I have a wife and two kids. Take what you want. No one wants anything to happen. All of these people have people who love 'em."

I tilled my head and frowned at him. "sorry about that. I'm sure we'll be outta here soon. We just want the money."

"What is this?" the manager said.

"You know what the fuck this is."

"Why?"

I pointed my shotgun at him. "Don't worry about it. You do what you're told, and no one will get hurt. I don't wanna have to use this," I waved the gun. "You'll be able to go home to your family. That's a good thing."

"You have my word," the manager said.

"What's your name?"

"Jim."

"Jim what?"

"Jim Cross."

"Okay, Jim Cross, tell the tellers over there to empty their cash."

The manager looked over at the tellers. "Give him what he wants."

The people Viggo and William were watching started to yell.

My brother turned to them. "Shut-up! We aren't gonna kill ya or anything."

William said to Jason. "They don't know that."

Jason said, "I just told them. Hey, why wouldn't they trust me?" he looked over at them. "Just because I have a gun you guys should trust me."

William said to them. "We're just a bunch of fun lovin' guys."

That seemed to calm the people.

The tellers went into their drawers and flung all the money on the counter. They acted as if we were going to shoot them at any moment. I told them to put the money in bags. After they gave us the bags I shoved the shotgun in Jim's face and told him to unlock the vault. I followed him back to the vault and told him to open it. He hesitated at first.

"Listen, that's not your cash," I told him. "You don't have to protect it. This place is insured, you're not. Do what you're fuckin' told, or I'll splatter you all over this place," I glanced at the gun, then back at him. "Had shot anything in awhile, think I should start with you?"

He nodded, then, did the combination to unlock the safe.

I'd never been in a safe.

"Please, please, don't hurt me," Jim pleaded.

"Sounds like a Country song," I laughed.

Inside the steel construction, there were tall stacks of money against the walls and in the center. My eyes grew big when I saw all that dough. I'd never seen that much in one place before.

"That's a lot," I said.

"It is," Jim looked at me.

"Good thing for you, we won't be taking all of it."

"Why not?"

"Too much."

"Maybe buy you some good faith with the cops when they arrest you."

I held up my finger. "See, that won't happen."

"You sure about that?"

I yelled for Jason and William to help me collect the loot.

Viggo stayed with the customers and tellers. After we got the money packed we took Jim back out to the lobby. We only took the money we needed to pay for Keith, and we took an extra two hundred grand for the hell of it. I still had bills and things to pay. The only time I got any cash was when Joe had me do a job, or when the band got paid for a gig. I had some money on the street. Compared to the other guys in the crew I didn't make much money. One of the guys told me that I needed to put more money on the streets. I was trying to get out of the life of crime.

"Everyone get on the floor!" Viggo yelled.

Everyone did as told except the bank manager.

I walked over to him. "He said get down on the floor."

"No."

"What?"

"You got want you want, just leave."

I hit Jim with my fist.

He dropped to the floor.

Blood started to fill his mouth.

I said, "See what happened, you fuck? I didn't wanna do it, but you gave me no choice." I looked up at the others in the bank. "Guy thinks he can manage every situation," I pointed at him lying on the floor. "That's what happens when people don't listen."

William, somewhere behind me called out. "We need to leave, don't have time for this."

I said, "Okay, people, we're gonna leave you. All of you made this a fine robbery. Glad none of you got hurt. Maybe we can do it again sometime, eh?"

"You sicko... Won't get away with this," the manager said, as he crawled back to his feet. "You'll be sorry."

"We'll keep that in mind," William shrugged.

"You guys are gonna get locked up," Jim said. "The cops should throw all of you scum in jail, toss the key in the river."

"That right?" Jason walked over to Jim. "Saying things like that makes men get lost."

The manager's eyes got wide. "I was trying to make a point."

"Well, keep it to yourself."

"Point taken."

Jason said to Jim. "You're a good guy. Keep up the hard work."

We got the bags of money and walked toward the door.

William raised his gun and squeezed off three shots in the air.

A few chunks of ceiling fell around us.

I turned to him. "What was that?"

"For effect."

"Effect?"

"Yeah, it worked, didn't it?"

"Not really."

He said, "Hey, man, you know, you try your best. Sometimes it's not my finest hour."

I laughed. "If you say so."

Jason said, "You guys crack me up."

"Thanks," William blurted.

Shootin' Noise

We ran out.

Out in the van, when we all got inside, Clarence hit the gas and we sped away.

When we were almost to the bridge police sirens rang out in the distance. I figured someone called in the robbery. The manager of the bank, I thought. After we left he must've called them. I turned in my seat, looked out the back window, and saw the faint image of a cop car. We had a good three miles to get to the other side. I was sure we could lose them as soon as we got to the other side. As soon as the bridge folds out to the road, there's a street to the left you can take that goes down a curvy hill, and then, you can blast your way down a two-mile stretch of nothing.

"I take it things went as planned?" our driver asked.

"They did," I said. "Had to get a little rough with the manager. he tried to pull some cowboy bullshit."

"Hate when that happens."

Viggo said, "We got what we wanted. No one got shot. Think things went pretty good."

I looked out the back window again. "We seemed to have lost them. They might have called ahead, set up a roadblock."

"Nah, man, they wouldn't do that," William said. "I'd think something like that would take too long. Those cops back there would've had to contact the cops over here, and set everything up."

"Wouldn't be too sure about that," Jason said

"Oh, well, what the fuck do I know? I look like a cop. I mean, I like donuts more than the next guy, but... I love bacon."

I laughed. "It is good stuff."

Viggo looked out the window. then back at us. "I got it!"

"Got what?" my brother said.

"The video."

"Oh, you finally think of who stole it?"

"When we were in the bank I kept turning it over in my head, trying to figure it out."

"And?"

"And I never owned it," he laughed. "I'd rented it a few times. Guess I got it mixed up. The hell knows what I was thinking."

"Not sure either."

"Here I was gonna blame that girl for taking it."

"Good, you got to the bottom of that one."

"I should go out and buy a copy. After all, all true fans have to own 'em all."

"Indeed."

The other guys verbally bashed Viggo for this for a bit.

When we got back to Viggo's house we got high and relaxed. I felt good about what I did, after all, it was for a good cause. A day didn't go by that I didn't think about Heidi.

After it was dark we went to one of Joe's protected dumps and torched the van.

Our work, the robbery, hit the news and papers the next day.

twenty-four

A day later we were back at Viggo's waiting for Keith to show. He was coming in from Memphis. We didn't know what to expect. I had this gnawing feeling that he would turn down the job. About an hour passed when we heard a car pull into the driveway. I looked outside and saw a black Mustang. An older man dressed in black slugged out. He looked at the number on the mailbox, then back at the house and shook his head. He walked up the drive and knocked on the door. Viggo let him in.

Viggo shook the man's hand. "How's it going, man."

"Can't complain. Had a pretty good drive down here," Keith said. "Glad I got the house right. I didn't even have to call for directions."

Viggo laughed. "That's good, buddy. I was sort of wondering about that. We know you're not losing your mind."

The man pointed his finger at Viggo. "Better watch it with that shit. I may be old but not that old. I can still kick your ass."

"Keith, you're breakin' my heart."

"Yeah, there ya go, going all cute."

Viggo smiled big. "That's what I do best."

"Nice one."

My friend laughed.

Keith looked at his watch, then at Viggo. "Made pretty good time. Only had to stop three times. I'd made a few sandwiches to bring along and brought some soda. If I had been thinking I would've brought some full gas cans with me. would've just put in the gas on the side of the road."

"That all? The last time I went up there I took five breaks. Hey, that's pretty good about the gas thing. I might have to do that next time."

Keith said, "You need to stop moving, buddy. You trade houses like boys in a schoolyard trade ball cards."

"I plan to stick around here awhile."

"Good," the man said.

Viggo introduced Keith around the room.

We sat at the kitchen table. Keith had a Vandyke with small patches of gray in it. His face had a few wrinkles. He looked like a man that had seen a lot in his time. Keith looked like a good guy. But he also looked like a guy who wouldn't give it a second thought to kill you if he had to.

"Good to meet you guys," Keith said. "You can never know too many people, that's what I always say," he looked at my brother.

Viggo put on a pot of coffee, then came back to the table.

"Thought you were gonna be here sooner?" Viggo asked the older man.

"Had some loose ends I had to tie before I left. I wanted to be here sooner, believe me."

"How'd that go?"

"Oh, you know how things go. We got it resolved. It's not perfect, but what is?"

Viggo shook his head. "I understand that."

"I'm gonna relocate here."

"When?" Viggo asked.

"Lookin' at a place later."

"What about until then?"

"Figured a motel would do."

"I can't have that," Viggo said. "You can stay with me. Have a spare room in back you can use."

"Sure 'bout that?"

"Of course."

"I wouldn't wanna put you out."

"No problem."

"If you insist."

"I do."

"Thanks."

"Can't have you staggering around homeless."

"Appreciate that."

"Don't mention it."

I said, "Why the move?"

Keith cleared his throat. "A change. The old woman split about six months ago, bodies fallin' around me. I figured it was a good time to move on. A friend of mine lives in town, and he was saying how this was a good place. When Viggo called, I thought it was a sign I should be here. Hope for the best, right?"

"Why'd Tammy leave?" Viggo asked.

"Said she couldn't stand me anymore."

"Really?"

"You believe that shit?"

"Crazy."

"Tell me about it," Keith said. "Hell, I dunno, it might be all my fault. She said I liked the bottle too much. Half the time she was bat-shit crazy. We'd been on bad terms for awhile. Guess it just got to the breaking point. I'm too old to settle with another broad, too old to date any-one."

"Somebody else may come along."

"Somehow I doubt that. I'm an old bastard, plain and simple. No gal wants any of that action. I have a past to face."

"I don't know about that," Viggo said. "We could always take you to Jo-Jo's across town for a tug."

"Or one of the girls at Highlife," I added. "We could introduce you to Smooth."

"Who's Smooth?" Keith asked.

"A whore we know," I told him.

"Thanks, but no," Keith grinned. "My dick might fall off if one of those dirty girls touched it. I surely don't want that shit."

"There are a lot more whores over there," I said. "You can take your pick. I can tell you from experience, they fuck like champs."

"I don't want any whores…had my fair share of that over the years. Hell, Tammy was one. That girl, she could fuck all day and night. The night we met, I'd only known her twenty minutes before she and I were naked."

"What's her number?" I smiled

Keith grinned. "If you want her, be my guest. She's quite the handful. Don't be surprised if she goes crazy on you."

"I can handle the crazy kind."

"You sure about that?" Keith asked.

"Don't have to worry about me. In my experience, all girls are a little fucked in the head."

William looked at me, hit me in the arm, then looked at Keith. "He needs a new girl. But if he doesn't want her I'll take her."

Keith looked amused by us like we were all old friends or something.

"It's true," I said. "I don't think I'm ready to get back into that stuff yet. That shit, man, it still hurts."

William said, "I get it."

"We're all sorry about that," Clarence said.

"It's okay," I said. "It wasn't your fault."

William leaned back in his chair, lacing his fingers behind his head. "There's always that one girl…that one at Highlife…what's her name?"

"Which one?" I asked.

"Umm... It'll come to me in a bit. I don't remember."

"You mean Madison?"

He raised a brow. "That's right. That girl, she's a fine piece of meat."

"How would you know, you sleep with her?"

"Nothing like that, I was just saying.'"

I said, "Well, shut the fuck up about it then. You don't know what the fuck you're talkin' about."

"Hey, man, cool down. I was just kiddin' with ya. Don't start actin' like a little dick, man."

"If you have to know, yes, we went out a few times. Yes, and all those times we slept together. She's a good girl."

"She has a sister?"

"No."

"Just my luck. Well, she hangs outs with those other whores up there. There's a chance."

I shook my head. "Madison's not like those other girls. She's better than them. She seems to have a good head on her shoulders. She's not crazy," I smiled. "That's not to say I'd ever back down from a challenge."

"If I could have all the pretty girls on Earth I would. I wouldn't deny beautiful ladies."

I laugh. "Deny them of that small dick of yours, huh?"

"Fuck you, you're the one with the small prick around here," William replied. "Anyway, even if I do have a little one I can still eat pussy. Every woman in the world loves a guy who can do that."

"Oh, yeah!" I agreed.

William shifted in his chair "You know that girl down at the club, the one with the blue panties?

"That can be a lot of girls up there."

"The one who takes the blue panties off during her dance? Sarah something... Blonde hair, nice tits. Never caught a last name."

I held my finger out in the air and turned it in circles.

"Okay, okay, what about her?"

"The other night I walked her out to her car in the back, and after we talked for a few minutes we got in her car. Next thing I know she pulls me on top of her. We start makin' out like crazy and I went down on her. I licked her dry. She was so sweet!"

"You guys fuck?"

"No."

"No?"

"That's right."

"Why?"

A shrug. "Thought she wanted to. After I licked her she pulled her panties up, and said I needed to go."

"She didn't even give you any head?" Clarence asked.

William shook his head. "No."

"Give ya a tug?"

"Nope."

"What was that?" Clarence howled. "She didn't even do anything for you? Man, that's a tough one. Don't think I would've admitted that to anyone. You should watch what you tell people."

"I dunno why she pulled the plug on everything," William said. "I thought she liked what I was doing to her."

"Guess she didn't."

"Yeah."

"Know what it could've been?"

"No idea."

Viggo said, "Maybe she remembered she had to go fuck some other guy. That girl, Sarah, she's a strange one. I've talked to her a few times. Trust me, you don't wanna get too involved with that mess."

"Why wouldn't I?" William asked.

Viggo said, "She was telling me about how she likes women."

"Lesbian?" William smiled.

"Something like that."

William lit a cigarette. "Fuckin' women!"

"Pretty much."

Keith busted out with laughter. "You guys are funny. Something tells me we're gonna become good friends. It's an important thing to have good people on your side in this line of work. There's a certain element of trust you have to have."

"That's what it's all about," Jason said. "We just love having a good time, no one can take that away from us. We welcome all. Good to hear you're gonna stick around. Good guys are hard to find. I gotta tell ya, it gets dangerous around here sometimes. People drop dead around here all the time."

"They don't know me yet," Keith grinned. "I'd like it to stay low-key for right now. I'm not looking to step on toes. I don't even know who runs things here."

"You don't wanna know," William said.

"I have to say, it'd be nice to know," Keith ran his finger through the lower part of his mustache. "Think my ways may catch up with me."

"That bad, huh?"

"I've had my moments."

"Could see where that'd come in handy."

"That's why I'm here."

The aroma of coffee flowed from the kitchen.

Viggo got up from the table and went into the kitchen. A few minutes later we came back to the table carrying a tray with a few cups filled with coffee. After he passed around the cups, he went back to the kitchen and came back with two small bowls: one filled with sugar, the other with dry creamer.

"Thanks, Viggo," Keith said. "What a fine host."

"The least I can do," Viggo sat down. "Anything for friends."

"Thanks."

William said, "I was thinking the same thing."

"Yeah," my brother said.

Clarence took a drink of coffee. "It's nice."

Viggo stood again and went to the kitchen, asking if we needed anything. We all told him we didn't. He came back to the table a few minutes later, sat down again, and lit a cigarette. We spent the next hour or so getting to know Keith, trading stories about this and that. We wanted to make sure we were hiring the right guy, a guy who'd never talk.

Viggo said, "Wanna get down to business?"

"Sure," Keith said, "Might as well get to it. That's why I'm here, right? Viggo didn't tell me much, and frankly, I don't care. I've learned long ago not to ask too many questions. If you want me to know everything, I'm sure you'll tell me. You need someone to do your dirty work for you, someone who's not too close. I don't mind, it's what I do. I've been doing this for a long time."

Jason looked at Keith. "Well?"

"Well," Keith said. "I was thinking about this on the way up here, and I'm willing to cut my price in half. Usually, it's half now, half later; but, I'm willing to take the cut. I figured with me moving here we'd most likely do future business. I like you guys - that goes far in these things. You need friends in this world. You guys seem trustworthy. If you're okay with Viggo that's good enough for me."

"How much?" my brother asked.

"Twenty Thousand."

The room grew quiet, and then Jason opened his mouth. "Well, everything can be negotiated, right?"

Keith sighed. "Guess so."

"We can do that," Jason said.

"Good" Keith took a drink of coffee.

"That was fast," I said. "At first I thought this was gonna be a hard thing to pull together. Thought we'd be discussing money for a few hours."

"How do you mean?" Keith said.

I thought about that for a minute. "We've never really hired anyone like you before. You know, the guy that does this type of thing."

The hitman took out a cigar from his shirt pocket, put it to his mouth, and lit it. "I'm flexible. Understandably, things come up. Never know what the day will bring. I'm looking forward to being here."

"You shouldn't step on any toes out here," Viggo said. "You'll learn a few things out here, I'm sure. Were you wanting to start a little business out here?"

A cloud of smoke came from Keith. "It's what I do. Over the years I've developed a nice set of skills. The thing is, you have to keep your eyes and ears open. It's all about getting that fresh start, right?"

I shook my head. "I know what you mean. Over the past year or so I learned a lot from the tough guys around here."

"Good. Things are, though, you have to know when your time's running out. You don't wanna find yourself in a ditch somewhere. Things heated up at home, so, that's why I'm here. I got myself into something that almost cost my life."

"What was it?" I asked.

Keith eyed me. "You don't wanna hear about that. Shit might give you nightmares."

"I can handle it."

"I don't wanna get into it now. Maybe later."

"Fair enough."

Again, the owner of the house stood and asked if we needed anything. We told him we didn't and he disappeared into the kitchen. He came back and told us he put on some more coffee. When he sat back down we continued talking.

"Who's the guy?" Keith asked.

I sat back in my chair. "His name's Joe Butler, our boss."

Keith's eyes got wide as he looked at me. "The boss?"

I shook my head.

"You want me to take out your boss?"

"That's why we called you."

Keith slowly shook his head. "I dunno about this, guys. Taking out a boss? There's a lot of risk, no? There's a lot to think about."

"Viggo said you're one of the best. We know everything that comes with this," I said.

Keith looked at Viggo. "Thanks for saying so," then back at us. "Still, something like this, it's a major piece of work. Something like this really could make people upset."

"We need an outside person to do it," I said. "We can't have this linked to us. If anyone ever finds out we're dead."

"Yes, you would," Keith said. "To do this I'll need a schedule of his daily routine. We need to catch this guy off his guard. We need to make sure this guy knows he can't control everything."

"Okay, we can get that."

"Think it would be better if I got him at his home."

"We can tell ya where he lives."

Keith let out a small cough. "That might be the best way to get it done. If he's at his house, he doesn't have his guys to protect him. Does he have any guards for the house or anything?"

"Nah, nothing like that," my brother said.

"Wife or kids?"

"Neither."

"That's good. Won't have to feel guilty about killing the guy. I've killed guys before that had children - that shit will eat you up inside. You feel bad for the kids - they never did anything to deserve being without a father."

"I'll have to keep that in mind," I said.

Jason said, "Johnny had a couple of kids."

"But they didn't like him," I said.

"How do you know that?"

"If they knew about his other life and how he treated people."

"I wouldn't be too sure about that."

"I have a hunch."

"Fair enough," Jason smiled.

"I remember hearing about one of his kids trying to kill him."

"I never heard that."

"I guess his one kid tried to shoot him."

"Tried?"

"The gun jammed."

"Interesting."

"I guess his son wanted some cash. Johnny didn't want to give it to him."

"Shit's crazy."

"I'm just sayin' what I heard. Not sure if it's true or not."

"Who's Johnny?" Keith asked.

William said, "Just a guy Sean got rid of."

"Ah," the older man looked at the drummer.

"Yeah, it doesn't matter. That guy was a poor fella," I said. "He messed with a few people he shouldn't of."

"I know a few of those," Keith said. "It's sad when something like that goes on. Some people think they know it all."

Viggo said, "Always have to have eyes in the back of your head."

"Or know the right people," William added.

Clarence said, "That can only take you so far, buddy."

Keith went on to tell us about himself. I guess he wanted us to know he was a level guy, and not going to go running to the cops the minute he left Viggo's. He told us about how much he hated cops. He told us about jobs he'd done for various people. He told us we could call a list of people for a reference. We didn't need to, plus, this wasn't the sort of business where you call other criminals regarding the acts of your associates.

"If I could ask you something, what did Joe do?" Keith asked.

"Revenge," I said.

"Revenge for what?"

I looked at my brother and the other guys, then I looked back at Keith. "I guess I should tell you. His lack of action led to my girlfriend's death."

I told him the whole story: Nick and Max, the night at the club, Heidi's death, everything. I told him that if Joe would've acted when I asked Heidi would've still been alive.

"Looks like I came at an exciting time," Keith said. "Guy gets out of jail wanting to run things again. I have a feeling a lot more people are gonna have to die."

"Afraid that's the way it's gonna go," I said.

"Just remember not to die."

"Yeah, thanks."

"I'm here to help."

I gave him a nod.

We talked for a few more hours, laughing, joking, trading stories. I felt like we could trust him. We needed not to let anyone know he was in Arkansas just yet. He had to do the job, then, after awhile, we could let other people from the gang know who he was. As far as anyone would know, no one knew how Joe was killed.

Keith told us he had over sixty kills under his belt.

I told Keith I'd go with him to get Joe. He made things personal.

I told him that we'd still need him and everything, but I wanted to be the one to pull the trigger. I told Keith how I wanted things to go.

twenty-five

For the next few days, we followed Joe Butler's every
move at a distance. We used a car William boosted. We
couldn't run the chance of being seen. After staking out
the clubs and his house for about a week, it was agreed
the best place to hit him was at night in his house. Even
though I hated Joe, I had to kiss his ass until he was
gone. Every time I saw him after the night at the doctor's
I wanted to kill him. I had to look at his face and smile,
nodding, laughing, at his stupid jokes. Truth was, he de-
pended on us. If it wasn't for my friends and I Joe
would've been killed or locked up for life.

"Sure you wanna go through with this?" Keith asked,
sitting in a car across from Joe's house.

"Why?"

"Hindsight is one of our best friends," he said. "I'd hate
to see this end badly. I mean, I get it, you're pissed at
this Joe guy, sure. I've been there before. But this could
start a chain of events that you're not ready to handle.
You could get hurt."

"I know what I'm doing."

"If you say so," he turned his head to look out the passenger window. "Got wind once a friend of mine had orders to kill me. Guess he didn't think about things.
Guess he only had money on his mind."

"What happened?"

He turned back to me. "What do you think? I killed
him. It was him or me. The years of friendship didn't
matter to him when it came down to it."

"Why are you telling me this?"

"Today's his birthday."

"Really?"

"Yeah," he muttered. "He would've been fifty-seven."

"Sounds like he had a good run."

"Until I put him in the ground."

"Well, there's that..."

He said, "We had the same boss at the time. The boss, Chuck, didn't like me much. Didn't help matters I slept with his wife. He put the hit out and gave it to my best friend. He was drunk one night and told me."

"I couldn't imagine that."

"It wasn't fun. I was faced with what to do. On one hand, I could've killed him, on the other I could've ran."

"Why didn't you run?"

He shrugged. "That's the thing I've been turning around in my mind ever since."

I thought about that for a minute and took out a ciga- rette. "Regret can eat you from the inside out."

"Indeed," Keith said. "I feel sorry about that now," he looked at me. "I think about that all the time."

"Damn."

"I was just wanting to make sure you wanted this."

"I do."

He turned his head and continued to look out the win- dow

Joe lived in a white two-story on the side of a hill. The house was pretty nice. I'd been in it a few times.

"Ready for this?" I asked.

"Always."

"Because I can go in first if you need me to."

"I'll be fine," he looked at me. "This guy, he has no weapons in the house. Anything I should know about?"

I said, "I wouldn't be surprised if there were guns and shit hidden in there. He's had a few people shoot up the house before. Two times he's had people break in. There was this week here I kept an eye on his house at night. I was parked across the street."

"I see," the hitman said. "What would you've done if shooters showed?"

"I'm not sure," I said. "There wouldn't have been enough time. I would've had to go it alone."

"And probably die."

"Maybe."

"I think the nearest payphone is at the gas station over there," I said, as I pointed in the direction of Joe's house, indicating to Keith there was a street on the other side of Joe's. "It would've taken me like ten minutes to get the call in."

"Good, you didn't have to do that."

"I would've probably let whoever just killed the guy, let him suffer."

Keith laughed. "Damn, he made you mad."

"He did."

"I hear ya," the man looked out the window again.

"We can't have any mistakes," I said.

"I figured that much," Keith said. "You sure he's in there by himself? I will, but I don't wanna kill a bunch of people tonight. I'm not really in the mood for that shit."

"But you kill people for a living."

"And your point?"

"It shouldn't be a problem for you."

"I do this all the time, but even hitmen have a heart. I'm not a total monster."

"I'm sure some think of you like that."

"Like a monster?"

"Yeah," I said. "What would you say about yourself? If someone asked what you were full of, what's on the inside, what would you say?"

He looked at me. "Regret."

"That can be a tough one."

"It can sometimes."

I looked at him. "Now is the time to focus on this."

"You don't have to worry about me."

"Good thing."

"I've been doing this for a long time. Is there anything else I need to know before going in?"

"Not that I can think of."

We looked toward the house again. About five minutes later the living room light went out. A minute later the bedroom light flickered on and then went out.

Keith turned his head to me. "Looks like we're all set."

"Guess we'd better get this thing taken care of."

"Give me twenty minutes. After I tie him up with rope, knock him around a little, then you'll make your entrance."

"No problem."

"Got a gun, right?"

"I always have one on me."

"That's good. You never what could happen."

"The amount of people who hate us, it can come anytime."

"Everyone needs to make themselves look tough."

"A lot of people think we're a joke."

"Those people, these are the ones you have to put in their place."

"I dunno, this whole thing is a little too much sometimes. I try to only do things to people that hurt me or someone I know."

"Ever been shot?"

"Not yet."

"You stay on this path, it'll happen sooner or later."

"I can't wait."

He took out his gun and made sure it was loaded. He opened the car door and got out. He walked across to the house and headed toward the backyard. I watched him until he disappeared around the side of the house.

I lit a cigarette and turned on the radio.

Ten minutes went by, not a sound from the house.

The street was quiet. I looked towards the front of Joe's house. A few minutes later, a bright light started to come through the back of the car. At first, I thought it was just some crazed drunk. I looked in the rearview mirror and saw a police car behind me without its siren turned on.

I was fucked, I thought.

As he approached the car I rolled down the window.

A lump started to form in my throat.

"Help you with anything?" I asked.

The officer, a short, brown-haired guy looked like he was disgusted at me for something. "What are you doing out here, sir?"

"Oh, not much," I said. "I was just taking a drive. It's a nice night out. Might as well take advantage while I can, right? The girlfriend and I argued. Just had to get outta the house," I smiled at him. "Women, they can drive you crazy. I just come out here to clear my head."

He leaned closer to my window. "You have any identification on you?"

I looked him in the eyes. "Sure, I do."

"Hate to ask, but it's my job."

I started to get nervous.

At that exact moment, I couldn't remember if I had anything outstanding he could get me for. I have to say, I wasn't the best at keeping up with things like that.

I handed him the card. He told me to wait in the car while he ran my identification. He came back and handed me my card.

"Everything's clean," he told me. "You're free to go."

"Thanks. Sorry about the trouble. I'll have to remember to not take these late drives."

"That would be best," he said. "We've been getting reports of a lot of perverts in the area. They like to sit in their cars and wait for a pretty little something to come along. There are a lot of sick people out here. I could tell you stories about the shit these guys do."

"Why's that?"

"Victims in these cases usually end up pressing charges. After everything, the guy's left in jail alone. The girl doesn't want anything to do with him. Most of the time I feel sorry for 'em."

"No, no, that's not me at all," I said. "I can take care of myself when it comes to the ladies. I get plenty."

"Good to hear. We have enough already."

"That's too bad."

"It is," he gave me another look. "I'll let you go this time. Just remember about the perverts. This is your warning. Go and tell your friends not to drive around here at night. We want a nice place here. In the future, if you see anyone who looks suspicious please inform law enforcement."

"Will do," I said. "People like that don't deserve to be on the streets. They're a menace, a plague."

"Okay, then. Glad to hear you say things like that," he patted the roof of my car. "Have a good night."

"You do the same, sir."

"If you see anything give us a call."

"Will do, sir."

He walked away to his car and got in.

A minute later his engine started and the bright light started to fade as he rolled away. I leaned back in my seat and closed my eyes for a few minutes. My eyes came open and I realized forty minutes had gone by and Keith wasn't back.

I got my gun from the glove compartment. The first thing that ran through my mind was Keith was dead, that

Joe had gotten the better of him. If I was gonna go into the house I needed to be prepared.

After I got out of the car, I started to head in the direction Keith went in. I noticed to gain entry into the house he punched a little hole in the widow of the back door, and then, he reached his hand in and unlocked the door. I turned the doorknob slowly and it opened.

It was dark when I entered. There wasn't any sign of light anywhere. I had to feel my way around as I moved. When I got to the living room, a little moving light from a passing car poured through the two big windows. I looked up the spiraling staircase, and I could see a yellow glow at the top of the stairs, underneath a door. I walked up the stairs to the door. When I got to the door I stood for a minute. I thought about kicking the door down, running into the room, and shooting. I placed my hand on the doorknob and turned it.

Keith was standing in the center of the room. Joe was tied up in a chair with his bathrobe on, hands behind his back, sock in his mouth. Once he saw me he started moaning. I looked around the room.

I looked down at the rope Joe was tied with. "Where'd this come from?"

"He had it in his closet," Keith said.

"Had rope in his closet?"

"Didn't ask him why it was there."

"Who knows? He's probably into some freaky sex games or something."

Keith laughed. "This day in age, wouldn't put it past anyone," he patted my shoulder.

"Some people you never know about."

"I know that's right."

"Some sick folks out there."

"And you think you know someone..."

"On second thought, he doesn't look like someone who

does that sort of thing."

"I wouldn't know. You can never tell. People, lead double lives all the time. It's a crazy thing to think about."

"I try not to."

I looked at Joe. "And what should we do with you? Hope that sock's clean. Oh, Joe, why are you makin' us do this? Things didn't have to be like this. Hope you know what I'm doing here."

Joe rolled his eyes at me. After he gave me a long look he shook his head.

"Good," I said. "I wanna make sure you know why you're gonna die."

Keith looked at me. "Thought I was gonna shoot him? I'm the hitman."

"You didn't kill him, though."

"I snuck in, and wasn't expecting him to attack me."

"Expect the unexpected."

"Thanks for the advice," he took out his gun and looked at it, ran his hand over the barrel. "Where were you?"

"Would've been here sooner, but I had a run-in with a cop."

"A cop?"

"He thought I was a pervert."

"Why'd he think that?"

"Because I was sitting in the car. He told me they had problems with perverts hanging around. That's why I was late."

"At least you didn't get arrested."

"That wouldn't have been good."

"Not at all."

"You guys would've had to break me out."

"I'm sure we'd die doing that."

"You think?"

"No doubt in my mind."

"Good, it didn't happen."

"They wouldn't take me without a fight."

"That's the only way to be."

The older man let out a big smile. "That's pretty good."

I said, "We gonna finish this or what?" I looked over at Joe. "You stupid fuck!"

Keith called over to my former boss. "This kid is mad at you. I feel sorry for you, my friend, real sorry."

We walked closer to Joe and pulled our guns. I tore the sock out of his mouth. As soon as I did, he spat in my direction.

"Joe, Joe," I said, "that wasn't very nice, was it?"

"Don't give a fuck," Joe muttered. "Just get it over with if you're gonna kill me."

"We'll get to that soon enough," I said

Joe gave a hard swallow. "I took you in, schooled you in the business, and this is what you do? And for what? All this for some bitch?"

A grin ran across my face. "Pretty much."

"You don't know what you're doing."

"I think I do."

"You'll regret this."

"I don't think."

I looked down at the floor, then back at him. "Why didn't you do anything about Max and Nick? I came to you, asking for your permission to get rid of them. You didn't want to, and Heidi got killed along with all of those other innocent people. Tell me, what sort of sick fuck does something like that?"

Joe hung his head. "Thought it was something that would blow over. Didn't know anyone would get hurt."

"But they did."

Beads of sweat ran down Joe's face. "I…I…was just doin' what I thought was…"

"What?"

He just shook his head as his eyes lowered

"And James, he didn't have to die," I said. "He was your friend."

He looked at me. "You won't get away with this, hope you know," he snorted. "You know, people will find out, ask questions, whatever. You'll end up having to tell this story, and when you do, that'll be it. You'll start a shit-storm of a war, kid. You can forget about Nick and Max, you'll have Sal and the others to deal with," he grunted a little. "Something else you have to think about-"

"What's that?"

"When our friends on the inside get out, that'll be another thing."

"We can deal with that."

"Oh?" Joe said. "And you know everything, smart guy? A lot of those guys like me. If you think killin' me will solve your problems, then be my guest. I don't think you have it in ya," he looked at Keith. "And you, you know, I've been in this game a long time, and I've never come across you. I don't even know your name."

Keith said, "My name's not important."

"Well," Joe continued, "you must be new, buddy. Hope you know what you're getting into with this crowd. Think if I'd known who you were, hell, I'd of probably killed ya by now. I hope you guys know what you're startin'. It'd be nice to know the name of the other guy who's gonna end me - don't think that's asking a lot."

"Shut your mouth!" I yelled.

We walked closer to him.

Joe started to urinate on himself.

I said, "Would you look at that? You pissed yourself. What, you scared?"

Joe was silent. He shook his head slowly.

"Things didn't have to be like this," I lowered my voice to him "Ego got the better of you," I looked Joe in the eyes. "Anything else?"

"Piece of shit."

"I should've killed you sooner. You fucked things up for me. I shouldn't have ever been a part of this. I never wanted this."

Joe gulped air. "I guess everything's my fault? You're in this world of dirty thugs, and I'm the reason you stuck around? Give me a fuckin break, guy. I should've let you get killed that night outside of the bar. You've always been weak. People, they'll find out about you tonight," he let out a sigh. "I'm willing to forget this whole thing if you let me go."

"I'm not falling for that line."

"What's it gonna be? Your pick! The other guys find out. When you shoot me, you need to turn the gun on yourself."

"Yeah, yeah, yeah, just keep it up. Last time I checked you're the one at the disadvantage."

Joe rocked the chair back and forth. "Man," he looked over at Keith, "you make a good knot," he jerked his shoulder to the side. "I can't even get out. If I had to guess, you were in the army at some point."

"I was," Keith said.

"Nice. How many years?"

"Ten."

"Not a short run?"

"Not really. I've known guys who were in for longer."

"Same here."

The next thing I knew Joe jumped out of the chair, leaving the rope to drop around him, and lunged at Keith, knocking him to the ground. Joe threw the first punch, then a second and third. Keith was able to get Joe's throat. On the other hand, he hit Joe hard on the side of the face. Joe fell off the man. Keith pulled himself on top of the mob leader. Keith pounded away with his fist. He asked if I wanted to give the guy a few licks. I told him I did. Keith pulled Joe to his feet. I smiled before I hit him in the face, knocking him to the ground. I took him by the back of the neck and flung him against the window. For a split moment, I thought I broke it. I got close to him and hit him three times in the face. I let go and he put a hand to his face. He was about to say something, then, I kneed him hard in the belly. I didn't let him drop to the floor. When he hunched over I hit him again on the side of the face. He managed to get to his feet and face me. With a mouth full of blood he told me he could go for much longer.

Keith and I aimed our guns at Joe and fired. Keith fired two times and I three. His body fell to the floor. Blood started to trickle from the bullet holes onto the white carpet. The carpet was damaged now: it wouldn't be of any use to anyone.

"Is that good?" Keith looked at me.

"Yeah."

After a little bit, Keith opened his mouth. "Let's get outta here. The idea of sticking around after I do a job tends to freak me out a little."

"I'm right behind ya."

We turned, walked out of the room, and started down the stairs. About halfway down I stopped and started back up the stairs.

Keith turned around. "What are you doing? We should go, man."

"We already killed him, might as well rob the place. He won't miss anything."

"Good point," he said. "Let's get what we can and leave."

We spent the next hour trashing the place, taking whatever we wanted: cash, guns, drugs, anything we could get our hands on. We had to make a few trips back to our car so we could get all of the guns loaded.

As we drove away I wondered who'd find Joe.

I drove Keith back to Viggo's house. When we got to his house Viggo asked how everything went. We told him it went well, and then showed him everything we stole. When Viggo saw everything we had his eyes got big.

"You leave anything in the house?" my friend said.

"He wasn't gonna use it," I said.

Viggo shrugged. "Got a point there. You gonna pawn 'em?"

"No," I said. "I was gonna keep everything."

He looked at me. "Well, sure, you don't wanna use the guns around any of the other guys. What if they recognize one?"

I thought about that. "Good call."

Viggo laughed. "What would you do without me, Sean?"

"I don't know," I laughed. "The drugs, though, we can unload them."

"Without a doubt. There's always a market for that shit."

Viggo invited me to stay for a beer with them. I looked at my watch, saw the time, and told myself I didn't have anything else better to do. Besides, after you kill your boss, you should always reward yourself with a nice cold beer.

After we got a beer, the three of us sat around his kitchen table. Viggo asked us about Joe, about if we left anything behind that could be traced back to us.

"No," I said, "Everything went as planned. Gloves, masks, they're in the car. No fingerprints in the house, nothing. He made it easy for us."

Keith said, "Yeah, at first, he tried to put up a struggle. Had to get some rope and tie the poor fool to a chair.

Found a dirty sock and stuffed it in his mouth."

Viggo smiled. "I would've loved to have seen that."

"No you don't," Keith said. "No one ever likes that shit."

I looked at Keith. "Why'd you take the job?"

Keith said, "This is what I do. There's no going back for me. I'm in it till the end of my days. This is the only thing I've ever seemed to be good at."

Viggo shook his head. "Think I'd of still liked to have seen it. I didn't like that motherfucker at all. He got too full of himself."

"He did that," I said.

We drank the rest of our beer and got more.

"What now?" Viggo asked. "I mean, should we be nervous about the outcome of all of this?"

"We'll have to see," I said. "We'll be ready if there's any backlash. Shit, I don't think we'll have a problem."

Viggo shook his head.

I said, "But, no one will ever know what we did. Everyone will assume Max or Nick got to him. The feud they had, it would make sense. That's what I was thinking when I thought about all of this. It should be okay."

"I hope," Viggo said.

Keith took out a cigar and lit it. "The Stone Monkey guys are the only other guys who know, right?"

"Yeah," I said.

"You sure?"

"Yeah."

"You better be," he said. "I know you're still pretty new at this. I don't wanna see you makin' mistakes."

"Thanks for the concern, but I'll be fine."

"If you say so."

I looked over at Viggo and gave him a nod. "You get the money yet?"

"I got it," he jumped up, went into another room, and

came back carrying a black bag. "Here ya go," he threw the bag on the kitchen table, in front of Keith. "You can count it, make sure it's all there."

 "I will," Keith unzipped the bag. "Thanks. This will come in handy. Buying a house down here, that'll help."

 "Glad we can help," Viggo said. "If there's anything else just let us know."

 "I'll do that."

 We continued drinking and talking until dawn. I was feeling tired and told the guys I needed to go back to my place to get some sleep.

twenty-six

That next day I got the call from one of the guys in the crew. He said we were having a big meeting at the warehouse. He didn't tell me over the phone, but, I knew what the meeting was about. The whole way over there I was thinking it didn't take any time for them to discover what happened. I knew going into this meeting I had to play dumb. I couldn't even act too shocked: they would see through that and know I was somehow involved. I had to be calm and cool.

When I got to the warehouse Sal was in the parking lot smoking. He looked upset. As I got out of my car I nodded at him. Sal nodded back as he mashed his cigarette stub out on the ground with his shoe. I walked through the doorway of the warehouse and saw that my brother nor any of my little crew had shown up yet. A few of the other guys were sitting around a table visiting with one another. I asked if they knew what the meeting was about. Nobody had a clue. I walked outside and lit up a smoke.

Sal walked over to me. "Hey, kid."

"How's it going?"

"Been better."

"What do ya mean?"

He looked at me. "A new day brings new challenges."

"What does that mean?"

"You'll find out."

"Huh?"

Sal walked inside.

Tony was still in the parking lot.

I called over to him. "What do ya say, Tone?"

He walked over to me. "Craziness. You know how that goes?"

"You can say that again."

"No one ever said this wasn't boring."

I could tell he was a little somber like he had something on his mind he didn't wanna tell me. He wasn't as chatty as normal. His eyes lowered as I talked to him.

"What's the matter?" I asked.

He took in a chunk of air. "Just been a rough few hours."

"Why's that?"

"Sal will tell you inside."

"I wanna know now."

"Think you can handle it?"

"Try me."

He shook his head and patted me on the shoulder. "You'll know soon enough. That's why we called this meeting."

I thought for a minute. "I noticed. Where's Joe? Shouldn't he be here? What is this?"

He stepped closer to me, in a low voice. "Someone got to Joe."

"When?"

"Sometime last night or early this morning," he pointed to the door of the warehouse. "We're gonna tell them."

"Thanks for that."

"We look out for our own."

I said, "Wow, that's some shit about the boss. We have to get to the bottom of it somehow."

"We should."

"Any ideas who it was?"

He didn't say anything, just shook his head and walked inside.

I looked at him as he shuffled along.

I just had to keep my cool and have hope that no one ever got to Keith. I knew Keith was in the life - for that, I didn't know if he could be trusted. Everyone has their price. I know, we told him he could be trusted, but still, you never can be too sure.

I walked back inside the building. Sal told us to take a seat, that he had something to tell us. I think the other guys had an idea of what was going on when Joe wasn't there. Maybe they were thinking Sal was going to kill Joe.

After a little while everyone else from my little crew showed up. As soon as they walked in they saw me and came over and took a seat. A few other people staggered in. After another ten or fifteen minutes passed, when it was clear everyone was there. Sal stood in front of us all.

"Thanks for getting here promptly today," he looked a little sad. "I hate to break you away from whatever you had going on this morning. I know, for me, no one better say a fuckin' word until I've had that first cup of coffee. That dealer, James, came by my house one morning... Not sure why he didn't talk to Joe, anyway, he came by saying, 'So and so motherfucker didn't pay me. I'm gonna kick his ass,' He went on like this for awhile. I finally look at the guy, 'Hey, dick, I don't give a shit. I have to have at least one cup of coffee before I can think about looking at anyone like you.' And you know, that son of a bitch is pretty damn ugly. I don't think his mom even liked him. Think she should've used a coat hanger to abort him. But we aren't here to talk about a cocksucker like that. We have a problem we need to talk about."

Everyone got quiet.

"Joe's dead," Sal broke the silence. "I found him this morning. Went to his house to pick him up, didn't answer the door, finally found where someone had broken into the back door, went in, and found him upstairs. He had a few bullet holes in him," Sal put both hands out in front of him. "Saw that, had to walk away," he lowered his hands. "That wasn't something I wanted to see ever. After I collected myself I came back in the room to investigate a little. Found nothing."

No one said anything at first.

Sal continued. "I have a few ideas on who did it. Guess we'll just have to see how this unfolds."

William said, "It could've just been someone else. Someone from Ted's crew, maybe? Max?"

"We'll ask him soon enough," Sal told us. "If it was him, it'll have to be dealt with fast. Could be they had nothing to do with it," his eyes darted around at all of us. "We have a good thing here. We have something big, that's more powerful than us. I'd hate to see all of this turn to nothing. We have to be strong in these times. Most of you guys are probably wondering about leadership. Well, I will be calling the shots for awhile."

Sal went on to tell us he'd have to pick a second in charge, that it would have to take a day or so to think about. He told us all to be careful, that we didn't know where this came from, that we all might be in danger.

Mike, one of the guys in the crew said, "No way they killed Joe last night."

Sal said, "And why's that?"

"I was at Hanger Al's last night, and they were there, Max and his brother."

Sal walked up to Mike. "They say anything to you?"

"Don't think they even knew who I was."

"I wouldn't be too sure about that. Could be they didn't want you to know they know who you are."

"I guess."

"How long were you there?"

"All night."

"How long was that?"

"About six when I got there. My girl and I left at midnight."

"And when were they there till?"

"Midnight. They had a band. Hell, they weren't that bad."

"They have anyone with them?"

"The band?"

"Max and Nick?"

"A couple of girls and guys. Looked like they were having a pretty good time."

"You're sure it was them?"

"No doubt in my mind."

"Interesting," Sal walked away from Mike. "Doesn't mean anything. He could've had a couple of his guys do it. We need to make sure of this before any sort of retaliation."

"So, what now, boss?" Mike said.

Sal was walking back and forth across the room, then stopped. "Yeah, Boss, I like the sound of that - it feels pretty good, I have to say. I like the way it rolls off the tongue."

Everyone told him he deserved it.

Sal said, "Joe and I went back a long time. This isn't something you just get over the next day. It takes time. Then again, it's the life we picked."

Nods went around the room.

Sal told us he'd have to think about who would be his second in charge. A few days later he called another meeting. He told us that he'd decided to have Tony be his number two. Sal said they were gonna have a party for Tony at Highlife.

twenty-seven

At the party, everyone was drinking and having a good
time. Sal doubled the amount of strippers for that night.
It was an open bar and a full buffet. The place got pretty
wild fast. Some of the dancers were taking some of the
guys in the VIP rooms for some fun. Sal asked if we
would play at the party. The band he had booked
dropped out at the last minute. As Stoned Monkey took
the stage, a small three-man brawl broke out: it didn't
take long before it was defused. I would later find out
the fight had to do with a woman. The three men were
told never to enter the club again. Stoned Monkey
played six songs before we took a break for a few drinks
at the bar. I was talking to Jason when Tony walked
over. He looked a little drunk.

"One hell of a party, isn't it?" Tony said as he sat next
to Jason.

"It is a good night, indeed," I agreed.

"Not bad," my brother said.

Tony said, "Guys have some pretty good music."

"Thanks," I said. "You liked it?"

Tony ordered a beer.

The girl cracked the top off of a cold one and set it in
front of him.

"We thank you for that," I said to him.

"Oh, yeah. You guys have something good there," he
took a drink. "It's always good to have something to fall
back on."

I shook my head. "That's what I was thinking."

He took another drink and slammed the bottle on the
bar. "Whatever happened with the album? Sal said something about you guys recording something. Said you

went to Texas."

"We did."

"How'd it go? When'll we get to hear it?"

"Not sure yet."

"Why's that?"

I shrugged. "Think they're bein' fucks. Our guy, Morris, he said he'd call when he has something. Guess there are some sort of changes going on in management. Just hope it's not bullshit."

"I know how that can be," Tony said. "Hope it works out for you guys," he took another drink. "Just don't write any songs about any of this."

"Don't worry," Jason said. "We wouldn't do anything like that."

Tony said, "I'd hate to dump you guys in a grave somewhere for turning rat."

"We don't do that."

"That's good."

I said, "I make sure all of you guys are gone first."

Tony let out a howl. "Think that'll work? You know people never forget. Maybe someone else. They don't joke around about that sort of thing."

"I've been told."

Around the bar, everyone was drinking and laughing. I lit a cigarette and looked around. I looked over at the strippers on stage shaking their shit for all of us. One of the girls, a blond beauty with ruby lipstick and wore a red-lace outfit caught my eye. As she swayed her hips from side to side, for a moment I thought of rushing the stage, giving her a jump in front of everyone. She let her top drop, leaving her white breasts to bounce free. Her pink nipples stood straight at attention. She did another dance to some song I didn't recognize the name of, then she walked off stage. As she walked away this guy grabbed a microphone and told us her name was Lilac-

Lilly-Pop: not her real name. I told myself I'd have to make an introduction to her.

"The place is crawling with fine ass tonight," I said.

"You can say that again, brother," Jason said.

One of the bartenders came back and gave us another round.

Tony said, "Sad thing about Joe, you know?"

"It just goes to show you that your life can end at any time," Jason said.

I grunted. "That's the understatement of the year. Never take anything for granted, that's for sure. Life's funny, you never know when it's your time. Glad Sal's the top guy now. Think people didn't like Joe that much."

"What do you mean?" my brother asked.

"I've heard a few things in the air," Tony said.

"A few things, like what?"

"A few back-door deals I'd heard about. That guy loved talking about people behind their backs. He was always talkin' about getting rid of people."

"Really?" I said.

"Yeah," he said.

"Guess you don't know people like you think you do. If that's true, I wonder what all he had to say about me."

"You have to wonder, but, hell, I wouldn't worry about that noise now. The only thing that'll get you is twisted inside."

"You think?"

"I know."

I grinned. "Yeah, well..."

Tony lit a cigar. "I know Joe changed throughout the years. Hell, when we first got involved with all of this, we were all pretty young guys. We stayed because of the cash... We were making a lot. None of us wanted to go back to any straight job earnin' bullshit money. Everything was so glamorous. Those were the days: violence,

women, and drugs, were all part of it. At first, I couldn't
get my head around the killing part of it all. Eventually, I
got right with myself about it. But, yeah, Joe and I were
good friends. Ask Sal, he can tell ya. There was a bunch
of us, some in jail, some dead. I was sad to hear someone ended him. Someone's gotta pay for what happened."

Jason nodded. "We'll get to the bottom of it."

"Sure we will. I'm just a little concerned with how long
it'll take," Tony looked over at Sal's table, then back at
us. "Look, all of this took us by surprise. I think Sal's
just trying to do the best he can. In times of darkness,
great leaders shine."

I said, "We'll be here."

"Yeah, we're your guys," Jason took a drink.

"I appreciate that, boys. Sure Sal does, too. I'll keep ya
posted on things."

"Good," I said.

Tony looked at us, took another drink, and looked at
some of the waitresses walking around. "I suggest the
two of you grab one of these girls and make your music."

I shook my head. "I already have a girl," then I patted
Jason on the shoulder. "This guy, he's the one who needs
a girl. The guy's spending too much time pulling himself. I'm surprised his thing doesn't break off."

Jason hit me on the arm. "Get fucked, asshole!"

"Dick."

My brother laughed. "Pussy."

Tony laughed. "You guys are funny."

"Big promotion, huh, Tone?" Jason lit a cigarette.

"Think it should've been sooner, but what can you do?
Guess it was sort of good James got taken out when he
did. He could've been where I'm at now."

Jason exhaled smoke. "So, Tone, gonna buy yourself a

new car or something?"

"Think I should keep it low-key for a bit. Don't wanna go around advertising myself too fast. I've never been the flashy type."

"Understandable," Jason said.

"And, even then, I wouldn't get big with it. I'm as simple as they come."

"Nothing wrong with that," I said. "None of that counts anyway. Family and friends, if you don't have those two things you may as well kill yourself."

Tony looked over at a table where a nice redhead was sitting, then back at us. "Well, fellas, duty calls. little slice of redhead over there has my name written all over it," he gave a nod to the girl. The girl smiled back.

Tony stood from the bar stool and stumbled over to her at the table.

I nodded. "Well, good for him. He deserves it."

"I guess."

"Where's our friend?" I asked.

"Who?"

"Mr. Memphis."

He stared at me. "Him? Our other friend told me he had to go back home for awhile."

"For what?"

"Didn't say."

"Thought he was here to stay?"

"Guess he had other plans."

"When'd he go?"

"Didn't think to ask. Had to be yesterday."

"Yeah."

"Man like that, you never know. And to think we robbed a bank to get his money. We could've been caught. If he does show up again, I'm not sure how well we'll get along. You don't wanna get to close to those guys. They're a sick deprived breed. Something's wrong with their brains."

I thought for a minute. "What if he rats us out? Maybe that was why he left?"

"He wouldn't do that."

"You think?"

"Oh, yeah, people like him, as dangerous as they are, they have morals. He won't tell. He'd be telling on himself. It's a 'code of silence' thing. Won't have to worry about him."

"Guess you're right. It just makes me wonder why he left is all."

"He'll show sooner or later."

"We'll see about that."

A bartender came over and we got a few more beers.

"You here from Morris?" Jason asked.

"Not yet. I dunno, he said he'd let us know something. Guess he's been busy. He might not have anything for us yet. The guy has more business than just us."

"Yeah, I know, I was just wondering. Hope he didn't get fired. No call or anything. He never even called to tell us when the album was gonna come out."

"Been thinking we might make another trip down there."

"When did you wanna go?"

"Not sure yet. Have to see if the other guys wanna join."

"I'm sure you won't have a problem getting them from this place."

I laughed. "I wouldn't blame 'em."

"Hell, we're just a couple of wild guys."

Just about that time, Sal called over to us. He wanted to say a few words about Tony. As we walked over to where Sal and the other guys were it became clear to me what I'd done. Because of me, the whole structure of the crew had changed: everyone was moving up, but I didn't know if I wanted this. As I sat in a chair by my brother I thought about confessing and leaving town.

Sal started to give a big speech about how great of a guy Tony was, and that he could go far in the business of ours. When Tony spoke I saw Madison out of the corner of my eye. She walked from across the club to behind the bar. She started waiting for people.

Sal stood and managed to quiet everyone. He asked Tony to stand beside him. Sal went on to say some words about Tony. I didn't pay much attention to what he was saying. I was more focused on looking at Madison.

Tony said, "Thank you guys. This means a lot to me. This is a good party, nice showing. I'm gonna try my best to do a good job," he looked at Sal, then back at us. "I'd known Sal since we were kids. He's a good guy. It was me, him, and Joe who wanted something better for ourselves. We all came from poor homes. We wanted something better. We told ourselves that we wouldn't stop until we had everything we wanted. Joe was a friend, and if it wasn't for him we wouldn't be here to-day," he cleared his throat. "Well, you know what I mean we're at this point because Joe was killed. What I meant to say was that he believed in life outside the rules. If you want something you have to take it and make it yours," he looked around the room. "There may be some of you who resent me being in this position, and I'm sorry, that's just how things go sometimes. If I could turn back time I would. We have to move on, the only way the pain will go away. Whoever did this, believe me, we'll find 'em," he paused for a moment. "I just want everyone to have a good night. Enjoy the fine drink and cheap women," he looked over at Sal and nodded. "Thank this guy," a laugh. "Need to get back to my

drink. You guys have fun."
 Tony shuffled over to his seat

 I stood and walked to the bar, took the stool I sat at before. As soon as Madison saw me she smiled. She walked over with a full mug of beer and put it in front of me.
 "How are ya?" she said.
 "Just a fun night of drinkin'."
 She smiled at the table I just walked from, all of the beer bottles. "I see that."
 "You?"
 "Oh, you're lookin' at it."
 I shook my head. "I know how that goes."
 "Yes, sir."
 "Someone has to do it. look at it like this, it could be worse. You could work in fast food."
 She ran a hand through her hair and smiled. "I wouldn't wanna do that no matter what they paid."
 "Can't say I blame you."
 "I've done my fair share of that."
 "That's why you have teenagers."
 "Cheap labor."
 "Exactly."
 "I scooped ice cream."
 I held my finger up to her. "That's the key. Fun times. See, mine was janitor work. I thought it sucked at the time. Looking back on it, it wasn't that bad. I was just an annoyed kid."
 "We had it good then. If I could be a kid again... Would be so fantastic."
 I smiled as I shook my head. I took out a cigarette. Before I could get my lighter Madison had hers and lit my smoke.
 "Thanks," I said.

"You're very welcome, sir," her eyes looked at mine. "Just pay me back later."

"I'd like that."

"Bet you would."

"I'd be crazy not to."

She licked her lips a little. "That means you're coming over tonight?"

"What time you leave here?"

"It'll be a late one. I'm thinking maybe two. We have to clean this place and all of that. How much longer are y'all gonna play?"

"I figure we'll play another five or six songs."

She folded her arms on the bar. "Guys aren't gonna play until close?"

"Sal said he didn't want us to."

"And you gonna do everything he says?"

"He has the crown now."

She smiled and whispered. "Wonder how long that's gonna last?"

I shrugged. "You can never tell. This thing, it's not the most legit life. Hell, some of the things I do, I'm surprised I'm not dead."

"Hope that doesn't happen."

"Me, too."

I took a drink of beer.

"Still wanna come over later?" she asked.

"I'll be there."

"I can't wait," she leaned over the bar and whispered in my ear. "I want you inside me so bad."

"You're in for a treat," I muttered back.

"I hope."

"Hey, babe, that's what I'm here for."

"I'm a fan."

She kissed me on the lips.

twenty-eight

She walked to the back and disappeared behind a door.
A few minutes later she returned, asking if I wanted another beer, commenting that I sucked the other one down
fast. I told her that I did. She went behind the door again.
I stared at the liquor bottles on the other side of the bar.
For a minute I thought of how great it would be to jump
over the bar and drink all of those bottles.

Madison came out of the door carrying a case of beer.

"It was pretty slow earlier," she brought a bottle of beer
over to me.

"That so?"

"Only made ten bucks. That's why I'm working now. I
wasn't scheduled tonight. Knew about this party, and I
figured I make some good cash."

"That all you made earlier?"

"Guess people didn't wanna come see me."

"I'm sure that's not true."

A smile. "You make me feel special."

"I do my best."

"I like it."

"Most girls do."

"There are others?"

"In the past."

"They better stay there."

"Don't worry, they will."

"If you lie, I know where to find a gun at."

"No need for that."

"You mean it?"

"Of course."

"Thanks."

"Always."

She leaned over the bar and kissed me. "I love you."

"The same to you."

"Come on, baby, you don't wanna say it?"

"Nothing like that, I love you too, babe."

"Glad to hear that."

Sal walked over and told me to get the guys together for a few more songs. I gathered up the other guys and went on stage.

Clarence said, "Glad to see y'all are still with us. Yeah, I like to see that. We've had a pretty good time tonight, think everyone will agree with that," he pumped his fist in the air three times. "Before we leave, we have a few more tunes. Enjoy."

I started running my fingers up and down the neck of my guitar. We started with a song called "Into Nothing." The next song we did was called 'Salute.' About half-way through my guitar solo, I looked over in the direction of the bar. Madison was busy mixing drinks. I glanced back, then, looked up again.

A minute or so later two guys walked over and plopped down on two of the bar stools at the end of the bar. Madison saw the two men and walked over to see what they wanted. I watched her as she talked to them. Both guys were short and skinny. I couldn't hear what they were saying because of the noise. After a little bit, I saw one of the guys grab Madison by the hand. Madison pushed him away. I took a sigh of relief. Just when I thought the two men were about to leave the bar, I saw what looked like shouting. The one man yanked Madison by the arm. She broke free and slapped the man. Before he had time to do anything, the other guy shot out his fist, hitting her in the side of the face. She dropped to the floor behind the bar. It was like I'd been watching a silent movie. As soon as Madison hit the floor I jumped off the stage. The other guys in the band saw what happened and followed me.

I ran over and grabbed the one guy by the collar, the guy that hit her. "Shithead, you just made the worst fuckin' mistake of your life!"

"Fucks your problem?" he yelled at me.

His friend rushed over to where I was. "Think you should mind your own business, don't you? Don't wanna see anyone get hurt."

"It is my business," I said. "I suggest you and your buddy leave."

I threw the man back, making him fall on the floor. A fist hit me from behind. I quickly turned and saw it was the other guy.

"You want some, too?" I said to him. "I'm not going anywhere. The girl you hit, she's my girlfriend."

My brother ran behind the bar and got Madison to her feet. "You okay?"

She wiped off some blood from her lips. "Yeah…think so."

I ran over to her and took her in my arms. "It'll be okay," I looked at Clarence. "Take her outta here. Go out the back door."

Clarence gave me a nod and led Madison to the back of the place.

I looked at both of them as they walked away.

The guy who hit me, I looked at him. "Guys shouldn't be treatin' women that way. Someone should teach you. Didn't your mothers teach you manners? Who are you guys? Don't think I've ever seen you two around here."

Sal called over from where he sat. "Got everything under control?"

"I'm fine," I said. "These two, they just stepped into a world of shit," I looked at both men. "Who are you?"

The one guy in, a black short sleeve shirt, the guy who hit Madison said, "The name's Turk, Shane Turk," he pointed at his friend. "That's Buster."

I nodded at Buster. "Gotta last name?"

"It's Gustus," Buster said.

I turned away from him for a minute, then turned back with a hard jab to the front of his face. Buster fell back against the bar. He didn't fall to the floor.

"That was for messing with my girl," I said.

Buster shook his head.

"What were you guys thinking?" I asked.

Shane said, "Just two guys lookin' for a good time, you know? We didn't mean any harm. How were we supposed to know that was your girl?"

I thought about it for a minute. "You're right. Just don't let it happen again. My friends and I, we don't think you wanna mess around with us."

As I looked at Shane, I clenched my right fist. I lunged at him, and swung my right fist, knocking him to the floor. I kicked him.

The next thing I knew Buster ran towards me. "You motherfucker! Thought we were good with you guys?"

"Now we're good, man! Now, you and your fuckin' friend, you need to get out of here. You might run across the same people here."

The two men stood side-by-side as my friends and I turned our backs.

"We'll come back and take that little pussy," Shane snarled. "Who are you to get in the way, buddy?"

Buster laughed. "Give that dirty bitch what she wants."

As soon as Buster's words hit my ears, I slowly turned around.

My friends turned when I did.

"Ah, boys, what did you do?" Jason flashed them his gun on his waist. "Wrong thing to say."

Shane snorted. "Gonna do something with that toy, boy?"

I walked up to Buster. "Say that again? Think I'm hard of hearing…I dunno. I could swear you guys disrespected my girl," I looked at Shane. "Both of you."

Buster glared at me. "You heard right."

I grinned. "That wasn't very nice."

The two men looked at each other and laughed.

"May have to teach you guys a lesson," I shook my head. "Not the smartest move. Guys must be dying to fight tonight, right?"

Buster let out a big laugh, revealing all of his teeth. "I'd love to see you try."

I took out my gun and hit Buster in the face with it. He dropped to the ground. A steam of blood came out his mouth. I picked up a stool and threw it down on him. I looked up just as Shane took a gun out and came at me. Next thing I knew Jason hit Shane and knocked him out of the way. Tony came over in a hurry and told us we needed to handle it outside, and that we were disrupting the other guests.

We grabbed the two men and went out the back door, over to a blue dumpster. The back lot of the club was surrounded by a solid wooden fence. A door was made for deliveries and whatnot. Sal and the other guys would park their cars out there sometimes. On that particular night, the only thing back there was us. When Madison saw us, she ran over and hugged me. I asked if everything was okay. She said she was fine.

Buster looked around the lot. "You know who we're with? We're with Ted across the bridge."

I said, "Thought you were new here?"

Shane wiped off some sweat and blood with his shirt. "We didn't wanna say. Just wanted to keep a low profile."

"I get that," I said. "We've all been there. No worries."

"Thanks," Shane extended his hand out for me to shake. We shook.

I turned my head, looked at Madison, and turned back to Shane and his friend. "I think it'd be gentlemen of you to apologize to the lady," I took Madison by the hand. "It's okay, babe. We just didn't know who these guys were with."

She shook her head. "I get it."

Shame and Buster apologized to my girl, saying they were sorry they disrespected her. "We were just messin' around," Shane said. "We don't want any trouble."

"Yeah, we don't want any trouble," Buster added.

My brother said, "You guys need to keep it that way."

I looked back at Madison and gestured for her to go back inside. "It's okay, babe, I'll be inside in a few minutes."

As Madison passed me she brushed her hand against my chest. When she got to where Shane and Buster were standing Buster leaned into her walking path. "If you want a real man to fuck, just call me," his fist flew out and hit her. As she fell back my brother was behind to catch her.

I took my gun out, shot Shane in the knee, dropping him to the pavement, and then I lunged at Buster, knocking him against the blue dumpster.

Shane was screaming in pain.

Jason picked Shane up from the ground. He hit Shane in the face and two times in the stomach.

I turned and looked down at Buster. He looked up at me as blood streamed down his face.

I looked over at Jason. "Think he needs a shot in the other knee?"

"He might," Jason replied.

My brother shot Shane in the other knee.

I looked at Buster again, picked him up, and let him see Shane. "I'm afraid this is the last time you're gonna see each other."

Shane begged my brother not to kill him.

"Please! We didn't mean anything. I'm... I'm... I'm... sorry."

"Too late for that," my brother barked.

"You don't know who you're fuckin' with."

"Shut up."

"We can talk about..."

Jason aimed his gun at Shane's face and shot three times. As Buster stood and watched Shane get killed, I put my gun against his head and fired once. Buster's body fell to the pavement.

The music and commotion inside were loud enough to drown the noise we made.

I gave a deep sigh as I looked at the two dead bodies. "Think we're gonna get a lot of shit for this?"

"Maybe," my brother said. "You can never tell about these things."

"How's that?"

"Things you thought were important might not be that. For all we know, these two were about to die anyway. They could've fucked around too many times. Who knows about Ted's guys," he laughed. "They're into some crazy shit. We could always put this on someone else. Don't think that'd be a problem."

I looked over at the back door. "Think I'll check on Madison."

"Good idea. I'll be here watching over our friends."

"Make sure they don't walk away?"

"Something like that."

I staggered to the door. When I got inside I found Madison at the bar. I asked if she was okay. She looked at me and told me she was. I kissed her and said there was a mess in the back we needed to clean.

We kissed again.

"You should stay in here," I told her.

"You gonna be okay?"

"I'll be fine."

"Stay that way."

"I just wanted to make sure you were okay."

"Don't worry, babe. Just do what you have to. Something happens to those two guys?"

"I'll tell you later."

We kiss again.

I walked over to Tony and quietly told him what happened out in the back lot.

"Guess all the noise in here, you couldn't tell," he lit a smoke. "Was gonna ask what happened with those two."

"Well, that's what happened."

He glanced at a stripper on stage, then back at me. "I figure this party's gonna be going on for a few more hours. Show me what you guys did."

We walked to the back door.

"Before we go out there," he said, "you sure they're dead? Don't wanna walk into any surprises."

I said, "Yeah, they're gone."

He turned the doorknob and we walked out onto the lot. Tony said he wanted to get a closer look.

We got closer.

He looked at the bodies. "Guess they pissed off the wrong people tonight, boy."

"They should've known better. You don't go around disrespecting women like that."

"Can't argue with you there."

I said, "We should clean this up."

"Yeah, it looks like it."

"Thought we were good after we talked to them, but then, the one guy hit her."

"She okay? I saw her inside."

"Madison's gonna be fine. Think she's just a little shakin'."

"That's understandable."

We stood in silence for a moment. Scattered traffic on the other side of the fence zoomed and hummed by.

"We might have a problem," I broke the silence.

"What's that?" he asked.

"These two guys, Buster and Shane, they're in Ted's crew."

His eyes got big. "That's interesting."

"They didn't tell us until we went out here. I don't want this to fall back on us."

"That would be good. Shit like that starts wars. None of us want that blood on these streets," he lowered his head for a minute like he was thinking, then back at me. "In this case, it might be best if we shifted the blame to someone else."

I shook my head. "Who could we put this on?"

"If anyone asks we can also play dumb."

"That's true."

"There's a lot of people inside tonight. Seems to me like un-named individuals can be pretty violent when they want to."

I stuffed my hands in my pockets and nodded to the bodies. "Got any ideas about what to do with these two?"

"Whatever you do, do it far away from here," Tony said. "No good havin' that around here."

"Should've thought about that before."

"You guys did the right thing, though. Motherfuckers should've known better than to pull that shit in a place like this."

"Our prints are on them. If they get dug up, they'll be able to leave our fingerprints," Jason told Tony.

Tony said, "I'd burn the bodies."

"Really?"

"Just make sure you go to a private place. Maybe at the warehouse or something. Wherever it is, it should be fast."

I shook my head.

Jason said, "Think anywhere along that road would be good. There's nothing there."

I thought about it, then said. "Those tracks over by Willow, no one ever goes over there. The drive wouldn't be so long. Just tryin' to do the best with what we have."

Tony said, "Sounds like a plan."

Jason and I talked it over some. It was clear he just wanted the situation to be over.

I said, "There supplies inside, things we'll need?"

"Yeah," Tony said, looking at his watch. "Man, it's getting late. Guess time got away from me."

We went back into Highlife. I told Jason we needed a few big sheets of plastic to roll the bodies in. After we wrapped them, I pulled my car around and opened the trunk. We loaded them, got in my car, and sped away to my brother's house. After getting the cans of gas and shovels we headed to where the abandoned train tracks were. Two old sheds were the only things in the area. In the daylight, the trees that surrounded gave off plenty of shade. The train track hadn't been active since 1988. All of the vegetation in the area was overgrown. It was the perfect spot to bury something you wanted to disappear.

As we drove up to the spot I turned off the engine. "Let's get this over with."

"Agreed," Jason got out of the car. "I don't wanna be out here too long."

We walked to the back of the car and I unlocked the trunk. It was a little hard to see because of the lack of light. After we dug two deep holes we decided not to burn the bodies. We didn't want to be out there any more than we had to. We dumped the bodies and covered them with loose dirt

twenty-nine

Two days later, on a cloudy day, they had Joe's funeral. For me, it was a day of mixed emotions. On one hand, I was glad he was gone, but, on the other, I questioned if I'd done the right thing. A lot of people from both sides of the river attended. Smaller crews from all around Arkansas were there. There were no enemies, just friends. A few of the guys got up one by one and gave a eulogy. It only occurred to me then that there were still people who had a lot of respect and love for Joe. As I was listening to everyone talk, I remembered that's how I felt at one time, after all, Joe was the one who mentored me. He was kind to me. If it wasn't for him I'd have been dead. If I had the chance to go back in time I'd do it the same way. After the services, a bunch of us went back to Highlife to drink.

"It's a damn shame," Rooster said, as he drank a mug of dark beer. "That guy was something else. I owed a lot to him. You know, he was with me on my first kill?"

"I didn't know that," I told him.

"I got so sick after. I was a little embarrassed by it all. Joe just patted me on the shoulder, and told me most people go through that."

"I know I got sick."

"Most people I know did. I guess Joe didn't. He said that he was colder than ice. Guess it's different for everyone."

"Mind me asking about your first?" I asked him.

He smiled into his mug. "Oh, man, thinking about that... Crazy days. It's funny, things we get into, know what I mean? One day you wake up not being a killer, by the end of the day you are one. I'd already been in the drug

game for awhile when it happened. This guy, he stole
some money from my brother. My brother had to pay the
guys above him, because of that one prick he didn't have
enough money. My brother told me this, it just pissed me
off. It hadn't been that great of a week for me, some
other bullshit... For another day. Anyway, I hadn't had
much sleep that week. Word was that someone wanted
me dead - this guy who thought I cheated him out of
dope. I was mad. When my brother told me about his
problem, I guess I just took my anger out on that guy.
Joe went with me. I dealt with the problem."
 "Damn."
 "Shit happens."
 "What happened to the guy who wanted to kill you?"
 "I got to him first."
 "You got lucky there."
 "Bet your ass I did."
 "Hey, at least you didn't end up dead."
 "That's right," Rooster said. "I'm here to tell the tale."
 The both of us laughed.
 A few of the other guys saw us talking and came over.
We spent the next few hours drinking and telling stories.
I found out about their pasts with Joe, and how they got
connected.

thirty

Six nights later, I was sitting with Jason in my car across the street from where Jerry Hale was dealing on Mullen and Brooster. It had been off-and-on rain all day. The dreary night sky was slowly clearing. Small pools of water dotted the street. We were there to make sure everything ran smoothly. A few nights before there'd been some people shot in the neighborhood over drugs. Jerry was a short skinny guy. He weighed about one-eighty-five. He was strong. Ultimately, we were there to back Jerry. If he got into a jam, we would help get him out.

A few people here and there were out on the street at that hour. The rain pretty much had people stay indoors all day.

"I tell you, man, I get tired of this shit," Jason said, as he lit a cigarette. "It's downtime like this that makes me wonder why I don't get into another line of work."

"What would you do?" I asked.

"I don't know. I should've finished school and become a teacher."

"You and me both."

"At least we have the music thing going on."

"Yeah, if the damn record label-"

"It'll all work out."

"Maybe."

"Oh, yeah, it will, man. You just have faith, brother."

"Thing that gets me, you have to think something's going on. We have a contract. All of this could go to shit, what then?"

"Go to another label?"

"That's the way I look at it."

"Hope it won't come to that."

"Me either, buddy."

I looked out the car window.

Jerry was across the street with a few customers.

"How's your lady doing?" Jason asked.

I looked at him. "Everything's fine."

"That's good."

I shook my head. "She was talking the other day about having dinner at her place. You and the other guys are invited."

"Sounds good. I'll bring a date."

"Who?"

He smiled. "Not sure yet," he laughed. "I have a list."

"I bet."

"Have to keep your options open."

"You have to make sure you don't get any dirty whores."

"Says you. I know you've had your group of whores."

I laughed. "Yeah, I know."

"Take precautions, that's all."

"Like wrapping your shit?"

"Exactly."

I lit a cigarette and looked out the window. "Don't know how we got stuck with this bitch work. I could be doin' better things with my time."

"Not to mention, I mean, come on, it's Jerry. A nice guy, but, I wouldn't die for him."

"Not everyone can be the same as you."

"You're right," my brother said. "I dunno, he's just not my cup of tea, I guess. The only reason I signed on to do this was because I knew Sal asked you to be here. Couldn't let you go in alone. I'd feel bad if something happened and you got hurt."

"Thanks. Don't think anything is gonna happen here, though. This shit's just protocol."

Jason nodded. "I get it. You hear who was doing the shootin' out here the past few nights."

I shrugged. "Not sure. I know some of the other guys asked around. They didn't get much information out of anyone. Everyone has their fuckin' code. Things like that get a little tricky."

"It was probably kids trying to make a name for themselves."

"Guess we'll find out sometime. Honestly, I don't think it's gonna amount to anything. I mean, we might find out it was just a little argument on a domestic level."

"That could be true. Good idea. Never thought about that."

"There's a lot of crazy folks out there."

Another laugh. "Don't I know it? I think we might be falling in with that crowd."

"I'm trying not to. Bein' around this shit every day, it has ways of twisting your mind. We need to stay focused on the positive. The band."

"Balancing the two could get hard, I'd think."

"It might. Something tells me we can never fully get out of this life, though."

"You ever get nervous about that?"

"About this stuff?"

"Yeah."

"At first. The cash came in handy. I had to come to terms with the other part."

"Would you want out when the music takes off?"

"Afraid there's no getting out of this. We've already killed people. We could end up in prison for life if someone wanted to use that against us."

He shook his head.

"But, yeah, I'd like to see this music thing be successful."

"At some point, you'll have to make a choice. None of

this 'both sides of the law' thing. At some point, you'll have to find what directions you wanna go down."

I exhaled some cigarette smoke. "When it comes to that, it'll be dealt with."

"Whatever it'll be, I'm all in."

"I appreciate that."

"We're brothers. We have to back each other. The other guys, I'm not sure about them. Don't get me wrong, love those guys to death it's just not the same."

As we continued to talk, I looked at Jerry through the windshield. A guy walked up to Jerry. The next thing I know the guy hit Jerry with a gun. Jerry fell to the ground. Jason and I instantly jumped out of my car and ran across the street. I tackled the man to the pavement. I picked him up by his shirt and hit him in the face three times.

"Wait!" he screeched.

"That guy you hit, not the best move."

Jason ran over to see how Jerry was.

It was clear Jerry had been knocked out.

Jason lunged at the guy. "You fuckin' maniac! Why'd you do that?"

The guy seemed a little shocked as he stood without a word.

"What's your name?" my brother asked.

No answer.

My brother asked again, but still no answer.

Jason took out his gun and pointed it at the guy. "Two against one. Tell me your name, or, I'll take a hole through you."

He held his hands up. "Wait…wait…wait!! Name's Cubby," he lowered his hands. "Maybe we can come to an arrangement."

"What arrangement?" Jason snapped. "We don't have anything you want."

Jason walked in front of Cubby, took his gun, and hit him two times. Cubby fell to the ground.

My brother looked at me. "This isn't good shit."

"We need to get Sal," I said.

Jason looked up the street. "I know there are two pay-phones over there," he pointed in the direction where a closed movie retail place.

"Guess one of us stays here while the other makes the call?" I said.

"Sure."

I laughed. "Wanna flip for it?"

"You'll lose."

"Sure about that?"

"You bet."

I dug into my pocket and brought out a quarter. "Call it," I flipped the coin in the air.

"Heads," Jason called.

The coin dropped on the top of my hand.

I looked at the coin. "…And it's Tails!"

He looked at the coin and shook his head. "Well, guess that's how things go."

"Thought you were gonna win, kick my ass?"

"Get the fuck outta here."

I chuckled. "There's always a next time."

"Hope that won't happen."

"That's wishful thinking."

"I know, right?"

My brother got into my car and darted down the street. As I stood waiting, I hoped Cubby wouldn't wake. I didn't wanna have to deal with him until I had my backup. I looked at him, and he started to move around. I panicked for a moment. The first thing I could think of was to hit him with my gun. He slumped to the ground. I walked over and kicked him a few times. About that time Jason came back in my car. He told me Tony and

Sal were on their way.

I looked down at Jerry and he opened his eyes. I crouched down beside him and told going to be okay.

About ten minutes later headlights came down the street. The car parked and Sal and Tony got up and walked over.

"Thanks for coming down," I said. "Sorry about this."

Sal gave a deep sigh. "Let's see what we have here," he went over to Cubby, who started to awake again. Sal picked him up by his collar. "Think you'll have to come with us."

"It…not my fault," Cubby muttered.

"Sure, buddy," my boss said.

By this time, Jerry was back on his feet.

Cubby looked over at our drug dealer friend. "I'm sorry, you have to believe me."

Jerry walked over to him and spat in his face.

Cubby opened his mouth to say something.

Jerry hit him a few times in the face.

Cubby dropped to the ground.

Tony walked over and unlocked the trunk of his car.

"What are you doing?" I asked.

Tony retrieved a bag and then walked back over to us. In the bag was a long length of rope, a pipe, and a roll of electrical tape. "This is how we get him outta here," Tony handed Jerry the pipe. As soon as he had the pipe he slammed it into Cubby's face. Blood bubbled from his mouth as a tooth hit the ground. He let out a moan. Cubby fell to the ground after Jerry cracked him with the pipe a few more times. Tony threw the roll of tape to me. I ripped off a long piece and put it over Cubby's mouth. I took the rope and tied his hands and feet. We carried the guy to my car and stuffed him in the trunk.

When we got to the crew's warehouse I commented to Jason about how much land there was out there, and how we wouldn't get bothered by any traffic if we buried the guy.

"We'll see what they want done first," Jason said. "Need to figure out what the deal is."

"Probably right."

"I'm always right," he chuckled.

"Really? Could've fooled me."

"Fuck-face."

"Asshole."

He laughed.

We exited the car just when our boss and his friend rolled up. As the boss looked over my shoulder, I popped the trunk of my car

Sal said, "Take him out. Need to get this over with," he shuffled to the warehouse door and unlocked it. Jason and I got Cubby out of the trunk. The guy struggled and moaned the whole time. It took all we had to get him inside the warehouse. Tony told us to place him in a chair in the center of the room. Once we had him in the chair my brother ripped the tape from his mouth. He screamed out in pain.

Jerry walked in from the outside.

To calm Cubby down I hit him two times. After he spit some blood, he looked at me with scared eyes

I snapped my finger in front of his face. "You know who we are?"

He said nothing.

"Hope you understand English."

The guy gave a nod. "I understand," he looked around the room. "Where am I?"

"We'll be asking the questions."

"Fair enough. That's the way it's gotta be, yeah?"

"It is."

A small smile started to cross his face. "You boys have

any whiskey? Worked up a thirst after those hits."

I shook my head. "None for you."

"That's a shame. I was hoping we could put this incident behind us, and have a few drinks. We could have a few laughs. I understand what this is," I'm reasonable," he looked over at Jerry. "Everyone needs a good knock-around now and then - it keeps us on our toes, keeps us prepared for those surprises around the corners. You walk around, and next thing, hit in the face by a fuck. As we spin, this whole thing is constantly climbing to the end."

Jerry said, "You're lucky I don't end you right now. I'm tempted to."

The man in the chair let out a big smile. "Now, is that any way to talk? Oh, I bet you wish you could. You'll never be able to, kid. You don't have it in ya."

Jerry said to the man. "Last I looked, you were the one tied to the chair."

"Yes, you have it all figured out. Guess everyone has their day in the sun. Better enjoy it while you can."

I turned my head and looked over at Sal. "You wanna take this one?"

"Sure," Sal walked over to Cubby. "My name's Sal, and you're in a world of shit," he pointed around the room to us. "See, these guys? They work for me," he looked back at Cubby. "They'll do everything I ask of them. They'll torch your whole world. They don't give a fuck, I don't give a fuck. It's all up to you. This is the last thing I wanted to do. This whole thing, it's made me a little cranky. I was at home watching a movie, bowl of popcorn, and soda, and having a little time to myself. I was about to put on another movie when I got a call about you beating one of my men. I haven't seen you around before. You must be a new addition to someone's crew. You tell me, I'll go easy on ya, kid."

Cubby turned his head spat on the floor and muttered something to himself. After he turned back towards us I asked if he was finished, then, I hit him.

"Oh, sorry about that," I stretched out my hand, as a small surge of pain ran through it. "We can go like this all night. If it were me in that chair, the idea of getting beat all night wouldn't appeal to me," I laughed. "I dunno, for all we know you could be one of those weirdos who gets off on pain."

Tony laughed, "I'd think the ladder."

"Sounds about right," Jason said. "Look at him, guy even looks like a sick pervert."

After a few more words Sal handed Jerry his gun.

Jerry aimed the gun at Cubby. "Shit, man, you could've killed me. Think you came pretty close. We can't let that happen again," Jerry lowered the gun. "See, this is what's gonna happen: I'm gonna put a bullet right in your shit-filled head."

"No, no, no, no, not this, not now," Cubby gasped. "You don't wanna kill me. I… I… you don't understand. Come on, man, just listen!"

"And why's that?" Jerry said. "Tell me why I should let you live after what you did?"

"It wasn't me," Cubby said. "Ted... he told me to do it. He told me to start getting your attention."

"The fuck you talkin' about?" Jerry said

Cubby said, "Ted Lavery, he said since Joe's out of the picture he wants to start taking things over. He's gonna run you guys out."

"What," Jerry lowered the gun again. "Better be telling the truth."

Sal said, "Why would he say that? We always had a good business friendship."

"Friendship burns sometimes," Cubby added. "The way I understood it, Ted and Joe Butler were good friends."

"Joe's out of the picture," Sal said.

"He knows."

"Then why wasn't he at the funeral?"

"Not sure."

"Guess he was busy."

"Couldn't tell ya. I was just doing what I was told. They don't tell me shit. I'm just tryin' to make my way through it all, trying to prove myself to those guys."

"Were you guys behind the shootings in that neighborhood, too?" Sal asked.

"We were."

"Why?"

"A few people who deal over there, we were tryin' to get 'em out."

"We deal over there."

"It wasn't you guys. It was these guys who lived there. I jumped your friend because I thought he was one of them. I was just doin' what I was told. My boss wanted to take that ground over there," Cubby took in some air.

"And he didn't think there'd be a backlash?" Sal looked confused.

"They never told me about any of that."

"Didn't you think about it?"

"Not really. I just figured whoever would just roll over. Never count on being tied to a chair. You gonna kill me?"

"Nah, I'm not gonna kill ya," my boss said. "I'm a nice guy."

"I appreciate it. This'll never happen again."

"You got that right."

"I tell ya what you should do," Cubby said. "You should wipe out Ted's crew."

"Why would I do that?"

"Cause he wants you dead."

"If it's true, that'll be dealt with. You don't worry about

our business.”

Cubby looked down at the ground, then, he looked back at Sal. “What are ya gonna do with me?”

“What do you think we should do?”

“Let me go.”

“Figured you’d say that.”

“We can forget this ever happened.”

“Don’t think we can do that.”

“Why?”

Our boss laughed. “You serious? Don’t forget, you tried to end that guy over there,” he nodded to where Jerry was standing.

Cubby looked at Jerry. “Sorry about that. Didn’t mean it.”

Jerry said nothing.

Tony said, “We should talk about this one, boss. We should make a plan on what to do.”

Sal looked at the guy in the chair for a minute, then, looked at us. “Let’s go outside. Try to figure out what we should do with this guy.”

We kept the door open when we went outside.

We had to make sure Cubby wasn’t gonna try anything.

“What do ya wanna do here?” Jason lit a cigarette. “Can’t let him go. He’ll go back and tell. I say we go across the bridge right now to crack some heads.”

“Nah, nothing like that right now,” Sal said. “We don’t wanna make that kind of noise.”

“Really? We need to stop this before it becomes a big problem. We don’t know what their next plan is. Come on, man, we can catch ‘em off their guard. Before they know what hit ‘em. They won’t be a threat. Send all the other crews a clear message.”

“I know,” Sal said. “We’ll let this go tonight. We need to think about this. Get a plan together. It doesn’t seem right. Something‘s not adding up,” he turned back to the open door. "We need to do something with the guy in there."

Tony said, "We can't let him go. No telling what he'll do."

Jason said, "You could always try to recruit him."

"I'll tell you now, I'll kill him if he joins us," Jerry blurted.

"That won't happen," Sal said. "We don't need him. Whatever we do we need to do it fast. His guys will be looking for him down the line."

Tony looked out onto the field beside the warehouse. "Yeah, they won't find him out here. No one comes around here. It shouldn't take that long to dig the hole. Just something that has to be done. It can't be helped."

"I'd love to do that," Jerry said. "You won't hear any sort of bullshit from me. He needs to pay."

"Guess we'd better get it over with," my brother said.

I looked through the doorway and saw Cubby struggling, trying to undo the rope. "Should we give him a last dinner or something?"

Tony laughed.

"Let's finish the job," Sal said, as he looked at Jerry.

Jerry nodded. "I'll have no problems with that."

Sal motioned for everyone to follow him back into the warehouse. Inside, Jerry was standing over Cubby. Just as I blinked my eyes I heard a loud crack. I discovered what happened was Jerry hit Cubby across the face with the butt of a shotgun. Out of the corner of my eye, I saw Sal stagger to the storage closet on the left side of the room. He came out carrying a shovel. As soon as I saw the shovel I knew what was gonna happen.

Sal said, "You wanna make this hurt," he threw the shovel to Jerry.

I had to turn my head: I couldn't bear to watch.

As I walked back outside to light a cigarette, the sound

of a shovel hitting flesh two times echoed through the warehouse. I heard the shovel hit the ground followed by three loud gun blasts.

After I finished my cigarette, I flicked the butt into the parking lot.

I walked back through the doorway.

The body of Cubby fell out of the chair. Blood started to pour out of one of the wounds. Smoke from the gun blanked the area for a moment, then dissipated. Sal went back into the closet and came out with two other shovels. He said we needed to bury the body. It didn't take us long to dig the hole. After we put Cubby in his grave we went back into the warehouse and had a few beers. We talked about what to do with Ted. It was decided Sal would call him and set up a meeting.

thirty-one

I was sitting on my couch, staring at some movie on TV when the phone rang. It rang three times before I picked it up.

"Hello?" I said.

"Sean?" the voice said.

"Morris, how the hell are ya?"

"Doin' pretty good. You?"

"No complaints. Just going day-by-day, makin' that money any way I can, buddy."

"That's all you can do," he said.

"Hey, we can all use more."

"I heard that."

"Lottery would be nice about now."

"Just don't forget about me."

I laughed. "What can I do for ya, man?"

"It's what I can do for you."

"Really? What? The record?"

"Something to do with that. Look, I talked to the guys at the label, they wanna sit down and have a meeting. Let the other guys know."

"I'm always up for a trip to Texas. When do they wanna have this little meeting?"

"Friday."

"Friday?"

"That gonna be a problem?"

"Not at all."

"That's in five days if you don't have a calendar with you."

"A lot could happen in five days."

"Just don't fuck me on this."

I laughed. "We'll be there."

"Thanks for that. How's everything else been?"

"About the same. Yeah, I'm glad you called. Jason and I were just talking about you."

"Well, that's nice."

"Can you give a heads-up on the topics of this meeting?"

"All I know is they're gonna talk about the album. Set a release date. Might have to sign a few things. Figure it won't be a big deal.".."

"Hope it'll be good."

"Sure it will."

I let out a sigh. "I'll let the guys know and call you back."

"Thanks."

"Oh, thank you."

"That's just what I do, I'm the magic maker. I make dreams come true."

I smiled. "Well, you could've worked your magic a little faster."

"What do ya mean?" You know all the bullshit that goes into this. A lot of talks and planning. The stories I could tell you."

"I'm just fuckin' with you."

"You know how it can get sometimes. Things get fuzzy. Business can get too much at times," a sigh came from over the phone. "You can only do your best, right? Keep on the right track and hold on. Oh, buddy, it's a crazy ride."

"I see," I said. "You wanna get into another line of work, friend?"

"Oh, not like that. This is a good gig right now. I wouldn't trade it for anything in the world. It just gets draining at times."

"I have an idea," I said. "What else is new?"

"Not much. Talked to Scott the other day. Said he wanted to know when you guys were gonna be back."

"Another party?"

"That's what it sounded like."

"We'll have to stop by their place."

"Sure they'd like that. They liked you guys the last time. They told me two days later. I was over there and they told me."

"That's good."

"It's always nice to make friends."

"Yeah."

There was a pause, then some static on the other end. "Listen, Sean, yeah just tell the other guys. I have a hot little honey over here. We're gonna party all night."

"Last thing I wanna do is get between a man and a piece of pussy."

"I'll get between those legs soon enough."

"Make sure and give me details."

"You got it, buddy."

"I'll talk to you later. Have a good time."

"Will do."

I slowly hung up the phone and walked back into my living room. I grabbed my guitar that was leaning in the corner and sat on the couch. I started to play this song I started writing the day before. A few hours later the phone rang.

"Sean?"

"Boss?"

"Call me back on an outside line."

I hung up the phone, got my keys, and ran out the front door. I drove down the street to the nearest filling station. I walked over to the payphone and dialed Sal.

"Sal, it's Sean."

"You at a payphone?"

"Yeah."

"Good. I called our friend on the other side of the bridge. Told him we need to set down, talk about that shit that happened at that one place."

"What did he say?"

"He was open to it. Wants to meet tomorrow at two. I don't guess the guy wants to come over to this area."

"Why do you think?" I asked.

"Who knows? Maybe it has to do with security."

"What's the plan?"

"The plan is to meet tomorrow about an hour before. I'll call you in the morning, tell you where this meeting is gonna happen. I already talked to the guys I want on this."

"Does he know what happened with the guy?"

"I don't know if he did or not."

"Think it might be a setup?" I asked.

"That's why I'm bringing you guys."

"Whatever you need, I'll be there."

"Good to know."

"Yeah, well...," I dug my hand into my pocket. "Anything else?"

"That's it."

"Okay."

"I'll give you a call."

"No problem."

Instead of going back to my place, I headed over to Madison's. We hung out and had sex. I left sometime after midnight. When I got back to my place I played my guitar for awhile, then, fell asleep.

When Sal called, he told me to come down to the club.

I saw my brother's car when I pulled into the parking lot of Highlife. I knew if I had Jason on my side during this, I'd have a really good shot of making it out alive. I'd walk with my brother to the deepest basement in

Hell. He always had my back and me his no matter what.

I walked through the front door. Viggo was sitting beside my brother drinking beer. I gave a nod when they saw me. I grabbed a stool beside Jason.

"I see you guys are already having a cold one, eh?" I said.

Viggo glanced at his watch. "Seems about the right time."

"I know that's right," I said. "I'm gonna have to join you guys."

"Might as well," my brother added.

I got the attention of the bartender and told him I wanted a beer and another round for Jason and Viggo. The guy filled three mugs, placed them in front of us, and walked away.

"Thanks," I told the bartender.

"Think nothing of it," the man said. "Just doing my job."

"Well, if you weren't here I'd have to pour my own," I added.

"You got a point there," the man gave a knock on the bar and walked away.

Jason raised his mug. "Here's to us: three of the richest guys in the world."

Viggo said, "I'll drink to that. And may it never go away."

Jason looked at me. "Before you came in I was tellin' Viggo about this girl I brought back to my place last night."

"Sorry, I missed it. I wanna hear. Lay it on me, buddy."

"Anyway," Jason said, "this girl wasn't like the others. I looked at her and saw a future."

I looked at him. "You serious?"

"I am," my brother said.

I laughed. "Get the fuck outta here!"

"I mean it. Would I mess around about something like that?"

"Maybe."

"Most girls, we have our hump and that's it. This girl, I dunno, there's something else there."

I took a swig from my mug. "Don't think I've ever heard that before. Why didn't you call me earlier?"

"She left just before I came over here. Thought it'd be sort of rude to talk about her when she was there. Might've pissed her off."

"Who's the girl? Anyone I know?"

"She works at the Century on Riverside. Name's Abby."

"Oh?" I got a surprised look on my face.

"You know her?"

"Heidi and I went there once, and she was working the from desk."

"Really?"

"That was awhile ago. I would've figured she got another job. She didn't look too glad to be there."

"And you liked all the jobs you had?" Jason said.

"Good point."

"If it were me, I don't think I would've lasted a week."

"Two days for me."

Jason smiled.

I said, "We're all gonna have to go out sometime. Sure Madison would enjoy it."

"So would Abby."

"We'll have to put that together."

"I'll let you know."

I said, "She knows about all of this stuff?"

"She knows we hang around with the guys."

"Guess that's better than anything."

"I'm sure if we continue she'll get the whole story."

"They always find out," Viggo intruded. "I've been down that road before."

I looked at Viggo. "A girl slept with you? Did you drug her?"

"Enough of that shit," Viggo snorted. "What are you talking about? I have a girl. Shows how much you know. I mean, we just started seeing each other last week."

I held up my beer mug. "My boys grow up fast. Hats off to both of you."

Jason said, "What's this girl's name?"

"Monica," Viggo said. "She's new to the area. Moved here from California."

"The fuck did she move here for?" my brother asked.

"She had a guy over there. They moved because he got a job offer. He cheated on her, so she split. Good for me, bad for him."

"Sounds like it," I said.

"Looks like we'll have to make that a triple date," my brother told us.

We continued to drink and talk.

Any time of day you could find a few guys from the crew drinking at Highlife: it was an oasis of sorts, an escape from the streets of North Brown Ridge. I heard all the latest gossip around me; about who shot who, who was fucking someone else's wife, and who got locked up. In a way, everyone was a newspaper reporter without the newspaper. Word traveled fast.

The door opened and Tony walked in with Sal. They took the two empty stools on the other side of me.

"How are we doing, boys?" Sal said.

"Can't complain," Viggo took a drink.

As soon as the bartender saw Tony and Sal he was quick to fill two mugs of beer for them.

"Thanks," Tony told the guy. "How's your family, Sam?"

Sam took some empty mugs from the bar. "They're

okay. Things can always be better. But you have to work with what you're given."

"You can say that again," Tony said.

"Wife's always bitchin' about money - what's new? The kids are doing better in school."

Sal said, "That's a good thing. The only thing you can hope for, your family, and loved ones, are all alive and taken care of."

"That's what I tell myself," Sam said.

Sal picked up his beer. "Thanks for the drink."

"No problem, boss."

"You're a good kid."

"Thanks," Sam said.

Tony said, "Just keep on the right track and you'll do good."

The bartender walked to the back.

Sal pointed his finger beyond the door, to the door that led to the back. "He's got something. A good guy. I'll set fire to anyone who talks trash about him."

Tony turned to Sal. "Might need to bring him into the fold."

The boss waved the idea off. "No, no, not him. He has his issues to work out."

"We can always leave it open, right?"

"Maybe. I'm not sure. Something may come up."

"He's strong," Tony said, "I'll give him that."

"Indeed," the boss agreed.

Viggo said, "He stole my bike when we were kids. Took me awhile to figure out who did it."

"How did you find that?" Jason asked.

"One of his little friends told on him."

"Oh, what are friends for, right?"

"No, shit. I was gonna go to his house and beat him up."

"Why didn't you?"

"I was grounded. My parents caught me ditching school one day."

"How'd that go?" Tony asked.

"Couldn't do anything for three weeks," Vigoo took a drink. "When I was able to do stuff again I was happier than shit. I was a growing kid, and the world was a huge candy store."

Tony howled. "And the boy picked through it all!"

I said, "Did he know the bike was yours?"

"Don't think so. I never told him. A friend of mine told me he saw him take it."

Sal rubbed his chin. "I can always call him out here, two of you can fight about it."

"That's okay. I'm not gonna do anything like that."

We sat at the bar and had another beer and some more laughs.

The five of us walked out into the parking lot.

"The guy called me and wants to meet at Stiggy's," Sal told us.

"I know where that is," my brother said. "I went there a few months ago. It was this party thing for a friend. It was fun. We got smashed"

Tony shrugged. "Maybe your friend's still there."

"He's dead."

"Did he die at the party?"

"No."

"What happened?"

"He was hit by a train."

"Guess the two of you aren't friends anymore."

"Guessed right."

Tony laughed. " That's a rough way to go. Things like that happen. When was this?"

"It's been about three years," Jason said.

"Sorry to hear that," Sal said.

"It was fucked-up. I guess he was drunk. I heard about

it a few days later."

"Was he into drugs?"

"Yeah."

"Dance with death, damn shame," Tony pointed his finger at Jason. "See, you guys need to stop doin' that shit. Look what happens."

"I know."

After we finished our drinks we walked outside.

I walked over and opened my car door, then looked over at Sal. "Should we be armed for this little meeting?"

Sal said, "I would if I were you. You always wanna be prepared. Shit might get sideways. Don't just wanna be holding your dick when shit hits the fan. You didn't bring your gun?"

"Point taken," I said. "We brought 'em with us. I didn't know if we should go in there with them."

All the time I'd been associated with the criminal element in North Brown Ridge I never attended a sit-down. I was a little nervous. You could never let on that you were nervous to anyone: it was a sign of weakness. The only person I could truly confide in was Jason and Madison. It's a dangerous world. You always had to be on your guard.

Tony said, "You know where we're going?"

"To Hell?" Jason smiled.

"Something like that," Tony said. "The bar, you know where it is?"

"Of course," Jason opened the car door.

"Okay, let's go. One thing I should tell you guys, is don't do anything unless we do. You guys get in there and hear something you don't like, don't start pullin' your guns and shit. I know how distracted you guys can be."

Viggo said, "What are you saying?"

"Hey, no offense," Tony said. "I've just seen you in action before. Some of the things you hear at this meeting you may not like. Just don't do anything you'll regret."

"I never regret anything."

Sal walked over to Tony's car. "Let's get this show started."

thirty-two

We turned down Doriman Street and drove nearly to the end of the busy street where the place was. When we were driving to the bar Jason was telling us a few things about the place. I was a little nervous about what he said. I didn't want to walk into death.

We pulled into the parking lot with Sal and Tony behind us. Everyone got out of the car they were in. I glanced around the area as we talked to the boss. I wanted to make sure nothing was outside - nobody waiting in the bushes or behind a car ready to take us out.

I tried to make out what was on the other side of the small dirty window on the wooden door.

We entered the place.

Two people were sitting at the bar. Cigarette smoke filled the room. A game show was on the television above the big bartender's head. As we walked up to the bar. I could tell by the look on the bartender's face he knew who Sal was. I'm sure the guy figured the other guys and I were part of his crew. The other guys sitting at the bar gave us a nod when we walked over. The two men quickly turned their heads back to the show.

"Help you guys?" the bartender said.

Sal walked closer and leaned over the bar to the man. "How are you?"

"I'm okay," the man took a full ashtray off the bar. "You?"

"Oh, I'm good. Never been better. Well, that's not true, I've been a lot better before."

The guy dumped the contents of the ashtray in a trash can behind the bar. "Yeah, I got that."

My boss laughed. "Seems to work like that."

The man looks over at us. "Guys need anything?'

We told him we didn't want anything.

My boss asked the bartender what his name was.

"Rick," the man said.

"Nice to meet you, Rick," the boss said. "It's always good to meet new people. Alliances are always wise to make - never know when they'll come in handy."

Rick gave a nod.

"You know why we're here?"

Rick shook his head. "To get a drink?"

Sal laughed. "No, no, not today. Ted in the back? We have a meeting."

Rick said, "I can call him. Not sure how much longer he's gonna be."

"That'd be nice of ya."

Rick walked across to the other end of the bar and picked up a white phone. He pressed a button, waited, then started to talk to someone on the other end. He hung up and walked back to us.

"Ted wants you to know how sorry he is. He should be out in about ten minutes or so. We got behind on things."

Our boss let out a grin. "No problem. I can understand that."

Rick looked over at me and the other guys. "Want something while you wait? It's free for you guys. Don't want friends of my boss goin' thirsty."

We all said we'd take a drink.

Sal looked at the two sitting at the bar. "And how are you guys? Good day to sit and watch some tube, eh?"

"It's almost over," a blonde-haired man said. "Have to leave in a bit."

"I wasn't trying to run you off or anything. Stay, relax, have another drink. Bet you're glad to get away from the wife for a bit."

"I'm not married," the man said.

"Good for you. Keep it like that. Women, they're nothing but a pain in the dick, friend."

"I'll keep that in mind."

Sal said, "You guys work for Ted?"

One of the guys, the blond-haired guy, looked at Sal. "Not me," he bumped his friend on the shoulder. "He does. I kept telling him to get out, that he doesn't want this."

Our boss said. "No offense, friend, but what the fuck do you know?"

The man's eyes got wide. "Now, listen, ass-"

"Now, now, now," Sal held up a finger. "I'd watch what I'd say if I were you. I don't know what you were about to say, but have manners."

I stood thinking we might have to fight for a minute.

"Sir, I didn't mean anything by it, sorry. Just having a drink," the man said.

Sal shrugged.

The conversation made the guy who was beside the blond-haired guy take notice. "Nah, my friend here, he wouldn't last. Took him on a drug deal once. Things got bad. He pissed his pants. He's a good guy, though. He's one of a kind."

"I bet," the boss said. "That's a rare thing these days," he nodded at the man speaking. "You are?"

"Hoover."

"Good to meet you."

"Likewise."

"I'm sure."

"So, what's your business?" Hoover asked.

"My business is none of yours."

"Fair enough."

Hoover was a bald man, about thirty-five, with tattoos up and down his arms. He wore a sleeveless white shirt with a thick gold chain around his neck.

"You been with Ted long?" Sal asked.

"Long enough," the bald man said. "I do whatever Ted asks."

"That right?"

"Got a problem with that, guy?"

"No problem from me," Sal said.

"You were one of Joe's guys," Hoover said. "Sad thing about him."

"It was," our boss said.

Hoover looked over at us. "Hey, I've seen you guys before."

"Oh, yeah," I said. "Where was that at?"

"Down at Blue Room. You and the other guys. Good music. I forgot the name."

"Stoned Monkey," my brother said.

"That sounds about right. Things were a little blurry that night - too much booze."

Jason cracked a smile. "It's all good, man. I know how that goes."

"You guys pullin' double duty or what?" Hoover grabbed a handful of peanuts from a little bowl on the bar and popped them in his mouth.

"Something like that," I said.

"Hey, no one can tell you how to make money," Hoover took a long swig from his beer bottle.

"That's what I say."

"So, that workin' out for ya?"

"We do okay."

"That's good," Hoover lit a cigarette. "You have to do something. , I tried once but couldn't stick with it. Never had patients."

"It takes some."

Hoover blew a chunk of smoke. "You guys, you guys, you sounded good. I was a fan, I'll just tell ya that right now. I caught you guys at another bar, too. Business called that night and had to leave early. You guys do private parties, shit like that?"

"Sure."

Rick, from behind the bar, put a few more bottles of beer out. "Anyone wants another?"

"I'll take one," Viggo walked over and grabbed one.

"Rock n' Roll!" Rick howled. "Anytime's a good time for it."

Tony looked at his watch. "He gonna come out, or what?"

The bartender said it was an important meeting Ted was in.

"And we aren't important? The fuck?"

Sal turned to him. "Hey, we can wait a bit. What do we have to do?"

The other man crawled off of his bar stool and threw some money on the bar. "It was good. Tell him I had to go. I'll catch up later."

"Will do," Rick said, as he took the money. "Have a good one."

The man turned to us, nodded, and walked out the front door.

Rick said, "That guy has problems."

"Really?" I said.

"Yeah. It's a shame. Someone lets himself get led down the road by booze."

"Why have him in here?"

Rick chuckled. "Tell me someone that doesn't need money. Hey, I feel sorry for the guy but I gotta eat, too. I don't mean to be rude or anything, but I gotta look out for me."

"I can understand that."

"But it's sad. He needs help. I'm not gonna do it. Wouldn't know the first thing to say, some bored bullshit about being happy, about how you don't-"

Just then, the phone on the bar screamed.

Rick walked over and picked the receiver up.

"Yeah?" he answered.

There was a pause while he listened to the other end.

"Yeah, they're still here. Hadn't gone anywhere."

Another pause.

"We have more than enough. How many?"

After another.

"Oh, no problem," he cocked his head to the side. "Whatever you want, sure."

Another pause.

"Sure I can get some," Rick said. "How much longer you guys gonna be?" he looked up at the ceiling. "I know," he laughed. "That remains to be seen. Know what you mean. If he thinks he can," another laugh. "Well, yeah," a nod. "Pretty sure. Okay, I'll let 'em know."

I looked at Tony and shrugged. "We being played?"

Tony shook his head. "Nah."

Rick, behind the bar, hung up the phone.

Sal looked at him. "And?"

"They'll be out in a minute. Hashing out a few new business deals."

"The power of greed," Tony blurted.

"The way of life, am I right?" Hoover said.

"I can drink to that," Sal said.

Hoover held his bottle in the air. "Here, here! The things every man chases."

"Indeed," Viggo said.

Hoover stood from his bar stool. "My friend, I gotta get on the road. Have a few stops to make."

"Duty calls," Rick retrieved his friend's beer bottle from the bar. "Have to do what you do."

"I might stop in later," Hoover started for the door.

"I'll be here," Rick said. "Won't go till about midnight."

"Damn, that late?"

"You know, no one else can do it."

"Why's that?"

"They all have reasons."

"Sounds like bullshit to me."

"Without a doubt."

Hoover said, "So, yeah, thanks for the drinks."

Before he walked out the door he told Sal that if he ever needed anything, wanted anything, needed an extra hand for work, to call him.

"You're with Ted, no?" Sal asked.

Hoover said, "Nobody can tell me how to make money."

"Okay, then," Sal told him. "I'll keep that in mind. Something may come up."

"Thanks."

"Anytime."

The drug dealer told us it was nice to have met before he staggered out the door.

A minute later loud music came from a car as it pulled out of the parking lot.

"You guys need anything else?" Rick asked.

Sal looked at us all, then, back at the bartender. "We're good."

"Good," the man said. "You need anything just say so."

A door opened from down the corridor. Voices began to make themselves clear.

"Looks like you guys are up," Rick muttered.

thirty-three

Footsteps clunked down the hall to where we were. A second later Ted stood at the mouth of the hall with two other men. Ted spoke with a rough voice. He was in a black suit and tie. The other two guys were normal street clothes. Ted's face was a little pale. He had a tired look to him. The man had dark rings under his eyes. White peppered his black hair. He introduced us to the guys by his side. Their names were Alex and Diggs. Ted explained how the two men were part of his crew, that they were two of his guns.

Ted said, "Two other guys were supposed to be here, but they got called away on other business. I'll be sure and tell them what they missed. Good, you could make it over here. It means a lot. Hope traffic wasn't that bad. I have to apologize, I had another matter I had to give attention to."

"That's okay," Sal said. "We were just getting to know everyone who was here, and Rick."

"Oh, I see," Ted said.

Our boss said, "Rick here his a good guy," he turned and smiled at the bartender, then back at Ted. "He does a damn good job."

"Thanks," Rick said to Sal.

Ted said, "I only have the best."

"I see that," Sal folded his arms. "It pays to have good people - people you can count on. You sure don't want anyone you can't trust."

"Oh, yeah, I've had my share I couldn't trust. Those guys had a way of disappearing. I tell all my guys about that."

The two bosses gestured for all of us to follow to the back room.

Rick called out. "You guys need anything just use the phone."

Ted turned. "Maybe a bucket of beers? That sounds good."

"No problem."

"You're the best!" Ted turned and continued walking.

When we entered the room Alex shut the door behind us.

"Yeah," Ted looked at us. "We better start this meeting. I have a lot on the agenda. Being boss isn't all fun and games, you know? A lot of times I end up looking the asshole."

Sal said, "I know how that goes. I just got this job and I'm already feelin' it. Let's get this show on the road. I'd like to be back in my neighborhood around five."

"You gotta hot date?"

"Nothing like that," Sal said. "I'd just like to be home."

Ted said, "We're gonna have to make some sort of progress here."

The room had three little tables along with a big round table in the center. As I walked across the red carpet, I got a little worried that we might all be shot.

Sal and Tony sat at the big round table across from Ted. We stood over them.

Rick came in with a bucket full of ice and beer.

"If anyone calls for me tell them I'll get back to 'em later," Ted told Rick.

"You got it, boss," Rick replied, then walked out of the room, closing the door behind him.

Diggs and Alex gave everyone a beer.

Ted said, "First off, I wanna give my condolences about Joe. He was a good man. You won't find many like him anymore. He was the"

"Best," Sal stepped in.

"Yeah, that's what I was gonna say. No one can ever replace him."

"I know," Sal said.

"We all know what happened. I was surprised."

"I'm the one who found him."

Ted's looked surprised. "Really? I bet that made an impression."

"To put it lightly."

"That's never an easy thing."

"Wish I was there."

"You know who killed Joe?" Ted asked.

"I don't," Sal shifted in his chair.

"That's a shame."

"If I did, I'd guarantee that person wouldn't be on this planet anymore. Joe and I were like brothers, like family."

"I can understand that, sure," Ted said. "Take it from me, no one in my crew had anything to do with it."

"I'm sure we'll find out. I'm not stupid, I know what this can bring. There was a bond there. You can't share something like that with just anyone."

"Funny how things happen, eh?"

Sal sighed. "Yeah. You know, you never expect the best people around you to die. You know it's gonna happen with all of this, but you prepare yourself fully. We were brothers. We were more than blood. You know the story of our past. You were there for a lot of it, you know how it was. Not sure if you ever knew this, though, he was the one who came with me for my first kill."

"I don't remember that the first guy you took out," Ted shook his head. "Never heard that story."

"It was the day after I turned twenty-one. I didn't wanna make it a big thing. It was in the papers."

"I'm sure you had your reasons."

"He wasn't very nice to a family member of mine. Had to teach him a thing or two."

"But he wasn't alive to use those skills."

"You do what you can..."

"I tell myself that every day."

"Last I knew, his parents hired someone to find the guy. Guess they didn't know about his double life. You know, I find myself thinking about him sometimes."

"In what way?" Ted asked.

"About what he'd be doing today if I hadn't killed him. Just think did I need to do what I did? I know, man, after I killed the guy I was sick for two days."

"That happened to me, too," Diggs interrupted.

Ted glared at him. "Who the fuck asked you?"

"I was just saying."

"When I want any of your insights I'll ask," Ted sat back in his chair.

"Sorry, boss," Diggs said.

"You better be."

"Won't happen again."

Ted hit his hand on the table and pointed his finger at Diggs. "If you open your mouth again, I'll go to your mother's house and rape the shit outta her."

Diggs smiled. "My mom died last year."

"Oh," Ted said. "You wanna join her?"

"Not really."

"Good."

Sal said, "That's a good guy you got there."

"He is," Ted confirmed. "All of my guys are good - well, most of them are, anyway. The ones that aren't, they went away."

"I see."

Ted pointed to Alex and Diggs. "Can't find guys like these anywhere."

"They have to be trained good, weed out the bad," Sal

shifted in his chair. "That's one of the things Joe and I talked about a lot - about how you have to be methodical about things, just can't go around shootin' shit. Have to think. Have to be smarter than bullets. These days, I see a lot of young guys who just want to act like gangsters, bangers, or whatever. Most of them, get put in their place. I hate to see it. But the circle goes 'round."

"Things have changed," Ted exclaimed.

Sal stood, walked over, and got a beer from the bucket. "I like to talk about those days. Man, we had some good times," he sat back down. "Thanks for the beer, by the way. You didn't have to do that."

"No thanks needed," Ted said. "I can order as much as I want."

"Sure that comes in handy."

"It does."

"Just say it's a business expense," Sal cracked the bottle open.

"I want my guess to feel welcome."

"Thanks."

The rest of us thanked him.

Ted went on to explain that his second in charge, Conley, couldn't make it.

"I'm sure he had good reasons," Sal said.

Ted continued. "Moving to this topic of Cubby: where's he at?"

Sal shrugged. "After he put that beatin' to Jerry, we returned the favor. He paid. He probably skipped town because he told on you guys."

"What did he tell you?"

"Told us you're the one who told him to be there. He said you wanted to take things over."

Ted lit a cigarette from a pack on the table. "Listen, Sal, I'm not here to waste your time. I know time escapes us all. I'm not gonna tell you what you wanna hear. Truth is, I don't like you and never have. The only reason I tolerated you was out of favor to Joe. I've always thought you were weak. I never thought you'd end up in the top seat - a seat you don't deserve. I liked Joe. He and I, no problems. We got along great. I say this to you, you better be on your guard. I'm not gonna show mercy to you or anyone connected to you. I figured with Joe out of the way I could take whatever I wanted, nobody wasn't gonna say a fuckin' thing."

"I'm not going anywhere."

Ted knocked his fist on the table. "Mark my words, you're finished."

"What about the arrangement?" my boss asked.

"Didn't you just hear what I said? With Joe gone, it nullifies everything from the past. Things change. See, I figure a little war might break out - a small price to pay for limitless wealth. Joe made it clear long ago not to go into his side. I always wanted it all. But I told myself I'd wait my turn. And, thanks to you or whoever, I don't have to wait anymore."

Sal said, "I could shoot you right now, end it here."

Just then, I pulled my .45 from my back.

Alex and Diggs pulled their guns.

Diggs snapped. "I'd think about that if I were you. Don't wanna mess around and have an accident."

My brother and Viggo pulled their guns.

"Make your move," Jason said. "If you kill me, I promise to cut one of you down before I go."

Diggs cocked his gun. "I'd like to see that happen."

"Just make your move," Alex cocked his.

"Fuck you!" Jason tore.

Tony gestured for us to lower our guns. "Okay, guys, we aren't gonna do this here. Not now. Don't get hyper!"

Ted told his guys to lower their firearms.

Ted said, "My suggestion to you, it would benefit you

to get out of it while you can. Get into another line of work."

"I don't think so," Sal calmly said. "You'll get your war if you want it. Be prepared to lose. I know how to get my hands dirty. We go back a long time, and it's a shame things have to be like this."

"I'm not goin' away that easy. What, you guys think you can come in here, in my place, and tell me how things are gonna be? This needs to end. I have news for ya, this isn't some sort of a democracy. The fuck you thinking? It's not like you can go to the cops or anything. The fuck you gonna tell them? They'll throw us both in the slammer. And I can assure you, if I go on the inside, you're not gonna get out," he shook his head. "It won't be a good thing. Your business would suffer greatly. Your crew, there'd be nothing left. The guys that are left, I'll give them a choice to choose me or death."

Sal said, "Listen, there's a lot to own. You can't possibly keep an eye on everything. Why not just keep things like they are? You still make good money, no?"

"That's not the point."

"What is the point?"

"Do you realize how many people work for me?

"Plenty."

"I can stretch my power over everything. I plan to use everything I have to destroy you guys."

"We wish you the best of luck with that, buddy," Tony said. "Like my friend said, that won't happen."

Ted exhaled a cloud of smoke from his cigarette. "That's what you say. I dunno, I think things are gonna get very bloody soon. I can only keep a leash on my guys for only a limited amount of time - and your guys are the same," he laughed. "We're all criminals. We have common goals. We just wanna make money and find peace. From what you say that'll be a rough road. I gotta hand it to you, you have a lot of fight in ya: I respect that. At the same time, though, I need to survive. I'll do anything to make sure that happens, old friend."

Sal sat back and folded his arms in front of his stomach. "Whatever happened to us? Like you said, yes, we are all criminals. I'm fine with the way things are. What good is it being king when you're six feet under? I'm sure you don't want that. Our crews, we've been doing this for some time now - yes, we've had our little fights here and there, but for the most part, it's been civil. This business with Cubby, I'm willing to forget about it, just a little bump in the road."

"A little bump?" Ted said. "He's missing. I don't know where he is, do you?"

My boss turned up both hands. "I don't have a clue. Most likely he ran off somewhere."

"Where would he go?"

"How would I know?"

"You just let him go after your feud?"

"We told him not to do it again."

"And you didn't make him disappear?"

"That's right."

"It just seems strange to me."

"Sorry, I couldn't be more help."

"Sure you are."

"Hey, I can only imagine how you feel."

"He was one of my best guys."

"You think he betrayed you?"

"I don't think that's the case."

"I'm sure he'll come back."

"He's gone from us. He won't turn up anytime soon."

"That's always the risk, right?"

"Guess it is."

"We all know what this was gonna be when we got into it."

"Did we? I didn't think about any of this back then."

"Why?"

"I was so caught up in the money and girls."

"That'll do it," Sal said. "Those things cloud every-thing. It gets hard to look passed them. I guess that's why I never got married."

Ted laughed. "You think that's the only reason?"

Sal said nothing, just took a drink of his beer.

The two forces talked longer. I just stood there thinking of leaving that place. I wanted to be with Madison. It seemed as though they kept talking in circles, not getting anything accomplished. To be honest, I was surprised Ted didn't interrogate anymore about Cubby. I guess he knew deep down what happened to him, that letting us know he knew would only make matters worse. The way they saw it, it was the price of doing business. It was a very "no questions asked" type of thing. Everyone knew the rules. For those who asked too many questions, you were sure to meet a bullet. You never knew who to trust. If the heat was getting too much for a fella they could turn on you in a heartbeat, bring you down with them.

Ted pointed his finger at my boss. "Just know you guys are on very thin ice with me. If something like this happens again we'll do to you what was done to Cubby."

'Understood," Sal said, as he took another drink of beer.

"Good."

"But we don't know what happened to Cubby. How many fucking times do I have to tell you?"

"Whatever you say."

The room fell quiet for a minute.

Diggs walked over to Ted, bent down, and whispered something into his boss' ear. The look on Ted's face grew confused. After Diggs walked back to where he previously stood, Ted cleared his throat.

"There's something you might be able to help me with," Ted said.

"And what's that?" Sal asked.

"Two other of my guys, Buster and Shane, no one knows where they are either. You or your guys know anything about that?"

Sal slowly shook his head. "Don't know. Never heard of those two."

"I'm working on it. We'll find out soon enough. If you hear anything let me know."

"I can do that."

"Make sure you do. I don't relish the idea of having these meetings. They're a pain in the ass. I had to stop what I was doing today to come to do this. While I was waiting on you guys something came up - that's why I had you guys wait. And what did we learn from any of it? Not a fuckin' thing. This was a waste of time, now, if you guys don't mind, I'm gonna go to my girlfriend's house," Ted stood.

Sal nodded. "Well, good for you," he looked at Tony. "I think we're done here."

thirty-four

We called the rest of Sal's crew to the club. Sal gave the other guys the highlights of the meeting with Ted, telling us all we needed to keep our eyes and ears open. He told everyone not to trust any talk on the street unless they knew the person well. I already knew a few dozen people who did business across the bridge. He told us we shouldn't ever underestimate anyone.

When you take part in a criminal enterprise you have to develop skills you can't learn in any school. You have to know how shady characters act and think. After awhile, things start becoming second nature.

After the meeting was over, we all went and got a drink at the bar.

I sat on the bar stool beside my brother.

"What's your thoughts on all this?" I asked.

"I think it's pretty fucked."

"I get the feeling nothing good is gonna come from this situation."

"I know."

"Just like all those gangster movies."

"What can we do, buddy?"

"We can always skip town."

"Where to?"

"I dunno."

"I'm sure we'll get through this."

"Think so?"

"Sure," Jason said. "It's always worked out before."

"I like the way you think."

"Not sure about that. You're sort of limited in your options. You can either be killed, or you can be the one doin' the killing."

I shook my head. "This shit, why did I ever get involved?"

"You told me the money was good."

I lit a cigarette. "I'd like to retract that statement. You can't spend money if you're dead. You're dead, you're gone, that's it."

"Yes, sir."

"We can go to Europe."

My brother laughed. "I'm afraid it's too late for that, brother. We have to ride this wild ride out."

"Why'd you have to say that?"

Jason called the bartender over and ordered some more drinks.

"Isn't it a good day to drink?" Jason said.

"Sure," I agreed.

"Of course it is."

"What are you doing after this?" I patted Jason on the shoulder.

"I was going to try to get in a nap."

"Really?" I chuckled.

"Didn't get much sleep last night."

"Why?"

"Not sure."

"You didn't get with a girl?"

"Nope," he said. "I'm afraid to disappoint you."

"Oh, not me," I said. "What, so you gonna get a girl tonight?"

"If I'm in the mood for it."

"Hell, buddy, you should always be in the mood for it."

Jason took a drink from his bottle. "Abby's the only one for me now."

"Really?"

"Oh, yes."

"Who would've thought, huh?"

"I know, right?"

"A big change from before."

"Had to happen sometime."

"I'm glad for ya, bro."

"I gotta say, at first, I was worried."

"How come?"

"She and I talked about it the other night. I sort of got the impression she didn't like what she heard. Said it was okay. But I could tell she had a problem."

"And she's a saint?"

He chuckled. "She's far from that."

"There ya go, then! Why the hell should she care about that stuff? Everyone has a past. You can't apologize for your life."

"I know."

"Crazy."

"Guess she was concerned about me being faithful."

"You could say the same thing."

"I didn't say anything about her past. I was fine with it. Shit happens. She's not doing that stuff now."

"That's good," I said. "She should do the same."

"That's what I thought."

"You never know with people."

"Couldn't tell ya."

I took a drink.

My brother unfolded himself from the stool, took out his wallet, and threw a ten-dollar bill on the bar. "Guess it's about time I move on. You know, that thing about moss not growing on a rolling stone."

I smiled. "I know what ya mean."

I threw ten dollars on the bar. "I'll walk out with ya."

When we got to his car in the parking lot we both lit a cigarette.

"Guess who I got a call from?" I said.

"Who?"

"Morris."

"What's been new with him?"

"He set up a meeting with us and the record company."

"It's about time they get around to wanting to talk to us."

"Yeah."

"I was starting to think they were gonna drop us or something."

I looked at him and shrugged. "They still might. Still haven't released our album."

Jason took his car keys from his pocket and put them in his hand. "When's this meeting?"

"The end of the week."

"Tell the other two?"

"Not yet."

He put the key in the keyhole of the car and opened the door. "Let them know about it. We'll take all of our gear down there, too. It'll be a good time."

"Okay," I said. "I'll give Morris a call and let him know we're coming."

"Sounds good," he got in the car and turned it on. "Well, brother, I'll catch ya later. I need to go and drift in the sweet arms of sleep."

"I'll let you know what I find out."

"Okay," he shut the door.

"Have a good one."

"I'll do my best."

I backed up from the car as he started off the parking lot. The next thing I knew he was gone. When I got back to my place I called Morris.

thirty-five

The next morning, I went to Sal's house to let him know we were going to be out of town for a few weeks. I had to go around to the back alley behind his house so if anyone was watching his place they wouldn't see me. When I first got there he asked if I wanted coffee and breakfast.

"Sure," I said.

"It'll be ready in a minute."

The kitchen was small, and it was stained with cigarette smoke. An old picture hung by a magnet on his fridge of him and Joe Butler. As I got closer to the picture I saw it was dated 1978.

"Picture's pretty old," I nodded to it.

"We went back at least ten years before that. He was a good man."

He opened a cabinet over the stove and took out two plates and two coffee cups. By this time the coffee finished brewing

He put the eggs on the plates, and we took everything over to the table to eat.

"So, you miss him?" I asked.

"Yeah," Sal took the lid off the sugar jar and scooped a spoonful out. "I think about him all the time," he dumped the sugar in his cup. "I'll never be half the man he was," he scooped out another spoonful.

"I think you're a good guy," I took the sugar jar when he was finished.

"I tell you what," he said, "when I find out who got to him, I tell ya, I'm gonna kill that motherless fuck. What's this world coming to, Sean?"

I shrugged. "Your guess is as good as mine. Hell, I

dunno these days."

Sal cut a piece of egg with his knife and ate it. "You might be right about that."

I took a drink of coffee.

"So, what's on your mind, Sean?"

"I got a call from our band manager, he set up a meeting with us and the record label."

"About what?"

"Not sure."

He looked at me. "Just don't let them screw you. It's been my experience that if anyone thinks they can take advantage of a situation, they will."

"Thanks for the tip."

"Don't mention it, kid."

"You going to be okay with us going….Ted and all of that stuff?"

Sal took another drink of coffee. "Oh, Ted will be dealt with in time. I'm pretty sure he'll still be here when you get back. How long will you be gone?"

"Probably a week."

The wall clock in his living room echoed nine o'clock.

Sal said, "I want you to do something for me, Sean."

"Sure," I said.

"I want you to ask around, see if you can get any information on who killed Joe. I wanna find this person and want them to pay."

I said, "It was probably Max."

"You sure about that?"

"I wasn't there, but I'd say it's a good bet."

"I wanna make sure."

"Okay."

After we were done eating, Sal took the plates over to the sink.

"That was pretty good," I said.

"Thanks."

I got another cup of coffee and went back to the kitchen table. I lit a cigarette. Sal walked over to the kitchen counter to a little TV and flipped it on.

"Guess I'll ask around, let you know if anyone knows anything."

"When you hear something let me know."

"Anything you say."

"Thanks, Sean."

I said, "You sure 'bout us going? I mean, we can always reschedule."

Sal shook his head. "Nah, it'll be okay. Ted, I dunno, he talks big, but, seems to me if he wanted to be a ruthless motherfucker he would've killed us at the meeting."

"Or?"

"He could just be toying with us."

We talked for awhile longer. He told me a lot about Joe and Ted. When I asked about what Max was like in those days, he poured some more coffee and told me a bunch of stories.

I asked him what he was going to do that day, and he just looked at me and said he was going to take a nap.

The next day Madison, the guys, and I left for Texas.

thirty-six (TWO WEEK LATER)

Madison and I were sitting in the bar of the Dentem Hotel next to the airport in Maxton, TX. I was on my second beer and Madison on her first. The bar wasn't crowded for a Friday night, just a few quiet people enjoying drinks. We were taking a break from the craziness on the third floor.

Our manager set up a few shows for us in honor of our first album's release. On the first day in town, we had a meeting with the label about our album and future projects. At first, we all thought,

Ostellio, our label, had given up on us before we began. There seemed to be a little breakdown in communication somewhere down the road.

The bartender left us a bottle of whiskey and said he had some stuff to do in the back. We thank him and he left.

"This is a nice place," Madison said.

"It is, isn't it? A nice place to get away."

"I've thought about getting a place like this."

"A bar?"

"Think it'd be nice."

"You work in a bar all day."

"I know. It would be nice to own one," she smiled.

I took a drink. "That could be interesting. You'd need the cash to get started. Somehow I think working at Highlife wouldn't split the bill. You'd have to figure out a way to get the money."

"Well, a girl can dream, right?"

"Yes, you can."

"I just think it would be nice."

I looked into her eyes. "I know I hadn't said it, but I'm glad you came along."

"I wanted to," she put her hand on my hand.

"Thanks."

"Anytime, babe!"

We kissed.

We talked and drank a little more.

I looked over at the lady at the front desk offering artificial smiles, signing people in and out, and chatting with everyone. She wore a white button-down, black slacks, a black vest, and golden hair. When she turned in my direction it was clear she had on enough Makeup that would make a clown jealous. I wasn't a great fan of makeup on women. I liked a natural look on a lady. I could tell she was a very friendly person. A man started to get vocal with the woman, something about him and the people he was with getting kicked out because of noise violations. The manager was called. After a few more words the guy stormed out the front door, cussing as he did.

Madison and I left the bar and went back upstairs

The next night we played at a place called BoxTox. The three-hour show was great. Everyone was glad to see us. I was surprised at how big of a reception we got from the people of Texas.

As soon as we came out on stage and saw all of those faces everything rang clear. This is why we do this, to bring joy to people. Clarence got on the microphone and started his normal routine of greeting the crowd.

Everyone started to roar.

After the show, we went backstage. Morris and Madison waited for us. I took my girl in my arms and gave her a long kiss. Morris told us he set up an interview. I looked at my watch: it was nearing three in the morning.

Morris said we had to be at the radio station at five. We decided to go to an all-night diner to get something to eat, and then, went back to the hotel to freshen up. After we were done we drove to the interview.

The building was a brick five-level affair that housed about a dozen radio and television stations. It was the media hub of the area. All of the professional types with their big grins and smiles looked over their notes as they chugged morning coffee. We walked into the studio as the guy who was going to do the interview started his morning show. The mixer of smoke and leather furniture filled the space. He began his daily address to his listeners, and then, he started talking about some local events around the town. From what he said that area of Texas was supposed to get rain later that day and not stop until two days later. He also mentioned something about a guy who got shot the day before at the local fair. He ended all of that by talking about a chili cook-off they were doing. After he gave his first address of the morning he flipped it to a song, got out of his chair, and walked over to us.

"Nice of you guys to show," he extended his hand to me. "The name's Jules," he shook hands around the room. "And Morris, how the hell are ya?"

The manager chuckled. "Oh, not bad ya know. Just trying to get by."

"I hear that. Same here. This place is a damn hassle most of the time," he hit Morris on the shoulder. "What the hell, huh?"

"Guess so."

Jules turned back to us. "This guy treatin' you guys okay? He hadn't sold you a world of lies, had he? You have to watch this awful son-of-a-bitch."

My brother said, "Yeah, it's been good. He's a good

guy."

"Good, that's good to hear. Morris is a pretty good guy. He knows I like bustin' his balls," he laughed. "Before I start can I get you guys anything?"

We told him we were okay.

"You sure?" Jules pressed on. "We have all kinds of booze and party favors. Sure you don't want anything? It's all good with us. No one minds around here. We're all addicts."

I nodded. "Maybe later."

Jules ran us through some of the rules the studio had regarding interviews. One of the biggest rules was that you couldn't cuss during the interview, but, in the event you did, Jules had a button on the control panel he could press to edit.

Jules leaned back in his seat as another song began. "I keep telling these scum I want a different shift. It doesn't do any good. They just tell me to stop complaining. All of these distractions... it's amazing I even have a life outside of here. I feel like I'm locked up half the time. Might as well blow my fuckin' brains out."

The song ended and he clicked on the "On Air" button.

He spoke into his microphone. "This morning I have a special treat for you," he said. "In the vast world of creativity, there are those that are going to last for years to come. I'm very proud to have the members of Stoned Monkey in the studio this morning."

"Thanks," my brother said. "We're glad to be here, Jules. We'd like to thank the people of Dentem for making us feel at home. You guys are some good fans. I dig everything about it."

"That's good."

"It's the truth."

"And I have to thank you guys for making our little community the last stop on your tour."

Jason said, "The thing that amazes me, is the idea people are just so perceptive to our music. You never know how people are gonna respond to things. I had a great time doing this whole tour. You know, I'd been waiting to do this for so long, it was a joy for me. The rush of it all."

Jules shook his head. "I remember the first time I heard your music. It was a Friday afternoon, I was about to go home for the weekend, and one of the assistants who works here dropped off some packages - one of the boxes was from Ostellio Records. I knew what it was. I knew it was some albums. I opened the box and started to dig through about fifty albums. All from artists who are already established. Then one, it read "To The Academy", from this group named Stoned Monkey. I asked someone what the hell this was. They said they're a new band. Not knowing what this was all about, I took it home. You know, I thought I should at least give it a try. I liked it. You never know if they're going to capture greatness or not."

"We're glad you liked it," Jason said. "At first I thought it was just a good way to pass some time."

Jules laughed. "And look at ya now."

"It's a little unbelievable in retrospect. I mean, hell, I was on a road not going forward. I was just there."

I added, "I'd have to agree with Jason. I didn't know what to do with my life. I met these other two guys in college, that's when we started playing."

"Education of music," William said.

"That's right," Jason said.

Jules leaned back. "Did you guys like your debut music? What did you think of the reception it got?"

"I'll take this one," I said. "We loved making it. We had a good time. But we didn't know what was going to become of it. We had no idea if people were gonna like it or not

Jason interrupted. "We had lots of fun during that time."

"We did that," I added. "Man, the stories I could tell ya. And that was just the beginning."

Jason continued. "' To The Academy' was an experiment for us. We got into this thing not knowing what the hell we were doing. At first, in the early days, it was just about the booze and women. I'd heard women love guys who are in a band. Well, I guess it's still about the girls."

All of us laughed.

Jules shrugged. "That tends to happen. It was probably just the newness of it all. When I first started in this business It was the same way. I just knew I always wanted to be on the radio."

My brother said, "Looks like you've done a good job so far. It makes a difference if you love what you do."

Jules gave him a look. "That's the best thing you can hope for."

I nodded.

William looked at Jules. "You think I can get some coffee? I need a pick-me-up."

"Sure," Jules said. "I know how that can be. Me, I'm a speed freak, myself."

"Thanks."

Jules unfolded himself from his chair and walked over to pour some coffee. He asked William if he wanted sugar.

"A whole can," William said.

He handed William the coffee.

"Thanks," the drummer said. "You don't know how much I needed this."

"No problem."

After a little while another song started playing.

Jules looked down at a pile of papers on his desk. He picked up the first five or six sheets and shuffled through them. "Hope you don't mind, I took the liberty of looking up some information on you guys."

"Hey, whatever you have to do, man," Jason said. "You have to do your job somehow, tracking down facts and whatever. If any of us were where you're at we'd do the same thing. It's all about being professional, right?"

Jules coughed and shuffled through the pages again. "It was sort of a tough job but we did it. Because you guys are new to the scene there's not much on you guys. We had to contact your label: they sent us some information. Guess they didn't have a lot either."

"What information did they send?" I asked.

"Not much. Just your name and where you're from."

"Well," I said. "There's not that much to tell. We're just a bunch of good people from Arkansas who love music."

Jules said, "You guys ever play in Memphis, around that area?"

"Lots of times. I love it over there."

Jason said, "I love Blues music. Of course, this album is more rock than anything, I like the histories you can tell behind it?"

"Any Blues recording in the future?"

"Most defiantly."

Jules went on to tell us about how he came to be in the business he was in. He said his family had always done things for radio.

William leaned forward. "For me, I just wanted to jam. I didn't know, or have any clue, people would even listen to it. Over the years we've developed a little fan base in bars and stuff. I didn't know if we were any good or not. Thought it was crazy when we first met Morris, and he was telling us he wanted to take us into the studio."

"Must've been rewarding," our interviewer said.

"It was pretty nice. It was like we were finally getting some kind of a break."

"Yeah."

We agreed.

They took a short commercial break.

The interview lasted for the next two hours. Jules asked all the right questions you'd ask a new band on the scene. After the interview was over Jules thanked us and said how much he enjoyed meeting us.

We shook hands and walked out of the studio into the hallway. A few people were hanging out and asked for autographs.

We walked out of the building. The morning air hit all of us. We started down the road as the sun began to cover us with its rays.

thirty-seven

We got back into town around nine that night. After I
got unpacked, Madison and I made dinner and then
made love. Early the next day I got a call from Sal. He
gave me a place he wanted to meet. He wanted to meet
at a place called River Way, a little diner that rested
along the river, about a mile away from the river bridge
that connected the two sides of Brown Ridge. The breakfast crowd didn't seem to have started at all based on the
look of the parking lot—it was pretty empty. Sal's car
wasn't in the lot. Of course, it was pretty normal for Sal
to take different cars to evade authorities. He usually had
someone drive him.

As I walked through the door of the diner a small bell
screamed. I looked around and didn't see Sal. I figured
he was probably running late. I walked over to a booth
by the windows and sat in one. The man behind the grill
was frying eggs, bacon, and some sausage. The bar had
six stools: four were occupied, while the other two sat
abandoned. The four of them were involved in loud chatter as a cloud of cigarette smoke lingered.

A waitress came over and handed me a menu. I thanked
her and let her know I was waiting on someone, and that
all I wanted was some coffee. A few minutes later she
came back with a pot of coffee. She said that it was fresh
and that they bring whole pots of coffee to tables. She
gave a smile and walked away. I poured a cup and
looked out the window. The sun made the water a fine
blue. A small white and red boat passed the window and
blew its horn. I thought it would be great to just get on a
boat and sail until I got to a secluded island somewhere.

I looked away from the window, glanced down at the coffee cup, picked it up, and took a drink.

I lit a cigarette.

A few minutes later the bell rang over the door. I looked over and saw Sal and Tony walk in. They walked over and sat across from me. Pretty soon after they sat Sal, said he had to go to the restroom.

Tony said, "The music man returns to us. How was Texas?"

"Wasn't bad," I said.

"That's good."

"What about here?" I asked.

"You know, same old stuff."

"I get that."

"Don't know if you knew this, but I lived there once."

"I didn't know that. What part?"

"A small place called Lothen."

"Never heard of it."

"It's over by the border."

"To Mexico?"

"Yeah."

"Why'd you move?" I asked.

"Had to set up shop there for awhile. This guy was lookin' for me because of this thing that happened."

"How'd that turn out?"

"Guy got shot in a bar fight."

"Damn."

"Worked out for me."

I laughed. "Sounds like it."

"I'd rather it were him instead of me, you know?"

"Wouldn't be a good day for you."

Tony flagged down the waitress for a coffee cup. She came back a minute later with a cup. She asked if we needed anything else. We told her we'd need another cup since our other friend was still in the restroom. She brought back an extra cup and left.

I said, "It's been a bit, how's our one friend and his brother?"

Tony raised a brow. "Oh, them? We haven't heard much from them since you've been gone. It's almost like they vanished."

"Think someone took them out?"

"We couldn't get that lucky. He's probably hiding somewhere. You can never really tell about guys like that," he waved his hand. "Well, when he shows we'll be ready."

A minute or so later, Sal walked over to the table from where the restrooms and payphones were located.

"Everything okay?" I asked.

"Why wouldn't they be?" Sal said.

"Oh, no reason, just asking."

"Thanks for the concern," the boss said.

I nodded.

Sal said, "How was Texas?"

"Exhausting," I said. "When we weren't playin' somewhere we were getting drunk - it was fuckin' great."

Tony laughed. "You should've let me tag along."

"Everything goes okay?" Sal asked me.

"I think so."

"When we gonna get to hear the opus?"

"I have a box of albums they gave me," I said.

"A whole box?" Sal laughed.

"Yeah."

"I guess Tony and I get a copy?"

"No problem."

"This album, when's it gonna be in stores?" Tony asked.

"Next week."

Sal raised a brow. "Next week? Good, that's good. You know, I was thinking, Sean, this could open a new door for us."

"What do you mean?"

"We can talk about it more later," Sal said, "I was thinking maybe we could get into the music business."

"This what you guys wanted to meet about?"

"Not only this. We can continue this conversation another time."

"Okay, then."

Tony grinned. "It's good to have ya back. How'd Madison like it there?"

"She loved it."

"Before too long she'll wanna move, no?"

The idea made me laugh. "Don't think she's ready for that. She likes it here too much."

"There'll come a time."

The waitress came back over with a fresh pot of coffee.

"I'm gonna leave this for you guys," she put the pot on the table.

As she turned and walked away my gaze followed her. "She has a nice look, a good wiggle."

Sal laughed. "That's one of the good things about being a guy," he nodded in her direction. "Those girls are what makes the world tolerable. Everything about a woman - their body, smell, hair, voice, soft touch, I love it all. The love of a woman is the greatest gift you can ever ask for."

I took another drink of coffee. "You may need to quit all this other bullshit and open a dating service."

"I don't think so."

"Why?"

"I like what I do."

"I see."

Sal glanced behind him, then looked across the room.

"What?" I asked.

"Don't want anyone to overhear," the boss said.

"Overhear what?"

"You never wanna let outsiders listen to your business."

"Oh," I cleared my throat. "I'm pretty tight-lipped when it comes to anyone I can't trust."

"Exactly. They'll run over, tell whoever-the-fuck. Before you know it you'll be pullin' a stretch up at Cornell," Sal said.

I blinked.

"Someone's big dick up your ass," he continued. "Something tells me you wouldn't like that."

"I'll pass."

He laughed. "I don't blame you," Sal reached for the pot of coffee. "Speaking of that, that's the other reason we wanted to see you."

"Why's that?" I asked.

Sal said, "A few people we know are getting out of prison?"

"What people?"

"Guys in the business."

"How many?"

"Three, maybe four."

"Maybe four?"

"Yeah, one of the guys, Rex Fuller, got in a fight with a guy a few days ago. From what I understand he hit the poor bastard a few times with a mop handle."

I rested both elbows on the table and clasped my hands together. "Damn, that's crazy. It must've hurt."

Sal smiled. "You think?"

"Seems if someone did that, he probably deserved it."

"Not sure. When guys get on the inside they seem to get tougher. It's like they all have to prove something. The fight could've been over something small."

"He gets more time?" I asked.

"Not sure. Maybe the other guys heard something," he lit a cigarette. "The guys that are gonna be out, I wanna throw 'em a party. We owe a lot to those men."

I picked my elbows off the table. "Of course. We could

arrange that, no problem. When are they gonna be here?"

"Next week sometime," he said. "At first Chris told me Monday."

"Chris?"

"Yeah, you know him?"

"I don't think."

"Chris Bailey, he's a nice fella. I'm sure you'll like him."

"But he's with us?" I asked.

"Yeah," the boss said.

"I'm always up for meeting new people."

"I'm sure he'll be glad to embrace freedom."

"I can imagine. I know I don't wanna get locked away for any amount of time."

"Can't blame you there," the boss said.

"I know when I got out," Tony said, "I told myself I'd never go back there. They'd have to take me out. Guys like us, on the inside, you could get gotten to anytime. You have to watch yourself in there. Protection is key."

No one said anything for a minute or so. I looked out the window again at the open water. The tree line in the distance complemented the river well. Anyone can always say what they want about Arkansas but the landscape is beautiful.

"Tell me more about this Rex guy?" I asked both of them.

Tony said, "Rex always did have a temper. He wouldn't ever back away from a fight, no matter how big the other guy was."

Sal looked at Tony. "Remember when he busted that guy's face open with a hammer?"

"Yeah, I remember," Tony said. "That was a bloody mess. I was up all that night cleaning that shit."

Sal shook his head.

"How'd that happen?" I asked.

Tony said, "He was workin' at this construction site. Some guy he worked with was messin' with his wife, and he got pissed. Confronted the guy. They yelled at each other for a bit. Rex picked the hammer up from a pile of wood and started to hit away."

"Did the guy die?"

"By the time they pulled Rex off him, he was gone."

"Damn," I said. "Nothing was done to Rex?"

"He knew some people, so, I didn't have to dig a hole for him."

I thought about that, then, took a drink. "That's crazy shit," I laughed, leaning back to the back. "So, why'd Chris get locked up?"

"Bad luck," Tony said.

I chuckled.

Sal frowned a little and shook his head. "He was involved in a truck hijacking eight years ago."

My mouth opened. "That's a long time. What happened?"

The boss lit another smoke. "It was him, Rex, and two other guys. They all got arrested a few days later. This girl of Rex's ratted all of them out."

"And those other guys are the ones getting out?"

"Yeah."

"Who are they?"

"Frank Boone and Matt Hope. They're pretty good guys."

"I can imagine," I said. "Well, what about Rex?"

"It had gotten out that his girl was the one who dimmed them to the cops. Guess everyone thought if his girl was a rat he would, too."

"Is the girl still around?"

"Yeah. Ellen lives in a little house in Cabot. I visited her a few weeks ago. After all this time she gets shunned by people. And so, some guys on the inside think Rex is a rat: that's probably what the fight was about."

The next thing I knew our waitress hovered over our table, and asked if we needed anything else. We told her I wanted a small plate of sausage and bacon.

"That all?" she said."

"Yeah," I said

"You sure?" she pressed on. "We have a sale right now on pie and slices of cake."

"That's okay," I said.

"You don't know what you're missing."

"I'll take my chances."

"It's your dime, babe."

She walked away and disappeared into the kitchen.

I looked at Tony and Sal. "Guess they need to push the pie around here?"

Tony said, "Whatever keeps people coming in. Supply and demand, that's what it's all about these days."

"They're all money whores," the boss said.

I sat back. "Always works that way."

thirty-eight

The next day, I had to run a few errands around the city. As I was heading home I decided to swing by Viggo's place. We talked and joked for about three hours. He asked about the trip to Texas. I told him the album was coming out.

Viggo got a call from Tony and told him that they planned a little gathering for us that night. I called the other guys and told them about the party. I drove over to Madison's and told her to expect a rowdy night at the club. She told me they had already told her about it, and that she was going to be behind the bar all night.

I stayed with my girl until she had to leave for work. When we got to Highlife and walked in, we heard the sharp sound of a pool stick smacking a ball. It was two men, one big, one short. They both looked as if they had been drinking all day. The tired look in their eyes told me they were still drunk.

"Want the next game?" the tall man asked.

I shook my head. "Nah, man, I'm good.

"You sure?" the short one asked.

"Pretty sure," I said.

"Your call."

"It's fine," I waved them on. "Don't worry about it guys."

"Your loss."

"I'll live."

The tall man offered me a cigarette, but, I told him I had my own.

I walked to the bar and ordered a beer. A few of the dancers, the entertainment, trickled in: they walked to the dressing room. For a minute I thought of the craziness that would ensue if I followed them.

I talked to Madison before she started her shift. I loved her. After Heidi died, I didn't know if I could ever love another girl. I loved everything about Madison. We talked about what we had planned for the next couple of days. We talked about going out to Midway and rent a cabin by Oak-A-Paw Lake.

We kissed and she went behind the bar.

A few minutes later some of the crew started to show.

I kissed Madison and told her I'd talk to her later.

My name was called out. I turned around and it was Rooster.

"There he is!" I said. "The man of the hour."

He laughed. "Why's that?"

I shrugged. "One never knows."

"I get that a lot," he sat on the stool beside me. "How the hell are ya?"

"Can't complain."

"Same here," he knocked his palm on the bar. "How's the beer tonight?"

"Nice and cold."

"Just the way I like it."

"Is there any other way?"

"Anything else is piss."

"Don't plan to drink piss."

"Think I'd pass on that party."

Madison, from behind the bar, asked if he wanted anything to drink. He ordered a beer and a shot of whiskey.

"Anything else?" she smiled.

"That'll be all for now," Rooster said. "This looks like it's gonna be an all-night job. I'll need some later."

"We're gonna be here for awhile," I said.

"Nice," he said. "When I first heard about this whole thing, I didn't know how long you guys would be here."

"I plan on staying till the sun comes up."

"That's the way to go about it."

"It's the best way."

"I'll be right here with ya."

Madison said it'd be a minute on the drinks, then walked to the back.

"Hurry back, honey!" I called after her.

"Love you," she replied.

Rooster turned to me. "That's a good girl you got there."

"I know," I told him.

"Don't let her go."

"I won't if I can help it."

He shook his head. "Girls like that, I'm sorry I let mine go."

"What happened to her?"

"She ran off with some asshole. I swore if I ever saw that bastard again I'd stomp him."

"That's a damn shame. Well, hey, you know I'll always

have your back, right?"

"Thanks, Sean."

"Don't mention it."

My girlfriend came back with the beer and whiskey and placed them in front of Rooster.

She looked at me. "Anything for you, babe?"

I nodded at the drinks in front of Rooster. "I'll have what he's having."

"Good choice," her sweet voice flowed through the air.

My girlfriend walked away again.

Rooster said, "So, they told me this little get-together was a celebration?"

"That's what I hear," I told him.

"Tony said you guys just got back from Texas?"

"Yeah."

"How long were you there?"

"Two weeks."

"Why?"

"Our album comes out next week."

"Oh, congratulations."

"Thanks," I said.

"See, you did something there that's gonna last forever."

"Yeah, our manager, Morris, set up a few shows for us."

"How'd those go?"

"Pretty good."

He took a drink. "I've never been to Texas."

"Really?"

"Not even for a party."

"You're not missing much. We were there for two weeks and only saw four towns, and judging by that I don't wanna see any more of it."

He laughed. "You just saved me a trip."

"But something tells me we're gonna make regular trips there."

"Why?"

"The record label is in one of the towns."

"Oh."

"Yeah, the recording of the album, the studio, and everything was great. After we got done recording it, this guy that helped us with it, Scott, had this kick-ass party at his place."

"That's pretty tight."

"Indeed."

"Bet you have some stories?"

"No really."

"Why the fuck not?"

I shrugged. "both times I went there, I was involved with a girl. You know, the first time I was with Heidi, and the next time 'round was with Madison."

He looked over at Madison, then me. "That's a fine woman you got yourself. My advice, keep a tight grip on her."

"I know."

"It's an important part of this world. Guys like us, we spend it dealing with the scum of the Earth. But everyone needs a living, right?"

I shook my head. "That's right. Nah, Madison's been good to me. I'm not gonna ever let anything happen to her. I'd die before that happens."

"That's the way it should be."

"Just hope she feels the same about me."

"She does?"

"She told you?"

"You can see it on her face."

I took a drink of beer. "So, how's business?"

"I have an end-game in all of this. You know, just like everyone else out there, trying to get enough cash to stay afloat, and then some for the retirement years. But, yeah, shit, the day people stop doing drugs, that's the day we cease to exist."

"Gotta keep meat and cheese in the fridge."

"That's right."

The more he and I talked, the more people piled in. He started to tell me about this business venture he wanted me to be a part of. Of course, knowing Rooster, it had to do with drugs. It seemed he had forged a somewhat friendship with a few guys down in Mexico. He explained what his role would be in this drug smuggling operation. I have to say, I didn't like where the conversation was going, especially, when he asked if I wanted to take part. I told him I'd think about it and then get back to him.

He finished his beer, told me he had to see some other people, and he was off into the crowd. I sat at the bar and ordered another beer. I looked over at Madison who was busy behind the bar taking orders. She looked over in my direction and blew me a kiss.

The band for the night were a few guys from Conway who called themselves Maniac Captains: they sounded pretty good. They played some covers, some originals - it all was good. I hadn't had the pleasure of hearing them before. The original material had more of a Southern Blues influence than Stoned Monkey, but, it was clear we celebrated the same style of music and got our Rock education from the same artists. The young guy on bass plucked hard and fast, like a madman on the edge of rage. The drumming, vocals, and guitar playing, were all outstanding. The guys wore nothing but black. The singer stood in one place throughout all of the songs.

Throughout the night, I had scattered conversations with pretty much everyone in the place. Sal got on stage and made a speech, saying how proud he was of my friends and me and what we achieved. Everyone applauded and went back to drinking, to enjoying the party and music.

I was sitting at one of the tables talking to Robert Spikes when I looked across the room and made eye contact with Madison. She was doing the usual, helping customers with drinks. She gave me a bright smile. I was still looking in her direction when two guys sat at the bar—the only reason I even took notice was because they obstructed my view of my princess. It wasn't too long before both men stood and walked away, leaving their full mugs of beer. After a bit, the two men returned and sat back down. Madison came back over, and it looked like they were talking about something. The two men turned around and looked at me as Madison pointed at me. They talked a little more before they left again. Like before, a little while later, they came back to the bar. They continued to drink and talk with each other. I didn't think anything else of it and continued my conversation. As the night drew on, people left and sputtered off into the city. Manic Captains finally stopped playing around 11:30, packed up their stuff, and left. Most of the guys from the crew had already gone. There were still a few people at the bar: a man and woman and the two guys from before. I walked over to the bar.

"Hey, babe," I said.

Madison looked at me. "Another beer?"

"Sure, why not?"

She grabbed one from the cooler behind her, cracked it open, then handed it to me.

"Appreciate it," I said.

"That's my job."

"Ah, but you're the best at it," I took a big swig.

One of the two guys sitting at the bar, a black-haired rough-looking fella looked at me, and said, "Your friend has been telling us about you."

"Well, hopefully, they were all good things," I laughed.

He shook his head. "Oh, it was very informative," he grinned. "I've always found it interesting, the people you meet, people you meet by chance or premeditated talks."

"What's your name?" I asked.

"Russ Miller," he turned to his friend, then back at me. "His name's Tommy, my brother."

Tommy looked at me and snorted. "We gonna have a problem here?"

Russ turned and hit him on the shoulder. "We're taking it easy. No brawls. Remember what you said earlier?"

Tommy grunted. "I see..."

Russ' brother had long dirty blond hair: he wore a white T-shirt and had tattoos covering both forearms. He looked at me with wild eyes.

I raised my beer to both of them. "Hope you guys enjoy yourselves."

"Don't worry about us," Russ said. "We won't have any problems, Sean."

Tommy looked at me. "Ain't it fun?"

"What's that?" I replied.

"The night... best time for things to get a little crazy. There's just something about how laughter and lights shower on the darkness."

"Guess so."

He let out a loud cackle.

I turned and walked away.

Sal walked up to me and said that he'd be calling it a night and that he instructed Madison and the cook in the kitchen to lock the place up. I wished him well and he shuffled out the front door.

My brother came over. We chatted a little before he left, told me he had a few new things, songs he had written, that I should read. After he left I went over to the bar where Madison kept busy washing drink glasses.

Tommy and Russ were still sitting there finishing drinks.

After they walked out, it was just Madison and I in the front area.

I told her I was calling it a night, and I kissed her on the lips.

"I love you," she said.

I told her the same.

I didn't get home until 2:00 am. I staggered into my place, threw my keys on the coffee table, sighed, and walked to the fridge. After I grabbed a beer I walked back into the living room. As I sat on the couch and stared at the blank TV screen a few crazy notes danced in my mind. I walked over to my guitar that was in the corner of my living room, picked it up, and staggered back to my couch. I plopped down and started to tune the instrument.

thirty-nine

I woke around 10:00 am lying on my couch. I blinked a few times as I stared at the ceiling. I sighed. When I stood straight I gave a stretch and lifted my arms wide and high. When my arms came down, I noticed my guitar was lying face-down on the floor. I staggered into the restroom to do my business and shower. After my shower, I called Madison.

No answer.

After an hour I tried again, the same.

The next thing I knew the phone yelled at me.

"Hello?"

"Hey, Sean," the voice said.

"How's it going, Sal?"

A sigh. "I'm glad I caught you. Hey, listen we have a problem here."

"What sort of problem?"

"Well, I'm down here at the club, is Madison there with you?"

"She's not here."

"Shit."

"What?"

"You live beside a payphone, right?"

"Yeah."

"Call me back on it."

"Everything okay?"

"Just call me back."

I put the phone down, got my wallet and keys, and flew out the door. I sped down to the gas station down the street. I called Sal back. He told me that when he came to open Highlife earlier he saw the cook, Steve, lying dead in the parking lot. Steve's car was still there along

with Madison's car. My girlfriend was nowhere to be
found. Sal said he searched both vehicles to try to find
anything in the way of evidence. I told him I'd try Madison on the phone again. I just figured that maybe she had
just been asleep or something. My boss told me he'd let
me know when he had any new information.

I sat back on my couch thinking for a few minutes. I
picked up the phone and dialed my girlfriend. After three
times of not getting an answer, I drove to her place. She
had given me a copy of her key, and I left myself in. I
called her name and didn't get an answer. The apartment
was silent. Everything was where it was supposed to be.
No signs of any sort of struggle or anything. I stepped to
her bedroom door and opened it. Her bed was neat. It
looked to me like she hadn't even been home. I started to
panic. I knocked on the neighbor's and asked if anyone
had seen her. I went back home.

A few hours later the phone rang.

"Hello?"

The voice on the other end. "Who's this?"

I took a deep sigh. "Who's this? You called me."

"This Sean?" the voice asked.

"Yeah."

I thought I recognized the voice.

"Diggs here," the voice said.

"Diggs? How did you get this number?"

"Your bitch gave it."

"Excuses me?"

"Your girl from the bar."

"From what bar?"

"Think about it!"

I held the phone tighter.

"Highlife?" I asked.

"There you go, bright boy."

"Why were you talking to her?"

Laughter came over the phone. "She just told me. The bitch is right here. Madison, right? Yeah, she's a pretty sweet thing, buddy. Think I may need to see how sweet she is."

I shut my eyes for a second, the bottom dropped, and I opened them again. "What are you doing? Don't hurt her!"

"Maybe."

"What's this about? If you hurt her I'll fucking kill."

"Don't jump too fast. I'd hate to see this sexy girl of yours get hurt. This is how things are gonna go: You are gonna come down to Ted's place. The same place we had the meeting the other time."

"Anything else?"

"Bring Sal, no one else."

"What's this about?"

"You'll find out when you get here."

"This some setup?"

"If you wanna see your girl alive again, you'll be here."

I thought for a second. "Listen, whatever this is, I'm sure we can work it out."

"You and Sal get here and we'll see."

"Okay, okay, I need to make sure she's still alive. Put her on the line."

"Hold on."

The phone went silent. A minute later I heard some distant talk on the other end, and then the other end picked up again.

"Here she is," Diggs said.

The next thing I heard was Madison. "Sean?"

"Madison?"

"Sean, what is this?" her voice was trembling.

"I don't know," I said. "Are you okay?"

"I'm okay. I... I... I... I don't know what they want. Just give them anything."

"I promise."

"I'm scared."

"I love you," I told her.

"I love you, too."

Diggs' voice came on the line again. "Just the two of you show, no one else. If you bring anyone else we'll cut your girl's throat."

"Don't do anything crazy."

"If you do what I ask I won't have to. You have an hour."

As soon as I got off with him, I grabbed my keys, and cigarettes, and ran out of my place. I sped over to Sal's place and parked in the back.

As I raced to the back door. He met me. I told him that I had to talk to him inside. Once we were inside, I told him about the phone call.

We decided to go in my cars

It seemed like it took forever to get to Ted's place. Sal and I arrived. Ted and his guys were in the parking lot waiting for us.

"Glad you could make it," Ted said when we got up to him. "We have a little problem."

"That we do," I said.

"I'm just glad you made it."

I eyed Diggs. "Where is she?"

Diggs nodded his head to the bar. "Oh, she's in there having a beer. She's doing good. We've been having to keep the other guys from wanting to lay with her. She's one foxy piece."

Ted told us to come inside. As we walked inside, a black car crawled into the lot. As soon as I walked into the bar, I saw Madison sitting on a stool drinking a beer. She was watching television. She let out a big smile when she saw me. I ran to her. We hugged.

"You okay?" I asked.

"I'm fine," she said.

"That's good."

"Are we gonna be okay."

"We will."

"What's this about?"

"I don't know."

The front door opened. I turned around to see Max and his brother.

I looked over at Ted. "What are they doing here?"

Ted extended his hand to Max. "Good you guys could make the trip," he looked over at me, then back at him. "Hope we can get this taken care of. I think that's what everyone wants, some sort of… um… a solution."

Sal said, "What is this guys?"

"You'll know soon enough, Sal," Ted smirked.

Ted told Diggs to take Madison to the back room.

We all followed.

Max, Nick, and Ted sat on one side of the table, Sal and I on the other. Diggs was busy tying Madison to a chair.

"Let's get down to it," Ted said. "Hope we can get done with this fast. I'm sure you guys are busy like I am."

I looked into his eyes. "You gonna let my girl go?"

"In time," Ted shrugged.

Sal said, "What do you want from us?"

Ted looked at me. "You met two of my guys last night."

"Who?" I said.

"Russ and Tommy."

"They're with you?" I said.

Ted continued. "They told me about you, about how impressed they were with you. When they found out you guys were together they called me. I told them to kidnap her. I thought she would make a great bargaining chip. I gather you don't agree?"

"No, I don't," I said. "Where are Tommy and his

brother now?"

"They got called out for business. They wanted to be here."

"It's a good thing they're not," I snarled.

Ted laughed. "Don't act like such a badass - that'll get you dead. The thought of that beautiful girl over there without her man would be heartbreaking. I'm sure if they were here there'd already be blood on the floor. I see some of myself in you, you know? Ask Sal how I used to be."

Sal shook his head. "Don't give us a fucking history lesson."

"You need to or someone will do it for ya, kid."

My boss glanced at me, then to Ted. "It was one of those… what you call it,…'a crime of passion'? I'm sure you can understand. Things happen. This kid didn't know who those guys were with, who they were connected to. Just let the girl go. I'm sure we can work something out. You can do this, Teddy."

Ted said, "I don't let many people call me that, you know?"

"I remember," my boss said.

"What?" I asked.

Ted looked at me. "This little fuck once, he challenged me whenever he could. He always called me that. One day I took a lead pipe to his head. It was a mess. It was a lot of blood to clean."

"I'd imagine so," I said.

Ted looked at me. "Don't test me again, son. I don't like when people lie. You aren't gonna feel it this time, but next time... you can ask some of the people in your crew, you don't wanna fuck around."

I looked over at Madison. She looked afraid. I started to wonder what we got her mixed up in. She started to weep a little. I called over to her and said everything would be okay, to trust me. But I didn't know what was going to happen.

"Let her go," I said.

Ted looked at Madison, then me. "Can't do that."

Sal said, "Why?"

Ted said, "That's why Max and his brother are here. See, you'll give Max what he wants or your boy's girl never walks out of this room."

Diggs stood in the corner of my eye. "I don't wanna do it, but I will."

I turned and showed him my gun. "I'll put you down before you pull the trigger."

"What do ya plan to do with that little toy?"

"Wanna find out? I'll kill you before you can take another gulp of air."

Ted looked over at Diggs. "There's no need for any of that. It's too early for blood. We don't wanna kill anyone, but if we have to, the world's full of monsters."

Sal said, "What do you want, Max? What's it gonna take to make everyone go home?"

Max looked at my boss. "I want everything you have. I understand we all have to survive here. I'm not some sort of a monster or anything. The world is made of compromise. You told me to go fuck myself, and I backed away for a bit. Not now. I want what I had before I went away plus interest. I'm owed that much."

"I disagree," Sal said. "I think you should get shit. You lost. You're the one who ended up behind bars. Why the fuck should I give you what Joe and I built?"

"I Don't get anything?"

"That's right."

"It was Joe who put me away," Max said.

"We all know that wasn't the case."

Nick said, "Last we heard Joe was dead. We don't think

he'd mind."

Ted called to Diggs. The henchman whipped out his gun, pointed it at Madison's head, and cocked it. "Say goodbye."

"Wait!" Sal held his finger up. "Don't hurt her. Max, maybe we can work something out."

Max nodded. "That's the smartest thing you've said in awhile."

"I'm sure you think so."

"You're a funny guy. Maybe I was wrong about you all these years, yes? No matter what, I still don't like you. I thought a lot about seeing you and Joe dead, used to dream about it every day in my cell. I wanted to be the one who killed Joe, but someone beat me to it."

"You didn't do it, that's what you're saying?" my boss asked.

"I didn't," Max said. "I know you must've thought I had something to do with it. I hate to disappoint."

"I didn't think anything."

"Sure you didn't. Think what you want."

"You know who it was?" Sal folded his arms in front of him on the table.

"Can't help you with that," Max cocked his head to the side. "If I find who it was I'll kill them for not letting me get the chance."

"If you hated Joe so much why didn't you get someone to get it done before?"

"I thought about it," Max said. "You have no idea how bad I wanted it done. I had a guy who'd do it, But I decided I wanted to do it myself. Something about waiting to get revenge. Surprise is key. I should dig him up to kill him again."

"It works that way?" Ted asked.

Max looked at Ted. "It might.

Nick said, "Hate to interrupt here, but can we get a

move on it? I'm hungry. I'm ready to get a nice burger and beer, don't know about you guys."

"We'll get there soon enough," Max said to his brother. "Have some patience."

Sal said, "We should divide some things up for ya, you think?"

"That would be good," Max said.

"I remember before you went away you had some of the drug trade in the city."

"That's right."

"Along Monday, right?"

"Yeah."

"A few of our guys work over there, Donnie and Zack. I don't think it'd take much convincing to let you have that area. We can always get them into something else. We'll have to talk with Ned McGehee and explain the situation. I'm sure he'll understand."

"Good," Max said.

"With that said," Sal continued, "would you wanna talk over the rest of it."

Max said, "That's why we're sitting here. I understand everything is about compromise. It's good business for all," he looked at me. "As for your bitch being here, I had nothing to do with that."

"What did you call her?" I raised my brow to him. "You wanna rethink that?"

"Don't get bent outta shape."

I looked over at Madison again, and she still had a gun pointed at her head.

"You guys did this," Ted said.

I said, "Let her go. Take me instead."

"You sure about that?" Ted gave me a stern look.

"Yeah," I said. "She shouldn't have to die because of us."

"You wanna get killed instead?"

"If I have to."

"Your time's coming, don't worry," Ted told me.

"Oh, I can't wait," I said

The next thing I knew I felt the cool metal against the side of my head; it was a gun, Diggs' gun. A knot grew in my throat. I knew I had to keep calm. I couldn't panic. If I reached for my gun I knew I was dead.

"You gonna do something?" I said, staring ahead.

"I won't have any problem pulling this," Diggs said coldly. "Those were my friends you killed."

"You plan to kill us all?" I asked.

"That's kind of the idea."

"I see."

Diggs lowered the gun and walked in front of me. "I don't know you. Don't wanna know you. I don't give a shit about any of this. I just do what I'm told. My boss, that guy over there," he gestured to Ted. "He told me if you don't do what he says to kill that sweet piece of woman of yours. I just follow orders. Don't ask questions. Just do what has to be done."

Nick said, "What are we doing here, guys?"

"We're wasting time it seems," Max commented.

Ted looked at Diggs and told him to untie Madison. After she was untied, he pushed her over to me. He pointed his gun at me, and I ran toward him and knocked the gun out of his hand. I hit him in the face three times. Sal walked over and pulled me off the guy.

Max said, "You two wanna beat the hell outta each other do it on your own time. We have things to do."

Ted said, "You guys make up, play like good little boys, eh? We are trying to discuss business. If you don't mind, could you guys wait outside? Guard the front. Make sure no one comes in we don't want here."

forty

I walked over to Madison and kissed her.

I took her hand, and we walked out of the back room to the front. When we got to the front door I heard footsteps behind us. I turned around and saw Diggs.

"You just messed up!" he pointed his gun at me.

I pulled my gun and fired at him.

When I fired my gun, I aimed at a row of bottles sitting behind the bar. The bullet hit one of the bottles, sending the liquid to the floor.

Diggs flinched. "Hey, I was just messing around!"

I moved my aim to Diggs. "I should put you down for what you did."

"What?" Diggs gestured to Madison. "Taking her? That wasn't my idea. Talk to Ted about that. I was just following orders. If I hadn't done it I would've gotten shot. I didn't wanna die. I'm not a bad guy. Just tryin' to get by in this mess. You should lower that thing."

I lowered my weapon.

"It wasn't personal," Diggs said.

"I bet."

"Believe what you want," Diggs lowered his eyes, looked at the broken glass on the floor, then looked at me. "Man, you're stupid. Look at this mess," he looked at the floor with the glass on it again. "We're gonna have to explain this."

The door to the back room burst open, and the men inside came out. Ted was ahead of the other guys and had a disgusted look on his face.

"What's going on?" Ted said. "We're trying to do business," he glanced over at the bar. "Someone shoots off one of the bottles?" He looked at us. "Speak now, or one of you will be on the floor."

"I shot the bottle," I said.

"Really?" Ted had a confused look. "Why would you do something like that?"

"Shooting practice," I said. "Your boy started it."

"How so?" Ted asked.

"He pulled his gun on us."

Ted stuffed his hands in his pockets. "Really?" he looked over at Diggs. "That true?"

"I was just playing around," Diggs said.

"Why?" Ted pointed at Madison, then back at Diggs. "We've already scared her to death. Do you think it's smart to push it anymore? I have to tell ya, that's not very good for business. We don't need people putting word on the streets that we treat women more unfairly than anyone else."

Diggs nodded. "Sorry."

"I need all of you guys to make up. You never know when one of you might need a favor from the other."

Diggs apologized, and then, we shook hands. He told my girl he was sorry for everything that happened.

Ted looked at me. "I gotta tell you, you got a tough girl there. Yeah, she can hold her own in a fight."

Madison said, "Appreciate that."

Ted asked if I knew how much the vodka bottle I shot cost. I told him I didn't.

"Top of the line," he said. "I know you're gonna pay me back. You're a good kid. You have a knack for this stuff, not everyone does. If you ever wanna jump ship, I can always use good men," he stepped closer to me. "I can't forget you killed two of my guys, though. I understand why you did it, but it still has to be sorted out."

"How we gonna do that?" I asked.

Ted looked at me for a few seconds. "Something will come up."

I nodded. "I get it."

"Glad you said that. In the end, all you have is family."

Ted invited all of us over to the bar to get a drink. As I walked over to the bar, Diggs gave me a dirty look. His boss told him to get a broom and dustpan to clean the glass. He also told Diggs he needed to mop the floor. Ted told Sal to make a toast. We brought our glasses together.

Nick said, "So, can we get this moving? We don't have all day."

"That's what I was thinking," Ted put his glass on the bar.

Sal told me that I needed to call someone to take Madison home. I used the phone on the edge of the bar to call my brother. Jason said he'd be there in about ten minutes.

"Sal, you know," Max said, "at the risk of putting this to bed, I'm willing to take a percentage of all of your business."

"Everything?" Sal said.

"I didn't stutter."

"That number won't happen."

"I'm thinking twenty might cover it," Max suggested. "You guys are doing pretty good, right?"

A loud laugh came from Sal. "Twenty? Shit, you want to put me out of business? Come on, that figure isn't gonna happen. I think you know that. I need to make money, too."

They took their drinks to one of the two tables sitting in the open area.

Ted said, "Just a thought here, it took God seven days to create everything, might wanna take your time with this. What's the big rush? There are plenty of things to iron out and a handful of days in the week."

Max looked at Ted. "What are you saying? I thought

you were on my side with this."

"I am. I just meant there are a lot of things to take into consideration. You can't just hash it out in one afternoon."

Max said, "We have to meet here every time. I'm not setting foot in any of their clubs: I do that I may as well kill myself."

Sal said, "I'll make sure you or any of your guys don't get hurt. Do you have any guys?"

"Yes," Max took a drink. "Yeah, we've been talking to guys, getting them to work for me. Now, guys, I don't wanna keep going in circles with this," he looked at Ted. "There won't be any of this 'take your time with this' bullshit," to Sal. "We get this done today or you won't like what happens. You need to decide what you wanna do, and how you wanna play this. I'm gonna get what I want no matter what. You'll be out of business real fast. Again, if I were you I'd hand over everything to me. Tell you what, I'll even let you stay on as one of my men. You got what it takes to boss for much longer?"

"I've been doing a good job so far. No, I don't think - look, that won't work for me."

"We're gonna have a problem, then."

"I guess we are," my boss said.

Max sighed. "Time for change. Change is always good, right?"

"Always right for one person."

"Well, if that's how it has to-"

"It'll never be you," Sal cut him off.

Nick said, "Now, we don't want a shoot-out over this. We need to set a good example for the young guys."

"Good example?" I laughed. "The first time I met you, you killed one of your guys. I don't wanna hear shit. And how old are you, anyway?"

"Had to prove a point."

I considered that for a moment. "I wasn't scared. Can't speak for my brother, but I'd imagine he would say you didn't intimidate shit."

Nick smiled. "You're just saying that."

"How do you know what I was thinking?" I asked.

He shrugged. "Just a guess," he laughed. "If you want, you should come by there, buy some dope. I'll give you a discount."

"I already have a guy."

"You never know. Your guy, your keeper of the beautiful poison might be found in a dumpster two days from now. He could skip town. Anything could happen. Some wild streets out there."

"I'll take my chances. I've always been one for adventure."

"I can tell."

"Oh, yeah?"

"Just something about you."

"Good... I guess?"

A car pulled up from outside, and a car door opened and shut. A minute later the front door of the bar opened, letting sunlight pure in. My brother closed the door behind him.

"And here's the other one," Nick said, as he looked at my brother. "Come on in! We're just talkin' about old times."

Jason smiled.

Ted walked over to Jason. "Welcome."

"How's it going?" my brother said.

They shook hands.

"Stay awhile," Ted said. "You want a drink?"

"That's okay," Jason said. "I just came to get Madison."

Ted said, "Oh, yes, your brother's beauty," he looked at Madison, then back at Jason. "I think she was getting bored. I dunno, I tend to do that to women. Guess that's why I haven't married yet."

"You sure that's the reason?" Max called from the table. Madison and I smiled.

"Hey, fucko," Ted shook his finger at Max. "That's right. Better watch that shit You shouldn't talk."

"And what are ya gonna do about it?" Max barked.

"I'll make it painful, no matter what it is."

"Nice."

Ted waved Max off and asked Jason if he wanted a drink again.

"Another time," Jason said. "I have some things on my agenda before I can relax. You know how things get, right?"

Ted said, "Yes, another time. I'm sure we'll still have booze here - well, that is if we don't lose the liquor license for the place. If we do, hell, I guess we can still have the stuff. That's what we do best, isn't it? Life outside the law - all fun."

My brother shook his head. "I guess."

"Yeah," Ted said.

I walked over to my brother and told him I appreciated him taking Madison home. Jason asked Sal if he wanted him to come back after he took my girlfriend home. Sal shrugged and told him he didn't need to come back.

Madison and I kissed.

I talked to both of them before they left.

"Let's get back to it, okay?" Max said.

Ted sat back at the table. "I shoulda got something to eat before I came down here. I'm hungry now. Shoulda brought something with me."

The guys around the room said they could eat something.

Diggs said, "Want me to pick something up, boss? I can go to Mello's, and get some sandwiches."

Ted looked at Diggs, "That sounds good."

Everyone said what they wanted. After Diggs took down the order on paper, he walked to the front door: he put his hand on the doorknob, and a bullet burst through the door. Diggs dropped to the floor. As soon as Ted turned to the door, the windows on either side of the door shattered as bullets poured in. We ducked, and took cover, as glass and other things exploded.

"What the fuck is this!?" Sal yelled.

Ted yelled back. "No idea! Just stay where you are. Don't fire back!"

After a few minutes, the bullets stopped, and a loud vehicle sped away.

Everyone got up from where they were.

"Everyone okay?" Sal called out.

Nick and I ran out the door to see if we could get a look at the vehicle. Looking back on it, it was probably a bad idea. I didn't know if I was gonna be shot or not. I guess I acted before I thought. When we got outside the car was already halfway down Rey Street. The color of the car was black, that's the only thing I could tell; no plate number, no model. I couldn't tell who was driving. I turned back to the bar, walked back, and felt defeated and in shock.

We walked through the door.

Sal was knelt over Diggs, "Oh, shit," he muttered. "This is fucked."

Ted came from behind the bar. "Here," he handed some towels to Sal. "Put these on it."

Sal put the towels on Diggs' bloody wound. "You'll be okay, buddy. Just hang in there. This'll be over soon."

Ted ran back over to the bar, picked up the phone, and dialed a number. He started to talk to someone on the other end. After a minute he took the phone from his ear and said, "What color was the car?"

"Black," I said. "That's the only thing I could get. It was too far down the street to make out a plate number or anything. I couldn't even tell what the model was. I could only see the back."

Nick told him the same thing.

"The fuck?" I said.

"Some crazy shit," Nick added.

Max ran over, knelt beside Sal. "He gonna make it?"

"Not sure," Sal said, pressing the towel on Diggs. "He needs a doctor, someone who knows what he's doing."

Ted hung up the phone and walked over to us. He said a doctor and another of his guys were on the way.

Nick looked at Ted. "The fuck was this? A setup or what?"

"A black car? It could be a few people. I'll get to the bottom of this."

"Better do it fast."

Ted pointed his finger at Nick. "I don't wanna hear it."

"Sorry, man, I just get a little pissed when people try to kill me."

"Oh, shit, they didn't even know you were here. Calm down."

"I tell ya," Nick turned and walked away, "this fuckin' guy."

"Hey!" Max leaped over to him. "We don't need this, now," he pointed to Diggs on the floor. "That guy on the floor, he might die. We can't let that happen. You aren't the one on that floor, so shut-the-fuck-up about it," he got closer to his brother. "We'll deal with this later, you know what I'm sayin'?"

Nick nodded.

"Who knew you were gonna be here?" I asked Ted.

Ted said, "I dunno, told a few people. They wouldn't have done anything like this, though."

"How you can be sure?"

"You gonna question me?" Ted raised his voice. "I don't know. Maybe someone was after you."

Nick said, "We could've died."

"You still want to?" Max asked him.

"I'll pass."

Sal looked at Ted, still applying pressure to Diggs' wounds. "You track these guys down... A swallow grave sounds about right."

Ted said nothing but nodded. "Just help him," he walked over to where one of the windows used to be and looked out. "The nearest cop building is a few blocks away. Those pigs will be here soon enough."

"I hate fucking cops," Nick said.

Ted turned to him. "You think we do?" he turned back to the hole in the wall. "In the interest of keeping us out of jail, could someone go outside, and see if any packages were left."

Sal told me to go look for anything.

I walked outside. In the parking lot, everything seemed normal. I couldn't find anything anywhere. The windows were shot out, and the building itself was peppered with bullet holes. I knew this wasn't good. I was a little afraid they'd come back. Clouds rolled over the sky. The police sirens penetrated the distance. I ran back inside.

"They're on their way," I said.

"Find anything?" Ted asked.

"It was all clear."

Within no time there were a few cop cars on the parking lot. They came in and called for an ambulance.

"I got my guy on the way," Ted told the cop.

The cop explained to him they needed to use professional help, and that Diggs could die. Ted agreed. He called his doctor back and told him not to come.

The EMT's came and took Diggs to the hospital. The cops, there were four of them, kept us for almost three hours asking us questions and whatnot. They asked us why we were all together. They wanted to know something like we were guilty.

"We were just talking about days past," Ted said. "Last I knew nothing was wrong with talking with people."

"That's all you were doing here?" the cop asked.

"Yeah," Ted said. "These are pretty nice guys."

"That so?"

One of the other cops came over and told them they got another call, and that they all needed to go. They told us they'd have to leave but would be back the next day to check things out. The cop told Ted to remain closed until further notice. They all got in their cars and sped away, sirens screaming.

Ted told us we had best get out of there. He said whoever did the shooting might be back, and he didn't want us to get involved. When Sal tried to press the issue more Ted just told him not to worry about it, that it'd get handled.

"Handle it with bullets, right?" Sal said. "Have an idea who it could've been?"

"With all the enemies we have, we'll figure it out. I know I should've been here. I was gonna go to my bitch ex-wife's house. I still have to get some of my shit from the house. The house I bought, mind you. I don't understand it: I bought the fuckin' house, and then after four years I gotta hand it over to her, why is that?"

Sal grinned. "Women, the cosmic wonder. My friend, I don't think any guy will ever crack that one. Just when you think you did, the game changes."

"I hear that."

After a few more words Sal and I walked out the door.

We walked to my car and I opened the driver's door and

got in. When my boss got in, he looked at the back wind-shield. "Your glass is shattered."

"What?" I looked at where he was looking. "Oh, fuck! What the shit!? My fucking car!" I turned around in my seat and hit the steering wheel with my hand. "You know how much that's gonna cost to fix?"

My boss glanced out his window, then back at me. "Could be worse."

"How's that?"

"Could've been in it."

"Yeah."

"Hope that makes you feel better."

"It doesn't."

"I gathered that."

I lit a cigarette and nodded to the bar. "Think I should get some money from them."

"What, for the glass?"

"Why not?"

"Those guys, I dunno about that."

"Why? It's because of them we're here."

"Some things you have to let go of, kid."

"I never give up that easy."

"I know."

The both of us exited the car.

Sal said, "Just let me do the talking. I know how emo-tional you get with these things."

"These things? Like this happens all the time or some-thing?"

He ran his hand through his hair. "These guys aren't happy with me at the moment. They hate you."

"Why do they hate me so much?"

He raised a brow. "You serious?"

"Yeah."

"Let's see, you kill two of Ted's guys, one being his nephew. You shot that guy Johnny, who was a friend of

Nick's. What's next, you gonna fuck his wife?"

"I don't think he has a wife."

He laughed. "He got a sister you could bang? That'd piss him off."

"I'm not sure if he has one or not. We didn't get to know each other that well."

Sal shook his head. " I get that."

I looked at the front of the bar, then back at Sal. "It's been an interesting day so far, might as well see if we can push it further."

"Ahoy! That's the way to be."

We started up the sidewalk, and Ted came out the door; he was followed By the two brothers.

Ted said, "Listen, guys, sorry this shit happened. I think you can appreciate the fact we'll have to do this some other time."

"So, when do we finish this?" I asked.

Nick said, "As far as my brother and I, we can hold off for a little while."

"While I respect our situation," Sal said, "I want this done as soon as possible."

"We still wanna give you time to think about our offer," Max said.

"The partnership? That's not gonna happen."

"What a shame," Nick said.

I asked Ted about the money for the window. He gave me an annoyed look and I dropped it.

forty-one

We were almost to Highlife before we broke the silence.

"I bet Madison was scared as shit back there?"

"She was," I said. "I need to go and check on her. I could tell she was pretty shook-up."

"That's a natural response. She's a good girl, too good for this shit. You can just drop me at the club if you want."

"Sure."

"Life's crazy. There are so many different roads, twists, and turns we go down. You think you know how it's gonna end - and, yes, we're all gonna die one day - but it's getting there that's the mystery. I could wake up tomorrow with a shotgun in my face... it's all over for me. Who the fuck knows? This is a dangerous game we're in."

"Nah, don't say that, Sal."

"Look it, we could've died back there. I don't wanna go out like no asshole. Every day I have to wake up and wonder, wonder if I'm gonna die or not. Even before the place got riddled with bullet holes, you know, I thought we were dead. I was thinking, 'Oh, boy, this is how it ends? I must've pissed someone off. I just hope they give me an open casket.' I didn't have time for a conversation with God, but I think he'd welcome me with open arms. Then he'd look at my rap sheet. He'd send me right to Hell to burn for eternity, and then some."

"That's a long time."

"I know."

"But I think I'd rather be in Hell partying with all the sinners, than in Heaven having no fun. I mean, what if they got that shit all wrong? Maybe Hell's the place to be and Heaven's stale and boring."

"We'll have to see."

"When our days are gone."

"You have to think, if there was a God he'd want to be showered in women. Who wouldn't? He's probably down there in a three-way right now."

I laughed. "It's that Mary chick, the both of them."

"Think he moved on since then."

"You think?"

"Sure. Once he discovered all the new types of women out there."

I pulled into the lot of Highlife and let him out. I told him I'd get back to him the next day. He said that he'd get a ride home from someone. With as many people that were there that night, he wouldn't have a problem finding one. It was an important thing in our organization to show respect for others.

I watched him walk into the club. I drove over to Madison's place to make sure she was okay. When I got to her place she was on the couch crying. I took her in my arms and told her everything was gonna be okay.